THE GREAT PACK

Chris Fox

For the readers. Thank you, all.

No Such Thing As Werewolves

Whenever I pick up the later book in a series I'm always torn. Should I re-read the first books, or just dive right in to the latest? I usually want to do the latter, but I can't always remember what happened in the previous books. The following section is for all those people like me who can't quite remember everything that went down in *No Such Thing As Werewolves, No Mere Zombie, and Vampires Don't Sparkle*. I've decided to recap it just like a TV show. For those who just finished *Vampires Don't Sparkle* feel free to skip to the prologue.

In an announcer voice 'Last time, on deathless…"

A giant black pyramid bores from the earth in Peru, and a team of soldiers have been dispatched to investigate. They encounter a werewolf dressed in Egyptian style clothing, which tears through their ranks before escaping. They bring in a team of scientists to help them investigate the pyramid, and quickly find the central chamber is full of very lethal radiation. They desperately seek a way into the pyramid's control room, while the escaped werewolf with the bad fashion sense (Ahiga) begins slaughtering innocents. Some of those innocents rise as werewolves, and a plague begins spreading across South America.

The desperate team of scientists recruits Blair Smith, a brilliant anthropologist working at a local junior college as a teacher. Blair finds a way into the inner chamber, where the team discovers a woman sleeping inside of a high tech sarcophagus the ancients called a rejuvenator. Unfortunately, the act of opening the door to the inner chamber injects Blair with an unknown virus and Blair dies (it's all very sad, really). Within hours he rises again as a werewolf and begins slaughtering his former companions.

Blair wakes up in a small Peruvian village not far from the pyramid, where he meets Liz, a beautiful young redhead from the United States. The pair are pursued by Commander Jordan, the leader of the forces controlled by the mysterious (terribly mysterious) Mohn Corp. Liz is killed and brought back by Blair as a werewolf, and we learn that female werewolves are much larger, and much scarier than males. The pair flees north, deciding that if they can get to California Liz's brother Trevor might be able to help them find some sort of cure.

Meanwhile Ahiga tries to catch up, because he realizes Blair has inadvertently stolen the key to the Ark (the pyramid). That key is required to wake the woman inside, who Ahiga refers to as the Mother. It turns out she's the progenitor of the entire werewolf species, and when Ahiga finally catches up to Blair he tells him that without her the world is doomed. He explains that the world is about to enter a new age. The sun will go through a Coronal Mass Ejection, which will wipe out nearly all technology. This CME will also activate a virus that will turn all the people who currently have it into zombies (oh crap).

Blair decides to be a dumbass and tells Ahiga to go screw himself. He and Liz continue on to California where they meet up with Trevor and begin investigating the werewolf virus. It turns out Trevor is a helio-seismologist who just so happens to be investigating a giant sunspot (what a coincidence, right?). He confirms that a CME could royally screw the entire planet, and agrees to help Blair and Liz get back to Peru to wake the Mother.

Before they leave, Commander Jordan and his comic-relief sidekick Yuri show up with a bunch of soldiers in power armor. They blow up Trevor's house and his '67 Mustang, but fail to catch Blair. The werewolves escape back to Peru where they gather some furry allies and invade the Ark. They battle Mohn Corp's ever growing army, and there are casualties on both sides. The werewolves win and wake the Mother, who slaughters poor Commander Jordan and every soldier under his command. It's very sad, because by this point we feel bad for poor Jordan.

In the epilogue, the asshole author (that's me) dropped a really, really messed up cliffhanger. One of the scientists had the virus that would cause her to turn into a zombie when the CME hits. Not only does she turn into a zombie, but Trevor gets bitten within the first 30 seconds of the zombie apocalypse. Poor readers were left wondering what would happen to Trevor.

No Mere Zombie

Did the asshole author answer the question right away? Nope, he made you wait until chapter 5 to find out what happened to Trevor.

The book opens in 11,000 BCE just before the Arks went into hibernation. Irakesh, the son of Ra (the Mother's greatest enemy), concocts a plan to sneak into the Mother's Ark. When it returned, he planned to steal the access key for the Ark of the Redwood, located near San Francisco.

Fast forward to the present. Jordan wakes up, his last memory the Mother ripping his arms off (ouch). He quickly realizes he's a werewolf, and has no choice but to join Blair, Liz, Cyntia, and Bridget in their fight against the endless sea of zombies washing over the world.

Led by Isis (the Mother), they attempt to save as many people as possible, setting up a refuge at a church in Cajamarca. Unfortunately, that plan goes to hell when Irakesh steals the access key and runs for it. Liz and Blair pursue, but have no choice but to turn back to protect the Mother's Ark when Irakesh sends an army of zombies to invade it.

We finally learn Trevor's fate. He's become a zombie, and can't remember who he is. Fortunately, Trevor quickly discovers he can grow smarter by consuming, you guessed it, brains. He begins to recover his memory, and is one of the zombies Irakesh seizes control of.

Irakesh realizes Trevor is smarter than most zombies, and begins grooming him as an apprentice. They head north, aiming for a Mohn installation in Panama that Irakesh learned about by snacking on an officer's brain. Cyntia, love sick for poor Trevor, leaves the others to go find him. She eventually catches up to Trevor and Irakesh, and is recruited by the deathless.

Cyntia begins feeding indiscriminately on zombies, people, and even other werewolves. Irakesh encourages this behavior, because he knows it will make her stronger. Of course it also makes her crazy, so maybe not the best long term plan.

Blair, Liz, Bridget, and Jordan pursue Irakesh knowing they must stop him and recover the access key before he can reach the Ark of the Redwood in San Francisco. Isis remains behind to repair the catastrophic damage done to her Ark during the final battle with Mohn in the previous book.

We get a new point of view character, Director Mark Phillips (that's THE Director). He's squirreled away at the Mohn research facility in Syracuse, New York, where Mohn Corp is experimenting on zombies and living in luxury. Unlike the rest of the world, all their technological toys survived the CME, including their nifty X-11 power armor.

It isn't all rosy for Mark, though. He's learned that the Old Man has some dark secrets. He's not what he appears to be, so Mark begins investigating. He dispatches Yuri to Panama to recover the nuke they'd intended to detonate in Peru, and to learn what happened to Commander Jordan.

Meanwhile Blair, Liz, Bridget, and Jordan are hot on Irakesh's trail. They arrive in the city of Medellin to find an encampment protected by werewolves. It turns out they know two of them, Doctor Roberts and Steve (aka Captain Douchey). They have a tense reunion, but it's broken up by an army of zombies sent by Irakesh to ruin their day.

Trevor, Irakesh, and Cyntia make it to the airport where Mohn has their secret facility. They find the airplane carrying Mohn's nuke, which Irakesh decides to steal. By now Trevor has developed the powers of a deathless, and has regained all his memories. Unfortunately, Irakesh is mentally dominating him. Worse, Cyntia is growing more powerful and more unstable by the day.

Blair and company finally catch Irakesh at the airport. There's a big battle with lots of pew pew pew, rawr, etc. Blair's side loses, Irakesh gets away, and Yuri arrives just in time to capture Jordan and Liz. They're brought back to Mohn corp in Syracuse.

Blair, Bridget, and Steve decide to pursue Irakesh, but not before Blair sleeps with Bridget (yes, his cheating ex. Poor Liz). They catch up with Irakesh in Larkspur, just before he finds the Ark of the Redwood. Blair once again gets his ass kicked, and this time the cost is higher. Bridget dies, and even though she cheated on him, we still feel bad because she redeemed herself at the end. Well most of us feel bad. Some fans wrote in to say the bitch got what she deserved. Heartless, people. Just heartless.

Meanwhile, Director Phillips continues his investigation of the Old Man. It turns out the Old Man is *really* old, nearly two hundred. He serves a deathless named Usir, a name we later learn is a synonym for Osiris.

The Director starts a brief civil war, freeing Liz and Jordan. He arms Liz with Object 1, a super-powerful magical sword. Of doom. Since that's a really long title, let's just call it what the Director does: Excalibur.

Yuri pilots Liz and Jordan to San Francisco, where they link up with Blair and Steve. They attack Irakesh on the Golden Gate bridge. During the fight Trevor (very predictably) breaks free from Irakesh and joins the good guys. But not before shooting Jordan in the face. Again. It happens like four times in the book.

Unfortunately, they aren't able to stop Irakesh. He detonates the nuke he stole, destroying a chunk of the Golden Gate bridge. He channels the energy from the explosion into the Ark of the Redwood, charging up the battery and giving him control of a fully powered Ark.

Meanwhile an enraged Blair attacks Cyntia, desperately seeking vengeance for Bridget. Cyntia's much stronger, and more powerful, so he comes out on the losing end. His body is shattered and broken, but before Cyntia can kill him Liz uses Excalibur to slay Cyntia and drain her essence.

The heroes are in pretty bad shape, especially Blair. He realizes their only hope is throwing everything they have left at Irakesh. Steve convinces him to give up the access key to the Mother's Ark, which powers up Steve.

Irakesh attacks, showing what a fully-powered Ark Lord can do. The heroes get their collective asses kicked, and it looks like this is going to be the last book since Irakesh has basically won.

Then Blair throws the hail Mary. He uses his shaping to alter Irakesh's helixes. Since Irakesh is a deathless, and the Mother designed the access keys to only work for werewolves, the key leaves him. It shoots into Blair, who is now a super-powered Ark Lord. He turns all the zombies on the bridge to ash, and kicks the crap out of Irakesh. The heroes teleport inside the Ark, where they imprison Steve and Irakesh.

Director Phillips calls Jordan using a satellite phone, warning him that the Mohn Corp is compromised. He lost his civil war, and the Old Man is handing Mohn over to a deathless named Osiris. They're heading to London, where Very Bad Things (tm) are happening.

Just to throw a little salt on the wound, the book ends with Steve telling Irakesh he can light walk (teleport) from the cell, so they can escape and head to the Ark of the Cradle, where Ra rules.

The cliffhanger for *No Mere Zombie* wasn't as bad as the one in *No Such Thing As Werewolves*, but we were still left with a lot of questions. You're about to get answers, because you're holding *Vampires Don't Sparkle*, the third book in the series.

I hope you enjoy it!

If you do, please consider leaving reviews for any or all books in the series. I'm an indie author, and reviews are vitally important to my success. You might also consider signing up for the mailing list to hear when **Deathless Book 4: The Great Pack** is available (or my other tie in series, **Hero Born**). If you do, I'm happy to give you a free copy of *The First Ark*, the prequel that explains a bit more about who the Mother is and where the zombie virus comes from.

Vampires Don't Sparkle

Vampires Don't Sparkle opens with a prologue showing Osiris, the super handsomest god ever, having his Ark jacked by his brother, Set. Instead of riding into the future with a sixty-inch TV and a fridge full of Guinness, he's now doomed to die alongside everyone else. He's pretty bummed about this, and slightly annoyed at his asshole brother, Set. But at least he has an awesome haircut.

Chapter 1 picks up after the incredibly lame cliffhanger at the end of *No Mere Zombie*. Not good lame, like having Trevor get fucked at the end of *No Such Thing As Werewolves*. No, this cliffhanger rightfully pissed a lot of people off, because Blair was stupid enough to let Steve and Irakesh live instead of killing them on the spot. That would have been the smart thing to do, right? It's what I would have done. But Blair isn't me. Blair was a borderline alcoholic junior college teacher thrust into utter chaos, then given godlike powers with no instruction manual.

Anyway, back to the story. Jordan and Trevor are helping to set up Angel Island, when they see a trio of strange light pulses fire from the Ark into the sky. They aren't sure what they are, and these pulses are never mentioned again. Astute readers pointed that out often in emails, and I promised there was a reason for the pulses. That reason is revealed in *The Great Pack*.

As soon as Blair realizes that Steve and Irakesh have escaped, he gathers his pack, and they pursue. Blair uses the Ark's light bridge to teleport them to the same coordinates used by Steve. They arrive in a strange place called The Nexus, which has been constructed by the Builders, the same people who constructed the great Arks (explained further in my Project Solaris spin-off).

Inside is a holographic figure who introduces itself as Ka. Those of you who read *The First Ark* will recognize Ka immediately, since it was Ka who helped Isis create the first virus. Ka tells Blair that Steve and Irakesh have gone to the Ark of the Cradle. This is a major 'oh shit' moment, because Blair realizes that Steve will sell them out to Ra. He wants to pursue, but I couldn't just make it that simple, right? It turns out the Nexus is damaged, and it's going to collapse unless Blair stabilizes it.

Trevor and Jordan catch up with Steve and Irakesh on the light bridge in the Ark of the Cradle. There's a brawl where it looks like Trevor and Jordan are winning, but then they're ambushed from the shadows. Anubis, the jackal-headed god, wrecks their faces and Jordan and Trevor are captured by Ra. Weak.

Meanwhile, the Director finally wakes up. For those who don't remember, he was captured by Leif Mohn at the end of *No Mere Zombie*. Mohn gives the Director a Bond villain speech about taking him to his master, one of the gods who survived from the last age. This god turns out to be none other than super handsome Osiris. =O (That's my shocked face). Somehow Osiris survived to the present without an Ark.

Osiris is super charismatic, and also totally not based on the author's six-year-old imagination of The Best Character Ever. He starts a slow mental chess game with Mark, starting with turning him into a vampire. Why? Well the title is *Vampires Don't Sparkle*, so clearly we need vampires. Vampires turn out to be a modified strain of the zombie virus, but they appear more human and prefer blood to devouring brains. They can also teleport, which is basically a short range version of light walking.

Back to Blair. He's stabilizing the Nexus when an intruder arrives. He ambushes them, instantly regretting it when he realizes it's Isis. She kicks his monkey ass, of course. Blair brings her up to speed, and Isis decides that they need a bold plan. They're going to invade the Ark of the Cradle and get Steve, and his access key, back.

We get our first villain cut scene, showing the evil, demonic Set. He looks like a cross between the aliens from X-Files and a bobblehead. He's annoyed that someone has stabilized the Nexus, which he wants to blow up because the Progeny of the Builders told him to. He vows to kick Blair's ass as soon as he learns who Blair is. The Progeny of the Builders are the original bobbleheads, and while we don't know why they're back, we do know that Set works for them.

Trevor and Jordan are brought before Ra, the mega-hot ruler of the Ark of the Cradle. Also, Irakesh's mother. She interrogates Trevor, asking him about Isis, and about his allegiances. In the end, she places a collar of Shi-Dun around Jordan's neck, and gives Trevor the leash. She also gives Trevor free run of her court, treating him as an ally. Steve is given to Irakesh like a pet, also wearing a collar.

Trevor isn't really sure what to make of this, and keeps looking for the catch. Jordan is understandably pissed, and assumes Trevor is joining the deathless side, since you know, he's a deathless. Trevor meets a few new gods, including Anput, Anubis, and Isis's son, Horus. In spite of himself, he finds himself becoming friends with Anput. Her husband, Anubis, even teaches him the basics of swordsmanship, starting with having Trevor eat a zombie, who was a skilled swordsman, to steal his memories.

This is common in Ra's court, and they even have a banquet where they eat interesting people and then share the memories they gain from consuming them. Ewww. During this banquet Trevor learns about sunstorms, which are more intense versions of CMEs. Ra takes him to an observatory near the top of the Ark, which is far more advanced than anything our age has produced. Trevor figures out that the Ark must be getting this footage from an installation in space, and spoilers— he's right. That's the Black Knight satellite first mentioned in *Hero Born*, and also addressed in *The Great Pack*.

Blair and Isis return to San Francisco to get Liz, but before they can leave, Isis insists that they must create guardians to protect their flock. Against her better judgement, Liz offers the gift to anyone who wants it, including a ten-year-old girl named Alicia. She's conflicted, but relieved, when Alicia is one of the ones to rise as a champion.

Now that the people on Angel Island are safe, Blair, Liz, and Isis assault the Ark of the Cradle. Isis knows that they're not going to be strong enough to overcome Ra and her entire court, so when they arrive she sends Liz and Blair to barter with the sorcerer-kings of Olympus. She's not entirely sure they've survived to the present, but if they are they'll be found in modern day Turkey.

Isis stays behind at the light bridge to battle Horus, her own son. The fight is short, brutal, and ends with Isis having no choice but to incinerate her firstborn. Ra is understandably pissed by Isis's attack, and mobilizes her forces to go to Olympus. This includes Trevor, who rides howdah on top of a giant undead elephant. Can you imagine how bad that thing would smell? Jesus.

Anyway, Isis wants to slow Ra down, so she uses the Primary Access Key to unleash the Ark's guardian. This guardian is a sand worm of colossal size, reminiscent of the worms from Frank Herbert's *Dune*. *Tips hat to the mighty Frank Herbert*. This sand worm attacks Ra's army, giving Blair and Liz time to reach Olympus.

When they arrive they're met by an old man in robes. He seems friendly, which just screams villain. We're all totally shocked when he turns out to be Hades, the Greek god of the underworld. Hades leads Blair and Liz into his foundry, where they meet the god Vulcan. They're building power armor that looks suspiciously like Mohn Corp's, but theirs is made from a strange dark metal.

Hades tells them that Ra's army is approaching. He can bargain with her, but they need to flee. Hades gives them a slipsail, a glittering silver vessel from the previous age. Blair wants to know what the catch is, of course. Hades wants them to ferry him up to Olympus. If they'll do that, then they can keep the ship. They agree, and drop Hades off right as a massive sunstorm washes over the floating city.

On the other side of that storm is Ra's army, moving to surround Olympus. Blair and Liz start flying away, but are pursued by the wolf-headed god Wepwawet. He's kicking their asses when Isis shows up. She slaps him around and dumps his unconscious body over the side. They start flying away to safety.

Jordan makes an escape attempt, but Trevor shoots him in the face (again). When that doesn't discourage Jordan, he uses the collar of Shi-Dun for the first time, inflicting unimaginable pain on Jordan. Trevor sees Ra in trouble, so he leaves Jordan to go help her against the sand worm. Jordan uses the opportunity to flee, and ends up running into Hades. Hades escorts him down to the foundry, and shows him the awesome power armor Vulcan has created.

Hades tells Jordan that the armor can protect him from the collar of Shi-Dun. Having no other option, Jordan accepts a set. He pilots the armor out, and sets off after Isis, Blair, and Liz. Isis flees to a set of caves in France that I learned about from a great Netflix documentary (Cave of Dreams I think it was called…I'm too lazy to go look it up).

We flash over to London, where Osiris is training Mark. He shows Mark footage of a demonic army marshaling from the First Ark. Set is finally on the move, DUN DUN DUN =O.

Ra finally catches up, and invites Isis to a parlay. Ra has learned from Hades that Osiris has gone rogue. She believes Osiris is the demonic ruler of the First Ark, and tries to convince Isis to help her take Osiris down. They're still discussing things when Osiris makes a super-handsome, stylish entrance. Isis responds by dumping a glass of water on his head, something nearly every reader also wanted to do in the hopes that it would knock the smug out of Osiris.

Osiris explains that Set took the First Ark, and that we're all really, really screwed. Set has been building an army for millennia, and is now unleashing that army on the world. He's kind of a big deal, even if he does look like a bobblehead.

Ra, Isis, and Osiris agree to cooperate. They're hammering out the details of just how screwed Steve is (he's going to be a present from Ra to Isis), when *gasp*…Set attacks the meeting. He's got dragons with fifty-caliber machine guns belted to their backs, plus masses of brutish demon-thingies (that's their official name).

Our heroes get their asses kicked, but Anubis volunteers to delay Set while everyone else escapes. He heroically sacrifices himself in a duel with Set. Everyone else falls back to a plane Osiris has waiting, just barely escaping Set's demonic army. They flee to Mohn's London HQ, but not everyone makes it. Set captures Steve, Irakesh, Jordan, and Wepwawet. Steve immediately volunteers to work for Set. Set makes the same offer to Irakesh, who earns his first tiny little sliver of reader sympathy when he says no. He won't be a demonic lackey to Set, so Set puts the collar of

Shi-Dun on Irakesh and gives Steve the control bracelet.

Both Wepwawet and Jordan are wearing the demonic power armor created by Hades, and we learn just how bad that is. They are controlled by the armor, and can't get out of it. They now serve Set, and will help him in his final battle against Isis and Osiris.

Set assaults Mohn HQ, but our heroes have laid the best trap they can. The Director leads the defense, which is designed to keep Set busy while everyone else assaults the First Ark. It works, but the Director is captured by Set. The others kill Set's wife, Nephthys, but Set arrives before they can assault the First Ark.

That's according to plan. Set is enraged, and Isis, Ra, and Osiris keep him busy while Blair and the others detonate the First Ark. Isis believes the resulting explosion will kill them all, but that the price is worth it to remove Set. His bobbleheaded-ness must be stopped.

Blair, Liz, and Trevor square off against Steve, Irakesh, and Wepwawet. This was one of my favorite fights of the entire series, because Captain Douchey himself is finally killed. He's incinerated by Blair, who gets revenge for all the jacked up things Steve did to him. Irakesh defects to their side, helping to battle Wepwawet. Finally, Liz kills Wepwawet and consumes his essence (because that won't have consequences, right?).

The First Ark explodes, and presumably Isis, Osiris and Ra are killed (I ain't saying). Everyone else escapes using the light bridge, and they arrive in the Nexus. At this point many people were sure the series was over, but I threw a massive curve ball in the epilogue. The light walk had been affected by the exploding First Ark, and they'd been flung five years forward in time. The world is a completely new place, and they have no idea what's changed.

So yeah, that's pretty much it. I'm sure I missed some stuff. Even as the author I can't remember everything that went down. If you think of anything I missed let me know and I'll add it. You can reach me at chris@chrisfoxwrites.com. On to *The Great Pack*.

The Great Pack

Wait, why am I recapping a book you haven't read yet? I'm not. This page is the very last hurdle you have to get over to get into the book, but before you get there I just wanted to pass something along.

I worked hard on *The Great Pack*. I studied Miwok tribal lore. I learned about the Amazon Rainforest, and their local legends. You're going to see many of those legends come to life. When you read about the Great Bear, for example, that's a real Miwok myth. It dates back to the tribe that proceeded them, the Awaneechee, who lived in Yosemite Valley thousands of years ago.

The same is true of the Mapinguara in the Amazon. That too is an established myth. As I've done in each preceding book, the events are based as closely as possible on real world lore. Why did I bring this up? Because over the last two years so many of you have reached out. You seem to love history and the idea of vanished cultures just as much as I do.

One last note. The first several chapters may feel disjointed, particularly if it's been a while since you read Vampires Don't Sparkle. New characters are introduced, and I show quite a few points of view. If you stick with it, it will all come together. I promise.

Anyway, thanks for listening to me ramble. Here's the payoff. Enjoy *The Great Pack*.

Prologue

The Liwanu awakened slowly, warmth seeping into long unused muscles through the rock above. That rock had been cold for innumerable centuries, since the sun had changed and robbed the world of its true power. Now, it was warm again. The time had come. The world was ready for his return.

He stretched, rising to his full height—well, his full height as a man, anyway. He'd slept in human form, as that had given him the best chance of surviving the long hibernation that had carried him to the present.

The Liwanu's shaggy black hair spilled down his back. His fingernails were long and unkempt. The furs he'd used for clothing had long since rotted away, leaving him naked.

No matter. He'd danced in the snow during the heart of winter; this lesser cold could not touch him.

The Liwanu yawned, walking sleepily to the mouth of his little cave. The entrance was still covered, which did not surprise him. He planted both hands against the warm stone, setting his feet against the floor as he began to strain. Pushing the boulder free was difficult—far more difficult than he'd have expected—but eventually, inch by agonizing inch, he forced it from its perch. It rolled free with a tremendous pop and bounded down the hillside into the thickly wooded valley below. The thunder of its passing resounded across the mountains, echoing into the distance.

A flock of ravens scattered into flight, winging up and away as they observed the boulder's passing. The sight of the agile birds winging through the redwoods drew a smile from the Liwanu. He knew the world must have changed greatly, but, whatever was different, at least that piece was the same.

The wind, too, was the same: bitterly cold on his skin. It whistled over the valley, singing in the high places, and caressed his nakedness as he moved from the cave mouth. The Liwanu blinked in the thin sunlight, walking up the hillside toward Tissaack's jutting granite crown.

The mountain was unchanged, the face of the young woman shedding tears down her granite slopes. Yet there were differences. What was that affixed to the back side of the mighty mountain?

The Liwanu leapt into the air, slinging himself from the tip of a great redwood. He bounded up the granite, landing in a crouch at the sub-dome beneath Tissaack herself. A pair of strange grey ropes extended up the back of the mountain, woven from something shiny. Every few paces a tree limb had been fashioned into a rung. It was a ladder, of sorts, allowing people to climb to the top of mighty Tissaack.

The Liwanu roared, lunging forward and grabbing one of the cables. He pulled, wrenching with all the fury the desecration wrought in him. The strange rope groaned, then pulled free from the rock. He yanked again, and again. The third yank pulled the rope loose, and the entire cabling tumbled to the rock near the Liwanu's feet.

His initial ire was sated, but he still longed to find whoever had done this.

The wind brought the scent of man: a whiff of long-worn leather. The Liwanu turned from the wreckage of the strange ladder he'd destroyed. A pile of strange-colored leathers lay not far from the trail. There were hundreds of them, mismatched and of all sizes. He approached, picking up a glove the color of a strawberry in summer. The glove was cunningly shaped, and far more supple than the leathers his own people had worked. The Liwanu slid his fingers inside of it, surprised by how well it fit. It protected his skin from the cold, so he fished through the pile until he found the matching one.

Then he peered up at the mountain. "Forgive me, Tissaack. I will return to remove all traces of man from your holy visage. First, I must learn what has happened to the Ahwahnechee. I will return to remove this desecration."

The Liwanu bounded up the rock face, extending long claws that bored into the granite. He was slightly winded by the time he reached the top—an unwelcome surprise. His slumber had stolen much, it seemed. He slowed his pace, catching his breath as he reached the flat part of the mountain, then walked to the edge, peering down into the valley below as he had countless times during his youth.

He had no words. Ahwahnee's sacred beauty had been blemished. Sinuous black lines stretched across the valley floor like snakes. They were choked with strange boxy vehicles that belched clouds of filth into the air. There were many upon many, in a bedazzling array of strange colors. Were they some sort of slipsail, as Mother had used?

The strange slipsails congregated around large structures, far bigger than any mud hut. Those structures were numerous, dotting every corner of the valley. Men moved in and out of those structures, their clothing a riot of colors. Some of those colors were new to him, the bright hues found nowhere in nature that he knew of.

The Liwanu growled deep in his chest. He leapt from the mountain, shifting into an eagle as he fell. His arms became wings, nimbly guiding his body down into the valley. A few disinterested faces looked up, each dismissing him in the same way.

The Liwanu glided to a perch atop a wooden post outside one of the largest structures. Strange glyphs decorated the sign. He wished Mother were here to use her magic. She could no doubt understand the glyphs.

The Liwanu shifted again, back to human form, hopping to the ground. Many of the humans were staring. More than a few pointed in his direction. He studied them with puzzlement. Not a single face resembled his people. Instead, some had pale skin, and their hair came in colors he'd never seen. A few had golden locks, and one had the deep purple of twilight. Some faces were paler, some the color of dried mud.

A woman in a dark jacket and dun-colored pants approached. She wore an odd hat with a wide brim. The Liwanu watched her approach passively. She smelled wary, but didn't seem hostile.

The woman said something, her voice rising at the end to indicate a question. He recognized none of the words, and simply shrugged in reply. The woman spoke again. This time he recognized a word: *Yosemite*. It was a more formal version of his name, the one used in early stories about his transformation.

"My name has survived the sleep between ages?" the Liwanu asked.

The woman seemed just as puzzled by his words as he was by hers, and her scent changed. There was more fear now. The people around him were growing restless, clustering closer. They were a confusing jumble of scents, and carried odd smells that burned his eyes and nose. He did not like them. They were all speaking at once, pressing closer.

Someone touched his shoulder, and the Liwanu lashed out.

He shifted back to his native form, dark fur sprouting all over his body. His hide toughened as bones popped and cracked. He grew in height, towering over the crowd of people. His face split into a broad, ursine snout. Black claws burst from his paws, and his teeth elongated into fangs.

The humans began to scream, and run.

The Liwanu gave in to his rage, chasing down the closest. He knocked the woman who'd first spoken to him to the ground, pinning her with a massive paw.

Then the Great Bear knelt to feed.

Chapter 1- Five Years Later

Yukon bounded over a rock, sending up a spray of snow as he dodged between two pines. Behind him the pack flowed: dozens of dogs, coyotes, and even a few foxes. They continued their ascent, making for the high places. Yukon paused, giving an encouraging howl to those behind him.

The howl was taken up by the pack, and answering howls echoed from the hills on the far side of the valley.

What news, brothers? Yukon thought at them. He shivered, his thick fur not even protecting him from the bitter cold.

Sunfur. You're Sunfur. It came in a dozen jumbled thoughts. They were tinged with awe and joy, something Yukon had come to expect when meeting new packs. Many had heard of the Great Pack, and longed to join it.

I am called Yukon. My pack and I are fleeing from many, many notdeads. They fill the valley below, and we dare not go back that way.

I am called Cloudrunner. The high places are not safe, thought back a coyote, an old matron, trusted by the others. He could feel her age, sense many seasons of memories in her mind. *You must risk the notdeads. Those who go further into the mountains do not return. Even now, we are fleeing to plains west of us. Better to lay down in the snow than face the Liwanu.*

Yukon could feel her terror, the lingering echo of packs whose song had been silenced forever. He peered back the way they had come, down the slopes winding into the town the humans called Sonora. Tiny black figures writhed between houses and shops, a sea of ant-like notdeads. Beyond them, he knew, thousands more choked the forest. He'd never seen a horde this large. It stretched for miles to both the north and south, blanketing the land in hungry death.

We cannot turn back. Yukon thought back, showing her what he saw below.

I mourn for us all, then, brother. The notdeads will kill many. The Liwanu and his children will kill all.

Yukon did not know that word, *Liwanu*—there were still many words he didn't know, even after the Mother had awakened him—but he could feel the meaning behind it, something like the growl of a terrible bear.

Yukon trotted a few steps in the snow, unsure what to do. *Thank you sister. We will move swiftly and try to avoid the high places as much as we can. We'll follow the mountains, until the notdeads are left behind. Hopefully, we are gone before this Liwanu can find us.*

May we run with you, brother?

Yes. Join our packmind. Be one with us.

Yukon bounded through the snow again, following the ridge to the north. He set a ground eating pace, loping through the snow with ease. The Mother had made him larger than any wolf, but the rest of the pack wasn't so fortunate. The smallest was a border collie, panting as she rushed along in the trail Yukon's passage allowed. He longed to slow, but dared not—not after Cloudrunner's warning.

The sun marched steadily across the sky until Yukon finally paused upon a tall hill. He stared down at the tiny town below, just a few structures near a lake that had been made by men. The water was thick with writhing black specks, and the shores teemed with them. This place was even worse than Sonora. How large could the horde be? Surely there was an end to it.

Yukon plunged ahead, knowing that if he hesitated too long the rest of the pack would pick up on his unease. He needed to be strong for them, to keep them moving lest they give up hope. He plunged down a steep slope to a snow covered road, then turned north again, pressing forward, feeling for more packs.

There were none. The hills were silent, save for the wind. Even the crows were missing, and they *never* stopped talking. The pack sensed the change, and the occasional yips and barks were gone. They moved silently, flowing through the trees like ghosts.

Yukon's heart raced. Something was out there. Something large, and very, very old. He sensed it out there, somewhere—and he knew that it sensed him, too. There was a sameness between them. Whatever it was, it had also been awakened by the Mother.

A lost brother?

The snow next to a huge granite boulder exploded into the air. A black-furred grizzly towered over the pack, standing many times the height of a man. It lunged at a German Shepherd, snapping her up in its jaws. She gave a single whimper, then the Bear flung her body into a pine tree. She fell and did not rise.

Yukon darted forward, barking at the Bear. Its gaze fell on him, and his pack sprang away. The larger members circled behind the Bear, while the smaller ones retreated into the trees.

Blood dripping from its muzzle, the Bear gave a thunderous roar as it lunged for Yukon. Yukon darted backward, but not quickly enough. Claws punched through his side, and he yelped as the blow carried him into the air. It flung him across the meadow, and he rolled through the snow at the far side.

Run, Sunfur. Run! Cloudrunner's voice echoed through the pack mind. *We will delay Liwanu, so you may live. The pack must live.*

Yukon knew despair. *No. Please. Do not do this.*

The pack howled. They swarmed the Bear, darting in from every side. Yukon could feel their fierce determination, their knowledge that this was a foe they could stop. They would die, so Yukon would live; they were gladdened by this.

Yukon hung his head in shame, turning from battle. Blood flowed freely from his side, leaving a trail he knew the Bear would be able to follow. He forced himself past the pain, running north along the ridge. He still couldn't risk leaving the hills, not while any of the pack survived. Many voices had gone silent, yet many more remained.

He redoubled his pace, running as he had never run. Alicia must be warned.

Chapter 2- Splitting Up

"Are we absolutely positive that splitting up is the best way to go?" Blair asked, leaning on his golden staff. The scarab-topped Primary Access Key hummed with power, comforting in the midst of so much chaos. He could feel it feeding pulses of energy into the Nexus, stabilizing its weakened matrix. The gems lighting the golden chamber glowed dimly, but it was better than it had been when they'd arrived.

They made a motley group: a mixture of deathless and champions, the ragged survivors of the battle for the First Ark. Now that the crisis was over Blair was already seeing the cracks start to form. Jordan stood apart from everyone, tree-trunk arms folded across his trademark black t-shirt. He hadn't said much, but kept darting glances at Trevor and Irakesh. Trevor clearly knew it, frowning back at Jordan each time the big man darted a glance his way.

Trevor stepped onto the light bridge, turning to face Blair. Trevor's skin was a little too pale, his eyes an unnatural green—but sometimes Blair could almost forget that he was deathless. "We've been over this. Yeah, splitting up is incredibly risky. Odds are good that at least one of us is going to run into more than we can handle. But with Ka essentially blind, we have no idea how things have changed in the outside world. We need answers."

He beckoned to Irakesh. Irakesh bobbed his bald head submissively, then moved to stand behind him.

Trevor smiled at Blair, "I can't believe you get to hang out with Liz, and I get stuck with fucking Irakesh. I feel like I lost a bet."

"You realize I'm standing right here, right?" Irakesh asked, glaring at Trevor.

"Let's focus, people," Jordan snapped. He walked to the edge of the platform, looking up at Trevor. "Keep your wits about you, and don't ever, ever trust that twisted bald fuck. Stick to the plan."

"I get it," Trevor replied hotly. "We'll use the Arks to check in with each other in three days. If we're unable to come physically, we'll use the Arks to project a hologram. If we miss each other we check again in another seven days. It's not a complicated plan, Jordan."

"Calm down, guys. The testosterone is making my eyes water," Liz said, smiling. She poked Jordan in the ribs. "Trevor's a big boy. He'll be fine." Then she darted onto the platform, wrapping Trevor in a fierce hug. "Be careful, bro."

Irakesh moved to join the hug, but Liz let out a low growl. Even in human form, it was menacing enough to make the deathless retreat.

"I'll be careful, Wizzer," Trevor said, mussing her hair. He released her, and she moved to rejoin Blair next to the platform. "Just keep Blair out of trouble." Trevor's face grew more serious as he turned to Jordan. "Good luck in South America. If you see Doctor Roberts, tell him I'm sorry about Panama."

"Good luck, man," Jordan said, extending a hand to Trevor. The pair shook, though there was clearly still tension between them. Trevor gave a nod, then the platform flared white. When the brilliance dimmed, he and Irakesh were gone—teleported thousands of miles in the blink of an eye.

"Guess it's my turn," Jordan said. He started walking up the corridor, back toward the central hub of the Nexus, where they'd first met Ka.

Liz lagged a little behind, still peering at the platform where Trevor had disappeared. Blair didn't blame her. She loved her brother, but circumstances always conspired to keep them apart.

Blair followed Jordan into the central hub, then up the passageway leading toward the Mother's Ark, which was located down in Peru. Thinking of the Ark reminded Blair of the Mother, and the sacrifice she'd made on the world's behalf. At least she was at peace now. She'd earned that.

"I can't believe you're going back to the place this all started," Blair said, eyeing Jordan as they made their way up the corridor. The walls were lined with glyphs, glyphs Blair could read now—not that he had time to study them. "I still remember Mohn's last stand down in the central chamber, when we woke the Mother."

"The universe has a shitty sense of humor. Now not only am I a werewolf, but I'm the guy running *her* Ark," Jordan replied. He shook his head, giving a sharp laugh. "It isn't really my style. I'd rather be finding

Mohn Corp. I can really make a difference there, with the Director gone. The Old Man might still be in charge, and he'll need all the help he can get. I never liked him, but at least he wants to keep humanity breathing."

"You'll make a difference in Peru," Blair replied. "There are more champions there than anywhere, and a lot of the tech survived. Those people will need a leader, and you can do that better than anyone except maybe Liz."

"I can organize a military, but I'm never going to have the Director's way with people. I'm not a bureaucrat, or a politician." Jordan's words were unapologetic. The man knew his strengths, and clearly didn't consider leading to be one of them.

"So don't be either. Be an Ark Lord. I wish you could see it from my perspective." Blair gave a genuine laugh. It felt damned good, dissipating some of the ever-present tension in his shoulder blades. "You seriously underestimate how scary you are. You were the terrifying hit man who blew up Trevor's house and chased us all over the world. You headed up major ops for Mohn Corp. When *I* got tapped for all this, I was a teacher at a local junior college."

"Point taken," Jordan said. He gave Blair a rare smile as he paused next to the platform. "I've just gotten used to taking orders, not giving them. Maybe it's time for me to change that."

"Good luck," Blair replied. He offered Jordan his hand, and the burly man shook it.

"Jordan," Liz said, hurrying into the room. She gave the commander a hug, just as she'd done for Trevor. "Be careful."

Jordan seemed more than a little taken aback, but after a moment returned Liz's hug. "I will, Liz. You guys do the same."

He stepped onto the platform, and gave them a tight salute. Then the platform flashed, and he disappeared.

"Our turn," Blair said. He offered Liz his arm, and she took it. They walked in silence, enjoying each other's company until they reached the platform leading to the Ark of the Redwood. He turned to face Liz, taking her hand in his. "You realize that we're walking into more chaos, and we won't have a moment of free time."

"Oh, I don't know about that. I think we can find a *little* time," she said, giving a delightfully wicked grin. She leaned a little closer—almost close enough to kiss. "The rest of the world has survived for five years. I'm betting it can survive for one more night."

Chapter 3- Salvador

Nox shifted restlessly, the shuttle's strange black stone flowing to fit the contours of his grotesque body. The chair formed in the stone had a low back that allowed his wings to rest comfortably behind him, and parted to make room for his tail. It was as comfortable as any chair was likely to be, but no piece of furniture could make a three-hour flight anything but tedious —especially in a craft that had been designed both by and for another species.

The shuttle used the Builder's iconic pyramid, and from the outside it could have been mistaken for a miniature Ark. Inside, it was dotted with small forests of black obelisks of varying heights, each giving off a different blend of signals. Nox couldn't decipher them all, and he suspected that was part of why the grey men had given Hades the shuttle in the first place: it showed just how much more advanced they were.

Nox wasn't impressed. The shuttle was advanced, but not much more so than humanity had been before the fall. Flying across the world was something he'd done regularly, as the Director for Mohn Corp.

The primitive airplanes you used were hardly the same, Set-Dun. They did not allow you to cross the world in minutes, nor did they allow you to journey to other worlds.

The voice had a point. Nox touched the console, willing the holoscreen to show him the coastline they were approaching. A vast expanse of blue-green washed up against the South American coast. Beyond that shore lay a sea of impenetrable green, the largest rainforest in the world. How odd that he had returned here, to the place where the old world had truly ended. Back then it had been about containing the werewolf virus, a war they'd thought they could win.

How naive he'd been, about so many things.

Yes, about a great many things. You've started to think of yourself as Nox, just as I predicted. Your old life will become little more than a dim memory as the years pass.

Nox ignored the voice, pivoting his chair to face the shuttle's interior.

Several dozen corrupted deathless, each with a sinuous tail and leathery bat wings, were perched among the obelisks. The differences between them were indistinguishable to the naked eye—but for one notable exception.

Kali, a beautiful girl in her early twenties, was in human form. She had red-brown hair, and an easy smile. Almost everything about her screamed *girl next door*—including her Ugg boots and black yoga pants—with only one thing to spoil the image: her eyes were flat black, dangerous and unreadable, like a shark.

She leapt to her feet the moment Nox faced her, hurried over to his side, and gave him a warm, friendly smile. "Looks like we're almost there. You don't mind if I kill Camiero's family, do you? Nothing says 'you work for us now' quite like turning your wife and children to ash in front of you."

Other demons had begun to approach, roosting on pillars all around them. Unlike Kali, the other demons had all been corrupted by Nox. He'd obliterated their free will, leaving them no choice but to obey.

Nox ignored them. "No," he told Kali. He rose slowly, stalking toward her.

Kali merely pouted at his approach, but the other pair of demons both flinched.

"This trip requires subtlety," Nox said. "If we do the job well, Camiero will serve us without the need for a demonstration. Remember, time is the resource we are shortest on. We need to work quickly, and we cannot do that if we antagonize this man. If he resists, you may dismember him and his family, and we'll select another to rule here. "

Kali grunted, studying her manicured fingernails.

Satisfied that his orders were clear, Nox turned back to the holoscreen. They had broken from the clouds now, and a mass of lush green jungle dominated the western horizon. They were circling South America's eastern coast, moving south toward the Brazilian city of Salvador. It sprawled across a triangular peninsula, shielding the bay behind it from the ocean.

Sixteenth-century Spanish architecture huddled at the feet of massive modern resorts bordered by lush palms and wide white beaches. It reminded Nox a great deal of Hawaii, though the city was about a dozen times larger than Honolulu. Half the city sat at sea level; the other half was nearly three hundred feet higher. The two sections were separated by an escarpment, and linked by a series of elevators.

One of those elevators was slowly rising, and Nox could see dozens of people packed tightly inside.

"How do those still work?" Kali asked suspiciously.

"This city's proximity to the equator means it was barely touched by the CME, or the subsequent sunstorms. That makes it the perfect place for technology to survive." He pointed at the line of cars snaking along the freeways. "That should tell you why controlling this city is so important to Hades."

Nox guided the shuttle toward a large manor house atop the largest hill in the city. It was exactly the sort of place you'd expect a petty dictator to choose: ostentatious and completely indefensible, without even a tree line to obscure the place. Anyone with a rocket launcher and a bad temper could blow the shit out of the entire house from any of three dozen buildings within a mile. A professional sniper could surgically remove targets at will, executing anyone or anything that emerged from that house.

Nox shook his head, guiding the shuttle to hover just outside a bay window on the third story of the manor house. Deathless with assault rifles were scrambling now, blurring through the house in a panic. Nox willed himself to sink through the black stone floor, extending his wings as he left the craft. The black leathery membranes caught the warm tropical wind, and he glided toward the house. He immensely enjoyed flying; the feel of the wind along his scaly skin was a cool balm against the heat of accumulated sins.

You are still far too squeamish, Set-Dun. You balk at the simplest of necessities, the ever-present voice rumbled, deep in the recesses of his mind.

Again, Nox ignored it.

Kali's demonic form rippled through the shuttle's hull, and she glided toward him. "Are you certain about not killing the family?"

More demons rippled through the bottom of the shuttle, falling on the manor like deadly black leaves.

"You may 'encourage' anyone that tries to leave this place, but do not kill them," Nox ordered. He crashed through the bay window, scattering glass across an enormous living room as his clawed feet sought purchase on the marble floor.

Several uniformed men took aim, letting out bursts of automatic weapons fire. Bullets ricocheted off Nox's carapace, but he chose to ignore them as he walked toward a wide stairway leading down to the first floor. Camiero was somewhere below, probably surrounded by every bodyguard he could muster.

"W-what are you?" a frightened deathless said, dropping his rifle and backing away as Nox passed him. He stank of decay and fear.

The gunfire grew sporadic, as the deathless gave up attacking. By the time Nox reached the first floor, he could only hear it from outside— punctuated by a single scream, then silence.

Nox's eyes narrowed. Kali was pushing boundaries again.

Hades views you the same way you view that girl. He knows you plan to escape. The tone was amused. *Is it any wonder you see the same in Kali? She still serves her grey men masters; you have to know that. The pretense that she serves you only lives until we earn their displeasure. Then she will turn her flames on you.*

Nox spotted a stairwell leading to a basement, so he made for that. He paused at the top of the stairs, wincing as a flash of white-hot flame splashed the ground outside a window. He forced himself to ignore it, walking down the stairs.

Below waited three bodyguards, all deathless. All were dark-skinned, darker than he'd have expected. Each held his gun like a talisman, and none employed any of the shaping that might have allowed them to escape, or possibly even to harm him. These people had little to no training. If these were the best Camiero could surround himself with, then Nox questioned the man's usefulness. How had he maintained control here?

"Tell your master that Nox has arrived," Nox roared.

The name still made him chuckle inwardly. He was *the night*; it made him sound like a bad comic villain.

One of the guards disappeared through a doorway, while the other two continued to cower. Both had lowered their weapons, evidently realizing that they were unlikely to have any better success than their companions on the second floor. Those fools still lurked above, peering down at Nox from the landing above. It puzzled him that none used their deathless abilities. Those wouldn't have worked, but these fools couldn't know that.

"Who—or what—are you?" a voice asked, speaking from a few feet away. The air shimmered, and a deathless stepped from the shadows. He was dark-skinned and impeccably dressed. He wore a suit of the finest cotton, the type Nox would had greatly enjoyed before his transformation. His goatee was neatly trimmed, his cufflinks buffed. His tie was even tied with a Windsor knot.

This man, Camiero, had swum with the elite before the world ended. That could make this alliance much more palatable, and potentially fruitful —depending on just who this man had been, and who he had become in the new world.

Nox took three unhurried steps closer to the deathless, then extended a clawed hand. "You may call me Nox. I've travelled a very long way to meet you, Camiero."

Camiero took the hand, shaking it firmly, then released it. He met Nox's gaze. "You've invaded my home. You scuffed up the floor with your clawed feet, and shattered my window. You've murdered my guards, though thankfully not as many as you could have. Why have you come? What do you think you can gain from assaulting me?"

Nox was impressed. The man calmly stated the situation, calling Nox out without insulting him. He didn't threaten or posture, though both knew it could come to combat, depending on how Nox responded.

"My entry was aggressive, but I needed to ensure that I have your full attention," Nox explained. He folded his powerful arms, tail swishing behind him as he spoke. It coiled, ready to grab Camiero's ankle if needed. "I've come to offer you power. I can give you demonic strength, elevating you above all other deathless on this continent. I can provide an army of demons to help you conquer all of Brazil—and eventually all of South America."

"An entire army, you say? And you will simply give it to me?" Camiero's words were jovial, his half-smile friendly. There was steel underneath. "That is a very generous offer, but my mother had a saying: do not trust those bearing gifts, unless you understand what they seek to gain in giving them to you."

"Your mother was a wise woman," Nox said, smiling in spite of himself. "I won't sugarcoat this. Accepting this gift will mean serving me. You will be more powerful, but you will also be subservient. This entire continent will be yours to do with as you wish, but when I have need…you *will* accept my commands."

"I already have plenty of power." Camiero pursed his lips and walked to the nearby bar, withdrawing a crystal ewer and pouring himself a glass of what Nox guessed was Scotch. He didn't offer any to Nox. Swirling the contents of his glass, he seemed to gather his words. "That you are so open about the cost suggests that you expect me to accept your offer anyway, even though you know that I'll eventually conquer this continent without outside aid. Why else would you have chosen me to make this offer to?"

"You're very astute. I'm glad you live up to your reputation." Nox found himself liking the man. He walked to the far side of the room, staring through a wide bay window that overlooked the harbor. A body plummeted past, charred beyond all recognition. Nox winced. Kali's antics would probably make this more difficult.

Camiero joined Nox at the window, setting his glass down on a mahogany end table. "You're very good at this, Mr. Nox. You enter my home like a brute, demonstrating your strength. You do not threaten my life, but you *do* bring a butcher so that the threat is implied: join, or be wiped out. Those are my choices, yes?"

"Something like that." Nox turned to face Camiero. "I would prefer not to kill you, but if you refuse to serve me I will simply approach the next candidate. I've identified a dozen. Eventually, one will accept. That one gets to live, and to grow in power. The others, as you've deduced, will be... removed."

"And what is it you want on this continent, Mr. Nox? I've been aware of you for some time, but in the last five years you've never come to South America. Why now? What is it you are seeking here?"

Nox weighed the benefits of telling the truth. In this case, that seemed the most expedient method. Camiero was too intelligent to labor in ignorance. "I'm searching for something in the Amazon. To get it, I need the resources you command."

"You seek El Dorado, yes? The legendary city protected by the jungle? Yes, by your expression I can see that you do. Getting into the jungle will carry a high cost. The champions rule the trees, and they will destroy any deathless who enters. My best men are either slain, or flee."

"Let me worry about the champions," Nox said. He turned from the window, taking a step closer to Camiero. "I will provide you the weaponry with which your deathless can fight the champions. By tomorrow morning, a full battalion of my demons will arrive."

"I do not like conceding power, but I am no fool," Camiero said. His gaze was heavy with acceptance. "To refuse is to die. I will agree to your bargain, though I'm sure it carries a much higher price than I wish to pay."

"Far higher," Nox agreed. He extended his right hand, using a claw to slice open his palm. "Drink, and learn the cost."

Chapter 4- San Francisco

Liz dropped to a crouch, resisting the urge to gather the shadows around her. The platform they'd arrived on was well-lit, a familiar golden corridor disappearing into the Ark beyond. The silence was total.

Blair stood next to her, his eyes going momentarily glassy. It was creepy watching him bond with the Ark. Liz knew he could somehow see the world outside, and was probably scouting not just the Ark, but the entire Bay Area.

The immensity of that power was humbling. Blair was, in most senses of the word, a god. What would he be like in a decade, or a century? The gods were supposed to live much longer than that.

He is finally coming into his own, Ka-Ken, a voice rumbled in her mind. Liz blinked. The voice was different, familiar somehow.

You're not my beast, she thought. Liz wasn't alarmed, not yet at least.

Not so, Ka-Ken. I am very much your beast, though your recent actions have altered me, the voice rumbled. *You drained my essence during the battle at the First Ark. Such feeding through a Sunsteel weapon carries a heavy cost. By consuming me, you have preserved a fragment of my mind. That fragment has bonded with your beast. I am a part of you now, Ka-Ken.*

"Wepwawet." Liz was positive, even as she uttered the word.

Indeed.

"What about him?" Blair asked, blinking as he stirred from his trance. He scrubbed a hand through tousled blond hair badly in need of scissors.

"Nothing," Liz said, maybe a bit too quickly. She wanted a little time to figure out exactly what was going on in her own head before telling Blair about it. Otherwise he'd start probing, and they had more important things to deal with just then. "What did you find?"

"I scouted the surrounding area," Blair said. "There are definitely a few surprises. It's easier if I just show you."

He rested an hand on Liz's arm. She shivered, there was a flash of light, and then she was elsewhere. She wrapped herself instinctively in shadow, struggling to get oriented. It was dark, but a large moon hung in the sky above, reflected in the lapping waters of San Francisco Bay. She and Blair stood at the very top of the Golden Gate Bridge—what remained of it anyway. Blair gestured at the city itself, but there was no need. Liz was already staring.

Most of the city was dark, but lights came from the skyscrapers in the financial district. Several cars even moved down Market Street, and she could make out a trickle of figures moving up and down sidewalks. The city didn't look much different than it had before the world had ended. A casual observer would have no idea it was anything but a thriving metropolis.

"So, what now?" Liz asked, fighting to be heard over the wind. It was cold this high up.

Blair crouched on the rusted metal arch next to her, unblinking eyes fixed on the city. He shifted to werewolf form, the silver fur covering his body in the blink of an eye. Liz took the cue and went into warform as well.

"Most of the activity is around the ferry building," Blair called. "If you look across the bay, you'll see lights in Oakland, too. Not as many, but there are definitely people there." The wind howled, nearly drowning out his words. He closed his mouth, looking at her, and his words appeared in her mind. *My guess is that the deathless have seized control. Based on the concentration of people, I'm guessing their leader lives near the ferry building. We can probably learn more if we get closer.*

What about Angel Island? Liz thought back.

Blair's face fell, and he shot an agonized glance at the shadowed island. A cluster of trees still dotted the familiar hills, not far from the bridge. There were no lights there, but Liz couldn't see much else. Maybe that was a good thing.

Empty, Blair thought. *I don't know where everyone went, but no one has lived there for a long time. I checked a little ways into Marin, and the place is a wasteland. There are some zombies, but I didn't see any people. Not a single one.*

We need answers badly enough to risk going down there, Liz thought back, knife sharp anger slicing her patience to ribbons. *I'll ride your shadow, if you take us down to the city. We were supposed to protect those people. Someone down there knows what happened to them.*

Blair nodded, his wolfish face somber. He probably felt the loss of Angel Island as keenly as she did. *Give me a moment. With the Ark, I can scan on a much larger scale. I think I can locate their leader. May as well go right for the source.*

Her Ka-Dun closed his eyes, the wind rustling his fur. He stood there serenely, but only for the moment he'd asked.

His eyes quickly opened, and he gave her a toothy grin. *I've found her. Hop in. Let's go get those answers.*

Liz flowed into Blair's shadow, the familiar numbing cold washing over her as she vanished. Blair blurred forward, far faster than she could track. They zipped across the bridge, bounding into the air above the bay. The apex of their jump carried them over the charred crater where Irakesh had detonated the bomb, what felt like a lifetime ago.

Blair caught a rusted streetlight near the crater's edge, bounding from landmark to landmark as he crossed the city. He paused briefly atop the Palace of Fine Arts, then darted up Lombard Street. Liz didn't know the city that well, but she could tell he was making for the cluster of lights in the financial district.

The closer they got, the more deathless they saw. Most were inside buildings; without heartbeats, they were difficult to hear. But Liz could smell their putridity, lurking all around her. Hundreds of them—maybe thousands.

The foot traffic grew heavier as they made their way up Market Street, especially as they approached the ferry building. Beyond lay the bay, dark and silent save for a few lights on the skeletal bulk of the Bay Bridge.

"She's inside," Blair said, "holding court, it looks like. I probed a few minds, and they think of her as the Lord of San Francisco. They fear her, but they also respect her."

Chapter 5- Melissa

"How do you want to do this?" Blair asked, crouching low atop the building. It was only four stories tall, but that was enough to shield them from anyone at ground level—especially in the dark. The city felt empty, and though there were some lights it was nothing like it had been before the CME.

"These deathless are living their lives. It's some semblance of society, and societies have laws. Let's find out what theirs are." Liz shifted back into human form. "It's possible they might attack us, but I'm hoping you and your fancy key can evac us if things go south." She shot him a crooked smile, then leapt off the building, falling four stories to land in a silent crouch. A few deathless turned to look curiously in her direction, but no one moved to investigate.

"I guess we're just going to walk in," Blair muttered. He stepped off the roof, shifting to human form as he fell, and landed next to Liz, occasioning no more comment than she had.

Liz slid her arm through his. "Shall we?"

Blair gave a strained smile. Being here scared the hell out of him, despite the siren song of the Ark's power. They were in the stronghold of their enemy, with no idea who or what ruled here.

They joined a few figures as they flowed through the quartet of glass doors at the front of the Ferry Building. Blair could smell the deathless, and had little doubt that most could sense his true nature as well. A few looked alarmed, giving them a wide berth as they entered the high-ceilinged building. No one stopped them, though.

Blair remembered this place well. He'd come into the city often when he'd been dating Bridget, and they'd usually taken the ferry. That summoned the ghost of one of her laughs, and Blair remembered her death, not ten miles from where he stood. He looked at Liz, and smiled. Bridget would want him to be happy. More than that, *he* wanted to be happy. He'd come to grips with Bridget—both her life and death.

"The boat docks right at the back of the building?" Liz asked, peering through the glass.

"Yeah," Blair said, nodding at the one of the converted stalls. The deathless inside were dressed in business casual, exactly the sort of dress shirts and slacks he'd have expected at any large corporation. A few glanced at them, but most paid no attention. "I used to get coffee from the Roasters right there—the one it looks like they turned into an information booth."

"It looks so…normal," Liz replied, her gaze focused on a pleasant-looking Asian woman chatting with an older couple.

"Yeah." Blair wasn't sure how to feel. He was glad society was continuing, but this was still a lot to take in. Everyone around them was deathless. There wasn't a single heartbeat anywhere, except for Liz and himself.

Where were the living?

"That one is coming over," Liz hissed. Her grip on his arm tightened.

Blair turned his attention to the dark-haired Asian woman, who looked to be in her mid-twenties, heading in their direction. She beamed a white smile their way, and he noted that the teeth were normal. There was nothing to suggest this woman wasn't alive—if you overlooked the lack of a heartbeat. He was guessing she'd employed an illusion, as a faint whiff of power came from her. Blair could feel the signal, even if he couldn't pierce it.

"Welcome to San Francisco," she said, extending a hand. "My name is Melissa."

Liz shook her hand, then Blair did the same. Her palm was cold, but not icy. Her nails were neatly manicured, claws covered in a muted red polish.

"I'm Blair, and this is Liz," Blair said, seeing no reason to lie. "We're, uh, not from around here. At least not recently."

"I can see that. We don't often receive living guests." Melissa eyed them thoughtfully. There was no hostility, but her gaze was calculating. She finally indicated a trio of tables in front of what had once been the coffee shop. "Why don't we sit down and get acquainted? I'm sure you have questions."

Blair followed Melissa to an unoccupied table, sliding into one of the metal chairs. Liz did the same, catching his eye. She gave a short nod, and he knew her well enough not to need to read her mind. She wanted him to take point, and as the resident mind reader that seemed like a great idea. He smiled at Melissa.

"We do have questions. We used to live here five years ago, right after the CME." Blair chose his words carefully, trying to get the information they needed without revealing too much about who they were. "Our people were on Angel Island, and now that we're back we're trying to find them. As I'm sure you know, there's no one there any more. Do you have any idea where they've gone?"

He had no idea if Melissa had ever heard of an Ark Lord, though it was impossible for her not to know what the Ark was. Every deathless would sense the power there; it was impossible to miss.

"How very diplomatic." Melissa gave a musical laugh, crossing her legs as she leaned back in her chair. She smoothed her pants, avoiding their gaze for a moment. When she looked up, her smile had become coy. "You've asked for no information about this city, nor who I am. That would make it rude for me to inquire about your own identities. Unfortunately, I'm going to have to be a little rude. I sensed a great surge of power from the Ark out in the bay. Minutes later, you happen to walk into my office." She gestured expansively at the glass wall bordering the bay. "It's magnificent, isn't it? A pyramid built by beings we neither know or remember. At least, beings *I* don't know."

Her meaning was clear, but Blair avoided it, shifting the discussion. "You're the Lord of San Francisco?"

"That's my title, yes," Melissa replied, giving a self-deprecating eye roll. It was well-practiced, clearly honed in whatever life she'd had before becoming deathless. Marketing, probably. "Melodramatic, but I'm part of a larger council. There are Lords throughout Northern California, most of them loosely allied with each other. It's a bit like feudal Europe—a bunch of tyrants bickering over power. That bit, you get for free. If you want more information, you need to share. Who are you, and what's your connection to the Great Ark?"

"I'm Blair and this is Liz. The surge of power was the activation of the light bridge in my Ark."

That got her attention. Melissa licked her lips, blinking twice. Then she rose gracefully. She had no heartbeat to read, but her nervousness was clear enough. "*Your* Ark? I see. Will you follow me? I can give you a brief tour, and show you where your friends are. I'm willing to do that in good faith, provided you agree to extend me the same courtesy."

"That all depends on what happened to the people on Angel Island," Liz said. She rose slowly, dangerously. She took a half-step closer to Melissa, looming over the shorter woman.

"Please, I don't want to this end in bloodshed. So far as I know, your people are alive and well," Melissa said, raising a hand to forestall Liz's advance. "It's much easier if I show you. I can explain everything."

Blair caught Liz's gaze, and raised a questioning eyebrow. Liz glowered, but fell into step with Melissa. Melissa relaxed visibly, then led them deeper into the ferry build, into a hub of activity. Most of it centered around a huge diorama that had been constructed in the center of the plaza. It was set out on sixteen tables, each showing a section of San Francisco. Suit-clad deathless with tablets moved hurriedly between the tables, tapping away at their screens without looking up.

"This is our logistical headquarters. We organize salvage missions throughout the city, stripping everything from old cars to medical equipment. Those are brought back here for processing and distribution," Melissa explained. She led them among the tables, into what Blair guessed must be the processing area.

Half a dozen booths had been set up around the doors leading out to the docks. The doors opened, and a beefy deathless set two big boxes at one of the booths. The clerk scurried over and began unpacking a variety of cell phones and tablets.

Deathless at other booths were processing books, clothing, and jewelry. Blair noted the conspicuous absence of food. There were no canned goods, no boxes of Twinkies.

This wasn't a group of humans recovering from the apocalypse. These people were deathless. He couldn't afford to forget that.

"We're nearly there." Melissa strode past the last pair of booths, pausing at a makeshift office in what had once been the information desk. A sixty-inch monitor hung from the rear wall, displaying a Windows desktop. Melissa gestured at a pair of chairs, then sat. "Please, join me. Being in charge affords me a few perks, and my ginormous monitor is one of them."

"How do you have working computers? You shouldn't even have power, after the CME," Blair blurted.

Melissa eyed him curiously, and Blair had the sense he'd given something away. Then he realized he'd forgotten about the time gap. San Francisco might have already had power for years. "The CME damaged a lot of the power grid, and it fried most unprotected electronics. When I say most, I'm talking upwards of ninety-five percent. But that meant that five percent still worked. We started processing material within months of the CME, and have been restoring services ever since. We've had help."

She faced the monitor, so Blair did the same. The screen now showed something he'd never expected to see again: Google Earth. The map zoomed in over the Americas.

"About two years ago a ship arrived with gifts," Melissa explained. She zoomed in further on Brazil. "Apparently, electronics closer to the equator were much less impacted than the rest of the world. Brazil sent us ham radios. They were dropping them off in every city, from San Francisco to Tokyo."

"You have the internet. Why do you need ham radios?" Liz asked. She was goggling at the screen, and Blair imagined he wore the same expression. These people had *internet*.

"Our internet is much more limited than you might think." Melissa's disappointment was clear. "Google, Facebook, and Apple were all headquartered here. We were able to restore the internet in the Bay Area, but not much further. It's a pale shadow of what you remember from before. The maps you're seeing are all from archived data. There are no more satellites, so if the world has changed we're unaware of it."

"You were going to tell us about our friends," Blair said. He badly wanted the intel she had, but right now the most important thing was finding their people.

"Indulge me for just a minute more," Melissa said. The screen zoomed in again, this time over northern California. She wiggled the mouse over each area as she spoke. "This is the most organized power block in Northern California. We're called the Lords of Silicon Valley. Don't blame me; I didn't get a vote on the name. Our territory extends to the Altamont Pass, and stops at the Sierras in the east—and not because they're big mountains, either."

"Then why?" Liz asked.

"Because people who go into the mountains don't come back. They get mauled by giant bears. We've had entire scouting parties disappear; after a couple years of trying we finally gave up. And that's hardly the only anomaly. A lot of old things have woken up, and we're only just beginning to understand them." Melissa's tone shifted, colored by the first real bit of fear Blair had seen her exhibit. She shook her head, seizing control of the conversation once more. "You asked about your friends. When I first rose to power in San Francisco, they were still on Angel Island. After a rather unfortunate misunderstanding, they moved north. They've settled here." She wiggled the mouse pointer over a town about forty miles north of San Francisco.

"Santa Rosa. Didn't you use to be a teacher there?" Liz asked Blair.

"Yeah, and I know the area really well." He turned to Melissa. "Thank you so much for your time, Melissa. We need to go find our people. I hope you don't consider us rude if we leave."

"I—see," Melissa said. She eyed him calculatingly. "Would you be open to a meeting in the future? I am sure the other Lords would like to meet you, as we're now neighbors."

"Liz?" Blair asked.

"We're willing to meet," Liz allowed, "provided everything you've told us is true." She leaned over the table, staring hard at Melissa. "Otherwise, Blair and I will be back to talk about it."

"Do you trust her?" Liz asked, her disembodied voice originating from the shadows to his right. Blair looked out over the valley below, the place where he'd lived for over a decade. Sonoma County, the heart of wine country. So many memories.

"I trust her to look after her own interests," Blair replied, "and right now I don't see what she'd gain from making us enemies. I didn't probe her mind, but she let us go without asking anything." He focused his attention on Petaluma, the closest of the towns below. The moon hung low over the horizon, but it gave plenty of light to see, even without his enhanced vision. "It looks like she was telling the truth—or part of it at least. Do you see that row of cars? It looks like they've moved them into a wall from 101 to Highway 16. Those are defensive fortifications."

"Clever. Reminds me of what Roberts did in Panama," Liz said, her voice closer. She was standing right next to him, yet Blair could detect nothing, of course. Not without pinging. "I see a few lights down there, but nothing like San Francisco. I'm guessing they're lanterns."

"Whatever Melissa is doing to restore technology, I doubt she's willing to share." Blair continued to study the wall of cars, and after a moment spotted movement. The longer he looked, the more he saw. Instead of men with guns, though, the shapes were four-legged. A few trotted atop the wall of cars, but most prowled the darkness just south of the wall.

"I wouldn't expect her to," Liz said. "However nice she played, it seemed pretty clear that the deathless and champions are enemies. She may not actively be at war with our people, but she sure as hell chased them out of the Bay Area."

"Liz, I'm pretty positive we're in the right place," Blair said, unable to suppress his sudden enthusiasm. "Do you smell them? Those are dogs. Someone's made a pack, or multiple packs."

"Like Adolpho?" Liz asked.

Blair hadn't thought of the diminutive Peruvian since they'd first woken the Mother. Adolpho had been killed getting them inside, along with the ever-present pack of dogs always trailing after him. "Just like Adolpho. Do you think we should approach?"

"Yeah, but I want to be cautious. Let's find out what we're getting ourselves into before we let them know we're here. We have no idea what changed while we were gone, and the last thing I want is to be attacked by people that should be our friends." Liz's voice moved farther away as she moved down the hillside.

"All right," Blair said. He closed his eyes, willing energy to surge through him. It was just a bit, a tiny amount compared to the vast ocean of power offered by the Ark.

Blair shifted, this time into the body of a true wolf. His senses sharpened, and he reveled in his speed as he loped down the hillside. Having four legs was handy. He extended the energy, offering it in Liz's direction, and felt her accept; she too shifted into a full wolf.

It might not have been the fastest way to approach, but it gave them the best chance of seeing the patrols before they were spotted. Plus, if these packs did detect them, they'd react more favorably to wolves.

They loped silently through the night, eating up the few miles to the wall of cars. An owl screeched above. Several dogs barked in the distance. The wind carried the scent of rusted metal and gunpowder, overlaying canine scents—dozens of them, crisscrossed all around them. This place was well traveled.

They slipped across the final field, stepping cautiously onto the cracked asphalt. 101 had not fared well, and was now more potholes than freeway. Weeds grew everywhere, tall enough to provide at least some cover.

Blair crept along the wall of cars, prowling toward a narrow gap wide enough for a person to peer through. He could hear the heartbeats just beyond, dozens of them. They were too fast to be human, and even were that not the case, he could smell that they were dogs. Blair leapt silently to the top of the line of cars, creeping to the edge.

The moonlight showed dogs of all shapes and sizes, with just about every major breed represented. Most lounged around the asphalt in groups of two or three, huddling together for warmth. Then a tiny black-and-white

Shih Tzu shot to its feet and began barking furiously, rushing in Blair's direction. Dogs rushed forward by the dozens, barking at Blair.

Liz was gone, probably vanished into his shadow. She could pop out if he got into real trouble, but right now the dogs didn't seem to be much of a threat.

"They recognize you," a strong voice called from the shadows of a toppled freeway sign. The figure took several steps forward, until it was standing in a pool of moonlight. "They call you the whelp. That's a strange name, don't you think?"

The man was old, his voice like sandpaper. He had a long, grey ponytail tied with a simple piece of leather. His skin was mottled with age, weatherbeaten by years of backbreaking labor in the sun. Sharp brown eyes lurked under thick white eyebrows, like snowcapped peaks along his craggy face. Blair could sense something in him. The dogs quieted when he spoke and stared as he approached.

"It's not strange," Blair said, "if you ever met the Mother. I'm Blair, and my Ka-Ken is Liz." Blair felt an instant kinship with the man. He wasn't just a champion, but a strong shaper.

"I am John Rivers, of Petaluma. I've heard your name, Blair. All of us have. They say you left on a bridge of light to battle gods from the ancient world. There any truth to that?" The old man was calm, and if the mention of a Ka-Ken put him off at all he didn't show it.

"That's the gist of it, yeah," he replied. "We helped Isis deal with Set, and now we're back." Liz still hadn't appeared, which suggested she didn't share Blair's trust.

"You'll want to speak with Alicia, then." John reached into his pocket, then fished out a hand-rolled cigarette. He put it between his lips, then went still. Blair felt something stir in the man, and the cigarette's end flared to life. A tiny tendril of pungent smoke floated skyward. "She's our war chief. She leads the Great Pack."

"Alicia?" Liz asked, finally stepping from the shadows. She'd shifted to warform, nine-and-a-half feet of muscle and fangs. She had gained at least six inches of height after absorbing Wepwawet. "She'd be what, fifteen now?"

"Near enough," John said, eyeing Liz like she'd sprouted a third eye. "I can already smell trouble. You and Alicia are going to be like oil and water, especially since she's been spoiling for a fight since Windigo started picking off our people."

"Excuse me?" Liz demanded. She straightened, looming over John. John seemed unimpressed.

"John," Blair said, "we'd appreciate anything you can tell us about Alicia while we travel there. We should speak with her as soon as possible." Blair placed a hand on Liz's side, and she relaxed.

"Of course, Ka-Dun." John nodded graciously. "My pack should remain here to watch for deathless incursions, but I'll escort you to Santa Rosa. Can you blur?"

Chapter 7- Ark Lord

Jordan's hand shot to his sidearm as soon as he was aware of his surroundings. As he had expected, he'd landed on the light bridge platform. It was an exact mirror of the one he'd left, with no way to tell which Ark he was in—well, no visual way.

Something massive pulsed at the edge of his vision, a sea of power waiting to be tapped into. Jordan reached experimentally toward it, shocked by the depth of the reservoir. Blair had described the feeling, but this was the first time Jordan had experienced the true power offered by the role of Ark Lord.

He strode up the golden pathway, the diamonds in the wall flaring brilliantly to life as he traced a familiar route back to his quarters. He hadn't been here since their brief stay in Peru, before Irakesh had fled north with the access key. How long ago was that now? Two months? Three? He genuinely had no clue. Add in the five years they'd somehow missed, and anything could have happened here.

What do you expect to find within your chambers, Ka-Dun? The beast's tone was respectful, maybe even a little awed. Jordan understood completely. The Ark was that impressive, and the fact that he controlled it refused to take root.

"Those were prime quarters," Jordan replied. "If someone is living in the Ark right now, they'll be there. If not, I'd love to grab my second favorite holster. I lost my favorite somewhere in Turkey."

Ka-Dun, the key within you offers command of this most holy place. You may use it to sense anything within, including anyone dwelling here now.

"Well that's damned handy." Jordan stopped in the middle of the corridor, closing his eyes. He reached toward the well of energy again, this time trying to feel the Ark around him.

An entirely new set of senses sprang into his head. *It is thirty-seven degrees outside the Ark. The energy reserves are at 4%. The occupants of the Ark are applying a 12% drain to energy accumulation.*

"Occupants," Jordan said, eyes snapping open. "How many and where

—show me a map."

The Ark obligingly supplied a vibrant hologram near Jordan's head. It showed a three-dimensional cutaway of the Ark. Orange lights were displayed on several levels, some moving slowly up and down corridors. Four of those lights were making their way toward the light bridge, but he'd already made it past the intersection they were taking.

What will you do, Ka-Dun?

"If I'm understanding how the Ark works," Jordan mused aloud, "I could probably incinerate them all before they're even aware of me. They clearly know I'm here, but they're not necessarily hostile—and even if they are, they're still the best immediate source of intel. They know more than I do about the last five years."

Jordan shifted, and coarse blond fur instantly covered his body. His senses sharpened, and he could smell the intruders: three females and a male, all champions. That didn't cause him to relax, though. Quite the opposite—just because they were werewolves didn't mean they were friendly.

He blurred, kicking up a fierce wind as he zipped through the tunnels. It came effortlessly, and the universe slowed to a crawl around him. Jordan had never moved this fast. Maybe Blair had, but if so Jordan had never seen it. This bond to the Ark was incredible.

Jordan burst around a corner, kicking off a wall into the light bridge chamber. None of the champions seemed ready for a fight; their faces were more curious than alarmed. The lead figure was kneeling next to the platform, one palm placed against the golden metal. Her eyes were closed, and Jordan could sense some sort of signal flowing from her.

She was shaping.

That shouldn't be possible, Ka-Dun. Not so far as I know. Shaping is the purview of the Ka-Dun, as battle is the purview of Ka-Ken.

Jordan had essentially all the time in the world to examine the situation, and he decided to use that time. He darted over to the woman, kneeling next to her nearly frozen form. She was tall, with long dark hair—beautiful, but severe. Motes crawled through the air near her face, and her deep blue eyes were fixed with concentration. The signal wasn't coming from her. It was coming from the golden bracelet on her wrist. It was clearly sunsteel, with a triangular sapphire set in the center. It contrasted oddly with her homespun dress. The white fabric looked handmade.

The trio of champions behind her wore similar garb, all cotton and all handmade. None of the others had bracelets, or any other real jewelry. None held a weapon—though the fact that they were werewolves was weapon enough.

How should he best deal with them? If Blair were here, he'd probably just stop blurring so he could talk to them. That was the polite thing to do.

Unfortunately, Jordan wasn't a very polite guy.

He drew on the vast power at his fingertips, fueling the ability he felt most comfortable with: his telekinesis. He willed invisible bonds into existence, lifting all four champions into the air. Their limbs were pinned to their bodies, and as Jordan released the blur their faces melted into different versions of confusion.

"Hey, there. Name's Jordan. This is my Ark." Jordan walked slowly to stand at the base of the light bridge, staring down at the woman with the bracelet. "You look like you're in charge. How about you tell me who you are, and what you're doing here?"

Her expression—eyes wide, mouth hanging open—was comical. She licked her lips, blinking a few times before speaking. Then her features hardened to indignant anger. "I am Elia, high priestess of this place. We keep vigil for the Mother's return. I demand you release me."

"Yeah, no," Jordan replied. He shifted back to human form, and was mildly surprised that Elia could almost look him in the eye. They didn't usually make women that tall. "The Mother is dead. I saw it with my own eyes. Whatever it is you think you're doing here, there's no point."

"Save your blasphemies; we will not be swayed by them. You may be powerful, but we will fight you until our dying breath." Elia's eyes blazed, and if she could have burned him to a cinder on the spot he was pretty sure she would have.

"Eldest sister, I recognize this man," said one of the Ka-Ken, a pretty dark-skinned woman with long black hair. "Or at least, his name. El Medico spoke of him. He did leave with the Mother to battle the ancient evil."

"You know Doctor Roberts?" Jordan asked. He ignored the woman with the bracelet, moving to stand next to the woman who'd spoken. She was nearly as tall as Elia, with her hair bound in the same kind of ponytail Liz used. Her scent was heady and intoxicating, in some primal way.

"I do know him, Ka-Dun," she said, giving him a deferential nod.

"Tell him nothing, little sister. We will—"

Jordan gestured, and her jaw clamped shut. "Can you tell me where to find him?"

"Yes, Ka-Dun. He is the president of New Peru. He has led that nation for the past three years, ever since they declared themselves. Before that, he led and helped others. He is well loved here." The woman's familiar tone suggested she knew Doctor Roberts personally. That increased her value several notches.

"Do you have a name?" he asked, setting her gently down. He maintained the bonds on the others, including the struggling priestess. Her face had gone bright red, and her eyes promised swift death.

"I am Leticia. Most call me Leti, for short," she said, giving Jordan a low bow. She clasped her hands together, speaking in a soft voice. "Please, release my companions. We mean you no harm. We are here to honor the Mother, nothing more."

Jordan waved a hand and the others dropped to the floor. He turned to Elia. "I'm releasing you, for now. If you become a threat, trust that I will deal with it accordingly."

"Your very presence profanes this place." Elia spat the words. She smoothed her dress, an attempt to regain her composure.

Jordan didn't give her that chance. "I am fast growing tired of your antics," he growled. He took two steps closer, meeting her gaze. "It's my responsibility to run this place, and to protect the surrounding areas. If I have to, I can teleport you—and your friends—all the way to Lima."

"The most holy Ark belongs to the Mother, not some jumped-up cur," Elia snapped. She shifted in an eye blink, claws raking at Jordan's eyes.

He blurred, dodging the blow by millimeters.

Jordan raised his hand, slamming Elia into the wall with telekinetic force. He left her pinned there, plastered to the wall and unable to move. "Insults I'll tolerate. Violence? I don't think so. You attacked me. We're done here."

Jordan reached for the well of power, using it to do something he'd seen Blair do often. Jordan activated the light bridge, teleporting Elia into one of the cells on the lowest level. He powered the bars, trapping her there. Then Jordan turned back to Leticia.

"There are more of you in the temple, right?"

"Yes, Ark Lord. They will be greatly distressed by your arrival. May I ask what happened to Elia?"

"I placed her in the Ark's holding cells," Jordan explained. He felt a twinge of guilt, probably the result of spending too much time with Blair. The man's morals were rubbing off on him. "Listen, I'm sorry for how that went down, but she didn't leave me a lot of choice."

"I agree, Ka-Dun. It pains me to see her imprisonment, but even I must admit she gave you cause."

"Leti, gather your people in the central chamber. I need an explanation about what you're using the Ark for, and I'm sure your people will have many questions."

Chapter 8- Emotional Baggage

Jordan's shoulder blades itched from all the eyes as he strode up the thick red carpet now leading into the central chamber. These people had been busy. Tapestries showing fanciful but not very accurate depictions of Isis dotted the walls, covering the golden glyphs Jordan remembered. He blinked, realizing that wasn't the only thing they'd covered.

During the battle to wake the Mother, Jordan had been on the wrong side. He'd tried to stop Blair, and the resulting battle had done catastrophic damage to this room. The tapestries covered the walls where the worst of that damage lay, and he could still see a few pockmarks in the stone, probably from stray rounds.

"This way please," Leti said. She rested a gentle hand on Jordan's arm, guiding him to the steps of a small dais that had been erected next to the central obelisk.

Priests and priestesses had gathered in a semi-circle facing the dais, though every head was turned to study him as he made his way through their ranks. He read a mixture of curiosity, fear, and outright hostility. So many emotions, and he had no idea what he'd done to cause them—other than existing, and having the key to this place.

"Brothers and sisters, I'd like to introduce Ark Lord Jordan. He bears a sacred connection to this place," Leti explained. She paused, her large eyes scanning her companions. Most seemed to respect her, though not all. A few gave her the same hostile look they'd hurled in his direction. Leti squared her shoulders, speaking again. "Eldest sister Elia attacked the Ark Lord, and he used his powers to place her into the cells on the lower levels. He asked me to gather you all here to discuss his arrival, and what it means for us going forward."

Leti gave him a weak smile, then stepped off the dais. She moved to stand with the others, watching him expectantly. Jordan looked around at the assembled faces, considering his words carefully. He wasn't an orator. He was a soldier. There was no point in pretending to be what he wasn't, so he'd be what he was, without apology.

"The Ark is of enormous strategic value in the war Isis began. It will be necessary to humanity's survival on this continent, and I was entrusted with the access key by the Mother herself," Jordan began. It wasn't strictly true. The Mother hadn't given him the key—he'd taken it from Steve's corpse—but she'd certainly prefer him having it over that smug, arrogant fuck. "It's my job to find every champion on the continent, and weld us together into a cohesive fighting force. To do that I'm going to need a lot of help, help some of you may be able to provide. Since I realize that you may find working with me difficult, I'd like to clear the air. Why don't we start with your questions, and then we'll get to mine."

Several priests shifted uncomfortably, adjusting robes or clutching something very much like prayer beads. One man finally stepped forward. Mid-forties, salt and pepper hair. Average height, with the well-muscled physique common to every werewolf.

"I am called Adam. My title in this temple is eldest brother. We are led by eldest sister Elia, yet you've usurped this place and locked her away. Why? What could you possibly hope to gain? Please, if you wish our cooperation, free her immediately." The man's words were impassioned. Jordan had seen zealots before, but this guy had definitely drunk a double helping of the Kool-Aid.

"Sure," Jordan said. He concentrated, linking with the Ark again.

Far below, the light bridge activated, and a very irate Elia appeared near her companions in a flash of brilliance. She lurched, barely catching herself before finding her balance.

"Here's your eldest sister," Jordan said. "As for what I hoped to gain in imprisoning her, your sister tried to tear out my throat. I don't enjoy being attacked, especially without provocation."

"I had provocation," Elia snapped. Her eyes blazed, and Jordan felt her bracelet activate. Energy infused her words. He didn't understand what the thing did, but he could feel it affecting him. The shaping affected the entire room, faces going slack as they listened to Elia. "You profaned this most holy place. You invaded it, claiming that the Mother is dead. Your heresy is unwelcome, invader. Leave this place, or we will resist you."

"And here I was having a nice day for once," Jordan said, heaving a sigh. Elia clearly had no grasp of what an Ark Lord could do. He doubted any of them did. "Listen, I don't want to pick a fight, but if you attack me again I will put every last one of your furry asses in a cell."

"You cannot defeat all of us," Adam roared, shifting into warform. His clothes shredded, tattered white robes still clinging to his grey fur.

Jordan laughed. He couldn't help it. The idea that these people were going to try to stop him, when they hadn't even mastered shifting with their clothing…he just had to let it out.

"You think this is funny?" Elia's words were the opposite of Adam's, soft as death. "You mock us in the heart of our most holy place. There is only one recourse. Brothers and sisters, slay this man."

Jordan willed bonds around every assembled werewolf, hoisting dozens of Ka-Ken and Ka-Dun into the air with no more effort than it had taken with just a handful of them. It was frighteningly easy.

"Yeah, I guess laughing was pretty rude. Picking you up without asking is rude, too, and I'm sorry for needing to restrain all of you." Jordan began again, moderating his tone. "Let me make the situation clear for all of you. Five years ago, the Mother battled Set. Do you know who Set is?"

"The ancient texts speak of Set and his treachery," Adam allowed, cautiously. "You say that you fought at her side? A simple mindshare can verify that."

"Great. We'll do a mindshare. Here, have some emotional baggage." Jordan wasn't nearly so skilled at this as Blair, but what he lacked in finesse he made up for in brute force. He pushed his memories to every person in the room.

He remembered the days leading up to the detonation of the First Ark. He remembered being imprisoned in the demonic power armor. He remembered fighting Set, and watching allies die. He remembered the Director's final stand.

Jordan blasted those memories at the assembled priests in a firehose of information. Shocked gasps and cries filled the room. The transfer lasted for several moments, and when it was over Jordan released Adam's bonds.

The werewolf toppled to his knees, catching himself against the stone. He rose shakily, licking his chops as he stared at Jordan.

"Satisfied?" Jordan asked.

"Clearly Ark Lord Jordan speaks the truth, or the truth as he knows it at least. He did fight alongside the Mother, and what's more, he is her direct progeny," Adam said. His words had a profound effect on those around them. They began whispering, and their faces shifted from anger to awed reverence. "Please, Lord. Release us, and we will offer you no resistance."

"Do not presume to speak for the order, little brother," Elia snapped, glaring hard at Adam. "I am the eldest, and this place is my responsibility. I will not turn it over to this monster, especially not when he claims the Mother is dead."

"You saw his memories, Elia. It is the truth *as he knows it*," Adam replied. He was calm, and clearly unafraid of Elia. Whatever her bracelet did didn't seem to affect him. "Jordan did not see the Mother die, but she and her consort were placed in mortal peril against a superior foe. Jordan sees no way in which she could have survived, but then he appears to have no real knowledge of her true abilities. There is no sin in ignorance, Elia. He cannot be faulted for it."

"He imprisoned me." Elia's tone was as hard as ever, but her expression showed that she knew Adam had scored a blow. The others were nodding thoughtfully. "Even now we are held against our will. Are you willing to let this brute assume control of the most holiest of places, without a fight?"

"Is that a fight you believe you can win?" Adam asked, raising an eyebrow. "He bested us easily. Effortlessly. He can do this, because he spoke the truth. Jordan is an Ark Lord. He has the key to this place, the key created by the Mother. I am not suggesting we roll over like pups, but I am saying we must proceed carefully. Jordan should be offered respect and understanding, especially if he is willing to continue mindsharing. There is much we can teach him, and much in turn that we can learn."

"I put it to a vote, then," Elia retorted. The bracelet pulsed again, infusing her words with...something. "Will we cast this mongrel out, or accept his dominion over the most holiest of places? Choose carefully, brothers and sisters. Our faith is being sorely tested."

Faces hardened around the room.

"Wait." Jordan raised a hand to forestall Elia, lowering everyone to the ground. "There's no need for a vote. I need intel more than anything, and that means venturing out into the world. Leti mentioned New Peru, and that an old friend of mine is the president. I'll leave, for now. Leti can take me to meet with Doctor Roberts. After I have some answers, I'll return. When I do, we can have a more formal discussion about the fate of this place. Are those terms acceptable?"

"Definitely," Adam said, nodding. "We appreciate the courtesy. This matter will be discussed at length, and when you return we can sort out this…misunderstanding. Elia, I assume you have no objections?"

"None." Elia's eyes burned into Jordan.

He had a feeling she was going to make a bad enemy.

Chapter 9- Arrival

The very instant Trevor was conscious of his surroundings, he flowed into the shadows. Beside him, Irakesh did the same. He spent several long moments looking for threats; there were none, but what he saw was disturbing enough to keep his guard up.

The walls were tainted, covered in a chitinous black substance. The substance was unfamiliar, but it reminded him somehow of Set. It smelled faintly of decay.

"What do you make of it?" Trevor whispered.

"I've never seen the like," Irakesh admitted. The shadows around the deathless dissolved, and he crouched next to the wall near the doorway leading from the room. "It's demonic, without a doubt. But it isn't any form I've seen. It isn't Set's work, either. I don't know who, or what, created this."

"When you say its demonic...can the creator sense us?" Trevor asked. Arks allowed their owners to extend their perceptions, as he understood it. Maybe this stuff could do the same.

"I doubt it," Irakesh allowed.

Trevor noted the brief hesitation. "I'll try tapping into the Ark and see what I can learn."

"Wait!" Irakesh spun, rushing toward him. "Do nothing. Not yet. Interfacing with the Ark will use power, and this stuff might allow whoever put it here to track that usage."

"If that's the case, they already know we're here," Trevor countered. "They knew the instant the light bridge activated." He closed his eyes and reached out to the Ark.

Something massive responded. Trevor gained a bewildering array of new senses, but during his time in the IT world Trevor had been forced to learn new things all the time. This was just another unfamiliar operating system. All he had to do was figure out navigation, and he could tap into whatever the Ark was capable of.

Trevor thought about power reserves, and a response came immediately.

"We're at point zero two percent power reserves. That amount is dropping, and at the current rate this place will go dark in about six more months." Even as Trevor spoke, he was looking for more data. He willed the Ark to show him the area outside the Ark. "Holy crap. There are three pyramids hovering above the Ark. They aren't Ark sized, but they're bigger than a 747. There's also a small city floating above the pyramids, and it looks like the pyramids are feeding it power somehow. It's Olympus, though I've got no idea how Hades moved the city."

"What about the Ark itself? Are we alone?" Irakesh asked, his voice rising a quarter octave. He began pacing.

"Checking," Trevor said. He thought about internal diagnostics, and knowledge flowed into his mind. "Most internal sensors are disabled. Whatever this goop is, it looks like it's the stuff draining the power."

"So we're on our own then. Lovely. Simply lovely. What do you propose we do, Ark Lord?"

Trevor ignored the sardonic tone. He wasn't surprised that Irakesh's composure was slipping, but he couldn't afford to allow the same to happen to him.

"We have no idea who or what we're dealing with," he said. "Our first goal is to get more information about whoever's hijacked the Ark. That means manual recon, so stealth up and follow me." He flowed into the shadows again, moving through the door and up the corridor beyond.

"Do not be so hasty," Irakesh hissed from the shadows in the doorway. "We can still retreat. Let us use the light bridge and go back to the Nexus."

"I told you, this place is bone-dry. There's no way we can activate the light bridge. We're stuck here. Handle your shit, Irakesh. You said you wanted to live, right?" Trevor didn't wait for an answer. He continued up the corridor, straining to detect any threats.

As they approached the central chamber, he detected a warbling thrum passing through the walls. It was slightly off, more of a tremble than the humming purr he'd have expected. The Ark definitely wasn't doing well.

They emerged into a T intersection, the last before making the final ascent into the central chamber. Trevor froze.

A rhythmic clicking came from the corridor to the right. He knew Irakesh had enough survival instinct to stay hidden, so he waited. He was thankful he didn't need to hold his breath, and that he didn't have a heartbeat to give him away.

Three demons walked up the passageway—two men and a woman. They reminded him of Set, but had bat wings and long tails. All three demons were roughly the same size, and Trevor could sense their ability to shape.

The trio turned and headed up the corridor leading back to the light bridge. One paused briefly, looking suspiciously in Trevor's direction. One of his companions called out in a language Trevor didn't recognize, and the demon hurried to rejoin the others. All three continued up the corridor and out of sight.

"Those were corrupted deathless," Irakesh whispered from somewhere nearby. "I've seen their kind before. Given that you saw Olympus above, I'd lay odds we both know who is doing the corrupting."

"Maybe, but we can investigate that later. We need to keep moving. You lived here for centuries, right? What's the fastest way to get out? Is there a back route we can take? I have a feeling we're going to meet heavy resistance if we try to walk out the front door." Trevor was already moving again, trusting that Irakesh would follow.

"So far as I know, an Ark only has one entrance, other than the light bridge," Irakesh's disembodied voice mused. "Still, the Arks possess many secrets. My mother had millennia to learn this one. I am trying to recall if she ever let one slip that could save our lives."

"Yeah, well, do it quickly." Trevor stopped. There was no point in going further until they had a destination.

"Mother used to disappear sometimes. She'd do it on the lowest level, near the heart of the Ark. I tried to follow her many times, but the furthest I ever made it was a door two levels above the heart. I don't know what was on the other side, but I do know that no one else in the Ark was ever allowed inside. Mother engaged the full protections of this place, and more than one foolish lord met his end trying to delve into her secrets."

"Sounds important enough to warrant a look," Trevor said. "Lead the way." He shimmered into view; a moment later, Irakesh did the same.

"Of course, Ark Lord." Irakesh gave a half-bow. They headed up the corridor, moving quietly as death.

Trevor might not like Irakesh, but even he had to admit that his former master made a strong ally. He was both cunning and deadly, and his knowledge of the old world had proven invaluable.

Irakesh began to blur, so Trevor did the same. They zipped up corridor after corridor, making their way steadily closer to the heart of the Ark. The chitinous ichor along the walls never let up, coating everything they passed —until they arrived at a bare door, the only uncovered stone they'd run across.

"I'm guessing that's it?" Trevor asked, running his hand along the stone. It was warm to the touch.

"It is. I've never seen beyond this point, but the fact that this vile stuff doesn't cover it suggests it might be useful."

"Agreed. Stand back, just in case." Trevor raised a hand, and thought about the door opening. A moment later something pulsed—a bit of energy from the dwindling supply. The stone moved silently up from the floor, sliding into the ceiling until the doorway stood open.

Trevor didn't wait, plunging through and gesturing for Irakesh to do the same. The stone slammed down behind Irakesh. Trevor willed it to lock, and felt power move through the Ark once more. Whatever he'd done had sealed the room again, so—in theory—they were safe on this side.

It was time to find out what they'd walked into.

Chapter 10- Hades

Hades savored a spoonful of soup, a rich beef broth prepared by his cook. In life, the man had been a famous chef, beloved the world over. That was before Hades had corrupted him, using the demonic taint to eradicate both will and personality. He'd left only the qualities he found of use, which didn't include the ability to speak or think.

Hades waved his hand, and the cook scurried away; now he could enjoy his lunch in peace. It was something he strived to do daily, a ritual that afforded him time to think—in this instance, about circumstances in South America.

A great deal depended on Nox's ability to find the Proto-Ark, and Hades wasn't certain that Nox's plan to subvert this Camiero was entirely workable. Yet Nox had never failed; as much as Hades detested his underling, he had little choice but to trust his abilities.

Hades set the spoon in the empty bowl, placing it on the tray floating near his throne. He was about to depart the throne room for Olympus's library when he felt a slight tug on his consciousness. It came from the strange golden cylinder his masters had provided. Hades waved a hand at it, and a river of light burst from the top. It resolved into one of the pasty-skinned grey men.

"Hello, great emissary." Hades rose from his throne with all the grace he could muster, putting himself at an equal height with the image of the grey man that had appeared in his throne room. He offered a bow. "How may I serve you with my meager abilities?"

"Your enemies have been detected within the Ark," the grey man began without preamble.

"Are you certain?" Hades asked, trembling.

The image captured the creature's pasty skin and black, haunting eyes —but it failed to capture the utter terror one felt being in the same room with him, or the certainty that the grey man could peel apart the layers of your mind like an overripe fruit.

"We would not have approached you were we not certain," the grey man said. Its tiny mouth shifted to a frown. "There has been an incursion into the Ark of the Cradle. That incursion began with the light bridge activating, so whoever has invaded possesses the ability to control the Ark."

"Is it Project Solaris?" Hades asked, mind racing. Who else could it be? David might be able to control the Ark, and with the primary access keys missing he seemed the most likely cause.

"Unknown," the grey man allowed. It seemed angered by the ignorance. "You will send your demons to investigate. Find the intruder, and bring him to us."

"Of course, great emissary." Hades bowed low, then straightened, licking his lips. The skin was dry and cracked, a reminder that he'd not yet achieved true immortality. Nor would he, until he was a full Ark Lord. "I will report as soon as I have more information."

The grey man's image disappeared. They were often like that, using neither greetings nor goodbyes. They told Hades what they expected of him, and occasionally answered one of his many questions—though even that was done with their characteristic brevity—then they vanished until they needed him again.

Hades spoke a word of power, channeling energy from his crown to send his voice to every demonic servant in Olympus. Hundreds of demonic faces peered up at the palace, waiting eagerly for instruction. "Someone has invaded the Ark below. Find them, and bring them to me. You may subdue them, but I want them alive."

All over the city, demons leapt from terraces and ledges. They floated toward the Ark below like a massive swarm of bats, winging toward the entrance. Hundreds upon hundreds of demons descended past the orbiting shuttles of the grey men, down to the Ark itself. Whoever had made the mistake of coming here was about to learn just how large that mistake had been.

Chapter 11- Chamber of the Sphinx

"So we've stepped into a closet. Wonderful." Irakesh's sarcasm was even saltier than usual.

"Shut up," Trevor replied absently. He studied the little room, considering. What the hell had Ra used this room for? The walls, floors, and ceiling were all gold, just like the light bridge platform. "Irakesh, I've got a shaping question."

"What is it?" Irakesh asked, pausing mid-rant. His interest was apparent —and unsurprising. Irakesh seemed to love teaching, especially when he could lord over someone about their ignorance.

"Sunsteel conducts energy, right? The kind of energy we need for shaping?" Trevor asked. His idea wasn't fully formed, but he suspected he might know what this place was used for.

"Indeed. It is the single most conductive material for such energy, and sunsteel's molecular structure can be modified to create additional properties. You already know this. Why are you wasting time with such drivel?"

"This room is made from sunsteel. It doesn't appear on any of the Ark's internal sensors. This is a blind spot, but I think it's a lot more than that." Trevor knelt and pressed both palms against the floor. A trickle of energy began flowing into him. "I can directly access the Ark's reservoir from here. That means we can bypass the black goop that's stealing all the power."

"Can you siphon enough power to activate the light bridge?" Irakesh asked, perking up. His bald head shone like an egg under the soft light radiated by the ceiling.

"I doubt it. Any energy I broadcast through the Ark is going to be siphoned by the crap coating the walls. The further the energy travels, the more it will take. If the energy goes very far, the stuff on the walls will get it all." Trevor rose to his feet, frowning, and stared hard at the walls. There had to be a way.

Boom. Something thudded against the other side of the door. Trevor could hear muffled voices—lots and lots of muffled voices.

"The've found us," Irakesh said, looking even paler than usual. "I know I've been derisive of your abilities, but if ever there was a time for you to impress me, it's now."

"Give me a second." Trevor considered the problem. This room looked like it could be used to perform complex shaping. Why had it been built? How had Ra used it? "You said your mother came in here. How long did she stay?"

"I once spent an entire day watching the door. She emerged at the end of it, but I scurried away before I could see much."

"Your mother was surrounded by a court of murderous zombies, all trying to get one over on the rest. She stayed Ark Lord by being more ruthless and cunning than the rest, right? Why would she have come here for an entire day? This place isn't even big enough to lie down, so I doubt she was sleeping."

Boom. Boom. A crack spread through the door. *Boom. Boom. Boom.* More cracks.

"I don't know," Irakesh whispered. He'd shrunk against the far wall of the room, staring at the cracks in horror.

Trevor tuned it out. He focused on the Ark, willing it to give him a list of locations that someone had light-walked to. "It looks like Ra light-walked to a location about a mile away, somewhere southeast of here. She did it recently too, since returning."

"You think she traveled there from this room? That would mean we might be able to light-walk from here." Irakesh wore his hope plainly.

Trevor nodded, ignoring another wave of cracks. "We're out of time, so I'm going to give this a shot. Let's hope we're not light-walking into a pool of lava or something."

He thought about the light bridge activating and sending him to the same coordinates Ra had used. A high-pitched humming began, and the walls radiated light. It grew slowly in intensity, much more slowly than the light bridges.

Finally, there was a sudden pop. Trevor was wrenched away, staggering as he landed against a crumbling stone wall. The air was stale, and the room was enveloped in total darkness.

He rose quickly, raising a hand and creating a mote of green energy. It cast ghostly shadows on the walls, which looked nothing like the Ark. These were smoothly cut granite blocks, similar to what the ancient Egyptians had used to make the pyramids. Cubbies had been carved into the rock; each cubby held several books, their spines gleaming golden in the thin light.

Trevor glanced up, estimating the ceiling to be fifteen feet high. The cubbies went all the way up. On the far side of the room was a doorway, so Trevor cautiously approached. Irakesh followed a few steps behind, flowing silently across the thin layer of sand covering the granite.

The room beyond was similar. It held more cubbies, with many more books. In the center of the room was a granite pedestal, and atop that pedestal lay a scarlet crystal about the size of Trevor's hand.

"By Ra, we're in the Hall of Records." Irakesh's awe was apparent. He stumbled forward, slack-jawed. If not for the mouthful of fangs, he'd have looked like a tourist seeing the Golden Gate Bridge for the first time. "I'd thought this place merely a story."

"Hall of Records?" Trevor asked.

"Yes, a place I've heard myths about. This chamber was built long before my mother seized control of the Ark. She and Isis discovered it, and —if the legends are true—they used the knowledge they found here to overthrow the original Ra."

"Original Ra?" Trevor asked. "Are you telling me that your mother isn't the first?"

"No. She, Isis, and Osiris overthrew the original. The tale is a long one, but the relevant part is this: This place was built by a long line of sorcerer kings who used the Ark to enslave this land. My mother overthrew him, and took his place. I've always wondered what happened to the secret lore mentioned in the story. Now we know."

"That's great, but I'm not sure if it helps us." Trevor withdrew a book from a cubby. It was heavy—solid gold with maybe twenty-five pages as thick as his thumb. He opened the book. Every page was covered in a flowing script of glyphs. "Can you read this?"

Irakesh leaned over the book, pursing his lips. "No. I've never seen the like. The glyphs are maddeningly familiar, but it isn't our language. I suppose this must have been the language used by Ra and his people."

"If we can't read the books, we need another way out of here. Whoever controls the Ark is eventually going to figure out where we went, and I really don't want to meet whatever was beating on that door."

"You're an excellent motivator, Trevor Gregg. Perhaps the gem will give us answers." Irakesh walked over to the pedestal, touching the ruby gingerly with one finger.

A scarlet hologram burst to life directly above the stone. It was a tall man dressed in something like African tribal garb. He gave a smooth bow, and spoke in a deep voice. "*Oobaka con tiky.*"

"Tell me you understand whatever the hell he just said." Trevor looked pointedly at Irakesh.

"He's welcoming us to this place."

"*Ooconca bo baka,*" the hologram said, steady eyes staring down at them over a broad nose.

"We are the first since the usurper," Irakesh supplied.

"Does it know of a way for us to get out of here?" Trevor asked.

Irakesh and the hologram conversed for some time. Trevor hated not being able to understand what was said. Irakesh could and would screw him over at the first opportunity. Who knew what the two were saying to each other?

"You'll want to hear this," Irakesh finally said. He turned to face Trevor, a ghastly grin creeping onto his face. "He claims that he is the spirit of most holy Ra, and that the Usurper imprisoned him in the stone. The Usurper is my mother, of course. He does know a way to get us out of here, but I'm not certain I understand what he's telling us to do. He claims that we can pay honor to the Builders. All we have to do is take the gateway to the heavens."

Trevor stroked his goatee, staring at the holographic Ra. The language was wrapped in superstition. What did it mean in modern scientific terms?

He turned back to Irakesh. "While we were in the Ark of the Cradle, your mother showed me data from an observatory, and it looked like the same kind of data we'd pull from the Kepler or Hubble satellites. Maybe he's talking about that—some sort of orbital facility created by the Builders."

"If so, how do we use that knowledge? Considering how quickly those things found us in the Ark, I doubt it will take them much longer to locate us here. As you said, I do not wish to meet whatever is coming for us."

"Come on," Trevor said, blurring back to the platform they'd arrived on. It was a thin sheet of gold, perhaps six feet across, much smaller than a light bridge. Trevor knelt to touch the luminescent metal. "This thing is close enough to the Ark that I'm betting both are controlled by it. I'm betting this is the Gateway to the Heavens."

Irakesh blurred onto the platform next to him. "I hope you're right."

Trevor closed his eyes, and willed the platform to take them to the installation in orbit. He figured if that installation didn't exist, the platform would just do nothing. If it did exist, then hopefully it could whisk them into orbit.

The platform sluggishly hummed to life, but Trevor felt an enormous tug at his personal energy. It flowed out of him in a thick torrent, into the platform. He tumbled onto his side, twitching, as the platform continued to siphon power. The room began to hum, the surface of the platform radiating brilliant white light.

Chapter 12- The Black Knight

I feel like death warmed over, Trevor thought, then immediately regretted the pun. His mind was a terrible place.

They were lying on something very similar to the light bridge in the Ark—similar, but not identical. It had gemstones set in different areas, and looked a lot more advanced. Multicolored energy pulses flowed along the silvery walls of the room around them. Trevor could feel the signals in those pulses, but he couldn't understand them. They were information—he was sure of it—but they had some sort of encryption.

"Can you stand?" Irakesh offered a hand, and Trevor took it. Irakesh pulled him to his feet. Once there, Trevor was able to keep his balance. Barely.

"I'm fine," Trevor said. He wasn't. Whatever had happened back there had taken nearly all his reserves, and if he hadn't finally severed the connection he might not have made it. It would be a mistake to let Irakesh know that, though. Irakesh was bred to pounce on weakness. "Let's see what we can find."

Trevor hopped down from the platform, walking cautiously to the doorway. A corridor led into a high-ceilinged central room. That ceiling was a transparent dome overlooking Earth. The view was breathtaking.

The room was empty except for a quartet of consoles that stood about waist-high. They were adorned with a variety of gemstones, and Trevor was fairly certain he could interface with them.

Heavy footsteps pounded up one of the corridors, echoing into the room. Trevor instinctively reached for the shadows, and was shocked when they refused to obey. Had the platform drained that much of his power?

"I can't shape," he said.

Irakesh shot him a confused look.

A suit of power armor charged into the room, leveling a rifle in their direction. Trevor recognized the armor instantly. He would never forget the night that Mohn Corp had blown up his house, using suits of armor just like these.

Trevor sprinted forward, dropping into a baseball slide. The rifle roared, and two feet of flame came from the muzzle. In the back of his mind Trevor knew that gunfire in space was bad, but now wasn't the time to worry about it.

The bullet cracked into the wall behind him, and Trevor rolled back to his feet. He shoulder-checked the power armor, knocking both it and himself to the floor. Trevor tried to pin his opponent's arms, but his opponent strained against him. An arm broke out of his hold, and an armored hand shot up to wrap around Trevor's face.

The hand began to squeeze, and Trevor screamed. He tried to change to mist, but nothing happened.

Irakesh seized the helmet with both hands, and a shower of sparks shot into the air as he tore it away. The man inside elbowed Irakesh in the face, and Irakesh was knocked away. Trevor rolled to his feet, turning to face…a man that still haunted Trevor's dreams.

"Oh, fuck."

"Is right, Gregg," Yuri growled, circling Trevor like a panther. "Is time you and traitorous master brought to justice." He flicked his wrists, exposing identical sets of humming claws.

Trevor slid into a defensive stance, bracing himself for the charge. He was completely unprepared for the wave of electricity that arced across the floor, carpeting the area around him and Irakesh. It surged through his body and he collapsed to the deck, every muscle seizing. He was dimly aware of Irakesh doing the same.

"Get clear, Yuri," a young male voice commanded.

The electricity stopped. Trevor shook off the paralysis, struggling back to his feet. Yuri had retreated away from them just in time. A cylinder of pale green energy appeared around them, just large enough to contain both Trevor and Irakesh.

A man in his early twenties stepped into the room. He was wearing jeans and a t-shirt, and looked like he hadn't been to a barber in a while. His eyes were completely at odds with the slacker student look, though. They held a weight Trevor recognized—the kind left by the sacrifices you had to make in order to survive in a world ruled by monsters.

"Yuri, you said you knew them. Brief me," the man commanded. He approached the cylinder, staring impassively at Trevor.

"Is Trevor Gregg and Irakesh. Trevor is traitor to the Mother, enslaved by Irakesh. Thought Gregg had reformed, but clearly was wrong." Yuri's fire had faded, and his expression had gone rigid.

"I'm afraid you're incorrect, cretin," Irakesh taunted. "Trevor no longer serves me. Quite the opposite, in fact."

Trevor elbowed him in the side. "Shut up, Irakesh. You speaking never makes anything better. Yuri, and whoever the hell *you* are, how about we take thirty seconds to discuss this like adults? I don't know who you guys are, but I'm guessing you're affiliated with Mohn Corp. We were allies against Set. I fought alongside the Director."

"Mentioning the Director is not helping your case," the slacker said. He folded his arms, and his eyes took on a far away look. Trevor couldn't pinpoint exactly what he was doing, but signals shot back and forth between him and the wall. A lot of signals. The pulses slowed, and the man's eyes opened. "My name is David. I lead a group called Project Solaris. I've just checked out your story—as much as I could anyway. I've found a number of references to you, particularly in Mohn's records. Your designation seems to have changed quite often. First, you were an enemy, then a friend, then an enemy again. You don't sound like the type of person I want to trust—so give me one good reason why I should?"

"I can't." Trevor shook his head, smiling at the predicament. "You're right. I have no way to prove my allegiance, and you found me with Irakesh. Of course you assume I'm an enemy. I get it. You'll need to keep me locked up for a while. But at least make use of my intel. Let me update your files. What's the last thing they tell you about me? I'm betting it ended five years ago, in London."

"You're as clever as your files suggest. Yeah, I'm intensely curious about you. The carrot of knowledge is very effective, especially when you're offering it for free. Impress me, Gregg."

"Fair enough. Isis, Osiris—pretty much everything Mohn could field—

assaulted The First Ark, alongside a bunch of other gods. I'm sure you've seen the crater left in London."

"In England, you mean," David corrected. He gestured, and a holographic map appeared. It was Earth's near orbit, and they were looking at Europe. The French coastline looked familiar, but what had been southern England was now an archipelago of little islands.

"Holy crap. We took out a third of England." Even knowing it was mostly populated by the dead, Trevor was horrified. He'd participated in something bigger than America dropping the atomic bomb. That was what it had taken to stop Set.

"What happened to Osiris?" David asked.

"So far as I know, he died. Osiris, Isis, and Ra challenged Set. He was far stronger, and they knew they were going to lose that fight, but they did it to divert his attention while the rest of us detonated the First Ark." Trevor paused. "I know that makes us look bad, but trust me when I say it was the only way to stop Set."

"We've always wondered what caused the explosion. Osiris founded Project Solaris. We could use the old bastard's help, more than ever. I'm not sure we can win without it." David's already somber expression grew somehow more dire.

"Excuse my temerity in speaking," Irakesh said, raising a hand timidly, "but win which war, exactly?"

Trevor had forgotten how well Irakesh played servile when he wanted to.

"I'm asking the questions, for now at least. Cooperate, and we'll do the same. Where have you been for the last five years?"

David's gaze was focused on Irakesh, allowing Trevor to study their captor a little more closely. A bewildering array of signals continued to flow from him to the station. Trevor had experienced something similar when he'd bonded to the Ark, something that required him to possess an access key. How was this guy doing the same thing? Was he another Ark Lord? Who or what was he? He wasn't a werewolf, or a deathless.

"Of course, of course," Irakesh said. He gave his most cultured smile, which didn't seem to move David. "Trevor, perhaps you should explain, since anything that comes out of my mouth will be mistrusted."

"I'm happy to, but can I ask a question first?" Trevor asked.

"All right," David said, giving a noncommittal shrug.

"We're in an orbital facility right? A satellite created by the Builders?"

"We call it the Black Knight Satellite," David explained. His eyes narrowed. "That's all I'm willing to share."

"It's enough," Trevor said, struggling to contain his excitement. "I read conspiracy rumors on the internet, before the end. They talked about two satellites that had been orbiting Earth for thousands of years. This place proves those legends were right."

"I'm glad to see you're well-read, and that your reputation as a scientist seems to be accurate," David allowed. He gave an almost friendly smile. "Now then, you were going to bring me up to speed on your arrival here."

"All right, but you guys might want to grab some chairs. This is going to take a few hours. Are you familiar with temporal spacial dislocation?"

Chapter 13- Alicia

Liz couldn't remember the last time she'd been this frightened. The fear she'd felt when fighting Set had been close, but the idea of seeing Alicia again terrified her in a way even the monsters she'd battled couldn't inspire.

"Do you think she'll remember us?" Liz whispered to Blair. Bright moonlight showed a cracked driveway leading toward a house big enough to qualify as a mansion. Candles could be seen through a few windows, but for the most part the house was dark.

"She'll remember." Blair seemed certain. An ever-growing pack of dogs trailed behind him, the bold ones occasionally darting up to sniff him briefly.

The Whelp. It's the Whelp. The Whelp has come.

Dozens of voices washed over her, and she slowed her pace, struggling to make sense of them all.

It is the packmind, Wepwawet explained. *In time you will adjust. Whenever we are near a pack of significant size a packmind is born, so long as a Ka-Dun exists to control it. Each member of a packmind can communicate their emotions and thoughts with the others.*

"You can hear it, too?" Blair asked. He seemed a little surprised.

"Are they talking about you when they say 'whelp'?" Liz asked, trying to suppress a smile.

"Of course." He sighed, starting up the driveway again. "I don't know how they know, but I'm betting someone told them that's what Isis called me. Why couldn't I be the Douche Slayer, or Blair the Handsome?"

Liz's smile became a laugh. "Douche Slayer it is. Anyone who ever met Steve will hail you as a hero."

John Rivers lurked a few dozen paces ahead, next to the front door. He'd graciously given them space during the trip, though she had no doubt that he'd been able to hear every word they said. She didn't mind; they weren't divulging state secrets or anything.

Liz tensed as John opened the door and stepped inside. Blair followed, leaving her no choice but to do the same. Her feet resisted, demanding she bolt. She forced herself into movement, holding her breath as she entered.

The house was spacious, and looked even more so because it was completely devoid of furniture. A pile of blankets lay in one corner, but that was it. The place appeared empty, but her enhanced hearing made out the sounds of combat out back.

"If you'll follow me, please." John seemed unconcerned, so Liz nodded. John walked to a large sliding glass door, sliding it back and stepping onto a wooden deck.

The view was breathtaking. The moonlight painted the rolling hillsides white, showing her all of Santa Rosa. Familiar suburbia radiated out from a small downtown area. There weren't any lights, but she could hear hundreds of heartbeats below.

"I really missed this view," Blair said, joining her on the deck.

"Did you use to live here?"

"God, no." Blair laughed and gave a self-deprecating smile. She loved the way his smile brightened his face. It took away some of the weight she'd seen accumulate during their time together. "I couldn't afford to live in Fountaingrove. But I remember when these houses were built. They did a showing, and I wanted to see how the other half lived. I loved the view so much that I'd sometimes park up the road a little ways. There was a Carl's Junior right across Highway 101, so I'd grab dinner and come park up here to watch the sun set."

"Eww." Liz crinkled her nose. "It's amazing you survived to the apocalypse eating that much grease."

The sounds of combat were louder. Hearing a female yell followed by a deep grunt, Liz walked to the edge of the deck and looked down at the yard below. Two women—an unremarkable housewife in her mid-thirties and a hard-eyed teen—were sparring. The housewife had just thrown the teen to the ground, but the teen flipped back to her feet with enviable grace. Midnight hair fluttered out behind her, and the moonlight caught her face.

Liz knew her instantly. Alicia's skinny frame had filled out, and she was taut with muscle. Hard lines framed her young eyes. The innocence had been burned out of her.

"The older woman is Kathy," John Rivers explained. He spoke quietly, as if not wanting to intrude. "She teaches Alicia to fight, though some might argue it's the other way around."

Alicia looked up, eyes widening when they met Liz's. Then they tightened. Alicia waved a hand at Kathy, and the woman gave a quick nod. She melted into the shadows, leaving them in private.

"You know, I didn't really believe. I couldn't. I thought the only way you could have been gone was that you were dead." Alicia's legs tensed, and she leapt the distance from the yard to the deck in a single smooth arc. She landed lightly a few feet from Liz. She was now tall enough to look Liz in the eye. "I guess I was wrong. You weren't dead—you abandoned us."

"Abandoned?" It was all Liz could get out. Her heart broke for Alicia. "I get that it looks that way. We up and leave, and don't come back for five years. But—"

"Here it comes." Alicia's sneer made her suddenly ugly. "I knew there would be a *but*. *But* we had to fight some big monster. *But* we had to save the world. But, but, but. What about us? You *abandoned* us. Almost everyone died—did you know that? Seven out of ten people on that island died the night the deathless came for us."

"You're right," Liz replied. The simple admission was freeing. "We left, and didn't come back. The reasons don't matter. We abandoned you. I'm so sorry, Alicia. I know nothing can ever make that right."

"You're right about that," Alicia snapped. Gathered tears made her eyes shine. "Nothing will ever make it right. You can't fix this, Liz. You can't bring back the dead; you can only fight them."

"I can't even imagine what you've been through, what you must have overcome to have survived this long. But I'm here now, and I'm not going anywhere."

"I don't believe you," Alicia said, but a hint of hope lurked there.

"You don't have to believe me," Liz said. "I understand that trust will take time." She took a step closer, offering her hands to Alicia. The teen took them. "Let's use this packmind. Show me what happened. Then I'll show you why Blair and I couldn't come back sooner."

Alicia's mouth opened to speak, but she hesitated. Her eyes were searching, and Liz felt like there was a chance, a crack in the wall this poor young woman had been forced to build.

"Fine. If you're serious, then I can show you. The packmind will only pass impressions, but your Ka-Dun can share the memories between the three of us." Alicia nodded at Blair, who'd been standing silently against the rail a few feet away.

"Liz?" Blair asked. He placed a supportive hand on her shoulder. She loved him for that, and a million other reasons just like it.

"Do it. I want to see what she went through."

Alicia awoke with a start, sitting up inside the dome tent. She touched the top to find the fabric wet to the touch. It must be after midnight. What had awakened her? It wasn't her bladder, which was the usual cause.

A muffled scream came from near the docks, until it was abruptly cut off.

Alicia hurriedly unzipped the tent, ducking into the chill night. Thick fog had covered the island, as it did every night. It was the perfect time for an ambush—even she knew that, and she was only ten. Gun shots stuttered, tearing apart the night with brief flashes. Those same flashes also came from the docks.

A generator roared to life, then another. All over the island, floodlights sprang to life, giving some definition to the fog. She could see shapes now —trees and people, and probably worse.

Alicia knew what she had to do. This was why she'd accepted the gift from the Mother: to defend her people. Mostly she hadn't done anything yet, though. She was still learning to use her abilities, still learning to fight.

Erik wouldn't let her anywhere near a battle like this, but he wasn't here to tell her no. She was going to get involved. It was time to help save people, whether they liked it or not. Alicia shifted, her t-shirt splitting at the seams. Oh well, she hadn't much liked it anyway.

Alicia hadn't learned how to use the shadows yet, but she was still pretty sneaky. She crept closer to the commotion, trying to figure out who was attacking, and maybe why. Several dozen figures moved in the mist around the docks, but there was no sign of any boat. They must have come out of the water. Hmm. Alicia used her claws to scale the pine tree she'd been crouching next to, and she scanned the mist on other sides of the island.

"Oh no," she whispered. "I have to warn them."

Alicia dropped to the ground, sprinting between trees as she headed toward the summit. She sucked in a breath, yelling as loud as she could. "They're on the south shore! Hundreds of them. They're coming up behind us. We have to run."

A stern voice spoke in her mind. *Alicia. You must be quiet, or the notdeads will find you.*

A large shape trotted out of the mist. Yukon's golden fur was drenched. His wet scent was powerful, familiar, and comforting.

"We have to help them."

No. Yukon replied, the single word carrying more mental force than he'd ever used with her. *We must flee. We can only save a few. We will head to where the sun sets, then swim across the cold water. We can go north. There are hills there, where we can hide.*

"But so many of these people will die. Erik can—"

No. Yukon bared his fangs, growling. *Erik battles the notdeads. He slows them, so that his death can save his pack. But he will not survive.*

"I have to help him." Alicia turned, sprinting toward the docks. Erik would be where the fighting was hottest. He was their strongest male; with the Mother gone, putting him in charge made sense.

Not that anyone had asked her opinion.

Please. Yukon's sending was softer now, further away. He hadn't followed her. *If you go down there, I will lose you, too. Please. We have to save what we can. We have to live. We have to be there when she comes back.*

Alicia slowed her pace, suddenly unsure what to do. She could see the dock clearly now, could smell the gunpowder and blood. Could smell the faint decay carried by the deathless.

Then she caught a whiff of Erik. Her ears went erect, and she strained to find him. Finally she spotted him, fighting a trio of deathless by the docks. He clutched his side, blood leaking through his fingers as he bared his fangs at his opponents. Several bodies lay near his feet.

One of the deathless lunged, and Erik's entire demeanor shifted in the literal blink of an eye. He blurred faster than Alicia could track, seizing the deathless's head between his furry hands. Then he tore, ripping the head from its shoulders. The deathless toppled to the ground, and both its companions backpedaled. They'd realized that Erik's weakness was a ruse.

A short Asian woman strode out of the mist. She held some sort of gun, cradling it tightly in both hands. The weapon barked, and a stream of thunderous slugs tore into Erik's unprotected back. He staggered forward, already turning to face the woman. He blurred, but she blurred, too. The Asian woman's arm came up and a cloud of dazzling green light burst over Erik. Erik screamed, tearing at his skin. It burned and bubbled, and he writhed in agony.

We are leaving. Yukon's voice was forceful again, and his mouth settled over her arm. The teeth dug in enough to hurt, and he dragged her back toward the northern shore.

Alicia clung to his fur, unable to stop the tears. They rushed passed several dozen people who were fleeing into the water.

"I can help these people," she said, forcing herself forward. She wiped at her eyes, composing herself, and raised her voice. "Gather around me. We're going to swim together. I'll be there to help people get across."

"Where are we going to go, kid?" an old woman asked, scowling at her. "This place was supposed to be safe. The land outside is even worse."

Pay her no mind, Ka-Ken. You are a champion, and your age matters not.

The beast was right. She wasn't just a little girl. She was a werewolf, and she could help these people. "If you want to stay here, you do that, lady. Anyone who wants to live, get in the water. We're getting out of here."

Chapter 15- Yukon

Blair quietly slipped through the still-open sliding glass door, gently closing it behind him. Liz and Alicia sat huddled together on the pile of blankets in the corner, deep in quiet conversation. He didn't want to intrude on the moment, so he gave them what privacy he could.

It is a bitter thing, Ka-Dun, his beast rumbled. *Being a champion requires difficult choices, and many sacrifices. The young always struggle the most with such things.*

"Yeah, poor kid has been through a lot. But she's also accomplished a lot." Blair stared out at Santa Rosa, still trying to adjust to the lack of lights. The CME had knocked this place back to pre-industrial revolution technology, for the most part. There were no working cars, at least that he'd seen. No working electricity of any kind. It was the polar opposite of San Francisco.

Goldenfur comes, a small canine voice thought at him through the packmind.

Goldenfur, repeated another.

The packmind buzzed with a dozen overlapping voices. *Goldenfur. He comes.*

Blair shifted almost without thinking, using his muzzle to search for scents. The dogs sensed something, and seemed more excited than alarmed. Their tones were respectful, in some cases awed. Perhaps it was another Ka-Dun—whomever had assumed control of the truly massive pack that seemed to be roaming Sonoma County.

He comes, the voices chorused.

A four-legged figure flashed in the moonlight, bounding across the freeway in a slow blur. A cloud of dogs flowed silently in the leader's wake, fanning out to all sides. There was a rightness to the pack, and part of Blair longed to join it, to seize control of it.

The figure bounded closer still, crossing Industrial and starting up the hill to Fountaingrove. As it approached, Blair could sense the power radiating from it. The scent was familiar.

Could it be? He didn't dare get his hopes up.

Golden fur flashed up the hillside below, cutting across the grass. It blurred closer, finally landing on the balcony next to him.

Blair shifted back to human form, seizing the massive golden retriever in a hug. "Yukon, you have no idea how good it is to see you." He buried his face in Yukon's fur, grinning as the dog's tail thumped against his leg.

Blair finally released the retriever, taking a step back to look at him. Yukon was massive, almost horse-sized. He had a dark scar on his right side, a patch where no fur grew. The wound was scabbed over, and still healing.

I knew you would find your way home eventually, whelp, Yukon thought at him, giving a canine smile. *I did not expect it to take quite so long. It is good that you are here. Alicia will not admit it, but we need help. We face a foe we cannot vanquish.*

"What foe?" Blair asked. The last thing they needed was another enemy.

Yukon's fur began to ripple, his bones cracking and popping in a very familiar way. His body rearranged itself, the process happening as swiftly as Blair could have managed. Where Yukon had stood was now a broad-shouldered blond man in his mid-twenties. His jaw was covered by a thin beard, and brown dog eyes stared back at Blair.

"Why don't you come inside," Yukon said, "and we can tell Alicia as well. This is not a tale I enjoy repeating."

Blair completely failed to process what he'd just seen. He could only stand there, gaping. "You just shifted into human form. Yukon, where the hell did you learn to do that?"

"From watching you," Yukon said. "I was changed by the Mother, just as you were. She gifted me with far more abilities than I could have dreamed." He gave Blair a warm smile, clapping him on the shoulder. "The longer I've had these gifts, the more intelligent I have become—but I will always see the world differently, I think, even now that I can live like a man. I am still dog."

Blair wanted to ask about a billion more questions, but Yukon opened the sliding glass door and stepped inside. As he did, Liz and Alicia rose from the table as one. Alicia walked to him first, kissing Yukon lightly on the cheek and giving him a friendly hug. "Welcome home, my friend. I can already tell I'm not going to like hearing this. Sit. Let's talk. How were you wounded? Windigo?"

"No, not that murderous spirit," Yukon said, shaking his head. "The pack and I were forced east by a horde of notdeads. We had to flee into the mountains to escape. We encountered the Liwanu, a Great Bear spirit. Many were killed, and I was hurt." He touched his side gingerly.

Yukon moved to a spot near the blankets. Settling into a comfortable cross-legged position, withdrawing a pipe from his pocket, he packed a small wad of green into it, then set the pipe on the ground next to his leg.

He looked up soberly at Alicia. "We came back through Windsor. It had been attacked. Teegan is dead. We found pieces of him all over the town square. Windigo used his blood to scrawl a message. No one is safe. Windigo's scent was everywhere, but we couldn't find him. He toyed with us, letting a few dogs see him. He'd draw them off, then kill them. We lost eleven in three hours." Yukon seemed spent from his speech. He picked up the pipe, withdrawing a red plastic lighter from his windbreaker. He lit the pipe, inhaling deeply. "It has not been a very good week."

He passed the pipe to Alicia, who merely held it. She stared down at her lap. "I don't know how to stop him."

"Who is this Windigo?" Liz growled. Blair shared her anger.

"Not who," Alicia corrected. "*What*." She licked her lips, finally looking up from her lap. "Windigo first showed up about a year ago, though we'd heard rumors about it for years before that. It started out somewhere further north, up in the forest near the Oregon border. He—if it is a he— made his way south, wiping out towns as he went. He picks victims off one by one, until people panic and flee. Once they do, he hunts them."

"There was a Ka-Dun named Monte, up in Humboldt County," Yukon interjected, taking the pipe back from Alicia. "His pack had many dogs, and looked after many, many people. They lived in a town called Garberville. He and his pack disappeared. Only the scent of their blood remains." He hung his head sadly.

Alicia took up the tale. "Now Windigo is here, and the attacks are getting worse. The problem is, we can't ever find him. Like Yukon said, you get a whiff of his scent, but almost no one has seen him. We can't be everywhere at once, so he just waits and strikes where we aren't. I don't know what to do." The teen's shoulders sagged. "People are scared, and some are already talking about leaving. I've warned them that they'd just be hunted—and even if they weren't, where would they go? They can't go north. To the south are the deathless, and we already know what they'll do to us. Yukon scouted east, and it sounds like we'd have to deal with this Bear. We're pretty much trapped. That means we have to stay and fight. I'm willing to do that, but I just can't come up with a way to stop Windigo. I need to give my people hope, show them we can fight back."

"We'll figure out something, Alicia," Liz said. Her conviction sounded total. "Blair is an Ark Lord. He can bring incredible abilities to bear. Whatever this Windigo is, we'll beat him."

Blair didn't share Liz's confidence. He had no idea how to find Windigo, much less stop him. There never seemed to be a shortage of enemies they had no idea how to fight.

Chapter 16- Windigo

Windigo lurked within hearing, using his host body's natural mastery of the shadows to avoid detection. Even the vigilant dog who'd chased him around Windsor was unaware of just how close he was. Windigo studied the new arrivals, intrigued by their relative strengths. The copper-haired Ka-Ken was the most powerful he'd ever met, possibly the equal of the legendary Jes'Ka.

The Ka-Dun was of even more interest. The sandy-haired man was unremarkable in almost every way, but he blazed like a bonfire. His power was immense, and Windigo had only seen it once before. That power was the same wielded by Windigo's creator, a thousand millennia ago. Never since that time had he encountered a being like this.

"I must have that body," Windigo whispered, giving a ghastly smile. Who was that Ka-Dun? Yukon and the child Ka-Ken already seemed to know who the new arrivals were.

He listened as they spoke of the Great Bear. Windigo was familiar with him, and unsurprised to hear that the Bear had hibernated to the present.

"Blair is an Ark Lord. He can bring incredible abilities to bear. Whatever this Windigo is, we'll beat him." The Ka-Ken's words were sweet nectar, confirming Windigo's hopes. That was why the Ka-Dun brimmed with power.

An Ark meant near-limitless power. Windigo could feed endlessly, growing ever stronger.

Never had he hungered so for a host, yet never had he faced such dangerous quarry. The Ka-Dun were far more adept at defending themselves than a Ka-Ken or deathless. They even possessed the ability to unmake him, if they were strong enough. Fortunately, no real memory of Windigo had survived to this age. What people knew of the "wendigo" was disjointed, and often contradictory. They didn't suspect his true nature—not yet, anyway. If he played the game as well as he should, they'd all die in ignorance.

He cocked his ears, listening again. They were talking about Isis. The

Ka-Dun believed she was dead.

Windigo had heard tales of Isis, and had been very careful to stay away from her. She was even more dangerous than the Ka-Dun she had birthed.

With her dead, Windigo had a chance—a chance to get and keep the Ark. Yet how could he safely bait the Ark Lord? What he needed was a host strong enough to threaten the Ark Lord. The Ka-Ken could certainly do that, but her defenses to his shaping would be considerable.

No, he needed something physically powerful, but mentally vulnerable.

Windigo's face split into a too-broad grin. Yukon had given him the answer: he could possess the Great Bear, then lead it back here to begin slaughtering the Ka-Dun's companions.

Windigo turned east, leaping from the roof and bounding silently into the night. He would reach the mountains tomorrow, and after that it wouldn't take long to set a trap for the Bear.

Chapter 17- Medico Roberto

Jordan sized up the compound below, impressed by the pragmatism of whomever had built it. The wrought-iron fence surrounding the main building was perfect for keeping out militia—or zombies. Beyond the fence was a hundred-foot stretch of brick, with nothing to use for cover. An attacker who breached the gate would have to charge across that space to reach the house. Snipers would pick off most before they made it.

The building was three stories of dense stone, ringed on top by a crenelated wall. That stonework looked ornamental, but Jordan knew better. The architect had known warfare, and he'd built this place with it in mind. Form was important, but only where it didn't interfere with function.

The current occupant wasn't blind to that function, either. Jordan saw two men prowling the deep shadows atop the roof. He could feel the power within each of them. They were shapers—Ka-Dun. He was certain of it. If there were males that he could see, then there were almost certainly females he could not.

You've grown, Ka-Dun. You perceive much.

"What did you say this place was called?" Jordan asked Leti. She'd paused a few feet away to drink from her canteen.

"We call it the Government Palace, or the House of Pizarro. It was built in the fifteen hundreds, by Governor Castille. It has served the government all that time. Before the end of the world, our president lived here, and our congress met to pass laws. Our people thought it fitting that Medico Roberto took up residence," she explained. Leti replaced the top on her canteen and slung it over her shoulder. "It is important. Symbolic. It shows that our people have survived, that we have not lost who we are."

"What are those obelisks?" Jordan asked, pointing at one of the twenty-foot-tall black pillars spaced around the wrought-iron fence. "I can feel them broadcasting some sort of signal."

"I do not know. I would guess they are some sort of alert system, but they could be a weapon. Medico Roberto has kept their true nature secret." Leti began walking toward the front gate, which was manned by another pair of males.

"That's smart," Jordan mused. "If your enemies don't know what you're capable of, they'll be more reluctant to attack, and less prepared for whatever your countermeasures are."

The more he saw, the more pleased he was with how Doctor Roberts had handled his deployment. Either he had smart councel, or he'd turned that enormous brain of his toward basic military strategy.

The pair of males at the gate watched them warily as they approached, but both relaxed as they got closer. One smiled and waved. "Leti, you haven't been home in too long. El Medico will be most pleased to see you."

"Hello, Javier," Leti replied with a smile. She walked over and gave him a fierce hug. "It is good to see you, my friend. I have brought a guest to meet with El Medico—one he will wish to see immediately."

"And who will we be presenting?" Javier asked, disengaging from Leti. His eyes became calculating, though the smile was still in place. He studied Jordan, probably sensing a lot more power than he'd expected— enough power to be a real threat.

The power Jordan could draw from the Ark seemed dependent on distance, but even several hundred clicks out the energy still felt endless.

Javier's unnamed companion had retreated to the guard house behind the fence, and was speaking into a walkie-talkie. Probably reporting to his superiors in the house, exactly as he should.

"My name is Jordan." Jordan stepped forward, offering Javier his hand. "Roberts and I go a ways back. Your boss doesn't like me, but he'll want to hear what I have to say anyway."

"Why don't we let him be the judge of that?" Javier asked. He stared down at Jordan's hand, so Jordan finally dropped it. "I have heard your name, Commander. It has never been spoken fondly, I can promise you that."

Leti seemed surprised by the exchange. He put a hand on Javier's forearm. "Javier, please. Give him a chance. He is the Ark Lord, and we will need his aid."

"You are the lord of the Ark?" Javier snorted. "You are nothing more than a hired butcher. The Ark should belong to El Medico. He's a wise ruler, unlike certain others who bear a mantle they clearly do not deserve."

"You don't like me. I get that." Jordan folded his arms, staring coldly down at Javier. "But I'm going to go see Roberts. I'm done talking with underlings."

"I can summon a dozen more champions with the press of a button," Javier sneered contemptuously. "Your empty—"

Jordan had had enough. He took a step closer to Leti, drawing a squawk from her as he scooped her into his arms, then blurred, fueling it with all the strength offered by the Ark. Hopping over the fence, he sprinted across the bricks, then leapt into the air, kicking through a window on the second floor. He rode the spray of glass into a large library and landed in a crouch.

The walls were covered with shields, each bearing a colorful pattern or symbol. Seven people were seated around a large table, their chairs cut from heavy mahogany. Jordan could sense the power emanating from the people around the table, and two of the males were slowly turning their heads in his direction. Both were strong enough to pierce his blur. The first male was older—at least sixty-five, Jordan would have guessed.

The second figure was familiar: Doctor Roberts.

Jordan released the blur. "Hello, Doctor Roberts. I'm sorry about the window."

"Jordan," Roberts roared, shooting to his feet. "How dare you barge in like this, unannounced? Who the hell do you think you are?"

"Me?" Jordan asked. He set Leti down.

She blinked at her surroundings, clearly shocked at her sudden change in location. To her, no time had passed and they were still at the gate.

"I'm your neighbor," Jordan said. "Lord of the Ark of the Mother."

"You? She chose you?" Roberts asked. He seemed to deflate, sinking back into his chair. After a moment he composed himself, turning to the other figures at the table. "Leave us. Jordan and I need to talk. Alone."

Jordan nodded at Leti. "She stays."

"Fine," Roberts snapped. "Everyone else, out."

The other figures rose, filing reluctantly out the door. Their faces were filled with curiosity, and he couldn't blame them. It wasn't every day an Ark Lord came crashing into your board meeting, or whatever they'd been about.

Roberts waited until the door closed before speaking. He turned to Jordan, scratching at his ever-present beard. It was just as wild as the last time Jordan had seen him. "You can control the Ark?"

"Yeah. How I ended up with the key is a long story, but the short version is I'm the Ark Lord." Jordan kept his tone light. He didn't want Roberts to think he was being insincere. "From the little Leti has told me, you're surrounded by enemies. Seems like you might be in need of a little help."

"She's right about that, and she doesn't know the worst of it." Roberts turned to Leti, giving her a respectful nod. "No offense meant, Leti. There are just things I haven't been able to tell you."

"I take no offense, El Medico," she replied, giving a graceful bow.

She sat in one of the recently vacated chairs, so Jordan did the same.

A figure appeared on the window sill, the muzzle of his machine gun raised in Jordan's direction. Jordan blurred to the right, dodging a stream of bullets as they punched into the chair he'd been sitting in. He had enough time to identify Javier, then Roberts blurred in between them.

El Medico seized the gun, yanking it from Javier's grasp. "Stand down, Javier. Now."

Robert's authority was absolute. Javier relaxed, but his gaze was fixed on Jordan. There was hatred there. Jordan really needed to work on his people skills.

"Jordan is my guest now." Roberts patted Javier on the shoulder. "You've done well Javier. Thank you."

"As you wish, El Medico. I will head back to my post." Javier glared daggers at Jordan. Then he turned without another word, leaping back down into the courtyard.

"Dammit, Jordan," Roberts said, "you make trouble wherever you go. You're like a tornado." He gave a heavy sigh, returning to his seat. "I hope you understand the intensity of my dislike for you. Every last time I've run into you, my life has gotten more complicated, and I have a feeling this is no exception. Unfortunately, you're right. I need you. Why don't I bring you up to speed on what we're doing here, and you can fill me in on what you've been doing the last five years."

"Sounds fair." Jordan nodded. "You want to start, or shall I?"

"I don't have time to care where you've been, to be honest. Let's start with my problems, and then we'll get to how you can help me with them," Roberts said. He eyed Jordan coldly, but at least the animosity was familiar. "Those problems are twofold. First, the deathless have been consolidating power on this continent. Every day, their empire gets closer to us on both the northern and southern border. We're surrounded."

"I thought that this continent had the highest concentration of werewolves in the world," Jordan pointed out.

"It does, but we're still drastically outnumbered. There are hundreds of millions of deathless across the continent, and only a few thousand werewolves. Most of those werewolves struck off on their own to carve out tribes. Only a few hundred stayed in New Peru. We're surrounded and outnumbered."

"What about the Amazon?" Jordan asked. "Doesn't the jungle protect your flank?"

"It does, to a degree. The Amazon is controlled by Leti's people, but that's not as much a blessing as you might think. They're religious zealots with their own carefully cobbled-together dogma." Robert's contempt for the order surprised Jordan. "Still, they're allies, of a sort. I allow them to occupy the Ark, and they leave us alone. If we're invaded, I'm fairly confident they'll send at least some help. I don't think it will be nearly enough, though."

"Okay, that's a grim tactical situation. What's the second problem?" Jordan asked. He wanted to know the entirety of what he was doing with before he started analyzing the problems.

"Sobek. You've heard of him?" Roberts asked. He waved a hand, and a muffin floated off a tray and over to his hand. Jordan watched the signal carefully. This one he knew intimately, and he was confident that his command of telekinesis was greater than Roberts's, even without the Ark.

"Yeah, I've heard of him. Neither Isis nor Osiris had anything good to say about him. How is he an issue?"

"About a year after Isis left to help you in your latest war, a ship showed up in port," Roberts explained. "It had a cargo of black stone cut from Easter Island. Sobek claimed he'd made a deal with Isis, and that he'd deliver a shipment annually for the next decade." He paused to tear a piece from the muffin, tossing it in his mouth. He chewed thoughtfully for a moment. "Do you remember why you recruited me for that initial dig, Jordan?"

"Of course," Jordan said, a little more forcefully than he'd intended. "You're a geologist—one of the finest in the world before it ended. Now? The leading expert, without a doubt."

"I examined this stone and learned a great deal about the properties that made it so valuable in the previous age. Here, look at this." Roberts withdrew a smooth black stone from his pocket and tossed it to Jordan.

Jordan plucked it from the air effortlessly. "What am I looking at?" He held the stone up to his face, studying it. It was warm to the touch, and he could sense faint energy inside of it.

"This stone is unique, so far as I can tell," Roberts said. "It's a type of volcanic rock, which turns out to be one of the best materials for containing the energy we utilize for our abilities. The same energy that we get from the moon, or that the deathless get from the sun. The rock makes an excellent storage mechanism for that energy. It's slow to charge, but will hold that charge indefinitely. In the case of Easter Island, it's been building that energy for hundreds of thousands of years—maybe millions. Since it was out in the middle of the ocean, there was no one like us around to tap into it."

"So you're saying that this stone is a battery, basically?" Jordan asked. That seemed the relevant takeaway.

"Essentially. A battery that we can build functionality into, using shaping."

"Like the obelisks surrounding the perimeter," Jordan said, snapping his fingers. "They're sensors, aren't they?"

"I shouldn't be surprised that you figured out the technology so quickly, given your background with Mohn. Yes, the obelisks are my invention. They detect certain wavelengths, such as the kind we use when shaping. That's not their only use, of course. They are also weapons—weapons we have not yet had to test."

"So Sobek is dropping off this stone. That's a good thing, right?"

"It was at first," Roberts allowed. "The problem is that he's growing suspicious. Sooner or later he's going to attack—and without someone of your strength, we're powerless to stop him."

Chapter 18- Anna

Trevor rose from where he'd been squatting next to the energy field. He began pacing, a precise five steps from one corner of their cell to the other. David had somehow modified the field to keep out sound, and it seemed to block *all* types of signal. None of Trevor's shaping had affected it in any way.

They had no way of keeping time, but Trevor was fairly certain a couple days had passed. They might have already missed their first check-in.

"Will you please stop doing that?" Irakesh said. His voice was jarring after the prolonged silence.

"What else would you like me to do?" Trevor asked, though he did stop pacing. "David holds our fate in his hands—and with Yuri egging him on to jettison us out the airlock, I'm not liking our chances."

"That is a very serious problem," Irakesh said, in a languid, relaxed voice that suggested the opposite. "But we can do nothing about it. Absolutely nothing. All planning is pointless. So we wait. That waiting may feel unbearable, but I promise you it will pass eventually. I have a great deal of experience with patience. For my eighth birthday, my mother locked me in my chambers for a month. Every day, she slid a tray under the door. It contained the day's food and a note. It said 'Be patient, and this will pass.'"

"Wow," was all Trevor could manage. "That seems incredibly harsh."

"Indeed it was," Irakesh said, "but consider the lesson—and consider how early in life I learned it. I have learned a great deal more about your world and the people that dwelled in it. Your children had no patience. Even your adults had none. Everything was about instant gratification." He gave a toothy smile. "My mother taught me the value of patience, and I have never forgotten it. I have no need to pace. If we are here for weeks, so be it."

"If you're so patient, then why does my pacing bother you?" Trevor shot back, then smiled. That had scored a point.

There was movement down one of the corridors, beyond the area that had been cordoned off for their cell. Trevor raised a hand to silence Irakesh, who subsided with a nod.

David and Yuri strode into the central room.

"Hello again, Trevor. Irakesh." David nodded to each of them in turn. "I've been doing quite a bit of research on the two of you. Your stories check out—but there are some disturbing gaps."

"How did you fact check us? The internet is gone," Trevor asked.

"For the most part, you're correct," David offered. He smiled, approaching the energy barrier. "Before the end, Mohn launched a dozen satellites into orbit. Ten of those satellites are still operational, and a number of factions all over the world tap into those satellites. Opening that communication leaves those systems vulnerable, and I'm able to breeze in and find out what I need."

"You're a hacker?" Trevor asked. It seemed so odd for something like that to still exist.

"Of a sort. I have abilities, I believe you'd call them shaping." David held up a hand, and electricity crackled across his fingers. "I can generate almost any type of signal or wave, and those signals can be used to do all sorts of things. Before the world ended, I was a software engineer, so the first thing I learned to do was tap into electronics. The internet was my playground, and the few remaining systems still are."

"That's how you know what happened to Mohn Corp." Trevor moved to stand at the edge of the containment field, as close to David as he could get. "You monitor everything, and they probably have no idea you're even here."

"No," Yuri corrected, speaking for the first time. "They know satellite orbiting earth." He stepped closer to the barrier as well. "Don't know how to find. If we broadcast signal, they find."

"So you can listen, but not talk?" Trevor asked.

"Precisely," David said. He seemed pleased that Trevor was able to follow along. "We do a great deal of listening, and deploy Solaris's teams to deal with the things we're able to tackle."

"What are you, exactly?" Irakesh asked, finally rising to his feet. "You are neither god nor sorcerer, so far as I can tell. How did you get your abilities?"

"Not by choice, that's for damned sure." David's face hardened. "Before the world ended, I was an abductee. As far as the world was concerned, that made me crazy, but it was the truth. We call them the grey men, and they experimented on thousands of us across the globe."

"Why? What were they trying to create?" Trevor asked. The idea that aliens existed was something he'd been comfortable with long before the world ended. He'd never given much credence to alien abduction cases, though, because most weren't credible.

"We call ourselves supers. Cliché, but hey, it fits. Those of us that survived the testing found we had an array of strange abilities. My wife can phase through walls, and even teleport. I can manipulate almost any signal, and I've met someone who can throw a tank like a baseball."

"Yeah, but why give you those abilities?" Trevor asked. "It doesn't make any sense. They're creating their own enemies."

"I get the skepticism. I asked the same thing, trust me." David gave a weary eye roll. "The grey men were trying to create someone with my specific subset of abilities. I can simulate their technology, and I'm a *Homo sapiens*. The grey men have another name, something you might recognize. Have you heard of 'the progeny of the builders'?"

"Shit," Trevor said, his enthusiasm dampened. "Ka used that term. And so did Set. So these grey men are the Builders?"

"Their forerunners, I think. The grey men were an early expedition sent to ready the Earth for their recolonization. Their goal was to access the Ark network left behind by the Builders, but when they returned they found that those Arks had been modified. The woman you'd call Isis created a sort of lock for each Ark. Those Arks can only be accessed with someone possessing the right key." David paused. "You know exactly what I'm talking about, don't you?"

"Sure," Trevor allowed. "I have one of those keys. I know two more people who have them as well. If I understand what you're saying, when Isis made the Ark keys she blocked these grey men from repossessing the

Arks their ancestors had created?"

"Yeah, that's it exactly," David said. "Isis basically changed the locks, coding the Arks to our DNA. They were experimenting on humanity, because the Arks have been modified to recognize our genetic structure. They'll only accept an Ark Lord who started off human. The grey men know that, and have for a very long time—several thousand years, at least."

"Why do they need the Arks so badly?" Irakesh asked. "Surely their power has grown since leaving our world countless millennia ago."

"Because the grey men aren't infallible. They came back to Earth assuming they'd have access to the Arks, and apparently they needed the Arks to send a message back home. Their own ships are too weak to generate a pulse strong enough to reach their home world." David raised a hand and a shimmering holoscreen appeared.

Trevor recognized it instantly as a solar system, but it was unfamiliar to him. "That blue one is their world?"

"Yeah, so far as we know. It's about fourteen light years away. Their ships can transmit a signal at a little slower than the speed of light, but the Arks are capable of generating a message that will travel much more swiftly. Unfortunately, the grey men were able to do exactly that. Five years ago you may have felt a pulse of incredible power being fired from the Arks."

"Yeah," Trevor said. "We saw that, and had no way of explaining it at the time. You're telling me that was these grey men phoning home?"

"I'm afraid so. We tried to stop them, but they found a way around us. It turns out there are seven Arks, one for each continent. During Isis's time, she created a lock for six of them. The seventh was buried under Antarctica, and didn't have the same genetic safeguards. The grey men are in control of that Ark."

"Wait a minute. Does that mean the grey men can get into the Nexus?" Trevor felt himself tensing. "David, we need to warn my friends. Blair and Jordan have to know about this. When we separated, we agreed to meet up there. They've already used the Arks to communicate through the Nexus."

"Oh my god," David said. His face had gone ashen. "We've got to stop them. Yuri, go to the lab and tell Anna to get prepped for deployment."

"I won't be gone long." Blair took Liz's hand, giving it a quick squeeze. "At least one of us has to stay. You know that."

"I know." Liz looked up, eyes full of emotion.

Blair drew her into a tight hug.

"Be quick," she said. "I just can't shake the feeling that if you leave I won't see you for months. Every time we separate, it takes forever to find each other again. We've really just found each other. I don't want to lose you."

"You won't." Blair kissed her hand. "I may be back in an hour. I just have to meet with the others so we can compare notes."

She gave him a smile, and then he was off. He fueled his blur, leaping from hill to hill. He had no idea how fast he was going, but he crossed Rohnert Park and then Petaluma in a matter of minutes.

Along the way, he felt hundreds of canine minds reaching out. They were curious, but he was in a hurry. Introductions could come after he was back home. For now, he needed to get to the Ark before the sun set.

It had already sunk to the horizon's edge, barely visible over a cluster of eucalyptus trees. Blair redoubled his speed, blurring straight up 101 freeway. He blew through Novato, then San Rafael, and finally into Larkspur.

The Ark was visible now. He could have simply light-walked from Santa Rosa, but it was important that he learn the terrain in this new world. That required him to see it, even if briefly.

Besides, he'd missed these rolling hills, the oak forests to one side, and the redwoods closer to the coast. This place had always been home; he was excited that it would be again. He and Liz had finally come home, and he wasn't about to let some emergency tear him away—assuming there even was one.

He paused in Larkspur, stopping in the parking lot where he'd battled against Irakesh, Trevor, and Cyntia. The place was even more ruined— every window shattered and the roof sagging inwards. Rust covered everything, even the weights inside the gym. Behind the gym was the bay, and dominating the bay was his Ark.

Blair closed his eyes, connecting to the Ark. He willed it to light-walk him directly into the Nexus, and the Ark thrummed in response. A familiar flash carried him into a moment of vertigo, then he was standing on the light bridge in the Nexus.

"Ah, Ark Lord Blair." Ka's pleasant voice came from the far side of the room. The green hologram gave a jerky bow, polite as always. "You are the first to arrive. I am awaiting your companions. If you'd like to wait in the central chamber, that's where your friends will go after arrival."

Blair nodded his thanks, then started walking in that direction. It didn't take long to reach the large, round chamber. He tried to stop himself, but he looked up anyway.

The cracks in the glass dome were no worse than they had been five years ago, but they were still just as alarming. Above that glass lay the entire weight of the ocean, so deep that it was pure, inky blackness.

A lifelike hologram flared into existence a few feet away, and Blair was surprised to realize it was Jordan, not Ka. Jordan started to offer him a transparent hand, then stopped. "I almost forgot I can't touch you."

"You couldn't come in person?" Blair asked.

"It would have been a hassle," Jordan explained. "There's a lot to catch up on, but I'm down in Lima helping Doctor Roberts. They've elected him president." He gave an affectionate smile. "That guy is exactly what this country needed."

"Tell him I said hey." Blair returned the smile. He missed the bristly-bearded geologist. "Looks like Trevor's the last to arrive."

"Pardon me, Ark Lords." Ka cocked its bulbous head. "The readings I received from the Ark of the Cradle when the light bridge was activated are quite alarming. The Ark's reserves are at critical levels. It is approaching total failure. Given that state, he may not be able to activate his Ark's communication array."

"Ka, can you record our conversation?" Blair asked.

Ka bowed again. "Of course. I am already doing so. I hope this is acceptable."

"If Trevor arrives after we leave," Blair said, "I want you to play the conversation Jordan and I are about to have. That will catch him up on our news."

"Of course. I'm happy to comply," Ka replied—happily, of course.

"So what did you and Liz find?" Jordan asked. He folded those tree trunk arms against his chest.

"Angel Island was blitzed by a settlement of deathless," Blair explained. "The survivors fled north, to Santa Rosa. I don't know if you remember—"

"Stop talking," a new voice said. "Right now."

A new hologram appeared, this one a young man in his mid-twenties. He had tousled hair, a little too artfully arranged to be accidental. A thin beard ran along his jawline.

"Yes," he said, "you heard me right. Shut up. The Nexus's communications network isn't private. All the Arks can tap into it. The grey men are listening, and so are a couple Ark Lords."

"Who the hell are you?" Blair asked. He shifted to warform, prepared to summon the staff if needed.

"And who the hell are the grey men?" Jordan added.

"We've got to make this fast, so please try to keep up. My name is David. I can save you, but you're going to have to work with me, all right?"

"Why should we do anything you say?" Jordan asked. His right hand wrapped around a holographic side arm. "You want cooperation. Start talking."

"Like I said, we don't have time. The grey men will already be on their way. Listen, I've got your friend Trevor. How do you think I knew to be here? He told me about your meeting. I realize trust is in short supply, but you've got to give me a little. Like I said, I can save you, but I need your help to do that. Are you with me?"

"Okay, I'm on board," Blair said.

Jordan looked askance at him, then turned and nodded to David. "What do you need us to do?"

"It's best that you get off the line, Jordan. Then we can close the communications array. I'm going to come down to the Nexus. I'll bring Trevor with me. We're going to appear in the chamber you're standing in, so don't freak out. Give us a couple minutes to get our gear together."

Chapter 20- Meetings

Trevor rose to his feet as Yuri re-entered the central room with a new figure in tow. He blinked in surprised, shocked to realize he knew the woman David had referred to as Anna. "Anput?"

"By Ra, you're right," Irakesh said. He gave a warm laugh. "Aunt Anput, it's good to see you. Surely you can convince David that we're no threat, and should be released."

"Why would I do that, nephew?" Anput asked. Her hair fell in artfully coifed waves, and she wore a pair of glasses highlighting gorgeous brown eyes. "You are one of the largest threats I have ever encountered. Your reckless actions put Isis and Ra at odds, and nearly cost us everything."

She approached their makeshift cell, stopping just outside the energy barrier, then delivered a warm smile to Trevor. "You, on the other hand, I am most definitely willing to vouch for. David, you should let Trevor out immediately. He's a capable ally, one that I trust."

"I was already planning on it." David waved a hand, and the wall before Trevor fell away.

He stepped through, offering Anput a hand. She ignored it, sweeping him into a hug. He could feel her pressed against him, triggering that odd feeling of lust. Given that he was basically a walking corpse, it was damned odd. It was part of her vampire heritage, something she'd inherited from Osiris.

"Thank you," Irakesh said. He stepped forward, but David waved a hand and the energy field reappeared. Irakesh bumped nose-first into it, falling back with a curse. "Are you really going to keep me imprisoned? I serve Trevor. Anput, surely you recognize the Collar of Shi-Dun."

Anput gave a musical laugh as she inspected Trevor's wrist. "You've enslaved him. This might be the single most beautiful thing I have ever seen—Irakesh forced to serve a man he detests."

"Collar of Shi-Dun? Explain," Yuri asked. He stood near the back of the room, a near-silent shadow until he spoke.

"The collar controls the actions of the person wearing it," Anput said.

She gestured at Trevor. "Whoever wears the bracelet is in control. Trevor can force Irakesh to do just about anything."

"Explains situation," Yuri said. He gave a grim smile. "Glad to see Trevor still ally. More glad to see Irakesh wear collar. Like dog."

"Trevor," David said, "are you okay with leaving Irakesh here? No offense, but I don't want him in my backfield. The rest of us will head to the Nexus." He wiped a lock of hair from his eyes, eyes hardening. "There's a high likelihood that the grey men will respond in force. If they do, you're going to want one of these."

He reached inside his coat, withdrawing a small golden boomerang, and handing it to Trevor.

Trevor hefted it experimentally. It was heavy, and just a little larger than his hand. When he wrapped his hand around the center portion, the two tips jutted out on either side. "It's warm, and I can feel power within it. Is it sunsteel?"

"Near enough. You supply the energy. The weapon enhances it, firing a beam that disintegrates anything it touches. The more energy you supply, the more powerful the beam." David aimed his weapon at the wall, and twin beams of green shot from it. They converged just past his hand, slamming into the wall in waves. "That was the lowest intensity, which would still kill an un-enhanced human. A full blast can disintegrate just about everything I've shot at. There are some defenses, but not many."

"Got it. I assume our opponents will be using something similar?"

"Stole from them. Grey men use same," Yuri confirmed. "David, should alert Jillian?"

"No time. We'll have to go with who we have. Everyone get close," David ordered. Trevor stepped closer, as did the others. "Okay, hang on. We're going."

A familiar white flash emanated from David, the same type Trevor had seen when using a light bridge. There was the instant of vertigo, then he was standing in the Nexus's central chamber. Blair was there, but there was no sign of Jordan.

"You said you can save us. Start talking," Blair said. He was still in human form, but his voice carried even more authority than it had just a few days ago. Trevor had rarely been as glad to see anyone.

"Wait a minute. Professor Smith?" David asked. His eyes widened. "It is you. Oh my god. *You're* Ark Lord Blair?"

"Do I know you?" Blair seemed unmoved, shrugging at Trevor. "What's he talking about?"

"I was one of your students at SRJC. I took Anthology 1A with you. Then, about six years back, I stopped by with my friend Jillian. We told you she was writing a book, remember?" David asked, clearly hopeful.

"I think so. You were asking why pyramids appeared all over the world throughout history. At the time I thought you were writing a cheap thriller. It wasn't research for a book, was it?" Blair asked.

"Nope. Turns out we were looking for the Arks before we even knew what they were. Listen, I realize we don't have time to catch up. We need to move quickly." David turned to the center of the room. "Ka, get your holographic butt out here."

Ka obligingly shimmered into view. "How can I help you, David?"

"Monitor the Antarctic light bridge and let us know the instant it activates. Track the arrivals, and give us numbers and location," David ordered. Trevor was impressed. He sounded like an experienced battlefield commander, despite his age.

"Seven grey men have already arrived," Ka replied cheerfully. "They are making their way toward the central chamber. At their current rate they will arrive in one minute and twelve seconds."

"We need to decide what we want to do right now," David said. He stared hard at Blair. "We can fight them, and we'll probably win. Doing so will give them information about you, though—things they may not already know. They'll transmit everything they learn back to their collective as it happens."

"So we want to wipe them out without showing them everything we can do." Blair shifted in the blink of an eye, suddenly becoming eight heavily-muscled feet of silver fur—with teeth. "I'm betting they're familiar with champions by now. That means blur should be safe to use."

"Perfect." David nodded. "I gave Trevor one of their weapons. I'll hang back and let you engage. I'm not bad in a fight, but I've heard legends of what the two of you can do."

"Yuri melt faces, too," Yuri said. He trotted to the far side of the room, dropping to one knee and taking aim at the doorway.

"I'll hang back as well," Anput said. Her body darkened, then disappeared as she slid into the shadows. "It's better they don't know I exist, especially if they're working with Hades."

Trevor slipped into the shadows as well, gliding to a position about fifteen feet from Yuri. Their fields of fire would overlap, and since Yuri couldn't see him it was important to stay out of his line of fire.

Something was approaching. He didn't hear anything, but Trevor could feel something with the ability to shape getting closer.

These grey men are powerful shapers, his Risen whispered. *Perhaps more powerful than you. Their strength will not be easily overcome. Utilizing surprise is vital. The moment they enter, we must destroy them. Do not hesitate.*

Trevor didn't reply, though he did agree. These fuckers had to go. He gathered his weight, doing a running jump at the wall above the doorway. He grabbed the wall, sinking his claws into the marble, and hung there, suspended over the door. Aiming the strange boomerang, he waited.

He didn't have to wait long. The first grey man leapt into the room, a golden boomerang clutched in each hand, and began firing pulses of green, walking the gunfire across the room. The first blasts zipped in Blair's direction, but he blurred right, then lunged with his claws. The grey man crossed its arms in front of it, a golden wall of force appearing just in time to ward off Blair's blow.

The grey man seemed completely unaware of Trevor's presence. Trevor lined up the shot, just like his dad had taught him as a kid, then poured every bit of energy he could summon into the boomerang. The green beam was thicker and brighter than the shots the grey man had fired, but seemed otherwise unremarkable—until it struck the grey man in the back of its oblong head, vaporizing it. The body tumbled into the room, its boomerangs clattering across the floor.

Trevor had only a split second to react as another grey man appeared in the air a few feet away. Its boomerang was already firing, a stream of deadly green coming right for Trevor's face. Time slowed, and he tumbled slowly backwards as the pulse advanced toward his face. It was still coming quickly, despite the blur.

He threw himself down, kicking off the wall to add just a bit more speed. The pulse passed millimeters from his nose, blasting into the wall behind him. Trevor jerked his boomerang into line with the new attacker, squeezing off a hasty shot. The grey man disappeared, and the shot cored the wall behind it.

Blast it. Could these things teleport? He wished David had given them more information to go on.

Trevor vanished, dropping silently to the floor. There was no sign of his attacker. No sign of any attacker.

"Brace yourself," David roared from the back of the room. Trevor grabbed the base of Ka's pedestal, just in time for a wave of pure force to sweep over him. Blair wasn't as lucky, catching the full brunt of the attack. He was hurled toward the wall, sailing in Trevor's direction.

Trevor extended a hand, and Blair caught it. Trevor swung him around, launching Blair toward the doorway. He blurred at the apex, adding to Blair's momentum.

Blair shot forward like a supersonic missile, sailing into the hallway. Two grey men suddenly became visible, knocked to the ground like bowling pins. Blair was on the first before Trevor blurred up the corridor. He lined up a shot on the second, ending it with a blast from the boomerang.

The last grey man appeared behind Trevor, ramming a glowing blue blade through his chest. It hurt, but he had no internal organs to destroy.

The blow would slow him, though.

"Gregg, get out of way," Yuri roared from behind.

Trevor smiled grimly, shifting his body to green mist. Two sleek black missiles shot into the grey man, a wave of fire ballooning outward. When it had cleared, the surrounding walls were covered in disgusting green residue.

"That's the last of them," David said. He rose from cover, trotting over to Trevor and Blair. "We've got to move quickly. They'll be back soon, and in greater numbers."

"Okay, Obi-wan," Blair said, raising a wolfish eyebrow. "What do you propose?"

"There's a lot I don't have time to tell you," David said. "You should head for the Peruvian Ark. I need to get back to the Black Knight, but I can send Anna with you. There's something in the Amazon that's of great interest to Hades, which means the grey men are after it, too. Anna can brief you on the entire situation once you're safe."

"Yeah, that's not going to happen," Blair said. He folded his arms, staring hard at David, then at Trevor. "The grey men are a threat, sure. But they aren't the only threat. I need to get my house in order. That means going back to Santa Rosa. You and Anput should continue to South America, meet with Jordan, and see what you can do. When I get a handle on what's going on in Santa Rosa, I'll come to Peru to update you."

"We'll miss you," Trevor said, "but I completely understand. Take care of Liz for me." He offered Blair a hand.

Blair shook it. "Thanks for understanding, Trev."

"Be safe, man, and tell Liz I love her." Trevor turned to Anput. "Lead the way."

Jordan appeared against the wall of the central chamber, spotting Elia across the room. She knelt, praying, at the feet of the statue of Isis. The bullet holes from the combat he'd instigated while still working for Mohn had been painstakingly repaired, though those spots were a slightly different shade of white.

"The real thing was much more feisty," Jordan said. He ambled toward her, trying to be as unthreatening as possible.

"Is. The real thing *is* much more feisty," Elia replied, rising gracefully. She turned to face Jordan, her entire body tense. Undisguised hatred smoldered in those eyes. "I tire of your blasphemy. I know that I cannot stop you—you have too much brute strength for that—but I do not need to listen to you profane the scriptures. What do you want, heathen?"

"I wanted to let you know I was here," Jordan said. "I'm going to meet some friends at the light bridge, and they might be coming in hot. Keep your people away from that room until I've dealt with the situation." Jordan moderated his tone, reminding himself that he couldn't approach every interaction like this was the military.

"What? You've invited yet more heathens to this holiest of place? I will not allow it. I will—"

Jordan did the least confrontational thing he could think of. He teleported. He didn't have time to deal with her shit, not right now.

He appeared next to the light bridge. They hadn't arrived yet, so he folded his arms, settling in to wait. Waiting was, and always had been, the worst part of being a soldier; he'd learned that long before he'd worked for Mohn.

All you could do as an enlisted was wait for orders. Those orders could mean your death, or the death of your friends. Yet the orders were never the worst part. It was the damned waiting, the not knowing what you were going to have to do in order to preserve lives.

Jordan didn't know who or what was coming across the light bridge, nor when it would happen. Would they be pursued by these grey men? What were their weaknesses? Their tactics? Jordan needed intel, but—like it or not—all he could do was wait.

So he did.

Sixteen minutes later the light bridge finally activated, its clean white light flooding the room. Three figures stood there, and Jordan was surprised to realize he recognized all of them.

He'd expected Trevor. He hadn't expected the other two.

Jordan recognized Anput from his time at the Ark of the Cradle. She had always been thick as thieves with Trevor, and had served Ra loyally. Her husband, Anubis, had been a royal pain in Jordan's ass.

The last figure was the most welcome, and Jordan moved forward to offer his hand. "You look like hell, Yuri."

"Eh, not so bad. Just older. Years tough," Yuri said. He shook Jordan's hand, his grip as firm as ever. His goatee had patches of grey now, but his hair was still dark and he still wore the same mirrored shades he'd always loved. "Good to see you, Commander."

"Welcome to the Mother's Ark," Jordan said. He released Yuri, and turned to the others. "Unfortunately, our stay here is going to be short. I can't take you further into the Ark just yet. An order of priests have taken up residence, and it will be simpler if we avoid them. Now, how about someone tell me what the hell just happened in the Nexus?"

"We have a lot to catch up on, Commander." Anput offered Jordan her hand like she expected him to kiss it. Jordan shook it instead. "I see you've grown far more powerful than at our last meeting. Hopefully you can help us win this war, Ark Lord."

"Which war, exactly?" Jordan asked.

"She's talking about the Builders," Trevor supplied. "What she and David call the 'grey men'." He gave Jordan a respectful nod, which Jordan grudgingly returned. "We engaged them in the Nexus. They're tough, but we took down a handful easily enough."

"*This* time," Anput said, frowning. "They are masters of adaptation. We do our best to hide our true capabilities, because every time they see us do something they either counter it or start using it themselves."

"I need a lot more basic information before I feel qualified to even discuss a war with these grey men," Jordan said. He folded his arms. "Trevor and I have been gone for five years. He might know some of what's going on, but I'm still in the dark about a lot of things. Yuri, what happened with Mohn Corp? Is the old man in charge of the Syracuse facility?"

"No." Yuri frowned, stress lines tightening around his eyes. "Syracuse gone. Old man dead, or worse."

"What happened?" Jordan asked quietly.

"Nox," Anput snapped. Her expression suggested that her hatred was personal. "He's Hades' chief enforcer. He took Mohn Corp apart in less than three months. His demons hit every facility around the globe, converting or destroying everyone. Everything Mohn had, Hades now has."

Jordan didn't like the implications of that at all.

"You'd know Nox by another name," Anput continued, moderating her tone. "Trevor, I suspect you'll recognize it too. Nox was once the Director, the most highly trusted member in Mohn's organization."

"The Director?" Jordan said. He sat down against the marble wall, slumping to the warm stone. "That's pretty much the worse news I could have imagined. If he works for Hades, we're in serious trouble."

"He's worked for Hades for five years." Anput spat. "During that time we've lost engagement after engagement. We've been powerless, while Hades has made deals across Asia and Africa. He's building a global army, slowly infecting every leader he meets with demonic taint. They have no idea the cost of the bargain they're making, and the fools are lining up to sign on. He's already got Syracuse as a beachhead in North America. Now, he's set his sights on South America."

"What does Hades want?" Trevor asked.

"Good question," Jordan added. "Set seemed unbalanced, but Hades was self-serving. What does he want? Global domination?"

"David was able to intercept some of their recent communications," Anput said. "They're after a city, maybe the first city to ever have existed. In that city is something called the Proto Ark. The problem is, we don't know why they need it." She brushed a lock of dark hair from her face. "Hades works with the grey men, and we're guessing that they're the senior partners in that relationship. They're mostly holed up in Antarctica, and seem to be letting Hades do the bulk of the work. I'd guess his first order of business is conquering every continent, but that can't be his end game. He's proven too intelligent for that."

"I'm still trying to get a handle on these grey men," Jordan said. "Are they an immediate threat? If so, are you trying to focus on them or on Hades?" He felt like he needed a flow chart to understand their various enemies.

"David considers the grey men to be the primary threat," Anput said, "and Project Solaris lacks the resources to go after Hades, even if they did consider him a primary threat. He isn't, so far as we can tell. He's self-serving and deceitful, but the grey men are paving the way for the return of the Builders. If they aren't stopped, we're going to have to deal with something even Isis and Ra never faced." She adopted a faraway look. "I've had a glimpse into one of their minds. The ones that left Earth before the last ice age are still alive. They make someone like Isis or Osiris look like a child."

"I can't even wrap my brain around that," Trevor murmured. "If these things have had millions of years to get stronger, there's no way we're going to be able to stop them. Not without one hell of an advantage."

"Gaining that advantage is why David sent me," Anput said. She looked from Jordan to Trevor. "You two are new players, and one of you is the Ark Lord of this continent. With your combined help, we might be able to reach this Proto Ark before they do."

"Maybe," Jordan said, and shook his head. "The tactical situation in Peru is grim. Brazil is encroaching on both the northern and southern border. There's a whole lot of deathless packing a whole lot of weaponry, and every last one wants Peru to burn to the ground. I'm not sure I can go haring off into the jungle. These people need me."

"Your concern for these people is laudable, but you have to realize what's at stake. Jordan, something came before the Arks," Anput said. "From what we understand, the Builders were the dominant race some 2.3

million years ago. They were far more advanced than humanity, and they built a city that housed the bulk of their culture. This was long before they created the Arks, perhaps hundreds of thousands of years. Eventually, for whatever reason, they built an Ark on every continent. Their numbers fell dramatically, until there were only a handful remaining."

"Why did they build the Arks?" Trevor asked. "Their placement doesn't appear random. Why were they constructed in the first place?"

"David has a theory," Anput allowed. "I haven't been able to substantiate it. He believes they built the Arks as a transmission network. When they decided to leave they beamed themselves to their new world as light, using the Arks."

"That's the light pulses David was talking about?" Trevor asked.

"Yes, it sounds like you witnessed them," Anput said.

"Yeah," Jordan said, nodding. He turned back to Trevor. "It was right after the CME, maybe a month or two later. The Ark beamed something into the sky, and we had no idea what or why. Is that what you're talking about?"

"That's it exactly," Anput said, soberly. "In that case, the grey men were beaming information. Information the Builders now have. In the distant past, we think they may have beamed their own consciousnesses."

"So this Proto Ark," Jordan broke in. "Assuming it still exists, where is it exactly, and what is it you think having it will do for us?"

"We believe the Proto Ark is located somewhere in the Amazon Jungle," Anput said. "That's backed up by the fact that Nox was recently sighted in Brazil, and that Brazil has launched a massive offensive into the jungle. They know the Proto Ark is there, and they're searching for it. We don't know everything it can do, but the fact that they want it should be enough."

"It's enough for me," Trevor said. "Jordan?"

"It's too thin. I can't leave on a hunch," Jordan finally said. "If this place is a threat, I need to know how."

"How about this, then?" Anput asked. "The staff that Isis used, the Primary Access Key? Both that and its mate were created at the Proto Ark. If the grey men are able to make another, then they'll be able to seize control of the entire Ark network. They'd be able to circumvent the security Isis put into place. Even were they not, do we really want them to be able to create access keys? Even a few would be enough to end the war instantly."

"Okay," Jordan said. "You've convinced me of the gravity of the situation. We need to get to the Proto Ark before they do." He gave a grim smile. "I think we can make that happen. I know just the person who can help us."

Chapter 22- Tricked

The Great Bear lumbered towards the colorful tent nestled atop a rise overlooking a nameless glacial lake. By day, its waters were the bluest thing he'd ever seen, though they were painted black under the heavy moon. The tent was bright yellow, visible from miles off. Yosemite could hear a single heartbeat coming from inside that tent.

"Awaken, child of man," the Great Bear roared. He rose to his full height, three times that of a tall man. His voice was thunderous, but he shattered a foot thick pine to punctuate it. "Rise, and be judged."

The heartbeat quickened, and then one of the wonderful zippers these moderns had invented began to unzip. The flap fell, and a woman emerged from the tent. She stared impassively at Yosemite, seemingly unconcerned by her impending death.

"What do you want, old Bear?" The woman's voice was crusted with age.

"Why have you come to the roof of the world? There is nothing for your kind here. Before I kill you, I would know your purpose." The Bear lumbered within easy reach of the woman, yet she did not flee.

"These lands used to belong to my people," she explained. "My tribe is called the Miwok. I figured I'm going to die soon, so I may as well do it somewhere pretty."

"You are of the Awanechee?" he rumbled, bending to sniff her. "Your legends tell you of the Great Bear?"

"That's right. The Awanechee came before the Miwok, but we're the same stock. Our legends tell of the Great Bear." She rubbed her gloved hands together to ward the chill. "They say that you were called Yosemite, a chieftain of your people, and that you earned your name by slaying a grizzly. Of course, those legends seem like they were off. They said you were a man, once."

"Your tales hit near enough the mark," the Bear replied. "I was born a bear, the largest to roam the mountains you call the Sierras. One day, a woman came to me. I attacked her, as I would any other human. She was prey, or so I thought. That woman became a wolf, and bested me. I was forced to retreat, but she followed. When she caught me she healed my wounds."

"You're talking about the earth mother." She nodded in recognition, waving for him to continue.

"Yes, the same. The earth mother changed me. She used her magics to shape me into a man. I was able to think as a man, to appear as a man." Yosemite moved to sit near the woman, his form still dwarfing her. "But I am not a man. I am Bear."

"Well, Bear, if you're going to kill me, get on with it," the woman taunted. "It's mighty cold, and I'm tired of listening to you yammer."

Inexplicable anger burst to life, coloring the Bear's vision. He roared, lunging for the woman. She made no move to flee, smiling as he took her life.

The Bear tore off a hunk of flesh, wolfing it down. He lost himself in the feeding, completely unprepared for the burst of scarlet light that came from the corpse.

He snorted, pawing at his nose as he backed away from the meal. His eyes itched, and his head hurt.

A thin, reedy voice sounded within the Bear's head. It was high, like the mountain wind. He'd not heard it in seasons uncounted. *You are a fool, old Bear.*

"Windigo," Yosemite growled. He rose slowly to his feet, peering around the snowy ravine. "Show yourself, trickster."

I can't do that, I'm afraid. Windigo taunted.

The Bear remembered the Mother speaking into his mind, and Ahiga had once done the same. Yet Windigo was no Ka-Dun.

"Where are you, demon?" the Bear roared. He spun around, still searching. Perhaps Windigo was in the shadows, somewhere. Like a Ka-Ken.

I was in the woman, you fool. When you consumed her, you opened yourself to me. Now I am in your mind. Already I am overpowering your defenses, and each time you sleep I will control your body.

"No," the Bear said. He turned in a frantic circle, still trying to locate Windigo.

I tricked you, Bear. Windigo's laugher echoed in the Bear's head.

"What do you want, trickster?" the Bear demanded.

You will leave these mountains, making your way toward the city that men call Santa Rosa.

"Why would I do anything you ask?"

Because I will kill every one of your children while you sleep. There are few enough bears in these mountains as it is. If you want to save your children, start walking west. Stay, and I'll ensure that your species is eradicated.

Blair briefly surveyed San Francisco from his perch atop Mount Burdell. He was about thirty miles north of the city, but he could be there in a few heartbeats. He could blaze through the deathless, extinguishing every last one of the lights.

Part of him longed to do that. Melissa certainly deserved it, after what she'd done to Angel Island. She could have come clean and told them. He'd have respected her for it.

That would have been most unwise on her part, Ka-Dun. You'd have slain her out of hand, and she knew it.

That was probably true. He would have killed her, and even if he hadn't Liz certainly would have. So, in a way, he couldn't blame Melissa for not telling him.

He *could* blame her for doing it in the first place, but now wasn't the time for vengeance. He'd meant what he said to Trev. He needed to get home, to Santa Rosa. It was time to rebuild, not to pick fights.

Blair turned from San Francisco, staring north. Below him lay Petaluma, golden hills forming a valley where dozens of farms had once lain. Most of that land was fallow now, reclaimed to some extent by nature. He could feel the minds prowling the darkness down there: dogs, coyotes, and a few foxes. They watched for threats, ready to alert their human allies if they found deathless.

He blurred from his perch, soaring down the mountainside to the valley below. Blair landed in a crouch, then bounded into the air. He flitted from building to building, the miles rolling by as he made his way closer to Santa Rosa. The wind tore at his fur, but he reveled in it.

High above, the full moon shone down, feeding him a trickle of power. That, too, felt good, though he didn't need it with so much more power readily available from the Ark.

Several minutes later, Blair reached Santa Rosa. The dark houses stood like tombs. He could hear heartbeats in a few, but most were empty. It would take decades to repopulate, assuming the world was able to go that long without yet another apocalypse.

Rebuilding was daunting, but if Alicia could shoulder the burden, so could he and Liz.

Blair blurred up Fountaingrove Parkway, leaping up the hillside to land near Alicia's house. He could sense Liz inside. Blair slowed, pausing outside the front door. He shifted back to human form then rapped three times. Several moments later he heard footsteps on the stairs—two pairs. The door opened to reveal Alicia, her long dark hair in a simple ponytail.

"You came back," Alicia said. She motioned for him to enter, giving a brief smile.

"You sound surprised," Blair said, hugging her as he stepped into the unfurnished home. "I was just exchanging news with the other Ark Lords we know."

"What's that stench?" Liz asked. She crinkled her nose in disgust.

"Oh, yeah, I guess I did get some goo on me," Blair said. Dark green blood had spattered all over his chest fur. He shifted back to human form, and the spots remained. They smelled like sour milk.

"Explain." Liz raised a copper eyebrow.

"All right, but let's do it outside so I don't stink up the house." Blair agreed. He walked to the back deck, opening the door and stepping outside. The others followed. "I met with Trevor and Jordan. Apparently, our use of the Ark communication network alerted the Progeny of the Builders, and possibly the other Ark Lords. We were warned by a guy named David who worked for something called Project Solaris. He claims that before the end of the world he'd been abducted by aliens that he calls the grey men. He was one of thousands of experiments."

"What kind of experiments?" Alicia asked, rather dubiously.

"The kind that gave them the ability to shape." Blair leaned against the wooden railing. He stripped off his goop-covered shirt, setting it on the railing. The cool wind felt good on his bare skin. "I saw some of what he can do, and I don't think he was lying."

"So where did the blood come from?"

"The grey men sent a scouting party when they realized someone was using the Nexus," Blair explained. "We took care of them. No casualties. Trevor is fine." He knew that was what Liz would most want to know. "They wanted me to go with them to South America to talk further about the threat, but I told them we have our own problems to deal with."

Alicia and Liz shared a look that Blair didn't much like.

"What?" he said.

"We received a messenger just a few minutes ago," Liz said. She bit her lip. "From Melissa. She says that the Lords of Silicon Valley want to meet in person to discuss a possible treaty."

"Wow."

"Yeah, I know," Liz said. She took his hand and he gave her a squeeze. "How do you want to play this?"

Blair considered that for a moment. "I think we should meet with them."

"Are you insane?" Alicia asked, her voice rising half an octave. "You have to know this is an ambush. They want to kill you and take the key to the Ark. You're just going to walk into their trap and let them take it?"

"You're right about it being a trap, but if we decline they'll just come after Santa Rosa. We need to respond with a show of force, let them know that we can't be pushed around," Blair said. He rose from the railing, turning south to peer in the direction of San Francisco. "A war is coming. A big one. We need to get our house in order, and that means one way or another we need to deal with these deathless. As soon as possible."

"If you want to go, I'll support you," Liz said. She gave him a tentative smile. "I don't mind admitting I'm afraid, though."

"I knew you'd leave again," Alicia snapped. She spun around, stalking toward the stairs to the second floor.

"Alicia, wait," Blair called.

Alicia, much to his surprise, stopped and turned to face him.

He followed her into the house. "Come with us. We're going to go down, deal with this threat, and then come back here to talk about whatever Windigo is. Liz and I are not going anywhere. We're going to help set things right."

"I'll believe that when I see it," Alicia muttered, but at least it was under her breath. She sighed, raising her voice. "Fine, I'll pack a bag. The messenger said tomorrow at noon."

"That makes sense," Blair mused. "That's the height of their power, after all. Where do they want to meet?"

"San Francisco. The Hilton in the Financial District," Liz said.

"Then I definitely like our chances." Blair smiled. "I think the deathless have no idea what a fully powered Ark can do, especially one that close."

Chapter 24- Hades

Nox smoothed his slacks, admiring himself in the suite's mirror. It had been a long time since he'd had access to the creature comforts of the business world. He hadn't realized how much he loved a good suit until he'd been without them for five years.

"Thank you for the use of your tailor," he said. "Do you have anything of note to report about your efforts in the jungle?" He didn't face Camiero, instead pulling his tie into a perfect Windsor. The humidity here would normally make a suit impractical, but since he no longer sweated he could wear a suit in any climate.

"Of course," Camiero replied. "I am happy to see you suitably attired. Regrettably, I have little progress to report. You have set a near impossible task, and I warned you that it would take a great deal of time." His eyes narrowed. "If I were a mistrustful man, I might assume that I was being set up to fail. But that would make me paranoid, would it not?"

"You're not paranoid," Nox said. "You failing is one possible outcome, and if it happens you'll be blamed for that failure. Honestly? I would prefer that it play out differently." He finally turned his full attention on the deathless and smiled, as warmly as he could manage. "There are two ways this plays out. You succeed, and I give you access to power you can only dream of. Or you fail, and I have to replace you. I have no desire to do that, Camiero. I have other tasks to attend to, and I cannot afford to get bogged down in an endless quest. We need to find the city, and we need to do it soon."

"If you are so interested in success, then why do you allow your pet demon to wreak havoc? She plays my lieutenants against each other, egging them on to kill one another. That thing is crazy, and you are a fool to let it run loose," Camiero raged. He leaned forward, stabbing a finger at Nox. "I also know that you've been meeting privately with my lieutenants."

"Kali is…a chore. I'll grant you that," Nox said, nodding sympathetically. "I'll try talking to her again, but I doubt it will do much good. She loves chaos, Mr. Camiero. And it is true that I've taken meetings with some of your underlings. If things do not go well, one of them will likely be your replacement. I won't lie about that. At the same time, it's important you understand that I *do* want you to succeed. Let's discuss your problems in more detail. Tell me about the invasion, and how we can speed it up."

"Very well," Camiero allowed. The deathless walked to a pair of plush chairs, sinking into the one closest to the window. It afforded a specular view of the ocean.

Nox took the seat across from him, crossing his legs and placing his hands in his lap. "You have my full attention."

"We sent a platoon of our best soldiers to seven different locations along the border of the forest. Each platoon had helmet-mounted cameras, and all were experts in stealth," Camiero explained. He reached into the end table next to the chair, removing a cigar from a mahogany box. He offered one to Nox, but Nox shook his head. "At first those platoons encountered nothing. They explored the jungle, looking for any champions, or any villages. They found no one. Nothing. Not a single sign of man, anywhere in the trees. They proceeded deeper, and the platoons broke into squads as they explored. The night after we changed deployment, we lost forty percent of our troops. The helmet cams show nothing, but there were ghostly sounds in the trees, and occasionally a scream. We've heard sounds consistent with werewolves, but we expected that."

"What happened after the first day?" Nox steepled his fingers, staring passively at Camiero.

"Our troops withdrew and fortified their positions. They prepared for night assault, and set both automated and living sentries. They knew what the werewolves were capable of, and were prepared for it. None of them need to sleep, as you know. They were as alert as they'd ever been in their lives." Camiero stopped. He scowled at the cigar, setting it on the end table. "The next morning everyone was dead, except for the sentries. The sentries heard nothing."

"Unsurprising." Nox sighed. "The werewolves know the jungle too well, and they have indigenous allies. We will never find El Dorado as long as they can keep us from the jungle."

"So what would you have me do then? If we cannot enter the jungle, then the task is impossible."

"You're thinking far too small, Mr. Camiero." Nox leaned forward and lowered his voice, smiling cruelly. "If we cannot fight them in the jungle, then we need to remove the jungle."

"Respectfully, I do not think that is possible," Camiero said. He shook his head sadly. "You do not understand the power of the jungle. Five decades of deforestation was reversed in the first year after the CME. The jungle is magical. It grows too quickly. If we burn a swath, that swath will return in days. Within weeks the trees will be the same height as before they were burned."

"I didn't say you had to burn the jungle," Nox said, "just that you had to remove it. Again, you are thinking too small. You are using the tools of an old, dead world. Tell me, Camiero, you are a shaper aren't you?"

"I have some powers, I suppose. I do not know that I would call myself a shaper," Camiero replied, shrugging, as if the ability to reshape the world around you were of absolutely no interest. It was one of the man's greatest failings.

"Then find me people who are. I want every deathless who is capable of shaping gathered and brought to this building. The first class will begin tomorrow morning, and I expect this place to be full. Am I clear?"

"Very," Camiero said. He paused, then cocked his head. "What will you be teaching them?"

"To use this," Nox said. He picked up the obelisk from the table, and tossed it to Camiero. "Hades, the god I serve, had them created. This will cause any plant life near it to shrivel and die. The more power you give it, the larger an area it affects. Gather another army, Mr. Camiero. I'm going to teach your shapers to kill the jungle. Then you're going to march all the way to the heart of it, and you're going to find me my city."

Jordan lowered the binoculars, handing them back to Rodrigo, the Latino man that Roberts had assigned to help him. He focused on the city itself, seeing it as a whole. Lima didn't look all that different from the last time he'd been here, except that there was far less traffic. Most of the cars had been removed, giving the city an open, quiet feel. Any pollution had long since dissipated, and the salty breeze smelled amazing.

Mankind had been reduced from a teeming mass to an exhausted remnant that couldn't quite fill the walls of a medium-sized city. Still, there were signs of progress. A crane clung to the side of a building, hefting a bundle of steel girders to a group of workers wearing hard hats. Towering over the workers was a white-furred Ka-Dun, who gestured at the girders. Jordan felt a faint stirring in the distance, as the Ka-Dun telekinetically lifted hundreds of pounds of steel. He maneuvered the girders into place, and the other workers swarmed around them with tools.

"Why did Roberts assign you as my liaison, Rodrigo?" Jordan asked. He turned to size Rodrigo up, and the man wilted under the scrutiny.

"Because he knows we've already met, and because there wasn't anyone else," Rodrigo explained. "I don't really expect you to remember me. We met back in the jungle, near the border to Columbia. You and your friends took one of our Jeeps."

Jordan's eyed widened in recognition. "I do remember you. We sent you to Isis, at the Ark."

"Ah, you do remember. Yes, I worked for the Mother, journeying with her when she sailed to Easter Island. I saw her confrontation with Sobek, though I was cowering in the hold at the time. After we returned, I asked her for the gift. Seeing that monster terrified me, and I vowed that I would help defend my people from things like him." Rodrigo straightened his baseball cap, a battered black thing with a faded gold police shield. "El Medico made me a kind of police chief, I guess. I'm not really cut out for it, but I'm what we have—well, *had*. Now that you're here, we finally have a real leader, someone who can put this place back together."

"Isn't that what Roberts is doing?" Jordan asked.

"Medico is a great administrator," Rodrigo said, "but he's a terrible field leader. He doesn't do well with the day-to-day stuff, but he's great at planning a future for our people. He relies on me to take care of most trouble, but I'm just not that good at it. People respect me, but I think a lot of them secretly pity me too." He avoided Jordan's gaze. "I'd like to learn to be better at this, but I haven't had anyone to teach me."

"I can definitely relate to that," Jordan said. "Most of being in command is about solving problems you've never had to solve before, all while making it look like you've done it a million times. I can't stick around, but I can spend the next few days helping you get organized." He shared the kid's feelings of inadequacy. "Listen I'm not really any sort of administrator, or leader. I was a *boots on the ground* kind of commander, who looked after squads, or at most a small installation. I've never done any of this before."

"You seem so confident," Rodrigo said. He looked confused. "I don't get it."

"That's the real secret," Jordan explained. "In America we had a saying: *fake it 'til you make it*. You act like you belong, and do your best to make that act become reality." He put a hand on Rodrigo's lower back, pushing to straighten his posture. "You need to look the part. Think and act with confidence, even when you don't feel confident—*especially* when you don't feel confident. You're going to make mistakes. Acknowledge that, but don't let decisions paralyze you. No leader is worse than an indecisive one."

Rodrigo nodded eagerly and squared his shoulders; if it looked a little forced, it was still an improvement over his previous slack posture. "I'd love some help with our biggest problem. I guess that would be the docks. Sobek will be coming in a week, and El Medico said we need to look as impressive as possible. I have no idea how to do that."

"We do that by showing Sobek that we're ready to fight," Jordan said. He peered out at the iron-grey waves, knowing the crocodile god he'd heard so much about was out there somewhere. Coming closer. "When he comes, we show him strength and organization. That's the only thing a predator like him will understand."

"The last time he was here, he told El Medico that he thought the Mother was dead," Rodrigo said. He adjusted his hat, pulling it down to shade his eyes from the harsh sun. He peered out from the brim, studying Jordan for a reaction.

Jordan gave him nothing.

"Is she? Dead, I mean."

"I don't know." Jordan sighed. "I think she is. I can't possibly see how she survived. But I didn't see her die, no."

"I like you already, sir. You give straight answers." Rodrigo smiled, starting toward the Jeep they'd arrived in. He slid into the driver's seat, waiting for Jordan to join him. "Do you have a title you'd prefer that I use, sir?"

Jordan considered that as he opened the door and slid into the Jeep. How did he want to be addressed? He knew what the Director would have said. Mark would have pointed out how much respect the right title carried.

For once, Jordan agreed.

"You can call me Ark Lord," he said. He glanced sidelong at Rodrigo as they sped along the empty road toward the dock.

"Yes, Ark Lord, sir," Rodrigo said. He guided the Jeep toward a large freighter laden with hundreds of metal storage containers. A crane was lowering one onto the dock, where a handful of people were waiting to unload it.

"What are they unloading?" Jordan asked. He leapt from the Jeep, using his telekinesis to carry him to the top of an already emptied cargo container. Below him, four people were unloading rough blocks of stone in a variety of sizes. The black rock looked fresh quarried.

Rodrigo leapt onto the crate, landing next to Jordan with a loud clang. "We call it the Mother's rock. Not terribly inventive, but it stuck. Sobek sends it four times a year, to honor an agreement he made with the Mother."

"El Medico mentioned that the stone had interesting properties," Jordan said. He hopped down, walking over to a pile of stones. The four men looked up at him curiously, but when they saw Rodrigo they just shrugged and kept working.

"I don't understand it. You can see a few of the ways we've employed it, though." Rodrigo pointed to the obelisks ringing the docks, about a hundred feet apart. "It's a security system, of sorts. It can detect the dead, and will alert any shaper in the area. There are other practical uses, too. Some shapers carry them as a sort of battery they can draw on." Rodrigo withdrew a smooth rock that fit in the palm of his hand. Jordan could feel a trickle of energy in the rock.

"You have champions guarding the entrances to the city, right?" Jordan asked. He'd seen patrols, but wanted confirmation.

"Yes, they move across rooftops mostly. They're both an early warning system and a mobile defense force."

"I want to set up better fortifications at every major freeway entrance to the city. I want a store of these batteries and a squad of unblooded at each. Make sure they're well armed. In the event of combat, they're to ensure that shapers are protected, and given access to the batteries." Jordan rattled off the instructions as they came to him. "Who coordinates patrols right now?"

"Uhh, I guess I do. We have people who watch over certain districts, but I only really check in with them if something goes wrong. I don't really have time to talk to them all," Rodrigo admitted.

"We need a command structure in place. I want you to get me a list of twenty-five people who you think can be taught to be leaders. How soon can you get that together?"

Jordan pulled on a black t-shirt, enjoying the feel of the clean cotton hugging his skin. It had been a long time since he'd had fresh clothes, much less a real uniform. He picked up the long-sleeved camo shirt from the bed, then set it back down. It would be too hot for that today, though he would have enjoyed the stylized black pyramid patch on the shoulder. A sign of his rank, Rodrigo had said when he'd dropped it off.

Jordan picked up his sunglasses from the nightstand and exited the room to the hotel's courtyard. Before the fall this hotel would have cost several hundred dollars a night. The locale had been set up to cater to tourists, but the same qualities that made it a great hotel also made it a suitable command location.

The building ringed a wide courtyard, completely enclosing it. That courtyard was mostly manicured lawn—or had been once. Now the grass was patchy and brown. The olympic-sized pool was dry and covered in debris. The courtyard was large enough for troops to run laps or spar. He could drill here, and that made it perfect.

The building was also more secure than most hotels. There were only five ways in or out; four of those were heavy steel doors at the corners of the building, and the fifth was the lobby. The lobby was the least defensible, but also had covered positions for snipers. Anyone who walked through those doors would be picked off, and if the place was breached they could evacuate in any direction.

"Good morning," Rodrigo called from the yard below, waving up at Jordan. "The men are assembling now, Ark Lord." He'd dropped the "sir," as Jordan had requested.

Jordan understood the habit, both in the military and local police. The word was one they knew, and calling Jordan "sir" would be comforting—but only in the short term.

They were building a new world. He needed to teach them a new way of looking at it.

He gave an approving nod and leapt from the balcony, landing in a crouch near Rodrigo. It still amazed him, his ability to do things like that. Any normal person would have broken a leg, or worse. He rose, joining Rodrigo as the younger man started for the field where the others were gathering.

As they approached, Jordan studied the arrivals, a mixture of men and women. Most were dark-skinned, which made sense given where they were. A blond woman stood out, and an Indian man. There was an Asian couple who stood almost back to back, glaring at their neighbors as if daring them to say something.

Jordan could feel their relative strengths. Some, like the Indian man, were powerful beacons. Others, like the blond woman, were so weak he could barely sense any power in them at all. The Asian couple lay somewhere in between. A few were stronger than the Indian, none were weaker than the blonde.

He'd never seen this many werewolves together, and the varying levels of strength were definitely intriguing. Liz could probably tell him exactly why there was such a difference, but he was fairly sure it had to do with the relative strength of the virus.

Jordan counted swiftly, unsurprised when the count ended at twenty-five. Everyone was here. He sucked in a breath, then launched his best drill sergeant bellow. "Good morning, whelps. My name is Ark Lord Jordan. Not Jordan. Not Sir. Ark Lord Jordan. If I'm in a very good mood, which I'm not likely to be while working with you lot, I may allow you to call me Ark Lord. I've adopted the unenviable task of turning you into an army capable of protecting this city."

"What gives you the right to talk to us like that?" the Indian man called out. He stepped forward, balling his fists.

Jordan extended a hand, pushing downward. The Indian man fell to his knees, struggling against the unseen force Jordan had generated. "Did I fucking stutter? 'What gives you the right to talk to us like that, *Ark Lord.*'"

The Indian man shifted into a dun-colored werewolf, straining to take a step toward Jordan. Jordan released him, allowing the Indian to charge forward. He waited until the man was inches away, then accelerated into his most powerful blur.

Jordan twisted, grabbing the Indian man around the neck and flinging him face-first into the turf—not an easy feat when in human form, but the telekinesis gave him an unfair advantage.

"What gives me the right," Jordan continued, turning his back on the Indian, "is power. I can feel all of yours, and I'm betting you can feel mine."

The Indian roared, rising to his feet and blurring toward Jordan. He was strong, but Jordan could have bested this Ka-Dun long before he'd become an Ark Lord. His foot shot backwards, shattering the Indian's kneecap. Jordan sidestepped the larger werewolf, dodging to the side as the Indian collapsed with a yelp.

"Some of you are stronger than others, but don't let that be a determining factor in your success here. Even the weakest can grow in strength, and I'm going to teach all of you how to do exactly that." Jordan shifted into his warform, blond fur erupting all over his body. He reached down to help the Indian to his feet. "I've fought alongside Isis, the woman you call the Mother. I've battled gods more powerful than you can possibly imagine, beings that were tens of thousands of years old. I survived by learning and adapting, and that's what you're going to do. Now, what's your name?"

"Vimal," the Indian spat.

"You're powerful Vimal, the strongest shaper here. If you're as stubborn as you look, you might surpass us all one day." Jordan turned back to the crowd.

He had their attention now. Some were curious. Many were afraid. All eyed him warily, unsure of what he'd do next. Excellent. That was the exact mental state that opened them to learning.

Jordan turned to the blond woman, the weakest. She was tall, just shy of six feet. She had a runner's lean frame, and unlike almost every other werewolf she had a pistol belted to her thigh.

"You," Jordan boomed. "What's your name?" He walked over to stand in front of the woman, staring down at her.

The woman snapped to attention. "Alison, Ark Lord," she replied.

"Why do you wear that weapon?" Jordan asked.

The woman squirmed under the attention; she licked her lips as she searched for an answer. "To even the odds, Ark Lord."

"Shift."

Alison shifted into a golden-furred female, just a few inches taller than Jordan. She was barely bigger than a male, tiny compared to a Ka-Ken like Liz. Jordan extended a hand toward the stack of crates he'd had brought in that morning. He levitated a bulky sniper rifle from the box, and the weapon shot to his hand.

He handed the rifle to Alison. "The sentiment is good, but that sidearm is too small to put down most threats we need to deal with. This weapon, on the other hand, can put something down and make it stay down. You can explode a man's head like a watermelon, and that includes deathless." He clasped his hands behind his back. "Take to the shadows and find a suitable sniper location along the roof of this building."

Alison's face went red and her gaze fell to the floor. She whispered something that sounded like a prayer, then, ever so slowly, she sank into the shadows. Jordan waited, pacing back and forth in front of the other werewolves. They'd formed a rough line without him having to ask. Progress already.

"Can anyone among you tell me where Alison is?" Jordan asked. Then he waited. No one spoke. Moments passed. Still nothing. "So, despite the fact that she's the 'weakest' person here, she's in a superior position. She can pick you off, and not one of you can stop her. Am I wrong?"

Heads shook, but no one spoke.

Jordan continued. "There is a way to detect her, a way pioneered by Ark Lord Blair. That's something I'll be teaching, but right now I want you to focus on the importance of knowing your strengths. Alison is an incredible scout, and in the next few weeks she's going to learn to become an incredible sniper. We're going to capitalize on her strengths."

"We'll be doing the same for each of you." Jordan paused, stopping in front of the Asian couple. "We are going to start working on teamwork, beginning with pairing off. Every Ka-Ken pick a Ka-Dun from the lineup.

Pair off, people."

They started to pair off, women up and down the line picking their prospective partners. When it was done there were three females without a male. That drew a pleased smile from Jordan. It would encourage competition, and few things motivated soldiers like competition.

"We'll begin with the basics. Males will learn to blur, or improve their blurring. Females will work on mastering the shadows." Jordan's voice boomed across the courtyard. For the first time in a very long while he was actually enjoying himself.

Chapter 27- We're Going

"Please do not do this," Yukon asked. Blair sank a little under the weight of that stare, those dog eyes in an all-too-human face. "What if you do not come back?"

"We'll come back," Blair promised, clapping Yukon on the shoulder. "Listen, I won't lie. This is dangerous. I know there's some risk. The thing is, *not* doing it is a bigger risk. There's a much greater threat out there than a few ambitious deathless. We need to either make a deal with these guys, or wipe them out. We can't afford to hide in Santa Rosa, waiting for them to attack."

"I know," Yukon admitted, shoulders slumping. He dropped his gaze, scuffing the carpet with his bare foot. "The pack and I will look after the flock while you are away. What should I do if Windigo attacks?"

"Do what you can," Alicia said. She gathered Yukon into a hug, resting her head against his chest. "We won't be long, I promise. You know I will always come back. Always."

"If we're going to do this," Liz said, "let's do this. I hate long goodbyes." She took a step closer to Blair. "Can you light-walk us all the way to the city?"

"Yes, the trip will be instant. Are you ready, Alicia?"

Alicia reluctantly released Yukon, wiping quickly at her eyes as she moved to stand next to Liz. "I'm ready."

Blair gave himself a once-over, deciding he looked as close to an Ark Lord as he was going to get. He wore a comfortable dress shirt over a pair of designer jeans that Liz had found for him. It was more upscale than he'd dressed in a while, and the ladies had followed suit. Liz was wearing a pair of wonderfully tight jeans, and a simple blue blouse. Alicia wore a nearly identical outfit, but her blouse was green.

"Okay, let's do this." Blair concentrated, pulling at the Ark's well of energy. He willed that energy to coalesce around them, channeling it in a pattern of signals that was very familiar to him by now. They disappeared, instantly reappearing at the destination Blair had envisioned.

Blair had stayed at the Hilton once, after taking Bridget to see *Wicked*. The trip had been memorable, and he remembered the place well. The entire first floor was glass, with plenty of exits in all directions. They'd appeared outside the hotel's front doors, along Market Street.

The instant they arrived, a delegation of deathless approached—six men and women in black suits, all Asian. They carried submachine guns, but the weapons were lowered and the guards appeared relaxed. One of them nodded toward Blair. "They're waiting inside for you, Ark Lord."

The doors slid open, and Melissa glided out to meet them. She wore a bright red dress that hugged every curve. Elegant and practical, it flattered her figure without restricting movement.

"Blair, Liz, thank you so much for coming. We weren't sure you would. Who is this lovely young lady?" she asked, smiling warmly at Alicia.

Alicia bristled, her fingernails elongating into claws. "This young lady remembers you slaughtering her family on Angel Island. My name is Alicia. Remember it, blood whore."

Melissa's smile slipped a bit. She darted a glance at Liz, then back to Alicia. "Please forgive me. I don't wish to stir up old animosities. We're here today to try to find a way forward for both our peoples."

Behind her a number of well-dressed deathless were filing through the lobby, into a conference room. Melissa turned, gesturing for them to proceed. "This way, please. Most of the delegates have already been seated. Everyone was excited to meet you."

"Everyone?" Liz asked. Her eyes narrowed. "How many people are in that room?"

"About forty," Melissa said, eyeing Liz sidelong. "That's every lord, and their retinue. I hope that isn't a problem?"

"It's fine," Blair said, following Melissa.

She led them toward the conference room, stopping to greet other deathless every few paces.

Blair sucked in a nervous breath, then stepped into the conference room. A wide, oval table dominated, with something like twenty chairs arrayed around it. More chairs lined the walls, most taken by hard-eyed security people.

He spent a few moments studying the people at the table. That was where the power players would be. A few people had noticed his entrance, but most were still unaware. They were finding seats, and Blair got the sense that a lot of very subtle political maneuvering was happening.

Then a whisper passed through the crowd and eyes shifted to him and his companions. Most had a hungry look he didn't much like.

"Ah, you must be Ark Lord Blair," called a handsome man at the far side of the room. "I'm Carter, the ruler of Mountain View." He moved to the conference table, taking a seat at the head. "Please, make yourself comfortable. We have a great deal to discuss."

Chapter 28- Deathless of Silicon Valley

Blair studied Carter as he settled into the large mahogany chair on the opposite side of the table. Carter's eyes glittered like a predator's, and his slick dark hair added to the image. Blair guessed he was of Korean, or perhaps Chinese, descent. There was something off about him, a nearly undetectable scent of corruption. It was different from the cloying decay some deathless gave off.

Liz moved to join Blair, sitting to his right. Alicia kept her eyes downcast as she walked to the other side, sitting on Blair's left. He could feel the terror emanating from her, and knew she was close to bolting for the shadows—which was understandable, given everything she'd faced.

Even Liz looked anxious, clenching and unclenching her hands as she sat. She was clearly ready for a fight.

"We're so pleased that you accepted our invitation," Carter said. He motioned over his shoulder, and a man in a black suit brought him a silver tray loaded with wine glasses. Carter took one, and the servant began circulating amidst the crowd. "I realize this must be awkward, being in the stronghold of your enemies."

"Not really. This isn't the stronghold of my enemies. It's the very heart of mine." Blair eyed the servant as he approached. The wine was a cabernet, but there was something off about it. Something foul. It had been tainted in some way. He took a glass, but didn't drink.

"I'm not sure I catch your meaning," Carter replied. He seemed amused. "You are surrounded. Every deathless here rules his or her conclave through force. All earned those positions by being the strongest, and the most ruthless. We represent the most powerful deathless within three hundred miles. Your companions sense it—the younger one is about to wet herself—yet clearly this doesn't trouble you. Why is that, Mr. Smith?"

"You seem to know a great deal about me," Blair replied, ignoring the question. "I know very little about you and your companions. That's why I came. I want to understand my neighbors. Right now, my neighbors seem to be a threat. Am I correct in that assessment, Carter? Because if that's the case we could have just met in a field and settled this. Why all the pretense? Why try to intimidate me?"

Expressions of surprise filled the room. Those faces included Liz and Alicia—especially the latter. Alicia was looking at him like he'd just sprouted horns. The people in the chairs along the wall began readying weapons, several guns cocking in rapid succession.

"You're much more blunt than I'd have expected from a junior college teacher, especially one without tenure," Carter said, a little too smugly for Blair's tastes. "Do you really believe that the Ark gives you that much power? That you can overpower all of us at once?"

"Am I going to have to?" Blair asked. He rose slowly to his feet, then gave Carter a grim smile. "Before you commit to attacking me, I'd give careful thought to the consequences."

"Oh, I have, Mr. Smith. Believe me when I say we all have. You possess a key, an access key more specifically. My benefactors have told me about this key, and that if I kill you, then I can take it." Carter mimicked Blair, resting his elbows on the table in the same manner. "They have also blessed me with abilities far beyond any deathless you've encountered, I can assure you of that."

He is tainted, Ka-Dun. That is the scent we detected.

"Demonic abilities come with a price, Carter. A heavy price. I wonder if you understood just how heavy when you accepted it." Blair heard the other deathless begin whispering; they sounded confused. "Ah, I see your people had no idea."

Carter rose, smiling confidently. "I'm sorry I won't have more time to get to know you, Smith. I think I like you."

"Come on, Blair. We're leaving," Liz said. She rose to her feet and started for the door, but nearly a dozen deathless moved to block her path.

"The pleasantries are done, then?" Blair asked. He waved at Alicia to rise as well.

"I'm afraid so, Mr. Smith. Now we get to business." Carter said. He motioned at his security people, and most began removing pistols from their jackets. A few flexed their hands, extending long black claws. "Before we begin, I will give you one chance. Give me the key of your own free will, and I will allow you and your companions to return to Santa Rosa. As long as you do not come south of Petaluma, we will leave you in peace."

"You'll wipe out Santa Rosa the moment he gives you that key," Alicia snapped. She shot to her feet, moving to stand next to Liz.

"She's got a point, Carter," Blair said. He slid his feet apart into a combat stance. "What would stop you from attacking Santa Rosa if I were stupid enough to just hand the key over?"

"You are not our chief enemy, Blair," Carter said. "We've been at war with Southern California for three years now. The desert along Highway 5 has become one large battlefield, and we've watered it with a lot of blood. I need the power to wipe out those fools, and the Ark will allow me to do that. I'd have my hands full, trust me. There are other threats as well. If I ever want to expand over the Sierras, then I need to deal with the bears. Both are greater priorities than your tiny little town. You have no important resources, and after you give me the key you won't be any kind of threat."

"You know," Blair said, "there was a time I might have been dumb enough to trust you. I might have turned over the key, because I believed it was the only way out of the situation. I assure you, that time has passed." He extended his right hand, willing the primary access key to show itself. Gold flowed along his arm, pooling in his hand. It slowly elongated, until it formed the familiar scarab tipped staff he'd inherited from the Mother.

"You aren't the only one with Builder-made toys, Smith." Carter reached into his jacket, and removed a golden boomerang just like the ones the grey men had used. "Since you aren't amenable to my terms, I'm afraid it's time to eliminate you."

Chapter 29- The Power of An Ark Lord

Blair didn't wait for Carter to finish speaking. He pulled immense power through the primary access key, but instead of blasting his opponents as he'd done in the past he channeled the energy inward. If he wanted to win this fight, he needed to be the fastest person in the room. It didn't matter how powerful these deathless were if he could kill them before they attacked.

The blur thrummed through him, singing as it never had. He was near the heart of a fully charged Ark, and drawing that power through the most powerful artifact he'd ever encountered. The room seemed to freeze. If any of the deathless seated around him were blurring, he couldn't tell. They were simply too slow.

Then Carter's facial expression changed. Slowly at first, like he was moving through molasses. Then faster, until he was moving at almost normal speed. Blair was shocked. The idea that this deathless could match his super-fueled blur was mind-boggling. What had his "benefactors" done to him?

You must deal with him quickly, Ka-Dun. Before he launches an offensive.

I couldn't agree more, Blair thought. He aimed the staff at Carter, fueling an ability he knew deathless couldn't normally defend against. Blair plunged into Carter's mind, shattering his mental defenses. There was a moment of Carter's started surprise, then Blair was in.

He floated in near darkness, lit by a sea of glowing dots. Most were further away, tiny pinpricks. A few were close enough to see more clearly, each a frozen image or a scene slowly playing out. Memories, these ones very recent.

Blair began to examine those memories, following the flow back to a large cluster from just a week ago. He plucked one out, letting it unfold.

"Do you really think you can beat an Ark Lord?" Melissa asked. She sat across from Carter, just the pair of them.

"Is that why you came to see me, Melissa: to talk me out of this? It is the

perfect plan, and it was voted for unanimously. Attacking this Ark Lord will no doubt result in a number of deaths, so those who survive will all better their lots. They'll be able to expand territory."

"I know the arguments. That's not what I'm asking. What if he's more powerful than you think? What if he just incinerates you? You haven't met him. I have."

"Your concern touches me." Carter gave a bitter laugh. "You are far too sentimental to be a deathless, Melissa. Your squeamishness is a weakness, one that other lords will exploit if you let them. I will hear no more talk of this. We're going to kill the Ark Lord, and I am taking that key."

"It's your funeral," Melissa shot back. "You didn't feel the strength of the Ark." She rose to her feet. "And it isn't weakness; it's social intelligence. Fear isn't the only way to amass power, and sometimes it's the worst way. If I'm right, you'll pay the price for your arrogance soon enough."

"You'd better pray that happens, Melissa. After advocating for a treaty, you've lost almost all your influence. Your underlings are already readying themselves to take advantage of your fall."

Blair released the memory, considering the import as he proceeded deeper into Carter's mind. Melissa was deathless, but she was smart enough to work with her enemies. That boded well, if he chose to let her live.

Another memory flitted by, this one catching Blair's attention. He grabbed it, watching it play out.

Carter backpedaled, then shrank against the wall when he ran out of room. He cowered there. This demon thing, whatever it was, had found him in the heart of his inner sanctum. It had batted aside his defenses like he was a child.

"W-what do you want?" Carter stuttered. He wanted to stop cowering, to stand proudly, but he couldn't. Something—some force exerted by this monster—robbed him of his will. He'd never been this terrified, and if he'd had a beating heart he was positive it would have stopped.

"My name is Nox. You've heard of me, I see." The demon walked closer, its leathery wings expanding as it approached. Behind it, a tail flicked like a snake, something golden curled within it. "You can stand up now. I release you."

The fear vanished, and in that moment Carter realized the fear was artificial. He'd been shaped. In its wake flowed a tide of anger. "I've heard of you. You work for a god. Hades, right? What the hell are you doing in my office?"

"I can bring the fear back, Mr. Carter. Do I need to do that?" the demon asked calmly.

"No," Carter said, gritting his fangs.

"I've come to bestow power upon you. You crave power, do you not?"

"Of course I do, but no one gives power without getting something in return. Why are you willing to help me, and what do you get out of it?"

Blair could feel the deathless's suspicion, but also his greed. He wanted the power Nox was offering, even before he knew what it was.

"I gain a powerful servant, one capable of ruling this entire continent," Nox said. He extended a hand, using one claw to slice a shallow gash in his palm. Black blood bubbled out. "All you have to do is drink. You'll be far more powerful than your rivals, and in a year you will rule the Lords of Silicon Valley. In five years, you'll rule California. Ten, the entire western sea board. You'll live for centuries, Carter. Wouldn't you like to do it as a god? Rule this continent in the name of Hades."

Carter's lust was overpowering, but a morsel of caution remained. "What will the blood do to me?"

Nox uncoiled like a serpent, his tail wrapping around Carter's neck. It yanked him closer, and Nox used one massive arm to pin Carter in place. He forced his palm against Carter's mouth. "Here. I'll show you exactly what it does."

Fire raced through Carter, a fire that Blair recognized. It was the same he'd felt when he'd grasped the hand of the past. The hand had infected him with the werewolf virus. Nox had just infected Carter with a similar virus, something that seemed to be overwriting his deathless nature.

"Tonight will be rough, but in the morning you will feel much better. You'll be aware of the new strength I've given you, as well as the link between us.

I can find you anywhere, Carter, never forget that. You belong to me."

Blair fled from the memory. Carter had been a pawn of Hades, right here in his back yard. Worse, Nox might be aware of Blair's arrival. It was a troubling possibility, but Blair let it go for now. Sifting memories was valuable, but he needed to deal with Carter and his deathless council.

Blair glided deeper into Carter's mind. In the distance he saw a massive figure, and he recognized it instantly. It was Carter's risen, and in a few moments it was going to attack him. Blair didn't give it a chance. He crossed the space between them easily, shaping a net of energy as he approached. Then he released the net, entangling the risen. It began to shrink, growing smaller and smaller until it was no larger than an emaciated mouse.

"What did you do to it?" Carter whispered. He appeared near Blair, looking like a human in his late twenties. He looked normal—handsome even.

"It doesn't matter," Blair said. He turned toward Carter, and raised a hand. "You won't be around to see it."

And energy flooded from Blair, obliterating Carter's mind.

Chapter 30- Mercy

Melissa had known it was a mistake to antagonize Blair. She cringed when he withdrew the staff, its power stronger than the sun itself. She could feel the vast reservoir of power he was pulling through it, more than she'd ever seen shaped before. It made everything she'd done, everything she'd learned, seem like first grade basics.

Carter was powerful, suspiciously so. He'd been nothing but a two bit lord, unremarkable in all ways. Then suddenly he'd exploded in strength, toppling the then-lord of Palo Alto and claiming the city for his own.

Melissa had no idea where Carter had found his power, but it wasn't even on the same scale as the energies Blair wielded.

She tried to blur, but even as she fueled her abilities the conflict was over. Carter slumped to the desk, eyes glassy and unseeing. Then Melissa was slammed onto the floor, along with every other deathless in the room. The pressure cracked one of her ribs, and she cried out in pain. It was strong enough that she wouldn't have been able to rise, but she didn't even try. The last thing she wanted was to draw Blair's attention.

Footsteps rustled against the carpet as Blair slowly approached. He stopped right next to her, squatting low enough to peer into her face. "Hello, Melissa. You're not my favorite person in the world, did you know that? You lied to me about Angel Island. You didn't tell me that you wiped out my people, and drove the few survivors north. Why is that?"

"I-I didn't want to poison relations," Melissa pleaded. Another rib cracked, and she cried out. "Please! I knew how Liz would react, how you might react. You said it yourself: it's a larger world and we're going to need allies. I didn't want to jeopardize that."

"So you omitted some very important facts," Blair said.

The pressure on Melissa vanished.

"This is the bitch that attacked us that night," the teenage Ka-Ken said. She stalked over to Melissa, glaring down at her. "Tell me we're going to kill her. To kill them all."

"We're going to kill most of them," Blair said. "But not her. She gets to live, and I'll tell you why. I'll tell everyone why." Blair gestured with his staff, and a pulse of potent golden energy rippled outwards. It washed over Melissa, the other deathless, and out into the city beyond. As it grew, she could feel it touching thousands of minds—then tens of thousands.

Hear me. I am Blair, Lord of the Ark of the Redwood. You are hearing this because you live in the lands surrounding my Ark. I lay claim to the lands currently controlled by those who call themselves the Lords of Silicon Valley. If you live there, you are now one of my vassals.

An image flowed into her mind, overwhelming her own senses. She could no longer see the world; instead she saw as if from Blair's eyes. His hand came up, and fire poured into every deathless in the room—every deathless except her.

Carter, her rivals, and even her friends burst into white-hot flame. A heartbeat later there was nothing left but ash.

I have removed the former lords. This will no doubt tempt many of you to make a power play, to try to fill their shoes. By all means try, but first I want you to know three things.

First, Melissa, the Lord of San Francisco, just got a promotion. She's in charge of the entire Bay Area, and she has my full support. Oppose her, and you are opposing me.

Second, this continent belongs to the living. If you encounter a living person, or a champion, they are to be given safe passage north to Santa Rosa. Fail to observe this, and I will find you. Trust me, I will know if you misbehave. The consequences will be dire.

Lastly, I want you to know that there are greater threats in the world than just deathless and werewolves, threats that we will need to stand united against. I have no desire to wipe you out. I'd prefer you as allies. Only you get to choose whether or not that happens. Oppose me, and justice will be swift. Work with me, and there's no reason we can't coexist.

Blair's thundering voice finally stopped, and the power tickling Melissa's mind disappeared. She was left staring at Blair and his companions. Both Ka-Ken watched Blair in awe, an expression she was probably mirroring.

Melissa rose hesitantly to her feet. "Why did you let me live?"

"I meant what I said," Blair explained. His staff flowed back up his arm, disappearing into his body. She could feel its power merging with his. "I'm going to need allies. Greater threats are coming, and if you can get the deathless to fight along side me, you get to live. You have as much free room to maneuver as you'd like. I don't care who you backstab, or what you have to do to maintain control here. Mark my words, though: if you backstab me in any way, I will simply wipe out every deathless in the Bay Area. All of them."

"You could really do that, couldn't you?" Melissa whispered. She felt something between awe and horror. "Trust me, Ark Lord. I will do nothing to jeopardize your support. You give me your mandates, and I promise I will see them enforced." She meant every word, praying that he would sense her sincerity.

"Good. Then we have an understanding. My people and I are leaving. If you learn something you think I need to know, send a messenger. Otherwise, wait for us to contact you."

"Yes, Ark Lord," Melissa said. She gave a deep bow, mustering all the respect she could—respect she felt to her core. Blair was terrifying, but he might be exactly what this new world needed.

The Great Bear bent to rip a mouthful of flesh from the deer's carcass. Feeding brought some small comfort—momentarily at least. Deer were his favorite prey, and he reveled in the hot, salty blood as it dribbled down his fur. The cold didn't bother him at all, not like it did when he was a man.

Each day he'd woken up in a strange place, further from the mountains he'd called home. During the day, he'd press farther west, toward the town Windigo had demanded he reach. He'd settle down to sleep, waking the next morning as if he hadn't slept.

The Bear lumbered to a nearby stream, drinking deeply. He studied his reflection as he rose from the water, horrified by what he found. Tiny antlers had sprung from his temples, the first visible sign of Windigo's corruption.

It will not be the last, I can promise you that.

"Why do you torment me, demon?" the Bear demanded. He did not understand what was happening, and that terrified him.

Windigo was a target he couldn't fight.

Remember that, Bear, and perhaps one day I will let you go.

The Bear's muzzle shot up, sniffing the wind. Power rippled across the land, the kind of power not seen since the days of the earth mother herself. The Bear stood up on his hind paws, staring across the mountains toward the city that men called San Francisco.

"What is that?" he murmured, unable to understand what he was feeling.

That is the power of an Ark Lord, one who wishes everyone in the land to fear him. Windigo answered. *It is a blatant display of power, meant to cow all who see it into serving. He is a threat to us both.*

"Perhaps this Ark Lord will be strong enough to stop you," Yosemite roared, smashing a sapling with a titanic paw. "I will not listen to your lies, Windigo. I know you for what you are, remember that. Nothing you say will sway me. I am no pawn. This Ark Lord has no reason to come to my mountains, and is no enemy of mine."

He soon will be, Windigo taunted, *because he is my enemy, and I control you. When I am through using your body, the Ka-Dun will have ample reason to hate you. I can promise that.*

"No," Yosemite snarled. "I will not let you."

Oh, little Bear. You are so amusing. What makes you think you can stop me?

Chapter 32- Sobek

Jordan peered out through the windshield. The wipers were working overtime to keep it clear of rain. Lima's perimeter now had machine gun emplacements at every major checkpoint, each shielded by sandbags. At the closest encampment, Jordan saw a backhoe digging a trench behind the emplacement. He was impressed by how much Rodrigo had accomplished in the week he'd been away.

"The batteries you requested are being installed in those holes," Rodrigo called over the wind. He pointed down to the encampment Jordan was already watching. "We've explained to every champion how they will be used, and they have all begun drills to practice."

"Very nicely done." Jordan rarely gave praise, but this was earned. "Is the delegation for Sobek ready?"

Jordan knew he was the last to arrive, but he'd been spending most of his time getting ready for the trek into the jungle. He needed to leave as soon as possible, and that meant he couldn't give Sobek's arrival the time and attention it deserved. He'd had to do something he hated: delegate. Fortunately, it looked like Rodrigo had been a good choice.

"They're assembled. Shall we go there now, Ark Lord? Sobek's vessel was spotted about twenty minutes ago. It will be here shortly." Rodrigo gestured at the Jeep, moving to the driver's side.

"Yeah, let's get over there," Jordan answered. He climbed into the Jeep, still marveling over how much of the old world had survived here. From Blair's brief description, it sounded like Santa Rosa had reverted to *Little House on the Prairie* levels of tech.

They sped through the nearly empty streets, occasionally passing other Jeeps. Jordan recognized the Asian couple in one, and Alison and her Ka-Dun in another.

"They are on hourly patrols," Rodrigo explained. He turned onto the broad thoroughfare leading down to the docks. "We have twenty-four hour coverage. The people already feel safer, and the men take more pride in their city. Before, it was about how strong each werewolf was. Now, it is becoming about how strong we all are."

"That's the real secret to effective leadership," Jordan replied. It was a direct quote from the Director. "Teach people to invest in the organization instead of themselves, and they will become the organization."

"I'm so glad you came to Lima, Ark Lord," Rodrigo said. He gave a gap-toothed smile as he pulled into a parking spot next to an empty dock. "You are a real leader, sir."

Jordan barked out a laugh. "I'm just imitating the real leaders."

The Jeep's door opened with a groan, and Jordan stepped onto the wet concrete. They'd parked near an empty pier, long enough to contain a cargo hauler the size of the one Sobek was supposed to bring. Rodrigo approached the crowd of people waiting around the edge of the dock, so Jordan followed. Several wore orange raincoats and looked to be dock workers. The rest were dressed like soldiers, and Jordan was surprised to find he recognized all of them. If the downpour bothered them, they certainly didn't show it.

"Salute your Ark Lord, whelps," Vimal barked. He snapped to attention, and the others mimicked it almost perfectly.

"At ease," Jordan said, returning the salute. He strode down the dock, stopping next to the Indian man. "I admit I'm a little surprised. I expected some resentment after our first few sessions together."

"Not at all, Ark Lord." Vimal's dark face had his usual lack of expression. "You've shown me the value of cooperation, and demonstrated that you are an able leader. I am proud to follow you."

Jordan extended a hand, and Vimal shook it. "I'm proud to have you."

"Ships sighted," bellowed a voice from above.

Jordan turned to the water, scanning. A cluster of grey specks was approaching through the sheets of rain. He counted eight. That wasn't a stone shipment. That was a show of force.

"Give me your binoculars," Jordan said to the closest uniformed werewolf.

Six of the ships were destroyers, the kind of warship that could bombard a shore from miles out. The last two were freighters, each loaded with colorful cargo containers. Those last two vessels were pulling away from the main group, heading toward the dock. The destroyers didn't approach, but the implied threat was there. The ships were perfectly capable of destroying Lima without closing to visual range. The only reason to get this close was to intimidate. Sobek had a navy and wanted them to know it.

"Attention," Jordan boomed. The troops fell into line. Jordan glanced at the approaching vessels. They were moving more quickly than he'd have thought possible. "In a few moments Sobek and his delegation will arrive. We will be courteous, but we will not grovel. This is our city, and we'll defend it with our lives. Show these reptiles the power of the wolf."

He delivered a tight salute, and the men returned it. They gave a ragged cheer. "Ark Lord!"

Jordan turned back to the boats, waiting patiently as they got closer. They were moving far more quickly than any vessel that size should have been capable of. He couldn't see any obvious sign of an engine or propeller, so Jordan had no idea what was powering them, until the ships reached the dock. When they were close, Jordan could feel a deep thrum of power coming from each. Those things were powered through shaping.

Of course, Ka-Dun. Such was common during the Mother's age. Sobek was one of the pioneers of such shaping. Long before the slipsail mankind plied the waves with wooden vessels.

The boat slowed as it closed with the dock; the last five feet took nearly a full minute. Then the boat finally stopped, and a five-foot-thick rope was tossed over the stern. The dock workers rushed to affix the rope. Once they had, a ramp extended to the dock.

A trio of bipedal crocodiles, more reptile than man, descended. Their skin was scaly and tough, their eyes black and unreadable. Their mouths were full of fangs, and Jordan could see bits of flesh still stuck between them. Not the most hygienic crowd. That was made even more obvious by the stench when they approached.

"Who leads these mongrels?" Sobek boomed in a deep, discordant voice. His tail slapped the deck with a tremendous thud, and several of the champions jumped. Most kept their composure though, making Jordan proud.

"You already know I'm in charge," Jordan said. He walked calmly to Sobek, ignoring the pair of crocodile warriors flanking him. Up close, the god smelled like rotting fish, bits of which were caught between his numerous teeth. "You can feel the access key, feel the strength I'm drawing from the Ark. Are you here to posture, Sobek? Isis said you were a petty god. Was she right?"

Sobek balled his scaly fists, stalking closer. He glared down at Jordan, who'd yet to shift to warform. The crocodile gave a low, deep growl. "You do not fear me as the other fools I've suffered. You carry yourself like an Ark Lord, and I can sense potential within you. Yet you are a young god, barely old enough to be off Isis's teat. Why don't you run and fetch her, so that she and I might discuss matters too important for your ignorant little mind."

"I think you misunderstand the situation, Sobek," Jordan retorted. "You are beneath Isis's notice, and you know that. She has far greater concerns, and doesn't have time for your posturing. She sent me, because you won't shut up about the fact that she's not come to see you personally." Then he shifted to warform, suddenly standing eye to snout with the crocodile god. "My ignorant little mind is what you're going to have to deal with—which shouldn't be that challenging since all you're here to do is drop off a boat full of rock."

Sobek's expression grew, if possible, more unreadable. He studied Jordan with those lifeless black eyes, silent for long moments. "The accord between Isis and I has reached its zenith. In five more years, it ends. Either we strike a new bargain, or we go to war. Isis must know this. Does she value our accord so little that she doesn't deem me worthy of her time? Is that what you are saying, little wolf? Such disrespect isn't like her. She was always one for decorum, even with her enemies."

"That's exactly what I'm saying," Jordan said. "She trusts you to keep your end of the accord. When it ends, then she will consider speaking to you. In the meantime, you deal with me." He crossed his arms, eyeing Sobek with a nonchalance he didn't feel. "She has other enemies, enemies you're well aware of. They take precedence."

Sobek was silent again. He worked his jaws, tonguing loose a piece of rotting meat.

"Do you know what I believe? Isis is dead, and you're covering. You are fumbling for excuses, because you know that our agreement died with her. This is all a ruse—one I refuse to entertain any longer."

"Maybe you're right. Maybe I'm lying in an attempt to stall for time." Jordan gave Sobek the most lupine grin he could muster. "You could always break the accord and find out. You might be able to best me in a fight, though given that I'm an Ark Lord and you're an errand boy for one…I guess we'd have to see. But let's just say you beat me, Sobek. Do you want to deal with Isis when she hears you killed me? Especially knowing that she's working with Osiris and Ra."

Sobek blinked. It was a small thing, but still the most human reaction he'd shown. He looked…uncertain. "Isis is working with Osiris…and Ra?"

"That's right. They set aside their differences, because they are aware of a common threat. If they've been scarce these last years, it's with good reason. Never let your enemy see you coming."

It might even be the truth. If Leti were correct, Isis might be alive and in hiding. So it wasn't a lie, precisely. That made it easier to sell.

"I remain dubious, little wolf god, but I will return to my master on the continent you call Australia. I will tell him of Isis's refusal to meet me, and we shall see what comes of it." Sobek turned without a word and headed back onto the boat. His minions followed, and the ramp ascended after them.

Jordan watched him go, giving a heavy sigh.

"Do you think he bought it?" Rodrigo asked. Rain pelted the brim of his ball cap.

"Nope. He knows we're bluffing, and soon his master will know it too. I don't know how they'll respond, but we'll save that for another day. At least we bought ourselves another few months."

Chapter 33- Research

Trevor was painfully aware of hostility from their hosts, a pair of champions who ran a little church on the north side of Cajamarca. They all but worshipped Isis—and thus Jordan—but they knew who the ancient enemy was. That ancient enemy was the deathless. From the sly glances to the sarcastic quips, the little old couple never failed to let Trevor know he would be purified in flame eventually. They maintained that Jordan was only keeping him alive to torture.

He steeled himself as he trotted down the stairs toward the door, knowing that Marguerite would be in the kitchen to the right. Sure enough he heard the chop, chop, chop of her cutting onions for that morning's chorizo.

"Good morning, unclean one," she called in her gravelly voice. She peered at him from under a mop of unruly white hair. "I see you have avoided judgment for another day. Do not trouble yourself, it will be along soon enough. I do not know why the Ark Lord considers you an ally, but the moment that ends my claws will find your throat. Would you like some breakfast?"

She held up a plate of chorizo, and it smelled heavenly. Unfortunately, Trevor lacked the right organs to digest normal food. She knew that of course, which was why she baited him with breakfast every day.

"Good morning, Marguerite. Have you seen Anput yet this morning?" Trevor gave her a friendly smile, knowing she hated that.

"The dead whore? Yes, she was up early. She left for the library." Marguerite had already turned back to breakfast, so Trevor slipped past her and through the door. He pulled on his ball cap, and added a pair of large black sunglasses. If he kept his mouth closed, most people assumed he was human until they got within arm's length.

He hurried up the walk and onto the road leading toward the library. This part of town wasn't very populated, with just a few families living in some of the larger houses in the residential section bordering the church. A woman gardening in her front yard glanced up at him, reaching suspiciously for the pistol belted around her waist. Trevor pulled his jacket tighter, and hurried on.

It only took a few minutes to reach the library, which was thankfully in good repair. Many of the buildings around it weren't, with broken windows and crumbling roofs. It was amazing how much the place had deteriorated in the last five years. Lack of maintenance was compounding, and most of the buildings looked like the wasteland from Fallout.

Trevor ducked through the double doors, which had been propped open on either side by heavily loaded book carts. The interior was well-lit with natural light, the sun streaming through skylights above. A few people prowled the stacks of books, and an elderly man walked past clutching a book on automotive repair.

Anput sat at a table bathed by one of the skylights. She had three piles of books in front of her, and was scrawling furiously in a notebook. A pair of glasses was perched on her nose, which drew a quiet chuckle from Trevor. Vampires, especially ancient ones, didn't need glasses. The only reason to wear those was for effect. It fit the image Anput wanted to play, the quiet, scholarly woman. Not a millennia-old vampire warrior goddess who part-timed as a succubus.

"Morning." Trevor slid into the chair across from Anput, picking up the closest book. "Genetic Justice?"

"It's about DNA banks," Anput explained absently, still scribbling in her notebook. "Most of the book is useless drivel about the inept legal systems you moderns seem to love so much. But it did mention several genetic repositories, places like the Ark where your people were storing helix maps —sorry, what you'd call genomes."

"I didn't realize you were a geneticist." Trevor set the book down, genuinely surprised.

"I wasn't when we last met. I found and devoured a nascent deathless who'd been an accomplished geneticist. From there I've studied the topic as often as I get the chance." Anput set her pen down, and turned to look at Trevor. She gave him the sultriest smile any man had ever seen, and a thrill ran through him. "The look I just gave you? The fact that I can make you feel lust even though deathless can't procreate? I understand how it works, how Osiris shaped Isis's original virus into the one I was given. We used different words, but both he and Isis were using genetics. They understood DNA and the genome, and how to modify them. They spent millennia practicing those abilities, and learning exactly how life worked."

"And you want to learn to do the same thing?"

"I already have. I've studied my own virus and the deathless virus very closely. I've even learned how the grey men shaped David and the rest of Project Solaris. The only one I'm not familiar with yet is the werewolf virus, but given where we are I'm hoping to rectify that." Anput took off her glasses and set them on her notebook. "We can discuss my theories later, though. You and I are supposed to be finding this lost city. El Dorado, I think your people call it."

"We don't have much to go on." Trevor leaned back in his chair. "My dad was really into gold panning when I was growing up. He loved the idea of El Dorado, and he even talked about coming to Brazil to hunt for it. It never happened, but I grew up with stories about the lost city. The truth is, no one has ever found anything. There's nothing to substantiate there ever having been a city out there."

"That tells us more than you might think," Anput countered. She picked up her glasses, tapping her lips with them. "If the Proto Ark is out there it would have to be absolutely massive. The fact that no one has ever found it suggests that someone or something is actively hiding it. Otherwise satellites would have found it."

"Point taken," Trevor allowed. He unrolled a map of the Amazon that he and Anput had been looking at the day before. "A Netflix documentary I watched said it might be somewhere up the Xingu branch of the Amazon River. I can't remember the explorer's name, but his last expedition ended here. He was never seen again, and most people assumed that the natives killed him. They were extremely warlike, and practiced cannibalism."

"That doesn't surprise me in the slightest," Anput said. She replaced her glasses, flicking her hair over one shoulder with the grace of a panther. "It's probably not so obvious to someone from this time, but I remember what

Isis's murderous little savages were like. It sounds like their descendants haven't much changed. For the record, it was she who introduced the cannibalism in the first place. They were mimicking her champions."

"They sound like a fun bunch. Did Isis know anything about this Proto Ark? Is that part of why she ended up making this continent her home?"

"I don't know." Anput frowned. Even that was pretty. "Ra's court lost contact with Isis when she came to these lands. Most of our wars with her took place when she lived in the land you call California. If she knew of this Proto Ark, she never told any of us about it."

"Well, apparently her champions have found and conquered the city, if Marguerite's rantings are accurate. They consider it a holy place. She's used racial memory before. Do you think that's the case here?"

"Quite possibly. Are you familiar with the legend of the Caipora?"

The sudden shift in topic caught Trevor off guard. "No." He shook his head. "What does that have to do with racial memory?"

"Just that Isis's tampering went far beyond memory. During the previous age this jungle was guarded by spirits called the Caipora. They were part of the reason my people only rarely tried to invade this continent." Anput pulled her knees up to her chest. "The Caipora are small, hairy, and mischievous. I believe they were shaped from the local populace. They were impossible to catch, and excelled at illusion. They were one of Isis's more inventive experiments."

"They sound like nasty little bastards." Trevor said. "I'm betting they died out. In the four decades preceding the first CME, the Amazon lost over 20% of its trees. In all that destruction someone with a cell phone camera would have seen a spirit guardian. No one ever reported one."

"That's because the gene that activated the Caipora went dormant." Anput reached for the map. "The Caipora have returned, and they're found in these areas, along the rivers that were most heavily traveled by the local tribes. They would have passed for normal humans, probably even interbreeding. They needed the energy from the sun in order to change, and now that the energy is back they've begun to emerge. The same has been true with dozens of other species all over the world. I've documented several myself."

"Wow." Trevor slumped into his chair under the weight of the implications. "I can see why you became a geneticist. In a lot of ways Isis was a literal goddess. That genetic manipulation was the biggest part of her power."

"It's a power you share, theoretically. You are an Ark Lord, Trevor. You can shape life just as she did, provided we can get you access to your Ark."

"We may not need to," Trevor replied. He leaned over the map, scanning the massive green jungle labeled Amazon. "If we can find the Proto Ark, there's every likelihood we'll be able to use that to do exactly the same thing."

"Suddenly all my work doesn't seem so theoretical," Anput said. She shifted uncomfortably in her chair. "I have a lot of research to do before we depart. I need to make sure I bring the right books. What if I could modify our virus at the Proto Ark? Think of it. We could become anything we wanted, manifest any trait we desire."

"It's tempting," Trevor agreed, and meant it. "But if we're going to get there, we need to buckle down and find the place first. Let's see what we can come up with before Jordan returns."

Chapter 34- Be Nice to Elia

Jordan was already having a bad day, and he knew it was about to get worse. He stepped from the Jeep, closing the driver side door and walking to the Ark's front entrance.

Leti exited from the other side of the vehicle, falling into step next to him. He could feel her hesitation; she didn't want to do this either. She'd brushed her long dark hair into a simple braid, but otherwise looked just as she had when he'd first met her in the Ark.

"I notice you're wearing the same clothing you usually do," he said. "What does the white symbolize?"

"I must approach as a supplicant, and the white symbolizes both purity and humility." She paused in front of him, adjusting his hastily assembled dress uniform. The stylized black Ark on his shoulder looked right there. "You, on the other hand, they must see differently. Not only as a warrior, but also as a leader. As the men in Lima and Cajamarca now see you. This is the Jordan they must come to know—a true Ark Lord, not a bully or dictator. Remember that South America is different from the United States. Many of us grew up under one dictator or another, and the corruption here was even more obvious than your own country. Leaders are tyrants and not to be trusted. You need to overcome that, somehow."

"I'm not off to a good start," Jordan countered sourly. "Elia hates me, and I've probably given her cause."

"She does, and her voice carries much weight." Leti turned and hurried toward the wide tunnel leading into the Ark. It pulled Jordan back to the first time he'd seen it, right after the Ark had emerged from a thirteen millennia nap. "Are you paying attention? Come along, Ark Lord. And treat this place with a little more dignity, or we will never be allowed to seek El Dorado."

"Can't we just go without her blessing? You seem capable enough." It was a half-hearted suggestion, and he followed her into the Ark.

"I cannot. I have never been to the city, nor am I allowed to yet," Leti explained with an air of exasperation. "When my people have proven ourselves, we are invited to seek the city. We must find it unaided, and when we do we become an elder—like Elia. Since I have not been given permission to go, we must obtain the help of someone who has."

They'd gone another hundred meters or so before they came to the first junction, one that Jordan knew well. From here, you could make it to dozens of locations in the Ark, including the light bridge and the central chamber. Last time he'd been here, this intersection had been empty. Now a pair of Ka-ken in human form stood impassively, each holding a golden dagger.

Sunsteel, Ka-Dun. They are armed for war, and consider you a foe.

"Why do you seek to bar our way? All supplicants are allowed to seek the Mother's wisdom," Leti said. It had the ring of scripture, and maybe it was.

"Eldest sister commanded it," the shorter woman said. She stared daggers at Jordan. "This one is to be escorted. He may be the lord of this place, but we will see that he causes no mischief. Come, Ark Lord. The eldest wish to see you." The way she said his title made it very clear just how she felt about it.

He looked to Leti, and she gave a short nod. Jordan fell into line behind the two women, following them like a prisoner as he was led through his own Ark. It was annoying, but the benefits outweighed any hit to his pride. He needed these people. The world needed these people. He couldn't afford to alienate them any further than he already had.

They were led into the central chamber, where a pair of elaborate golden thrones had been erected. They stood at the feet of the statue of Isis, as if bathed in her wisdom. Jordan smiled grimly. If Isis ever saw this, he had a feeling that one or both of the people on those thrones might not survive. Isis had a bit of a temper that way.

Elia sat on the right, resplendent in her glimmering white robe. The cotton she'd worn earlier was gone, replaced by the same kind of clothing Jordan had seen the Mother wear. Their formal wear, then? Her golden bracelet was still in place, and she'd added a golden necklace set with a knuckle-sized sapphire. Jordan probed it with his mind, unsurprised when he felt a signal. More of Elia's toys. At least now he knew the source of those toys, or suspected he did anyway.

"Eldest sister, we have come as supplicants," Leti said. She sank to her knees, prostrating herself before the thrones. After a moment Jordan realized he was supposed to do the same.

He gritted his teeth, imitating Leti's position. It was humiliating, and dangerous. Being in this position meant that Elia would never have a better shot at ending him. Outside of Liz and Isis, she was the strongest Ka-Ken he'd met.

That is the point of supplication, Ka-Dun. You are putting yourselves in their power, both figuratively and literally.

"It surprises me that this one can put aside his arrogance long enough to show deference," Elia said. She rose gracefully from the throne, approaching Jordan's still kneeling form. His skin crawled, and he longed to roll into a combat stance. "How did you domesticate him so quickly, little sister?"

Jordan knew the comment was meant to bait him. She believed he was susceptible to such things. He needed to prove otherwise. Jordan stayed where he was, refusing to give in to his instincts. After several more moments Elia glided her way back to the throne. She didn't speak again until after she'd sat.

"We recognize you as supplicants, little sister," Elia intoned.

"We recognize you as supplicants, little sister," Adam intoned, a heartbeat after Elia.

"Rise," Elia continued. "We will hear the supplicant's request."

Jordan climbed slowly to his feet, watching Leti as she did the same. He aped her body language as much as possible, trying for meek. He didn't do meek very well.

"I have been an initiate for two years," Leti said. She gave a short bow. "During my time I have learned much. I can walk the shadows, and slay silently. I know the Mother's catechisms by heart. My lineage is one of the purest in Peru, only two steps below Medico Roberto. I beseech you, allow me to seek the Holy City, that I might be found worthy."

"What say you, eldest brother?" Elia asked, turning to Adam.

"Why do you seek the city, Leti? Why now, at the precise instant the Ark Lord has returned?" Adam studied Leti shrewdly, and she held up under that scrutiny.

Jordan was proud of her. It couldn't have been easy.

"Because the Ark Lord needs to reach the Holy City. There we will find the tools necessary to carry on the Mother's war. Jordan was recognized as one of her champions. He is her direct progeny, created by the Mother to battle her enemies." There was an air of desperation to Leti's argument.

"So you seek to lead the Ark Lord to our holiest of places?" Adam asked. His tone was neutral, his expression the same. If he approved, or disapproved, nothing gave it away.

"I do, Eldest. It is the right thing to do, because I believe it is what the holy Mother would do. She made him a champion for a reason; she trusted him. He was there in the last battle between her and the ancient darkness," Leti said. The air of desperation dissipated. "We exist to honor her will, to see her decrees carried forth. The Ark Lord is her instrument, doing exactly that. He deserves our aid."

"You are not the voice of the Mother," Adam said, reprovingly. "Presuming to know her wishes is the height of arrogance. You are not ready to begin your seeking." He leaned back on his throne. "If you do not set aside your pride, you may never be ready."

"Well said," Elia agreed triumphantly, crossing shapely legs. "You are not ready for your seeking, Leti. Return to your studies, and do not speak to this man again. Are my wishes clear?"

"They are clear," Leti spat. She glared at the pair of them, bristling. "All too clear. It is not *my* arrogance that is the issue here. You seek to bar this man's aid because he was disrespectful. Because he neither knows nor follows our ways. Yet who among us can claim to have met the Mother? He has dined with her. Fought with her. His rebirth came at her hands. I *will* take him to the city. Nothing in the scriptures requires that I have your permission. That's a tradition *you* started."

Elia and Adam eyed each other uncomfortably. Elia finally looked at her, eyes flashing with the same hatred she'd shown Jordan. "If you do this, you will be cast from the Temple. You know that."

"If you are willing to place your own pride above the wishes of the Mother, then that is a price I must pay." Leti stood proudly. "As much as you pretend, you are *not* Her. I will let the city judge my worth."

"You will die in the attempt," Adam said, still emotionless. "The people will offer you no succor. We cannot stop you from seeking, but neither do we have to offer you protection."

"I cast you from this temple, Leticia," Elia roared. She rose from her throne, pointing accusingly at Leti. "You have until sunset to be gone from this valley, never to return. If you are seen here again, you will be treated as the ancient enemy."

Chapter 35- The Fate of Anubis

Trevor shot to his feet the instant he heard the rumble of approaching engines. He hefted his battered green backpack from the curb. The pack contained almost nothing—just a toothbrush, comb, and a couple changes of clothes. Not needing to breath, eat, or sleep definitely cut down on the number of things a guy had to carry.

"Marguerite, you've been a wonderful hostess," Anput said as she breezed into the kitchen from the stairway. She moved to embrace the old woman, who squirmed as Anput kissed her cheek. "I'll be certain to recommend this place to all my dead whore friends."

"Ugh, I'll have the stench of you on me for weeks. You did that on purpose, you deceitful whore. Get out of my house." There was no heat to Marguerite's voice, though. There might even have been a hint of affection. "You'll meet your death in that jungle. The Mother will never allow you to reach the Holy City."

Trevor didn't want to know how Marguerite knew they were leaving. If she knew, then everyone in Cajamarca knew, too. So much for a stealthy departure. Trevor gave a sigh as he headed for the door, not saying a word to the old woman as he stepped out into the chill morning. The sun was just cresting the horizon, its warmth feeding a trickle of power into his ever growing reserves.

Anput followed him to the curb just as two Jeeps pulled up. Jordan was driving the first. A dark-haired woman in a simple cotton skirt pulled up in a second Jeep, parking behind Jordan. She left the engine idling, meeting Trevor's gaze briefly. There was hostility there, but it was muted. She didn't like him, but her hatred didn't seem to run as deep as most other people he'd met here.

"Trevor, Anput, this is Leticia," Jordan said, gesturing toward the dark-haired woman. "She's a priestess of the Mother, and she'll be guiding us into the jungle. We'll take the first Jeep, and you two can follow us."

"Couldn't we all just take one vehicle?" Anput asked. Her tone was carefully neutral, but Trevor could feel the thinly contained heat. He shared the feeling. Were they so unclean that Jordan wouldn't even ride with them?

"We could, but I'm after redundancy. What if we break an axle? A second vehicle gives us spare parts if one breaks down. Once we enter that jungle, we won't be able to come back for help." He met Anput's gaze evenly. "I assure you, this isn't personal. If you'd prefer to change the seating arrangements, you can ride with me or Leti."

"I apologize, Ark Lord." Anput nodded stiffly. "Thank you for procuring transportation. I'd prefer to ride with Ark Lord Trevor. He and I still have a great deal to discuss."

"I'm sure you do," Jordan said, raising an eyebrow. He turned to Trevor. "I'm going to light-walk us, and the Jeeps, to the town of Pucallpa. According to Leti, that's a jumping off point into the jungle. Three days' hard drive will get us into the thickest part of the jungle. From there we'll be taking a canoe upriver. You two ready?"

"Yeah." Trevor nodded. Anput did the same a moment later. Trevor still felt irritated, though he had to admit that Jordan's logic was sound. He knew he was reacting emotionally based on past encounters.

Jordan's eyes closed, and Trevor felt a surge of energy from the mountains to the east. Light burst from Jordan, impossibly brilliant. It washed over all of them, Jeeps included. When that light faded, they were in a small clearing. Trevor stood on a patch of dirt, surrounded by towering trees, covered with vines. It was the kind of dense jungle he hadn't seen since Irakesh had taken him to Panama.

A wide, dark river, flanked by a wall of vegetation, disappeared to the south. Behind them lay a fairly advanced city, complete with a little airport. There was even something resembling a strip mall. It wasn't San Diego, but it was more advanced than he'd have imagined.

He'd also had no idea how humid it would be. A thick sheen of sweat already covered Jordan's face and arms.

Insects, macaws, and something that sounded to Trevor like monkeys all competed to be the loudest part of the jungle. It was a rolling wall of sound, hypnotic in an almost unnerving way.

"Being here reminds me of old times," Jordan said. "At least this time I'm not chasing your sorry ass through the jungle." To Trevor's surprise, he smiled.

"Are you okay, man? I think there's something wrong with your face," Trevor quipped.

"I smile now and again," Jordan said defensively. "Just not generally around you, because I'm usually trying to figure out the best way to kill you. Do you not remember shooting me in the face on the Golden Gate Bridge?"

"Yeah, uh, sorry about that," Trevor said. "In my defense, I wasn't given much choice."

"How about when you shot me again, outside Gobekli Tepe?" Jordan said. He poked Trevor in the arm. "You enjoy shooting me, so I don't smile around you. Getting shot sucks. It's totally unfair that you can just disappear into the shadows."

"Yeah, well you can monkey around inside my head," Trevor pointed out. "Seems a fair enough trade."

Trevor climbed back into the driver's side of his Jeep, and Anput slid into the passenger's side. Jordan rejoined Leti ahead of them. Jordan's Jeep rolled confidently forward, ambling up a steep trail leading over a ridge that disappeared under the jungle's thick canopy. Trevor guided his Jeep behind, allowing about fifty yards between them. They were paralleling the river, heading south.

"So what did you want to talk about?" Trevor asked.

Anput eyed him for a long moment before answering. She was unaffected by the sweltering heat; if anything, the humidity made her hair more lustrous. "I thought we could further discuss my theories on modifying the virus, but the truth is, that's just me stalling. I've been wanting to ask, but I don't really want the answer. Trevor, what happened to my husband?"

"We were ambushed in France," Trevor admitted. He eyed her side long. "He stayed behind to buy the rest of us time to escape. Anubis faced off against Set, and according to Irakesh Set cut him down. He died clean, if it's any consolation."

Anput was silent for a long time, so Trevor focused on driving. Finally, she licked her lips and spoke. "What of Wepwawet? I'd know his fate as well."

Trevor considered his answer carefully, buying time by focusing on navigating the treacherous trail. Jordan had left a cloud of dust in his wake, which billowed up around them. "When we attacked the First Ark, Wepwawet was still being controlled by Set. Isis, Osiris, and Ra went after Set. Their job was to delay him while the rest of us detonated the Ark. Your husband was sent to stop us. He confronted us in the Ark's central repository. Wepwawet squared off against Liz, and she was forced to kill him."

"Did Liz still wield Excalibur when she killed him?" Anput asked quietly, staring down at her lap.

"No, Osiris was wielding it," Trevor explained. "She did use the na-kopesh that used to belong to Irakesh."

Anput's head shot up and her eyes locked on Trevor. He eyed her sidelong as the Jeep bounced over another root.

"She used the blade to kill Wepwawet?" Anput asked. Her voice had an intensity he'd never heard from her.

"Yes, she drained his essence," Trevor said. "I saw her do that once before, when we were fighting a corrupted champion. I gather that makes her stronger." He didn't really understand the process. Exactly what were you draining when you took someone's essence? It might be explainable scientifically, but he had no idea where to even start with sunsteel.

Anput gave a bitter laugh. "It will have to do, I suppose. Draining a foe does more than empower the killer. If they drain all the essence they'll often absorb the consciousness of the person they slew. Part of Wepwawet almost certainly dwells within Liz. He was a powerful god, far too powerful to simply dissipate."

"Wow." Trevor wondered how Liz would deal with having wolf-headed god in her head.

Chapter 36- Mobilization

Nox watched impassively from the hotel balcony as the jungle below withered and died. He'd seen sections burned before, and remembered how the dense smoke had blackened the sky—how breathing had been difficult, and he'd needed eye protection.

This was somehow more terrible than even the wanton burning of ancient jungle.

Four of Camiero's best shapers had been deployed along the jungle west of the isolated city of Brasilia. Each held a staff cut from dense black stone. They wore golden bracelets, allowing them to interface with the Builder-created weapons. Nox could feel the tremendous flow of energy from each shaper, fed through the bracelets into the staff. The staff radiated that energy in all directions, and wherever that energy passed plants died.

The process began as a simple withering. Leaves drooped, then began to shrivel. Within moments, everything green was dead. Within a minute, everything within a thousand yards of the staff had become desiccated husks. Only the tallest trees remained standing, isolated husks to mark the grave of the jungle. The rest toppled with cascading crashes, so weak the dried wood could no longer support its own weight.

After that swath of jungle had been cleared, all four shapers blurred forward, and the process repeated.

It had been going on for three hours, and already they'd cleared tens of square miles of jungle—and they were not the only ones. This process was being repeated all along the border of the Amazon. By tomorrow they'd have done more destruction to the jungle than the four decades of logging before the CME combined.

"Glorious," Kali whispered. She stood behind him, and he had almost been able to ignore her presence. She cradled one of the obelisks, doting over it like a mother. "These things are incredible, and the jungle is merely one application. I can use these to amplify nearly any ability, including fear. You could break an enemy without evening needed to fight. The Builders are truly gods."

Nox longed to tear out her throat, horrified by how much she reveled in the destruction.

You only hate her because she represents the darkest parts of you, Set-Dun.

Nox found it interesting that the voice believed that. He detested Kali, that was true—but not because she was anything like him. She was the opposite, in fact. Everything he did was with cold deliberation. He was always working toward his goals, methodically plotting his next moves. Kali was a creature of passion, chasing whatever emotion caught her fancy. She could switch from passion to rage and back again in the space of a few heartbeats. That had proven lethal to far too many of Camiero's lieutenants. She'd roasted the last one alive using her pyrokinesis, a brand of shaping Nox had only encountered in the people shaped by the grey men.

It gave him a clue to her past, though he'd been unable to uncover anything further. She was tight-lipped, and the only people who knew anything about her were Project Solaris. It was a pity Nox hadn't been able to find their sanctuary, somewhere in orbit. He had no doubt it would yield all sorts of secrets, perhaps including a way to stop the Builders.

"What makes you think the Builders won't wipe us out the moment they arrive?" Nox asked. He didn't expect a logical answer, and wasn't disappointed.

"They've promised us power," she explained. "Their chosen will stand above the rest of the cattle. We will not rule, but I do not wish to. I merely wish to serve the masters."

Her tone was all devotion, which was odd for Kali. Nox had seen brainwashing before, but this went well beyond it. Somehow the grey men had shaped Kali's mind, instilling in her a slavish devotion to the Builders.

That terrified Nox, because if they could do it to her they could certainly repeat that process with others. His transformation by Set and Hades had changed him, but Nox still retained free will. Kali couldn't boast the same thing. Hers had been stolen, and Nox knew that if they didn't find a way to stop the Builders the same fate lay in store for the few slaves left alive after they invaded.

Of course, that was why he was here, after all. He and Hades both knew that one of them would betray the other at some point, but for now they were united in a common cause. Neither wanted to serve the Builders. Both knew the Builders would end everything. Right now they had no choice, no ability to resist. They worked alongside their would-be masters, learning everything they could about them.

If his mission succeeded, Nox might finally have the means to fight back. He *had* to succeed, because if he didn't the city's power would be taken by the grey men. He'd seen enough of their power to know that would mean the end of everything. They were master shapers, and—if he understood correctly—the Proto Ark was exactly the kind of manufacturing facility they needed to gear up for war.

"I like watching things die as much as the next demon," Kali said, "but I still have no idea what we're doing here." She sidled up to the railing near Nox, but took great care not to touch him. That was a lesson he'd taught her very quickly after meeting, when she'd assumed she could seduce him. "It will take months to clear enough jungle to reach the city—possibly years. The masters are not patient. They won't wait that long. Sooner or later they will intercede directly, and they are not gentle with those who fail them."

"It's touching that you're so concerned with my safety." Nox refused to give her anything else. Kali was unpredictable, but she was also cunning. She knew there was more to his plan, that what was happening here was merely a distraction. A smoke screen for his true plan to find the city. He had little doubt she was spying for the grey men.

Nox turned to the east, smiling as he spotted several black specks approaching. The B-949s flew low over the jungle, like fat birds. They contained hundreds of demons, the occupying force that he'd used to secure the area. The mechanized troops would arrive tomorrow, and in less than a week he'd bring the Anakim online.

The army wasn't the largest he'd ever assembled, but it was by far the most powerful. Whoever or whatever was waiting in the lost city had no idea what was coming for them.

Chapter 37- The Amazon

By the end of the first day, Jordan hated the Jeeps. The extra storage space was nice, but the further they proceeded the more treacherous the roads became. Twice they'd had to pick up the Jeeps and carry them through impassable stretches. He was convinced they could have moved faster on foot.

Or through the trees, Ka-Dun. As we did in the oldest days.

"Leti, I've agreed to trust you," Jordan began, "and I don't want you to think that I don't." He glanced across the Jeep at the brunette. The sweat stains on her shirt matched his, and her hair was slick with it. It looked good on her, and gave her an earthy scent he very much enjoyed. "Why did you insist we take vehicles? They're slowing us down. We can move faster on our own."

"Do not worry, Ark Lord. I am not Elia," Leti teased. She gave him a warm smile, brushing sweaty black hair from her forehead. "I invite questions. If our faith cannot stand the light of questioning, then it is no true faith. Your question is a good one. We take Jeeps for two reasons. First, because if we took to the jungles it would be disrespectful to our hosts. These are their lands, and we should not trespass any more than we already have."

"I'd like to avoid antagonizing the locals," Jordan allowed. "What's the second reason?"

"These Jeeps will be an offering," Leti explained. "When we reach the river, we will need to barter for a canoe, and the tribe that carves them will accept the Jeeps as payment." She withdrew a can of chili from her pack, using a single claw to slice it open. "I had forgotten how hot it is. It's like the jungle is trying to smother us."

Deep rhythmic howls came from the dense foliage to the right side of the path. More howls came on their heels, this time from the other side of the path.

"What am I hearing?" Jordan asked. He scanned the trees, but kept one eye on the treacherous path.

"They are called howler monkeys. They are harmless, for the most part. Sometimes they can be dangerous, in that they will lead predators to prey. After the predators kill and eat their fill, the howler monkeys scavenge the carcass. This is a new thing. They did not do it before the world changed." The way Leti said it suggested more fascination than revulsion. "It is the way in the jungle. All things must kill to survive. Even the plants fight to reach the life-giving sun. There is no truer expression of nature's price."

"Sounds lovely. If we're really being hunted by some sort of spirits, those things are going to be like a beacon." Jordan guided the Jeep over a small rise, bouncing sharply when he went over a thick root. God, he hated roots.

"If the jungle wishes us harm, there will be no hiding from it. Even making the attempt to hide would be perceived as hostile."

"You mean the natives, right?" Jordan asked.

"No, I mean the *jungle*. The jungle itself is alive. It has a consciousness. I do not know the science behind this thing, but I do not need to fully understand a thing to know how it is possible. Werewolves and zombies were nothing but fantasies five years ago. Is this so difficult to accept?" Leti stared up at the trees, spooning chili into her mouth. "This place is the largest biomass in the world. It is one of the oldest, one of the last remaining great jungles. Only the Congo rivals it, but the Congo is smaller."

"I respect this place, trust me." Jordan eyed the tree warily as they slowly picked a path down the hillside. More than once Jordan had felt like the Jeep was going to topple, but he knew from experience that the low center of gravity made these things like mountain goats. "I did a tour along the jungle in Columbia, back in the early nineties. We were hired to oust some guerrillas that were terrorizing local villages. We lost two dozen men in three weeks before we finally cornered them. It was one of the costliest operations I've ever been a part of. Those who know the jungle have a massive advantage over those who don't."

Jordan paused at the bottom of the hill, pulling off to the side of the trail to allow Trevor to catch up. He leaned out the side of the Jeep as the deathless pulled up alongside them. "Hey, Trevor, it's getting fairly late and I don't like the idea of doing this in the dark. That little cave looks like as good a place to camp as any. What do you think?"

"Looks safe enough. We can flee in two directions, and it should keep the rain off." Trevor angled his Jeep's wheels, backing it off the trail behind Jordan. He rubbed his lower back as he exited. "I know we're supernatural badasses and all, but that drive tore up my back. These Jeeps *suck*."

"It *is* a rather awkward means of travel," Anput said. She fished a large duffel from the Jeep's back seat and headed into the cave. "I'll get a fire set up so that those of you with a heartbeat can have dinner."

"Thank you," Leti said stiffly. She followed Anput inside and began setting up a green canvas pup tent—as far from Anput as it could get without being outside the cave.

Rain began to fall all at once, in an avalanche that drenched Jordan and Trevor. It rang off the Jeeps like giant drums, booming loudly enough that anyone within two miles who didn't already know they were here sure did now.

Jordan closed his eyes, raising his face to the rain. It felt good—warm. A damned site better than the awful humidity, at least.

"I have a feeling this is about to be the most awkward evening I've ever had." Trevor paused next to Jordan, his backpack in hand. "They don't like each other. And we don't like each other. Probably not the four I'd have picked to head into the jungle with. You know, Blair would have loved this. He's basically Indiana Jones, and the one time he'd get to find the lost city he chose to stay home."

"I get why. Blair has decided to take a stand. He's taking up the role of Ark Lord. I'm still trying to learn what that means, and I know he is too." Jordan reached into the Jeep and fished out his own pack. It weighed an easy eighty pounds, but he one-handed that without effort. Being this strong never got old.

"Yeah, he made the right call," Trevor said. "Besides, him going back means he's with Liz." He started toward the cave, but paused to wait for Jordan.

"That's where he should be," Jordan said. "I hope those two get on with it. They've certainly waited long enough." He tossed his pack against a rock.

"Dude, that's my sister you're talking about," Trevor protested. "Don't make me climb a water tower to defend her honor."

"I'm pretty sure Liz can climb her own water towers, but point taken. Still, I think she and Blair are good together."

"They need each other, I think," Trevor said. He sat down, cross-legged, and withdrew a .45 from his thigh holster. He swiftly disassembled the weapon, then reached into his pack for a well-worn cleaning kit.

Jordan withdrew his own sidearm, automatically beginning a nearly identical cleaning process. It was something soldiers did. Just like you'd yawn when you saw someone else yawn. Weapon maintenance saved lives, and every soldier who liked breathing tended to their weapon religiously.

As quickly as it had started, the rain stopped. In its wake came a million dripping sounds, as water trickled down lush vegetation. It was pleasant, almost hypnotic. Jordan enjoyed it as he finished cleaning his sidearm.

Then a piercing shriek split the silence—a weird, bestial wheezing noise. He started reassembling his weapon. Trevor did the same.

"Tell me you know what that was," Anput said. She stalked to the edge of the cave and peered out into the impenetrable jungle.

"It is a mapinguara." Leti rose from the tent and moved to join Anput. "You know they are close when you can smell the decay of the deep jungle. It is…unique. Few see a mapinguara and live, but I have heard them described. The smallest are taller than a man, and they can grow many times that size. They walk like a man, but they are covered in thick shaggy hair. Their arms are too long, and tipped with long claws. Their skin is said to be so tough that nothing can pierce it, and the older they get the tougher their hide."

"How old is the one we just heard?" Jordan asked. He was very glad they had Leti with them. Nothing beat local intelligence.

"That one was young. It was screaming at the rain. Mapinguara hate water. They will not cross a river, unless it is very shallow." Leti looked up at him, and he could see the concern. "If it is one, we are likely safe. If it is part of a herd, then we must flee. Many champions have thought to test the legend of the mapinguara, and the few who return usually will not speak of it."

"They have to have heard the rain hitting the Jeeps," Jordan said. "We either stand our ground or abandon the Jeeps and cross the river. I say we stand our ground. Three of us can blur, and Leti can walk the shadows. We set a watch, and if one of these things gets close we'll decide how to deal with it. We can run if we need to."

Chapter 38- Mapinguara

Trevor leaned against the moss-covered boulder, shadows wrapped tightly around him. So far as he knew, other than Blair's ping ability there was no way he could be detected.

Of course, the very fact that Blair had the ability showed that it was possible, so Trevor took no chances. He stayed vigilant, listening to the jungle.

It loomed outside the cave, a mass of shadowy shapes only visible because of his enhanced vision. Insects and spiders crawled across tree trunks, but nothing larger than a human fist. An anaconda slithered past, the jungle going silent around it. He even spotted a large cat in a distant tree. Jaguar, maybe?

During that first watch, Trevor had plenty of time to think. About Anput and her work on a modified virus. About Jordan, and the fact that most of the heat had gone out of his animosity. Trevor respected the man, even if they weren't friends. They'd become allies, and that was probably a good thing for this new world they were building.

"I find it interesting," came Anput's disembodied voice, "that Isis added the need to sleep to her virus. It wasn't present in the original deathless strain, nor in my father's modified strain. She added a weakness, and I have never understood why. I mean look at the Ka-Dun. Jordan is an Ark Lord, yet right now he is as helpless as an unblooded. It makes no sense. The only quote I've heard from Isis was that she felt it preserved the human soul."

Trevor considered that. Was she being superstitious? He seriously doubted it. "Isis has lived longer than any of us, even you. Deathless can choose to sleep, but we aren't forced to. We don't have that limitation. Maybe when enough centuries pass that blurs your perspective. Maybe you can't think like a normal human any more. Werewolves don't age, but they eat. They sleep. They can mate. They're still human, for the most part. Still connected to their former identity in a way I think we lose."

"I suppose there's some merit in that," Anput allowed. Trevor guessed she was no more than three feet away, but it was difficult to tell because she was enveloped in shadow. "If you were to tinker with your own virus, would you make the same change?"

"That's a good question," Trevor mused. "The pragmatist in me says that would be a terrible idea." He ran his hand along the golden boomerang David had given him, enjoying the weapon's faint warmth against his cool skin. "Honestly, though? Yes, I think I would. I've only been deathless for a few months, from my perspective. I've already seen how it's changed me, and I'm not sure I like all those changes. If I could reclaim a bit of who I was in life I think I'd leap at the chance."

A shrill shriek cut through the jungle, dropping a veil of silence. Even the insects ceased moving. Trevor stood poised, straining to hear anything. A cacophony of howling exploded in the trees all around their cave. Trevor spotted small forms flitting through the trees above.

Trevor blurred to Jordan's side to wake him, but the commander's eyes were already open. The big man unzipped his sleeping roll, climbing swiftly to his feet. He was still wearing his combat boots. "It's those damned monkeys again, isn't it?"

Leti had also risen, and was peering out into the darkness. "Yes, they are leading something toward us."

"I think we all know what they're leading here," Trevor said. He was still wearing the shadows, but neither werewolf jumped when he spoke. "There was an otherworldly shriek just before the monkeys."

"The mapinguara are not swift by our standards," Leti said, "but they are faster than an unblooded. At least one will be on us soon. More if we are unlucky." She fixed Jordan with an agonized stare. "I do not know what to do. If we stay and fight, we may die. If we run for the river we will arrive with no gift, and will not be able to make passage on the river."

"Can't we just swim?" Trevor asked.

Leti shook her head. "There are dangerous things in the water. We cannot risk it. We need a boat."

"Choice seems pretty clear," Jordan said. "We need to stay and defend those Jeeps. If we get into real trouble, we'll fall back into the jungle. If these things can't blur, we should have no trouble outrunning them. Trevor, you on board with that?" He faced roughly in Trevor's direction, his steely eyes roaming the shadows where Trevor lurked.

We should flee, Trevor's risen whispered. *There is no sense in risking our deaths.*

Trevor shimmered into view. "Yeah, I'm good with that. We've taken on some pretty scary things. Let's see how we do against this mapinguara. If we're going to be journeying through here for weeks, it will be good to know what to expect."

"I hope this is not madness," Leti whispered. She was still staring out into the darkness, and winced when another shriek split the jungle. It was close now. The monkeys went into a frenzy of howls.

"Child, if two Ark Lords cannot handle some unintelligent beast, the lot of us deserve to die." Anput's tone was sharper than Trevor was used to, putting the lie to her bold words. The vampire was frightened.

Trevor summoned the shadows once more, moving silently to the far end of the cave. He scanned the tree line, waiting. The clearing, if it could be called that, was about twenty feet across. The mapinguara would need to cross that to enter the cave, so that was where they had to meet it. He didn't know how tall these things were, but the cave was maybe eight feet tall. If the thing were large enough, they could use the cave defensively.

The monkeys grew bolder, several darting down to touch the stones above Trevor. Something crashed through the jungle, tree branches snapping loudly as it pushed its way into the clearing. The jungle parted long enough for something hideous to emerge. A stench of rotting vegetation and something worse filled the cave, so awful it made Trevor's eyes water. The stench worsened when the creature gave a deafening roar.

It lumbered closer, approaching the Jeeps. A stray beam of moonlight fell on it, giving the creature some definition. It had thick shaggy fur, and a sloth-like face. Its arms were too long, sharp grey claws touching the earth as it approached. Trevor estimated it at about eight feet tall. It wasn't quite as massive as a female werewolf, and it moved sluggishly, like it wasn't in any kind of hurry to devour them.

"How do you want to play this?" Trevor called to Jordan.

"You've got that grey man weapon, right? See how it feels about being shot in the face."

"Yeah, Anput has one too." Trevor obliged. He aimed the golden boomerang, willing energy to flow through him and into the weapon. He poured out as much as he could muster, trying to make this blast as powerful as the weapon could handle.

Brilliant green light lit the clearing like day as the tips of the boomerang built up a charge. A deep hum filled the jungle, then the weapon discharged.

It sent a bolt of crackling green energy right at the mapinguara's face. The beast fell back half a step, its features locked in almost comical surprise. Then the beam washed over its face, drawing an ear-piercing shriek of pain. The scent of charred flesh now mingled with the awful stench, and Trevor heard Jordan gag behind him.

Trevor kept his attention on his target. The mapinguara gave another shriek, but this one was more rage than pain. It scanned the cave entrance, its patches of steaming flesh still sending up tendrils of smoke, and lumbered forward, attention fixed on the only thing it could see: Jordan.

Trevor shot it again, this time in the side of the head. The shot elicited another shriek, and the beast turned to face Trevor's direction. Its eyes narrowed as it scanned the shadows, but it seemed unable to detect him. Trevor crept around the beast, studying the bald patch where he'd shot it the second time. That shot had done even less damage than the first—it had burned away fur, but the skin wasn't even reddened. These things were damned tough.

Jordan capitalized on the beast's momentary distraction, blurring toward it from the cave. He shifted in mid-air, coming down on the mapinguara's back. He worried at the creature's neck with his fangs, but was about as effective as a puppy chewing on a shoe.

The mapinguara's arm shot out, seizing Jordan by the neck. It tightened its grip, and Jordan beat frantically on its arm as he struggled for breath.

Trevor glided forward into a blur. Time slowed as he charged the mapinguara, dropping his shoulder like a linebacker. He took the beast behind the knee, ending the blur the moment he impacted.

The blow knocked the creature to the ground, and it released Jordan. Jordan rolled backwards, raising both his arms. The mapinguara was suddenly lifted into the air, and it gave an angry bleat like some titanic sheep.

Trevor was already rolling away, but the creature's clawed hand sank into the back of Trevor's leg. It dragged Trevor toward it, punching the claws of its other hand through his shoulder.

He suppressed the pain, blurring into a punch. His fist shot forward, but a fang-filled mouth opened in the creature's gut. Razored teeth clamped down around his wrist, and Trevor gave a roar that was more shock than pain. He shifted into green mist, swirling into the shadows.

Sluggish black blood flowed from the stump where his hand had been. It would grow back, but for now he was crippled.

"I think I've got it," Jordan called. He'd raised his arms higher, and the creature moved up about ten more yards. It flailed about, shrieking wildly as it sought to find purchase with its long arms. They tore at a few branches, but the mapinguara could do nothing but shriek as it rotated slowly.

"Telekinesis is so handy," Jordan said. He took another step back from the creature as one of its arms swiped the air near him.

"It's a temporary solution," Anput countered. She'd retreated to the cave mouth and was watching the mapinguara warily. "Sooner or later we'll want to leave, and you'll have to let it go. It will just come after us again, right Leti?"

Leti's voice came from the shadows in the cave's recesses. "I'm afraid so. Now that it has the taste of our flesh it will never stop."

"Then we have to kill it," Trevor said. "I have an idea about that." He stepped from the shadows, and the mapinguara instantly swiped in his direction. The claws passed within a foot of him, and he leaned back slightly to avoid the blow.

Bones popped as a new hand sprouted from Trevor's wrist. It happened with incredible speed, flesh weaving itself around bone until his hand was completely regenerated. Trevor switched the boomerang to his newly regrown hand, and then leapt at the mapinguara. He punched it in the gut again, and as expected the mouth opened. Trevor blurred, at the same time pouring power into the boomerang.

The jaws of the strange mouth were closing on his wrist, the fangs beginning to pierce his newly regenerated flesh. Trevor released the shot, and a beam of pure green shot into the creature's innards.

Trevor increased the power, firing a second shot, then a third. The beast thrashed wildly, writhing desperately to escape the pain. The mapinguara gave one more tortured shriek, then its convulsions ceased.

"You've done it," Leti said. There was awe in her voice. "You've killed a mapinguara."

Shrieks came from the jungle to the south, a mourning answer to the mapinguara's death cry. Another shriek came from the north, then a third to the south. Finally, a deep shriek came from the east. It was far deeper, and longer, than any of the others.

"They know what we have done. We must flee." Leti darted back into the cave and began stuffing her sleeping roll into her pack.

"We need to abandon the Jeeps," Jordan said. He'd also moved to pack his sleeping roll.

"Agreed." Trevor darted to his pack, pulling the straps over his shoulders. "We'll find something else to give the villagers at the river. I don't want to stick around to deal with a whole pack of these things."

"This way," Leti called from the shadowy jungle ahead. "It isn't much further."

Jordan trotted through the jungle, pulling up short when he reached the shore of a wide, lazy river. The moonlight was bright over the water, as there was no canopy to obscure it. Out in the middle of the water was a grassy mound not quite large enough to qualify as a real island. That mound was dotted with tiny huts, and several figures crouched around a smoldering fire.

From behind Jordan came more enraged shrieks, still distant but growing closer at a truly alarming rate. Apparently these things could move fast when they were pissed off.

"Leti, you know these people, right?" he asked.

Leti stepped from the shadows, in human form. "They are of the Muisca tribe. I have not met them personally, but I know their ways."

"Since we don't have a gift, what do you suggest?" Jordan asked. He tried to ignore the approaching shrieks. They had time. Not much of it, but enough to ensure they approached the situation tactically.

"If we approach without a gift, they will take it as a grave insult. Combined with your choice of friends, I fear at best they will send us away. At worst they may attack us." Leti climbed onto the base of a large ropey tree trunk that jutted out into the river. "Still, I do not see that we have any choice."

"Then let's be about this," Anput said, shimmering into view. She dove gracefully into the murky water, her powerful muscles propelling her toward the island with incredible speed.

Jordan waited for Trevor and Leti to enter the water, risking a glance back at the jungle. He had a hard time believing that those monstrosities would be stopped by a shallow river, but he'd seen stranger things. He dove into the muddy water, surprised by how warm it was. Tales of piranha lurked in the back of his mind, but he focused on swimming for the island. He blurred, but only enough to catch the others as they arrived on the shore of the little island.

The natives were already aware of them, and a group of dark-skinned villagers were advancing with spears. They wore little more than bright red loincloths and colorful body paint. Men and women were similarly garbed, and all held spears. They chattered in a language Jordan didn't recognize.

You can take that language from their minds, Ka-Dun. They are unblooded, after all. I know you are squeamish about accepting your position, but they possess something you need. It is to their benefit that you seek the city. Surely claiming their tongue is an acceptable price.

Jordan was mildly surprised by the long outburst. It was the most his beast had said in a long time. Its answers were usually short, and it rarely suggested he do something he disagreed with. That it did here was interesting.

The crowd of natives parted for a short woman, bowing as they stepped from her path. She shared their dark skin and hair, but there was something different about her. She walked with confidence and poise, and Jordan could feel the strength in her. "I do not recognize you," she said. "But I know the garb of one of you at least. You are a priestess?"

"I am, honored sister," Leti replied. She stepped forward, giving something between a bow and a curtsy. "We are supplicants seeking the city, and were hoping you might provide aid."

The dark-haired woman frowned, looking hard at Anput and Trevor. She eyed Jordan curiously for a moment, though her expression didn't soften much. "You bring the ancient enemy into the jungle, and you seek to lead them to the city? I imagine our elder sisters would take a very dim view of this."

"Then it's a good thing that you are not an elder sister." Leti gave a respectful nod.

The woman returned it. "I'm not, but if you are a fugitive then I can expect trouble from helping you," she countered. She gestured at her companions, and the villagers dispersed back into the huts. Most seemed reluctant to go, and almost all were still staring. "My name is Anhuaga. I protect these people from the jungle, and I am not willing to put them at risk

—especially not for the sake of people harboring the ancient enemy. Why should I help you? What gift have you brought that I should accord you any honor at all?"

There it was. Leti gave him an agonized look, and Jordan wracked his brain for a solution. They had a few weapons, and some basic gear. Nothing that these people would be interested in. They wouldn't care about guns.

Then it hit him.

"Can you excuse us for a moment?" Jordan asked. He took Leti by the shoulder, guiding her back to Trevor and Anput.

Anhuaga gave a cold nod. She could probably hear every word, but was at least polite enough to pretend that she couldn't.

"Anyone have a suggestion? Those howls are getting closer and I'm not really looking forward to fleeing downriver without a boat," Trevor said. He stared back at the jungle they'd emerged from. "Maybe we could have carried the Jeeps somehow. Maybe we can go back for them."

"I have another idea," Jordan said. He lowered his voice. "Both you and Anput have one of those golden boomerangs. I don't want to lose the firepower, but I'm betting these people would value them…especially once we show them what they can do."

"You want to trade a priceless piece of enemy technology for a canoe?" Anput asked. Her tone made it clear how crazy she thought Jordan was.

"Here," Trevor said. He reached into his pack and handed the golden boomerang to Leti. "Tell them that's the gift. Show her what it does. It will be most valuable for a female werewolf, since they don't have any external shaping. It can help her protect this place."

The idea that Trevor would give up a potent weapon without a second thought really cast him in a different light. Jordan had always believed that Trevor put his own needs first, above the group. Either he was changing, or Jordan didn't know him as well as he'd thought.

"Very well," Leti said. She walked back over to Anhuaga, and gave another bow. "Revered champion, we show our honor with the mightiest gift we can bestow. This weapon will help you defend these shores." Leti aimed the weapon at the sky, discharging a beam of pure green energy. It shot skyward, eventually disappearing into the dense cloud cover.

Leti handed the weapon to Anhuaga, who took it reverently. She studied the weapon carefully, then looked up sharply at Leti. "I see what this is about now. You've stolen artifacts from the temple, and you seek the city to acquire more."

"How dare you," Leti snarled, shifting into her warform. "My gift has accorded you great honor. Those weapons are not artifacts of the holy temple. They come from our enemies, foes the Mother opposes. You think I am some thief in search of treasure? I should tear out your throat for all your people to see."

Anhuaga shifted as well, growing into a dark-furred warform a few inches taller than Leti. She bared her fangs. "Threatening me in front of my people is unwise."

"Unwise?" Leti interjected. She walked brazenly over to Anhuaga, staring up at the Ka-Ken. "We are in the company of two Ark Lords. Either could incinerate you where you stand. They could wipe this place clean of life, leaving nothing but a memory. Accept the priceless gift we have given you, allow us to take one of your dirty little boats, and then we'll be on our way."

There was a tense moment when Jordan was positive Anhuaga was about to attack, but that moment came and went. Her posture softened, and Jordan knew she'd been cowed.

"Very well," Anhuaga snapped. Her gaze darted to Jordan, then away again when he met it. There was definitely fear there. "I grant you the gift of passage. You may take a single canoe. Leave immediately." Anhuaga slid the boomerang into a pouch sewn from crocodile hide, and turned coldly away. She stalked back to her people, who studiously avoided looking at them.

"It is the best we can hope for, I think," Leti said, apologetically.

"It's enough. Let's just take it and go," Jordan said. He started walking along the edge of the shore toward a trio of canoes that had been pulled out of the river.

Chapter 40- Bonding

"I wonder what this surprise is," Blair asked. He and Liz were waiting at the curb outside Alicia's house. The eastern horizon was just beginning to lighten, and only the stars in the western sky were still visible. The town below hadn't quite woken up, but a few figures moved between rows of houses.

"Got me. She seemed really pleased with how you handled San Francisco." Liz threatened a grin, but managed to suppress it. "Personally I think you went a little overboard, but if I were an Ark Lord I imagine I'd enjoy the theatrics, too."

"Yeah, yeah, I know it was over the top. In my defense I was a little pissed off." Blair gave her a sheepish smile.

Liz returned it, growing even more beautiful when her features brightened.

Footsteps sounded from inside the house—two sets. The door opened, and Alicia stepped out. Her hair had been pulled into a ponytail that looked suspiciously like Liz's, and she wore a baseball cap...also like Liz. Behind Alicia came a second figure, the one he'd met the night they'd come to Santa Rosa. John Rivers was one of Alicia's lieutenants, but he'd been away on patrol every time Blair had been here.

"Morning," Alicia called. She gave a cheerful little wave as she approached. "Thanks for coming so early. I hope you didn't have to cut anything short." Alicia gave a truly wicked smile, and Blair could only stand there blinking.

Yup, that was what she was implying.

"Nothing we'd be embarrassed about," Blair replied smoothly. "So what's this big surprise you have for us?"

"A home," Alicia said. She gestured at the house across the street from hers, an identical McMansion, also in good repair. "John Rivers dropped by my place last night. I'll let him give you the news."

"I'm almost never in Santa Rosa," John Rivers explained. He stepped forward and offered a leathery hand to Blair. "After what you did in San

Francisco, you've proved yourself in my book. If anyone should be living right next to Alicia, it's you. I was only given this place as a status symbol, but I don't really ever use it. Don't much like houses. So why don't you folks take it?"

"We're neighbors," Alicia burst out. It was such a stark shift from the hard-eyed teen he was already growing used to. "Yukon is already inside, and I've got a truck coming by later with some furniture. I don't really use it, but I'm told you old folks from before the end of the world like couches and beds."

"We can't accept this. It's too much," Liz protested. She stared at the house longingly though.

"Yes we can," Blair said. He took John Rivers's hand. "If you're really sure you want to give this place to us, we'd be honored to take it. This is an incredible gift, John. Thank you."

"No, thank *you*," John Rivers said. He had a firm grip and an easy smile. Blair found himself liking the guy even more. "We've been terrified of Melissa and her deathless ever since they drove us off Angel Island. I was one of the first people Alicia gave the gift to, but that happened after. I'll never forget running, too frightened to even look back. You've ensured that we don't have to worry about the deathless ever again, and that makes you a hero in my book."

"Thank you, John." Liz embraced him in a fierce hug.

"Why don't we let the lovebirds explore their new place?" Alicia suggested rather coyly.

"I can't believe it even comes with a dog," Blair quipped.

"He insisted that the Mother would want him to stay with you two," Alicia said.

John Rivers offered the keys to Liz. "Enjoy," he said, then he and Alicia turned back toward her place, heading up the walk to her door.

"Guess that's our cue," Liz said. She linked her arm through Blair's, and they walked up to the front door of a house far larger than Blair had ever dreamed of owning.

"Mowing this lawn is going to be a real bitch," he said, wrapping an arm around Liz's shoulder.

"Are you serious? You can blur." She slid the key home in the lock, opening the door to a cavernous living room. A large furry lump lay against the far wall, illuminated by the moonlight coming through the skylight above. Yukon's tail thumped on the carpet, and he rose to his feet as they closed the door behind them.

Welcome home.

"It's good to be home," Liz said. She knelt next to Yukon, ruffling the fur on his head. "I missed you, and I'm glad we finally have a chance to catch up."

Blair found himself studying Yukon with fresh eyes. It wasn't just his size, which was impressive. That sort of genetic manipulation he could get a handle on. What he didn't understand was how Isis had been able to give Yukon the power to shift into a human, or to grow so much more intelligent than a normal canine. When they'd been investigating the werewolf virus they had learned that dogs had the most malleable DNA of any mammal—but it still seemed incredibly complex.

A pulse of energy flowed into Blair's eyes, and he was somehow seeing *inside* the dog. A knot of energy tendrils had been woven into Yukon's brain, somewhere near where the prefrontal cortex would be on a person. A low rhythmic pulse was being broadcast from that knot. Blair probed the signal, feeling a surge of joy and contentment emanating from it.

You experience his emotions through the bond the Mother forged. During the last age such bonds were common. Sometimes they would be forged between a Ka-Dun and a chosen pack member. More often that bond was forged between Ka-Dun and Ka-Ken. This bonding enabled mates to work together with far greater efficiency. You should bond your female, but beware. Such a bond will last until your death.

"Blair, what is it?" Liz asked. "You're a million miles away." She was sitting on the carpet with her back against the wall. Yukon had his head in her lap, and she was scratching under his ears.

"Something my beast just said." Blair squatted across from Liz, searching for a way to broach the topic. "Yukon has some sort of bond with

Isis. I can see it, see how she created it, I think"

"Blair?" Liz asked—then she cocked her head, as if listening. Her voice quavered a little, and she gave a soft smile. "Did your voice explain to you how this bond was used? What it represented between a man and woman?"

She peered at him with those impossibly blue eyes, and there he found the answer to the question he'd been afraid to ask. "I know now isn't the best time, and that this is all rather sudden, but I doubt we'll ever have a better time. Liz, I'd like to forge one of these bonds between us. It's not marriage or anything, but in a way maybe it's deeper."

"We're going to be alive for a very long time," Liz said. "I can't think of anyone else I'd rather spend eternity with." She sat up straighter, with the best smile Blair had ever seen. It was like a tremendous weight had been taken away from her.

Blair stretched out a hand toward Liz, and began to pull at the energy offered by the Ark.

Allow me to guide you, Ka-Dun. His beast rumbled. Blair gave over control and a burst of complex signals flowed from his hand toward Liz. She tensed, eyes widening and mouth opening slightly.

The burst sped up, pulsing far faster than Blair could possibly track. He could only comprehend a fraction of what the beast was doing, but when it finished several minutes later he could see exactly what it had accomplished. Liz now had an identical knot, and Blair could feel one inside him as well.

"I can feel you in the back of my head," Liz said in wonder. She reached up and touched her temple. "You're in here. Your emotions. It's amazing."

"I can feel you, too. Hey, Yukon, how about you go for a run? I think Liz and I are going to need some alone time."

I will go rouse the pack for the day's hunt. Yukon gave a doggy smile, wagging his tail as he used a paw to open the front door. *Enjoy your alone time.*

The wind howled as Blair ran low and fast up the ridge. He bounded over rocks, reveling in the freedom his full wolf form provided. Having four legs made running not just effortless, but exhilarating. All around him the packmind echoed his emotions, sharing different flavors of joy and wonder. Dogs, foxes, and coyotes moved as one, flowing over the golden hills northeast of Sacramento. It was as close as Blair was willing to come to the Great Bear's territory.

A flash of golden fur appeared beside him as Yukon drew even. He loped alongside Blair, easily half again as large as Blair's wolf form. His sober brown eyes fell on Blair, dampening the joy.

They are ready to follow you. The Mother always intended you to lead the pack.

Blair turned from the hills, flowing down switchbacks along a steep ravine. He began circling back to the west, toward home.

I know, he thought back. *I intend to. I've been dodging this for a long time, but that time has passed.*

He leapt over a boulder, tongue lolling from his mouth as he sprinted through the snow. This was incredible. Dozens of dogs yipped and barked in his wake, sniffing at plants or marking territory. Yukon stayed even with Blair, loping along in wide strides.

Blair was silent, sniffing at the air with his powerful nostrils. He considered Yukon's words, and knew they were true. He needed to take up the reins of the pack, and to start rebuilding northern California. The war with the Builders was coming, and there were likely other threats out there, too. Windigo, at the very least, though Liz and Alicia had left in search of him.

Even now Blair could feel Liz somewhere to the northwest. She was tired, but happy.

So how do I start leading? Is there something official I need to do, some sort of shaping?

Yukon cocked his head, giving Blair a confused look. *You lead.*

Blair realized the problem. He was looking at this from his background as a junior college teacher. He was considering psychology and anthropology and culture, and a whole bunch of other factors that only clouded the issue. To a dog—or a wolf—there was only action.

If he wanted to lead this pack, then he didn't need to think about it. He needed to *do* it. Action was what he needed. So Blair acted.

He turned north to parallel the Sierras, diving off another rock and sprinting down the trail. Blair called to the packmind, to every last mongrel within a dozen miles. *Run. Run fast and free. We hunt for survivors. We are their champions.*

The pack responded with an outcry of joy, leaping eagerly down the hill after Blair. Their minds reveled at the connection, at the shared extension of their senses. In that moment, Blair finally understood what the Great Pack was. He understood why the Mother had created that pack, and the role it had filled during the previous cycle.

Such things cannot be explained, Ka-Dun. They must be experienced, his beast rumbled. It was clearly pleased. *Taking up this mantle makes all who share the pack greater. It makes us whole. You are that which bonds the pack together, and without you it will always be incomplete.*

Blair continued to run, reaching out experimentally to the packmind. Sharing this much of himself was difficult, especially since every time he'd ever lowered his guard he'd regretted it. Yet here the intermingling felt right.

To his surprise Blair felt other minds, not just dogs. Other champions ran with the pack, each the leader of a smaller pack. They had acknowledged his authority, glorying in the connection just as their canine companions did.

On and on they ran, fanning out through the trees as they began to climb in elevation. If they continued along this path it would bring them to Lake Tahoe eventually. Blair had no way of knowing how fast they were moving, but he'd have guessed twenty-five miles an hour for most of the pack. That shouldn't be possible for a normal dog.

They are not normal, Ka-Dun. You are shaping them, even without realizing it. When they are near you, they grow stronger—faster. This is an ability you can consciously control. You can make your pack much greater than it is now, a skill we will need for the battles to come.

That was an interesting revelation, one that made a great deal of sense. Somehow the Mother had shaped Yukon in exactly that way. He was at least three times as large as he'd been when she first discovered him, and had learned to shift to human form. Isis had somehow re-written his genetic code, and so far as Blair could tell she'd done it without the aid of an Ark. The virus she'd crafted, the one that had made him what he was, must have contained that same ability. He just needed to learn to use it.

Flee. Flee. Do not go to the high places. A frantic fox's mind called from the hillside above. It shared images of a massive bear slaughtering a pack of coyotes while the frightened fox hid in a patch of snow.

Blair pulled up short, sending up a spray of white. Yukon paused next to Blair, studying him with those large brown eyes, waiting to see how Blair would handle this.

Should he investigate further? Deal with this Great Bear? He glanced at the scars on Yukon's right flank, where the Bear's claws had swiped him. Yukon was strong, stronger than many Ka-Dun. This Bear was not to be trifled with.

Join us. You are safe. We are many. Blair thought back to the fox. He knew the rest of the packmind was listening, just as Yukon was. *We will lead you to our home, in the valleys where the sun sets. There are no bears there, and you will be safe.*

I do not believe so, mighty one, the fox thought back. *Soon we will reach the end of the trees, and the notdeads will catch us.*

We will protect you, from the bears and the notdeads, Blair thought back. He could feel the fox's skepticism, but there was hope there, too. The fox came closer, creeping toward their pack. A moment later, a small vixen darted after, following her mate.

Blair continued north. They would find other survivors, swelling the pack.

Chapter 42- Hunting

Liz filled her water bottle from the Russian River, though the trickle of water could hardly be considered a river. That was alarming. Droughts had been a problem her entire life, but they'd gotten worse in the years leading up to the end of the world. She'd always assumed that was due to mankind's hand in climate change, as the research overwhelmingly supported that conclusion.

In the five years she'd been gone the situation hadn't improved, despite mankind no longer producing the vast clouds of CO_2 they'd been belching out for two centuries. Perhaps the damage was already too severe, or maybe mankind hadn't been as responsible as they'd assumed. Whatever the reason, California's climate was definitely changing.

"Have you set up rain catchment systems?" she called to Alicia. It was the first time they'd spoken in over an hour.

The teen sat on a rock a few dozen paces away. She was staring down the hillside they'd just climbed, down at the pine forests bordering Sonoma County. A rippling sea of green covered the horizon to the north, extending over higher and higher hills as it approached Mendocino County.

She blinked at Liz. "What do you mean?"

"As our population grows, water is going to become more and more of an issue," Liz explained. She picked up her pack, sliding the straps over her shoulders. "We should start building cisterns. Every family should have one. You line the roof of their houses with tarps, and those tarps funnel rain water into big drums. My parents used to do that, and it would give them four or five thousand gallons a year."

"We don't really have water problems, though. There are plenty of streams, and we've got water filters from the local REI to use on stagnant ponds. Enough to last a few years, I'd imagine." Alicia hopped down from the rock. She picked up her pack, which was about half the size of Liz's.

"By the time we know there's a water problem, it will be too late. Droughts can last years, and the more water we have the more insulated we are."

They started back to the road, following Highway 101 toward the summit of yet another pass. Patchy clouds had clustered there, and Liz suspected they'd run into rain before the end of the day.

"I'll order it as soon as we get back," Alicia said. "It shouldn't be too hard, and it seems like a smart move." She quickened her pace and fell into step next to Liz. "I, uh, I wanted to say sorry. For being so rude when you and Blair got back."

"You don't have anything to apologize for." Liz tightened the pack's strap across her chest, distributing the weight a little more evenly. "We left, and didn't come back. You have every right to be angry. The things you accomplished…it's amazing, Alicia. I couldn't be more proud."

"Still, I'm sorry," Alicia said. She wouldn't look at Liz. "I'm finally starting to believe you guys might stick around, and that's a good thing because we need you. What Blair did in San Francisco…I've never seen anything like that. The way he handled those deathless, it was like they were children. He destroyed an entire roomful of their strongest leaders. It's just crazy, you know?"

"I know." Liz couldn't help but smile. "Blair is really coming into his own. He's a pretty amazing guy, and he will always do the right thing. In this case that means staying to protect everything you've built. Blair said he was going to do that, and he's as good as his word. So am I. We've been through a lot, and it's time to rebuild. Blair's position as Ark Lord gives us a lot of resources to do that."

"Do you really think we can get rid of Windigo?" Alicia asked. She brushed a lock of hair from her face, but the wind immediately blew it back. It made her look younger, a willowy young woman not far removed from a gangly pre-teen. But it did nothing to diminish the hardness in her eyes, a sobering look no one that young should ever wear.

"Honestly? I don't know." Liz continued up the hill.

The road finally leveled off as they crested the summit. They picked their way past a rusting gas station and a McDonald's.

"I don't really understand what he is," Liz said. "I've heard of the Wendigo, but everything I know comes from an episode or two of

Supernatural."

I can enlighten you, Ka-Ken, Wepwawet rumbled in her mind. *Windigo was known, even across the ocean. He predates the Mother's arrival in these lands. The tales I have heard suggest he predates mankind. We do not know where he comes from, only that he devours his prey and has an insatiable appetite. We believed him to be some sort of spirit.*

Alicia spoke on the heels of Wepwawet. "There has to be a way to stop him. After seeing what Blair can do, I believe that. We'll catch him, and after that we'll finally have some peace. I can't even imagine what that will be like."

She wore her hope plainly, and that scared Liz. That same hope left her vulnerable to disappointment.

"Neither can I," Liz said. She tightened her baseball cap to keep the wind from prying it off. "There always seems to be another threat, but you know what? We've dealt with them all, and we'll deal with this, too."

They continued up the road, descending into the first valley. It would take days to explore it all, but if Windigo was out there they were going to find him.

Chapter 43- The Great Pack

Blair closed his eyes, reaching out to the packmind. He swelled the boundaries, pushing them further than he'd yet tried. He called to every Ka-Dun within forty miles, inviting them to join him at the SRJC campus in downtown Santa Rosa—Santa Rosa Junior College, his employer once upon a time.

Answers chorused back as a veritable army of dogs escorted their Ka-Duns. They trickled in, clustering around the eternal oak tree he'd been waiting under. The tree stood in the center of a grassy field bordering half a dozen large, brick buildings, and had been there for as long as students had been attending SRJC.

Blair hadn't chosen this place based purely on nostalgia. SRJC had been one of the finest junior colleges in the nation, and the campus was comprised of sturdy brick buildings. They were a little weathered, but still in great repair. The apartment buildings around the campus hadn't fared as well, but that could be fixed easily enough.

"What do you intend to do, Ka-Dun?" Yukon asked. Today he was in human form, but he lay casually in the grass just like a dog. That fascinated the anthropologist in Blair. Yukon was a dog who'd become a man, and Blair was a man who could become a dog—or a wolf, anyway. Their origins changed their perceptions in so many ways.

"I'm going to do what you asked. I'm going to lead." Blair knelt next to the oak, picking up one of the scarlet leaves that had accumulated beneath the mighty giant. It crunched in his hand. "We have many champions, but from what I can see everyone is their own little island. We don't work together very much, outside those few pairs who've mated."

Leaves whirled in a sudden wind as John Rivers blurred up to them. A few moments later another Ka-Dun appeared, then another. Over the next minute and a half Blair counted nineteen arrivals. Most stood away from each other, respectful but distant. A few chatted with each other or exchanged friendly smiles, but there was definitely a distance between them, an aloofness.

Blair waited until the crowd had swelled as large as he thought it might. He walked slowly to the base of the ancient oak, then turned to face the sea of placid canine faces turned in his direction. Many of the champions were in wolf form, though John Rivers and a few others stood as men.

"Thank you all for coming, and coming so quickly," Blair began. He gestured expansively, taking them all in. "Each of you leads your own pack, some large and some small. You vary in power, and in knowledge. Yet we all share the same goal. We protect. We ensure a future for both humanity and for the Great Pack. This legacy was given to us by a woman who taught me much, a woman most of you know as the Mother."

Awed whispers filled the packmind, but many of the Ka-Duns stared at him impassively. They had heard what he'd done in San Francisco, but these warriors were proud. They were used to being the ones with the power. Having someone like him breeze in and demonstrate an Ark Lord's power couldn't have been easy, and Blair knew that if he was going to gain their support he'd have to first earn their respect.

"I chose this place as a meeting spot because of what it represents: a place of higher learning." He paused, letting his eyes roam across the assembled faces. They were curious now, even the hostile ones. "Isis made the Ka-Ken our warriors, which makes us the scholars. It falls on us to learn everything we can about shaping, and to share that knowledge freely. We will need those skills in the coming days. Shaping can do nearly anything, and I've seen some incredible innovations. I'm sure you all have, too."

A fiery-haired kid in his twenties stepped from the line, and walked straight up to Blair. He looked a bit like a young Trevor. "So that's it, then? You walk up like you own the world and we're just supposed to sit at the feet of the master like good little puppies? I don't fucking think so. Why should we listen to you? Because you control a big rock in the middle of the bay? Why don't you go back there and lord over your deathless buddies?"

Blair's beast gave a low, deep growl. *You cannot allow his impudence, or your standing in the pack will suffer, Ka-Dun.*

Blair took a step closer to the young champion. The kid was easily two inches taller than Blair, so Blair had to stare up at him. That position might be reversed in warform, but that wouldn't instill the lesson Blair needed to impart here. He needed cooperation, not obedience inspired by fear. These people needed to learn to trust him. At the same time, he couldn't allow them to perceive him as weak.

"What's your name?" Blair asked. He kept his tone even, expressing no emotion.

"Zee. Everyone else here already knows that, because we're a family." He poked Blair in the chest with a finger, hard. "You're a stranger. We don't know you. We don't need you."

"Zee, since you know everyone here, who would you say the best shaper is? The one with the best control over his pack?" Blair asked. He already knew what he thought the answer was.

"John Rivers is the strongest shaper," Zee said warily. "His dogs are bigger and stronger than the rest of ours, and he's got more of them. Why?"

"Because I didn't call you here to sit at my feet like I'm some sort of guru," Blair said. He poked Zee hard in the chest, just like the kid had done to him. "I called us here to learn together. I'm not very good at shaping animals. I have almost no experience doing it. So I intend to study under John Rivers, because he can teach me to be a better shaper. Many of us have our own specialties. I have a friend who is incredible at telekinesis. It's a talent, and I'm sure everyone here has something they're talented in."

"And just what are you talented in?" Zee asked. He leaned in, looming over Blair as he balled his fists.

"Speed." Blair blurred, punching Zee in the gut. The blow launched Zee across the grass, all the way into the side of a building fifty yards away. The brick cracked with impact, and Zee slumped to the ground. Blair blurred next to Zee's battered form, standing over him.

The kid glared up at him, one hand snapping his broken arm back into place. "You think that impresses me? So what if you're faster? You're just a bully."

"Let me be very clear, Zee," Blair said, dropping into a crouch. He spoke loudly enough that the rest of the Ka-Dun could hear. "Every last one of us has a responsibility. We must protect our packs. The best way to do that is if we come together as one. If we become the Great Pack—one united whole that exists to achieve a singular purpose: to keep our people alive. If we want to do that, we need to be strong and wise enough to deal with any threat. Trust me when I say those threats are coming, and our only hope of overcoming them is learning to work together."

"I stand with Blair," John Rivers yelled. Many of the Ka-Dun turned to face the older man. "We've kept this place alive over the past few years, but only just. We've taken a lot of casualties. If we don't want to take more, then we need to get better. We need to learn to work together. Clearly Blair has a lot to teach us. He's learned directly from the Mother, and he's got control of an entire Ark. We'd be idiots not to learn everything he can teach us. Are you an idiot, Zee?"

Zee glared back, trapped by the question. "You don't have any cause to make fun of me, John Rivers," he said. He rose to his feet, dusting himself off. "I'm not an idiot. No one here is. But it isn't smart to blindly trust this guy. We don't know him."

"We know that he stopped the deathless," John said. "We know that his Ka-Ken is helping to hunt Windigo. We know that Blair is strong enough to keep this place safe, and that the Mother trusted him." He walked over to stand next to Blair, wrapping an arm around Blair's shoulder. "I consider Blair a friend, and am proud to have him in the packmind. I know you all haven't spent time with him yet, but I urge you to come at this with an open mind. Blair can help us if we let him—help us build something lasting, so our children have a place to call their own. So what do you say, Zee?"

Blair offered Zee a hand, and the kid took it. Blair helped him to his feet.

"All right," Zee allowed. "I'll give this guy a shot."

Chapter 44- Learning

"Show me again?" Blair asked. He suppressed a sigh, rubbing exhaustedly at his eyes.

John Rivers peered at him impatiently. "Pay attention this time. You're an Ark Lord. This should be child's play."

"The Ark didn't come with an instruction manual," Blair protested. Then he caught himself. That was an excuse. He took a slow breath. "Just show me again. This time I'll get it."

John Rivers gestured at the cluster of dogs lounging on the grass. Energy pulsed through John Rivers, then a burst of complex signals flowed from his outstretched hand. It enveloped the dogs, and the change was immediate. The dogs leapt to their feet, muscles swelling and bones elongating. When the process was complete, the dogs were half again as large, and Blair could see the link between them and John Rivers. A steady signal was being broadcast, sustaining the change.

"I can keep feeding them power—making them stronger still, or just giving them more endurance," John Rivers explained. Some of the irritation had left his face. "The more animals I do it with, the more taxing it is. The most I can manage is about a hundred, but only for a short time. That's why we keep our packs smaller, at a size each person can manage. With your strength, you could manage hundreds. Maybe thousands."

The part where Blair shouldn't be struggling with *just one dog* was heavily implied.

Blair took several steps closer to the dogs, who eyed him with interest. He stretched out a hand, then quickly lowered it. He couldn't just keep trying the same thing.

"You can make them larger and stronger," Blair said. "How about faster?"

"I've shared my blur, but it's so taxing that I can only keep it up for a few seconds," John Rivers allowed. "Why don't we focus on the basics, though? Just make them a little bit larger."

Blair stretched out his hand again, but this time he ignored John

Rivers's advice. He didn't try to make the dogs larger and stronger; he'd already tried that several times with absolutely no luck.

But blurring was his speciality. It was something he excelled at more than any champion he'd met. If he was gifted in anything, then that was it.

A wave of signals burst from his hand, spreading across the pack. It was different than his last attempt, and he had more luck discerning the complex signal. It looked a good deal like his own blur ability, somehow transmitted to others.

Run, Blair thought to the packmind. *Feel the wind.*

The pack responded. The dogs bounded to their feet, blurring all over the grassy field. A Doberman tackled a Rottweiler playfully, and the two zipped all over the field, motion blurs in their wake. Blair could feel the enormous flow of power from him to the animals, but it barely taxed the flow from the Ark.

"There we go," he said. He gave a triumphant smile. "I can keep this up all day. I think I could probably do it for a lot more dogs, too."

"Wow," John Rivers said. He scrubbed his fingers through the back of his hair as he watched the dogs. "Now I can see how you took out the deathless. The amount of energy flowing from you is probably more than every other Ka-Dun could produce together. Now, that said, don't get all full of yourself. You need to get better at this. If we can teach you to make your pack larger and stronger, and then also faster…I feel bad for anyone we go up against."

"That's the real trick, isn't it?" Blair released the blur. "I can feel them, and I can see how and why the signal effects them. But I don't know what kind of signal to broadcast to make them larger. I mean, I can see what you're doing. I just can't seem to reproduce it. I don't know why."

"What about that mindshare thing you've been going on about?" John Rivers asked. "That's like the packmind right? I'm not very good at working with minds, but if you want to link, maybe you can learn how to do it that way."

"Worth a shot, right?" Blair asked. He closed his eyes. "Just relax a little. I'm going to initiate the mindshare."

The process had grown much easier since Blair had first experimented with touching someone else's mind. Blair opened himself, sharing a torrent of memories, thoughts, and his very identify. John Rivers did the same, and hundreds of competing sensations washed over Blair. He focused on John's time learning to shape, seeing how he'd first bonded his loyal chocolate lab, his pack alpha.

He saw how that pack grew, how John Rivers added coyotes, foxes, and dozens of neighborhood dogs. Blair watched the pack fight, watched them struggle to protect their tiny flock of humans. He watched as John Rivers struggled, and realized instantly why John Rivers was so adept at empowering his pack. John Rivers had *needed* the pack to be bigger and stronger, and had focused on making that happen. Just like Blair had *needed* to be faster, and so he had been.

Now, he needed to consciously control what he'd learned to do instinctually. Blair imagined that this was the Yoda-like lesson the Mother had always been too busy to impart. *Control.* He must learn control.

Blair retreated from John Rivers's mind. The older man watched him with wonder, apparently still reeling from whatever he'd seen in Blair's mind. "You've seen so much in such a short time. I had no idea. Everything you've been through. Everything you've had to sacrifice. It's…I'm sorry Blair. Thank you, for everything you've done to preserve this world."

"Don't get soft on me, teach," Blair said. He couldn't help but laugh. "Mindsharing is incredible. The effects will fade, but you'll always retain some of my memories. And I will retain a few of yours."

Blair turned back to the pack. He extended his hand, calling on the desperate need John Rivers had felt. The pack needed to be larger. Stronger. Power surged through Blair, and the signal he'd seen John Rivers use burst from his hand. The dogs began to grow, muscles thickening and bones extending. If anything, they grew larger than when John Rivers had tried to effect the same thing.

"You are really scary. You realize that, right?" John Rivers said. He was grinning.

Chapter 45- Books

Liz knelt next to the pile of desiccated entrails. They'd been left at the base of the stop sign near the center of the scenic town of Healdsburg. Awful runes had been scrawled on the sign itself, some sort of alien script that reminded her of the sigils within the Arks. Maybe Blair would recognize it.

"This is his handiwork?" Liz asked. She moved away from the grisly remains. They were old, but the stench lingered.

"Definitely," Alicia said. "Windigo picks off prey one by one, gradually emptying a town. He waits for people to flee, and everyone in the town can hear their screams. Then he leaves signs, like this. We don't know why or what they mean." She was trembling, her skin ashen. "Eventually, the survivors get together and try to flee. He hunts them. A few get away, but most think they were allowed to live so they could tell other places about Windigo."

"And the survivors never get a look at this thing?" Liz asked. She headed toward the little row of shops bordering a patch of green at the town center—a place where townspeople had probably attended everything from local concerts to farmer's markets. It stood empty now, the grass brown and dying.

The storefronts had a few broken windows, and the paint had faded a bit. But this place had been cared for, and recently—until whatever this creature was had slaughtered them in some sick game.

"Some have, but their stories conflict. Some say Windigo is an old crone with sharp claws. Others claim he's a wild-eyed Indian come to get revenge for the death of his people. The most common description is a tall, skinny monster with deer's antlers." Alicia walked alongside Liz, darting furtive glances inside the shadowed shops as they walked past. "We've guessed that maybe he's a shapeshifter, but we have no way to verify that."

"What sorts of abilities does this thing have?" Liz asked. She stopped in front of a bookstore. It was intact, no broken windows. Inside she could see shelves lined with books. She hadn't picked up a novel in months. It would be nice to curl up with a book, in between bouts of saving the world.

"Nothing has been confirmed, but we believe it can walk the shadows. It's fast, so it can probably blur. I guess it's most similar to a deathless, but we don't know how accurate those accounts are." Alicia peered inside the book store. "Why did you stop here?"

"Books are going to be vital to rebuilding. Without the internet, all our science, medicine, history…this is the only record." Liz checked the door, but it was locked. She gave a reluctant sigh, then kicked the door. The door frame splintered, and the door hung drunkenly inward. "I'd love to send a team up here to bring these books back. Is anyone using the Santa Rosa Library?"

"I don't think anyone has done anything with it," Alicia said. "They certainly haven't mentioned it to me if they have. I imagine it's in good repair. I could have someone check."

"That would be great. I'd love to start using it. Are you running any kind of schools?" Liz asked. She ducked into the book store, scanning subjects as she made her way through the shelves.

"We…really haven't had time," Alicia admitted. She stared at her shoes, her hair obscuring her face.

Liz stop and walked back to Alicia. She put a hand on her shoulder. "I'm sorry. I didn't mean to criticize. I know you've had enough to deal with. I'd just like to start thinking about these things. We're going to need schools if we want to build something permanent here."

Alicia nodded, visibly relieved. "There's so much to take care of. I get up early and go to bed late, but it always feels like I'm falling further behind. I hate being in charge."

"I hate it, too, which just makes me even more proud of you." Liz drew Alicia into a hug. "This new world isn't easy, and you've made the best of it. I wish I could say the dark times were over, but I can't. We have a lot of tough battles ahead. I can promise you this, Alicia: you'll never have to face them alone again."

Alicia returned the hug fiercely, but disengaged swiftly. She started wiping at her eyes, still avoiding looking at Liz, and cleared her throat. "Do you think we can find a book here on Windigo? I know there were legends about him, but nobody can give me details. Just vague recollections of Wendigo being cannibals."

"That's a great idea." Liz moved to the next aisle, scanning titles. She passed among the shelves, inhaling deeply. She loved the scent of old books. The place was pretty small, and the titles were eclectic. Most were used, probably recycled countless times through the community. "Here we are—myths and legends. Wendigo are a Canadian myth, I think."

"Doesn't seem very mythological to me." Alicia came around the corner, brushing a lock of hair from her face as she scanned the spines of books on one of the shelves. "Not when its leaving entrails outside."

"You said that this thing was constantly killing, right?" Liz said. She finally found a book with *The Wendigo* on the spine. It looked like a novel, and the copyright date was 1910. Not exactly current.

"Yeah, pretty much all the time. The attacks started about six months ago, at least far enough south that we knew about them. People had come down from Eureka before that, and they told tales of Windigo."

"So why did the attacks stop now?" Liz asked. "No one has seen Windigo for over a week. Doesn't that seem strange to you?" She thumbed through the novel, but it didn't look like it would be useful. She dropped it into her pack anyway.

"It is strange, but I can't imagine Windigo just leaving. I don't know why the attacks stopped, but I'm betting they'll start back up again soon. He's probably just toying with us." Alicia looked dejected. "I wanted to come home with better news, not news that we can't find him."

"I know, but we've looked everywhere I think we can. It's time to head back. If he makes another appearance, we'll deal with him."

Chapter 46- Struggle

The Great Bear was vanishing. Each day he slept, and when he awoke he was less a bear and more something dark. His fur had fallen out, and his body was wasting away. His arms were longer, as were his desiccated antlers.

But those weren't even the worst changes.

He hungered for flesh, and slaughtered anything that came near his path. The very instant he'd finished feeding, he craved flesh again; even now the hunger was driving him to find it. He wandered, Windigo's dark presence nudging him steadily westward. He knew that, but the pain and rage made it so difficult to fight. So difficult to resist.

Each day he slept longer, and today he was already growing weary. He'd risen just two hours before. How many more days would it be until he didn't awake at all?

Not long, foolish old Bear, Windigo taunted. *We have nearly reached the lands claimed by the Ka-Dun. Soon, you will help me take the key from him.*

The Great Bear had been a fool, so certain that he was the strongest predator in his mountains. Now he was the tool of a mad spirit—one that seemed determined to kill this new Ark Lord. The Great Bear had no love for the Mother's wolves, but didn't wish death upon them. They lived in their forests, and he roamed his mountains.

Yet you will kill the Ka-Dun for me anyway, Windigo whispered. *You know you can't stop me.*

The Great Bear lumbered through the darkness, finally breaking free of the tree line. He'd never come this far from the mountains, not in all his centuries. Before him lay long, flat floodplains. He'd heard of the river delta, but had never been interested enough to see it. The brown grass and the skeletons of many buildings did not impress him. This place was lifeless. He longed to turn around, to head back to the comforting granite peaks.

There is a refuge from all this, Windigo whispered seductively in the back of his mind. *Relax. Sleep. There is no pain in sleep.*

The Great Bear roared, punching a rotting wooden bench. It shattered into kindling, and he felt a little better. "I am still in control, spirit. You do not have me yet. Nor will I go quietly. I will fight you until I am no more."

That will happen sooner than you think, Mighty Bear. Each day I reshape your body a bit more. Soon you will become what I have made you: the devourer of man and beast. You will stalk this Ark Lord, and one by one you will kill his champions. You will strip away the Great Pack, and every last living thing between us and the Ark Lord.

"And then? You want me to devour the Ark Lord, don't you?" the Bear roared. He caught sight of his reflection in a pool of stagnant water, and knew despair. Windigo had not lied. He was hideous, more monster than bear. All in a matter of days. What would the changes be in another moon?

The Great Bear despaired. He was truly trapped, and had no idea how he might escape. He wished the Mother were here to aid him.

Chapter 47- Swarmed

Mournful shrieks came from the thick wall of jungle bordering the wide, slow river. Trevor sat in the front of the canoe, using an oar to keep them near the center of the dirty water. He estimated it at about seventy feet across, narrower than it had been for most of their trip.

"You thinking what I'm thinking?" Trevor asked, directing the question at Jordan.

"Yeah, this would be a great place for an ambush. The river is shallow, so if anything with a fear of water wanted to attack this would be the place to do it." Jordan tested the depth with his oar. "Those shrieks seem pretty personal. I'm betting the mapinguara we killed had family, and they're more than a little pissed about his death."

The shrieks stopped, and a veil of silence fell over the jungle. A moment later, rain began falling in thick sheets, muffling all other sound and dropping visibility to less than a dozen feet. Trevor could just barely make out the wall of vegetation, and that made him uneasy. The rain was warm, plastering his shirt to his skin. A steady stream of water dripped from the brim of his baseball cap, which was at least keeping it out of his face.

"Leti, what's beyond that bend?" Jordan yelled over the rain.

"I do not know." Leti's voice battled with the rain, and Trevor strained to hear her. "I've never been this far in. We are told little of the dangers of the jungle, only that if we cannot find a way to survive them, then we are not worthy of finding the Mother's city."

"These creatures are intelligent, more so than they look at least," Anput interjected. The rain had plastered her dark hair to her pale face. "You're right about this being a good place for an ambush. Leti, when you said they were afraid of the water, you didn't say why. Will the rain keep them away? Or is it something about the river that they don't like?"

"There are dangerous things in the water," Leti called back. "But I do not think those things could be a threat to a mapinguara. Perhaps one of the larger anacondas. They prowl the waterways."

Trevor glanced at the muddy brown water. Anything could lay under those depths. He hadn't seen anything, but before the end he'd loved river fishing. There were fish in there, he was sure of it. It made sense that there must be predators that preyed on those fish. An entire ecosystem, invisible to the surface.

The shrieks resumed, much closer now. They came from the north side of the river, all along the trees they were slowly passing. The others had gone still. Leti had her golden boomerang out, and Jordan had withdrawn his .45 from his thigh holster. The weapon was mostly an afterthought, but Trevor drew his own sidearm. The weight was reassuring, but he missed the boomerang.

A hairy arm emerged from the trees, slashing angrily at the water. The blow fell less than ten feet from their canoe, and Trevor caught sight of the beast's brutish face through the rain. The stench was overpowering. Another mapinguara slapped the water, then a third. Their shrieks reached a crescendo where the river was narrowest, but their reach fell short.

Trevor guided the canoe closer to the southern shore, gaining them another dozen feet. It still felt like the creatures were far too close—close enough to be a real threat.

"I really don't like the look of those things," Trevor said. He turned to face Jordan in the rear of the canoe. "Do you think we should ground the boat and chance going on foot?"

Before Jordan could answer, a thick, furry arm burst from the trees on the southern shore. It thumped against the side of the boat, but found no purchase. The force of the blow pushed the boat toward the middle of the river, safely out of reach. The failure seemed to drive the mapinguara insane, and it leapt into the water in pursuit of the canoe.

"Oh shit," Trevor said. He squeezed off a trio of shots, but the bullets glanced off the beast's hide. "That thing is a lot bigger than the one we killed. I think mama is pissed."

"She's gaining on us," Anput said. The vampire squeezed off a shot from her boomerang, but the green energy washed harmlessly over the mapinguara's thick hide. The stench of burnt hair filled the air, so strong that not even the rain could dampen it.

The water around the mapinguara began to thrash and churn. Trevor caught sight of silver bodies, and sharp fins. They were big fish; even the smaller ones were at least a foot long. Some of the larger ones were closer to three feet.

They swarmed around the mapinguara, which seemed to ignore them— at first. Then one of the fish leapt from the water, latching onto the mapinguara's lip. Trevor caught a flash of white fangs, and then the fish tumbled back into the water. A piece of the mapinguara's tough skin was missing, blood flowing freely from the wound.

The mapinguara stumbled, toppling into the water. Fish swarmed around it, tearing into the sensitive flesh around its eyes and mouth. Red froth filled the water. The mapinguara gave a pained shriek, disappearing below the surface. When it reemerged, patches of its face had been eaten away, and a fish tail jutted from its mouth.

More and more fish filled the water, and then something jerked the mapinguara from its feet. This time, the creature stayed under the water. Red-brown water frothed around the point where it had disappeared, and the thrashing reached a crescendo.

Then the water stilled. The surface sat unbroken. The only evidence that anything had happened was a slightly darker hue to the water, but that faded quickly.

"What the hell were those things?" Trevor said in a low, reverent tone.

"Piranha," Leti said, "but not like any I've ever seen. They were larger and faster than the ones I've heard tales of. I do not know how they pierced the mapinguara's hide, but at least we know why the beasts fear the water." She shuddered. "It is a bad way to die."

"Let's hope those things don't suddenly decide they like the taste of boat," Jordan said. He used his oar with long powerful strokes, propelling them further from the carnage.

Chapter 48- Report

Hades strode through the corridors of Olympus, smiling as he stared down through the balcony's glass floor at the Ark below. Tendrils of electricity crackled along the containment vessels the grey men had provided, feeding power into Olympus.

Not all the power, of course. The grey men kept the bulk for themselves, but had been willing to share scraps. A proud man would turn such scraps away. A smart man took them graciously, with an eye for how he might acquire more.

He studied the three identical crafts, each a floating black pyramid surrounded by a green nimbus of power. They looked like miniature Arks, but were clearly far more advanced. Those crafts could leave the planet and journey into the cosmos. Who knew what other feats the grey men and their Builder masters were capable of?

Hades folded his smooth hands under his golden robes, making his way past the dozens of demonic courtiers he now employed. He left them very little free will, and they universally cast their eyes to the ground as he passed. Some might argue that there was little point in ruling a mindless army, but Hades disagreed. None of his minions were decent company, but there was no chance they'd betray him. His servants with more free will, on the other hand, were an ever-present threat.

"Speaking of which, it's past time we received an update from Nox," Hades mused. The horned demons he'd just passed nodded enthusiastically, though it was doubtful they knew what they were agreeing with. Hades breezed past them, crossing several golden platforms until he reached the Orb of Vulcan.

The swirling globe of blue light was suspended over a golden disk, both objects crafted by Vulcan in the primordial days before Olympus had been constructed. Three such artifacts had been created, and two still survived. They allowed the bearer to communicate over vast distances, a feat that most had considered miraculous during his day.

Today such communications were more common, but that only made the orbs more valuable. So far as Hades knew, they were one of the few means of communications that the grey men were unaware of. They'd never seen the orbs, and he'd made doubly sure that Nox knew he needed to keep the sister orb a secret. Fortunately, Nox understood and practiced discretion. Nox reminded Hades a great deal of himself, though Nox had inherited some troubling moralities from his upbringing in this strange new world.

Hades sat gracefully on the golden throne, willing it to rise. It floated into the air, bobbing comfortably next to the orb. Through the transparent floor, he caught sight of a wild bolt of lightning, darting from the Ark toward one of the orbiting ships. The lightning was less frequent than it had been in the beginning, now that the Ark was essentially drained of power. Keeping it that way was one of his primary motivations, at least until he was able to obtain the key to that Ark.

The orb began to pulse, and Hades gestured. A signal burst from his hand, establishing the link. The orb flared bright blue, then the brilliance dimmed. Nox's head and shoulders were displayed within. He wore the garb that had been popular among the nobles of his world, a black suit with a white shirt. The tie around his neck looked confining. Hades would never understand how a man could willingly bend to such obtuse fashions.

"I hope for your sake that you have something of worth to report, vassal," Hades demanded. Dealing with Nox always angered him, and he struggled to master himself.

"I do, my lord." Those words were delivered through gritted teeth, but they *were* delivered. "Camiero's forces have engaged the champions along the entire eastern border of the Amazon. We've made seven incursions, and Camiero's forces are getting the worst of it. My projections suggest he'll have no choice but to pull out within three weeks. Less, if the werewolves get more aggressive."

"That should be plenty of time for you to accomplish your task, yes?" Hades asked. He raised both hands, adjusting the heavy golden crown. Sometimes he longed to set it aside, but he'd never willingly deprive himself of the strength and clarity it offered.

"I believe so," Nox said. His steely eyes grew even harder. "You realize the danger this puts us in, right? You sold me on opposing the Builders from the inside, but if we give them the Proto Ark we're as good as handing them the Arks themselves. They'll be able to make more keys, Hades. Is that really the kind of power you want to hand over?"

"I promised the masters that I would secure the Proto Ark," Hades said. All humor was gone now. He stared hard at Nox. "You know what they will do to us if they think we are stalling. Their forces are limited, but if they wanted to destroy Olympus they could do it. If they wanted to destroy the satellites you commandeered they could do it. The opportunity for us to betray them will arise, but until it does we have no choice but to capitulate to their wishes."

"Of course we have a choice," Nox snapped. It was a rare lapse of emotion, and Hades drew back in surprise. "I've learned that Ark Lord Blair has returned, along with his Ka-Ken. We could work with them, come up with a plan to wipe out the grey men. We could resist."

"We could," Hades agreed, "but we will not." He recovered his composure, straightening. "I sometimes forget how young you are. Tell me, Nox, what do you think the Ark Lords will do to us after the grey men are defeated? Both of us are demonically tainted. Both of us have already conspired with their enemies."

"They'd wipe us out," Nox said, "or try to at least. But they wouldn't do that until *after* the grey men had been dealt with." He shook his head, eyeing Hades as if he thought him a fool. "If we throw in with the grey men, we won't survive the arrival of the Builders. They're coming to wipe us out, and you know it. If we throw in with those resisting, we have a chance. If we work with the grey men, we guarantee our destruction."

"Not so," Hades countered. He gave Nox his most condescending smile. "We are a dagger at the belly of the grey men, and we know they bleed just as we do. The time will soon come for us to reveal ourselves, but until that happens we share a common goal. The thing most desired by the grey men is a Primary Access Key, yes?"

"Obviously."

"What you, in your youth, do not see is how desperate that makes the grey men," Hades explained. He urged his throne a little closer to the orb. "They will do anything to obtain a Primary Access Key, including making me an Ark Lord. Do you begin to see?"

"You're hoping they'll use the key you create to make you Ark Lord of the Cradle." Nox's eyes widened slightly, the only concession to his apparent surprise. "You really believe they'll honor their bargain, don't you?"

"Why wouldn't they?" Hades asked. He gave a roaring laugh. "They need allies, Nox."

"How so?" Nox asked dubiously.

"Ark Lord Blair was not the only one to return. You recall your friend, Commander Jordan?" Hades asked. "I've received word that he has returned, and is also the bearer of a key. Three Ark Lords have been sighted in total, one of them at the Ark of the Cradle itself. Your former companions are back, Nox. The grey men have larger problems, for the moment at least."

"I hope you know what you're doing," Nox said. "I will head into the jungle tonight. Once I'm in position, I will activate the beacon. You have until then to get me the materials to construct this key. Have them sent to my forward operating base in Brasilia."

The orb went dark. Nox often terminated the connection first. It probably made him feel some semblance of control, which Hades was happy to allow him.

Soon, Hades would have the means of securing himself an Ark. If the plan failed for some reason, he'd simply sacrifice Nox as an offering to appease the grey men. Either way, he'd emerge stronger.

Chapter 49- The Song

Jordan caught himself with a jerk, throwing his hands out to grab the sides of the canoe. He must have nodded off. At some point the rain had stopped, and a low mist had risen over the water. It was otherworldly, like sailing on clouds.

He looked over his right shoulder, then the left. The jungle loomed silently on both sides. There was no sign of pursuit, and there had been no other mapinguara. After the big one had gotten eaten, they'd apparently had enough.

He couldn't much blame them.

"How long was I out?" he asked groggily.

Leti was curled up on her bench, snoring softly. Trevor and Anput were conversing in low tones, but the conversation trailed off when he sat up.

"Maybe two hours?" Trevor called back softly. "All we've been doing is steering the canoe. No sign of pursuit."

"I miss anything interesting?" Jordan asked.

Anput eyed him suspiciously from the front of the canoe.

It was Trevor who answered. "We're talking about the viruses Isis created—specifically, how to modify them. Anput has some theories on how the different strains vary. It's all theoretical stuff, for the moment at least. We'd need access to an Ark, and a fair amount of time, to test any of her theories."

"It's good that someone's thinking about this stuff." Jordan dipped his oar in the water, propelling them forward with a powerful stroke. The mist swirled away from the boat as they drifted in near silence. "You're welcome to use my Ark when we're done here. I'd be happy to set you up with a lab, and I imagine Roberts could find a way to fund it."

"Wait, did you just ask me to be your roommate?" Trevor asked. He pulled his oar from the water and twisted to face Jordan.

"Crap, I guess I did." Jordan couldn't help but laugh. "I'm not asking you out for beers or anything. But you get the job done, and so far as I can tell you're fighting for the same reasons I am. I can't say we'll always be allies, but for now we need each other."

"And a bromance was born," Anput said. She gave a musical laugh. "While I'm glad that you two are working together, don't you think we ought to focus on why we're here? If you weren't so distracted you'd already feel it."

"Feel what?" Trevor asked. He turned to the jungle, scanning warily.

Jordan reached out experimentally with all senses. At first there was nothing, but after a moment he realized he could hear a rhythmic pulse, so faint it was almost imagined. "What is that?"

"What is what?" Leti rose sleepily to a sitting position. She stifled a yawn.

"That pulsing," Jordan supplied. "I can feel it, almost like a heart beat. It's coming from the jungle—to the southwest, I'd guess."

All sleepiness vanished. Leti sat fully erect, frozen as she stared in the direction Jordan had indicated. Lines tightened around her eyes as the hope bled away. After several moments, she turned defeated eyes on him. "I feel nothing, but I am familiar with what you describe. The ancient texts describe the city as singing. The song grows louder as the city approaches."

"Approaches?" Anput asked. She wore her skepticism openly. "The city comes to us?"

"Yes. It sounds impossible, but every one of my brothers and sisters have told the same tale. We do not find the city, the city finds us." Leti stared a challenge at Anput—one the other woman seemed ready to meet.

"It doesn't matter whether the city finds us or we find the city," Jordan snapped. Both women turned hostile gazes his way. "We're going to follow the sound of that pulsing. If the city finds us, great. Less cutting a path through that jungle. Trevor, can you beach us on the southern shore?"

Trevor nodded, using his oar to guide them toward the dark mass of trees. Mist parted as they glided forward, finally stopping with a thump against the trunk of a fat, squat tree with about a million roots.

Anput was the first out of the boat, blurring into a crouch against one of the trees. Trevor followed her, moving to a trunk on the opposite side of the canoe.

Leti rose slowly, and Jordan braced the boat as she leapt out. She transformed in the air, nine feet of dark fur disappearing into the shadows near the apex of her jump.

Jordan hefted his pack, using his telekinesis to stabilize the canoe. He hopped out, kicking off the tree and landing in a crouch. A wall of vegetation blocked his path.

Jordan sighed, then reached for the machete strapped to the side of his pack. He began hacking at the jungle in broad smooth strokes, cutting a rough path.

"What are you doing?" Leti's disembodied voice came from somewhere above. "That will take forever, and it will anger the jungle."

"You have a better idea?" Jordan asked. He slid the machete back into his sheath.

"We have already offended the land," she said. "We may as well take to the trees. We can move far more quickly, without damaging the jungle. There are many spirits here, and they do not take kindly to strangers— much less strangers who harm their jungle." Leti's voice was already growing more distant as she leapt from tree to tree. He could hear the trees creak as she landed, each time further away. "The faster we move, the more chance we will avoid them. We would do well to be away from here quickly. Do not worry about the deathless. I am sure they can keep up."

"Guess we're Tarzaning this bitch," Jordan muttered. He leapt into the air, kicking off a trunk to gain altitude. He used his telekinesis to extend the jump, then kicked off another tree. He caught a limb fifty feet away, then swung to another.

Well done, Ka-Dun. Do you not feel it? The exhilaration? We were meant to travel like this, masters of this place.

Jordan did enjoy the feeling of swinging through the trees. He lost himself in the motion, gliding through the jungle as fast as any monkey. After the first few jumps he shifted to warform, and the jumps became larger. He guessed he was moving at twenty-five to thirty miles an hour, which was great given how dense the jungle was. He could increase that speed, too, if needed. Blurring would easily allow him to top three hundred miles per hour.

Unfortunately, that kind of shaping would risk revealing their position. It was likely that natives already knew they were here, but no sense making it any easier for them.

Especially if Leti was right about the city finding them.

As they made their way through the jungle, the pulsing grew stronger. Jordan moved toward it, but kept an ear out for his surroundings. He heard the low *squick, squick* of insects, the occasional caw of a macaw. They did pass a single pack of spider monkeys, who gave a few curious calls as they passed.

There was nothing resembling a predator, no eerie supernatural presence oppressing the jungle around them. It all felt a little too easy.

Jordan landed on a branch, and held position. Several moments later Leti shimmered into existence on the branch next to him. "Why have you stopped?"

"Just testing a theory," Jordan replied. He stared in the direction of the pulse, but studied everything in his peripheral vision. If he was right, they were not alone. Something was out there, watching. "Do you feel the pulse yet?"

"Yes." A broad grin slid onto her face. "I began feeling it not long after we left the river. I will not lie, I was concerned when even the deathless heard the city before I did. I was concerned that I had been judged unworthy."

"You have," roared a voice from above.

Jordan recognized Elia's voice immediately.

A beam of intense green light shot down at them, dissolving the tree they were standing on, and they tumbled toward the jungle floor in a mass of burning tree limbs.

Trevor blurred to buy himself time to think. He examined the situation tactically, not liking what he found. A light-furred female in warform had appeared for a split second. One clawed hand was wrapped around a thick tree limb, while the other was pointed in Jordan's direction.

She discharged a beam of green light from the bracelet on her wrist. It seemed similar to the blast the boomerang fired, but this one was darker and more dispersed.

Even with the blur going, he barely saw the Ka-Ken before she began slipping back into the shadows. Trevor leapt toward the werewolf, firing a wave of radiation from both hands.

It wasn't nearly as lethal as the boomerang, but in this instance it proved just as effective. The blast caught the werewolf full in the face, and she tumbled limply from the tree.

Trevor kicked off the trunk of the tree she'd been in, watching as she fell. She disappeared into the foliage, so Trevor did the same. The jungle had gone silent. Dense, wet smoke came from the tree the werewolf had obliterated. It cut visibility, and overpowered anything he might have made out through scent.

The only visible person was Jordan, standing amidst the burning logs. He was in a relaxed stance, waiting.

"Hey, Jordan," Trevor called. He blurred to another limb, not speaking again until he was safely in a new position. "Remember that trick Blair learned back in Peru? The ping?" Trevor blurred again, moving to another tree.

"On it," Jordan called back. Trevor felt something wash over him, tingling at the edges of his mind. He recognized it as the prelude to whatever shaping Blair had used to touch his mind.

Jordan's weapon leapt into his hand and he began firing into the trees. Trevor blurred, following the path of the bullets. He grinned as he realized how Jordan was using them. The bullets weren't designed to kill—they couldn't. What they could do was give away the location of anyone they hit.

Trevor intensified the blur, following the first bullet Jordan had fired. It spun slowly through the air, finally stopping in midair about three feet above a thick tree limb. A few drops of blood fountained into the air, and Trevor fired off a burst of radiation at that location. The move exposed a blond female, her body spinning to the jungle floor.

Green flashes came from another tree, and a third female tumbled to the ground. That had to be Anput. She'd already fled back into the shadows, as had he.

Two more Ka-Ken lunged from the darkness near Trevor. He blocked a savage swipe from the first, but the second punched through his chest with a clawed fist. She bit down on his neck, roaring in rage. A third female appeared, then a fourth. Before either could attack, Leti lunged from the darkness, raging into them in a flurry of claws and teeth.

Another shot came from the trees—Anput with her boomerang. The blast caught Jordan and his two assailants, all three collapsing into a smoking heap.

Trevor came down on one of the werewolves Leti was fighting, digging the claws of one hand into the wolf's neck. He plunged the other into the base of her spine, ripping it out of her back. She screamed, swiping awkwardly at him. Trevor rolled away, disappearing into the shadows.

A pulse of invisible force exploded from Jordan, and Trevor was hurled into the air along with everyone around him. Jordan raised his hands, and the werewolves all hung in midair. Trevor was released, dropping silently to the foliage below.

"Elia, I'm pretty sure you're breaking rules—" Jordan was knocked from his feet by a dark green blast. The werewolves were suddenly released, each fleeing back into the shadows.

A similar blast caught Trevor in the back. The pain was blinding, and he was dimly aware of the ground rushing up at him. Trevor's cheek landed on the warm dirt, and his unfocused gaze settling on a black beetle scuttling across a leaf. His entire body spasmed, and he couldn't seem to make his muscles work.

"Ow." A second blast burned into Trevor, then a third. Blackness overtook him.

Chapter 51- El Dorado

Jordan blurred into a crouch next to Trevor's still-smoking body. It reeked of cooked meat, and worse, less identifiable things. He couldn't check for a pulse, so he decided to trust in deathless physiology. Either Trevor was "alive" or he wasn't. All Jordan could do was win this fight.

He willed a telekinetic bubble, covering both him and Trevor. It was the same he'd used to shelter the group on the bridge back in San Francisco. If it could hold a nuclear blast at bay before he was an Ark Lord, it should damned sure be enough to keep out a few laser shots.

As if in answer to his thoughts, a flurry of dark green bolts rained down, scattering across the surface of his bubble in iridescent ripples. Jordan could feel them sapping the bubble, but he fed more energy back into it. The Ark was much further away now, but he was still drawing a steady flow of power—enough to sustain the bubble indefinitely, if needed.

"Elia," Jordan roared. He spun slowly in place, scanning the trees above him. There was nothing to see, of course. "I'm not going to claim to understand your religion, but I find it hard to believe that ambushing people is considered kosher. If the city judges us worthy, then it finds us. That's how it works right? If we're not worthy, it will hide. So what do you gain out of attacking us?"

At first only the jungle answered, the returning buzz of insects.

Elia finally spoke, "You will not profane the Holy City with your heresy. I will not let you bring our ancient enemy into the very heart of the Mother's kingdom. You are a threat to everything we've built—one I will not allow to continue."

Another flurry of bolts came from the trees, rippling harmlessly off the shield he'd erected. Jordan said nothing, allowing it to continue for long moments. He glanced at Trevor, but the deathless still wasn't moving.

"You can't stop us, Elia."

Elia's form dropped through the trees, and she shifted to human form as she landed. The priestess stalked outside his bubble like a jungle cat. "Your strength has limits, and I am patient. When you drop that bubble, you die.

Your deathless friend is proof that an Ark Lord can be hurt. You are no tougher than we. You can bleed, and you can die."

"I can also kill." Jordan rose from Trevor's side and walked to the edge of the bubble. He stared at Elia through the oily surface. "I'm going to give you one chance, Elia. Withdraw, or I will end you. Don't make me do this."

"Wait," Leti said. She shimmered into view outside the bubble, dropping respectfully to one knee next to Elia. "Elder sister, I beg of you. Do not do this. It isn't right to interfere with a supplicant. I can feel the pull of the city. I can feel it getting stronger. It is not your place to judge. The city does that. Do you really believe the council will condone your actions?"

"You presume to lecture *me*?" Elia leaned closer to Leti and lowered her voice. "You are guiding the ancient enemy to the heart of our power. There is no greater heresy. Your actions are treasonous, and it is the duty of every sister to put an end to you."

Jordan was distracted by the sudden pounding in the distance. It wasn't like drums, not exactly. The same pulse they'd been following was at the heart of it, but there were more layers now.

Whum, whum, whum. Whum, whum, whum.

"We shall soon see which of us is right," Leti taunted. She rose to her feet, every bit Elia's equal. "The city comes for us both."

"You will be judged for your actions, little sister," Elia hissed. Her eyes leaked the kind of hatred Jordan had rarely seen. Then she vanished.

The rhythmic pulses were coming faster now, and they vibrated through Jordan. He could feel them in his teeth.

"Hey, you alive-ish down there?" Jordan asked, shaking Trevor's limp form.

"*Ow*. Those bracelets. So shitty. Would not recommend." Trevor climbed shakily to his feet. Steam still rose from the parts of his clothing that had survived the blasts, and much of his skin was charred. "What did I miss? That pulsing is intense."

"Leti, how close is the city, do you think?" Jordan asked. He dropped the telekinetic bubble, and hopped twenty feet into the air, grabbing a vine hanging from one of the upper limbs of a huge tree. A flock of parrots burst into flight, winging their way to new perches a healthy distance away.

"I do not know," Leti said. "Perhaps if we can get above the treetops?" She leapt into the air, bounding up into the canopy.

Jordan gave one last look around the clearing, just to make sure Elia was really gone. He sent a final ping, allowing the energy to ripple through the trees in every direction. It met resistance from Trevor and Leti, and a single other consciousness that he guessed must be Anput. There was no sign of Elia or her companions.

He followed Leti up into the canopy, surprised by how far he had to climb before he got above the trees. All around him lay an impenetrable green canopy. Their vantage was on the side of a gently sloped hill overlooking a valley. The only thing not covered in thick vegetation was the river itself, a muddy swath of brown snaking through the valley and disappearing between two hills in the distance.

"The pulse is coming from that direction." Jordan pointed toward a hill to the southeast. "It feels close, but I don't see anything."

"Nor do I," Leti agreed. She was perched atop a neighboring tree, maybe a dozen feet away. "I suppose we have no choice but to continue on."

Jordan nodded. He didn't like the idea of heading blindly into the jungle —especially knowing Elia was out there—but there just weren't any other good options. He released the tree, dropping toward the ground nearly a hundred feet below. The wind tore at his clothing as he fell, and Jordan smiled as the ground rushed up. He cushioned his fall telekinetically, but still sent up a huge cloud of debris.

"Show off." Trevor groused. "See anything?"

"Nope. Can't see a goddamned thing. Let's keep moving toward the pulse. We've got to be close."

Trevor nodded, climbing unsteadily to his feet from his perch on a giant root.

"You going to be okay?" Jordan asked. He couldn't resist taunting the deathless. "I could carry you—you know, if you need protecting."

"Fucker," Trevor shot back, but there was no heat to it. He melted into the shadows. "Lead the way. I can keep up."

They leapt back into the trees, quickly working their way across the valley. By the time they reached the top of the hill he'd seen, Jordan was covered in sweat. He wasn't tired, exactly, but this humidity was getting a little old.

Leti had gone a little ways ahead, and her excited call snapped him out of the endless swinging between trees. She was crouched atop a tree limb, pointing deeper into the jungle. Jordan bounded through the trees, landing on a branch a little below her.

"Holy crap," he said. They were the only two words he could find.

Before them lay a sprawling golden city. There were pyramids of all sizes, with dozens of obelisks made tiny next to them. Broad marble avenues flowed between the pyramids. Every inch of every structure gleamed gold. "Well, I guess that explains the El Dorado myth."

Trevor materialized on a neighboring tree. "This explains so much. Look to the right and left. See the edges of the field?"

"Field?" Jordan peered into the jungle, unsure what Trevor meant. Then he spotted it: about a hundred yards off, there was a shimmering white field that blurred the jungle around it. He looked the opposite way and saw an identical field. Glancing up, he saw it there, too, near the top of the canopy. "What am I looking at?"

"I think we're looking through a portal," Trevor explained. He pointed at the edge of the shimmering field. "If we went down there, I'm thinking the city wouldn't be visible. We can see it through this portal, and I think it's the portal that's giving off that pulsing."

Anput's disembodied voice spoke. "That would explain why no one ever found the city. It's not anyplace that can be reached directly, and the location of the portal is constantly changing."

"The city might not even be on this continent," Trevor mused.

"Mohn spent a lot of satellite hours scanning these jungles. Their search was kind of a joke outside their department," Jordan allowed. "We'd have picked up a city with this much metal a decade ago—longer, maybe."

"I think we're on to something," Anput said.

"But this leaves us with a lot of questions," Jordan said. "Who made the portal, and where will it take us if we step through?"

Leti dropped down to Jordan's branch. "I do not wish to sound like a zealot, but you must have faith, Ark Lord. I do not know what the city holds for us, but there is only one way to learn the answer. Let us see what the City of the Gods wishes us to see."

Chapter 52- Matron Davina

Elia's fury had not abated by the time they arrived at the Temple of Divine Winds. The pyramid wasn't the largest, and it wasn't the most powerful—but it was filled with people she trusted, people who agreed about the threat that this Ark Lord and his allies posed.

She cloaked herself in shadow, passing by the guards. She didn't have time for them; she needed to speak to the matron. Gliding silently through the temple, she finally stopped at a small chamber with a simple cloth door-hanging. That cloth had been shaped by the matron herself, woven from strands of gold. It absorbed signals and prevented anyone from probing into her quarters with shaping.

Elia ducked under the heavy cloth, stepping into a narrow chamber. It had the same small bed she herself slept on, one of many testaments that they stood no higher than their brothers and sisters, even if they were slightly closer to the Mother.

"Were you successful?" Matron Davina asked. The old woman sat at a tiny writing desk, scrawling away in a journal with a cobalt pen. The woman's long white hair screened her face, giving Elia only her neutral tone to work with. Was the matron angry?

"I was not," Elia admitted. There was no point in dithering. "We attacked the Ark Lord, but his defenses were potent. In time we could have overcome him, but the city chose to reveal itself. The portal was no more than a few hundred meters away, and I thought it best we not be discovered tampering with the Ark Lord."

"Very wise," the matron murmured. She still hadn't looked up, and her pen continued to scratch across the page. "If the council learned that you had interfered with a seeking, they would have no choice but to intervene. Part of your mission was stealth, was it not? The threat was to be eliminated quietly."

"Yes, but—"

"No *but*," the matron roared. Her head snapped up; her dark eyes fixed on Elia. "You told me you could do this thing. You gave me your word. You have failed. What will we do if the Ark Lord tells the council? How will you respond to that allegation? They will delve into your mind, and when they do they will see what you have done."

"Matron, I…" Elia licked her lips. She'd been about to make another excuse. Excuses would not help them. Excuses could not fix anything. "What would you have me do?"

"You will go to the rest of the council, immediately," the matron instructed. "You will tell them what you have done, and why you have done it. We see the ancient enemy as invaders, and were doing what we must to keep them from the city." She bent back to her journal, and the scratching began again. "I will not be able to intercede, nor will I admit to having met with you. The council may choose to punish you; if they do, that punishment will be far less if you are the one to bring the situation to their attention. You must get ahead of this if we are to have any chance of regaining control."

"As you say, Matron." Elia bobbed a curtsy and backed from the chamber. She had a feeling she wouldn't enjoy the interrogation the council would give her, but it was still possible they could salvage something from this.

Leti and her Ark Lord master were leading the ancient enemy into the city. Couldn't Elia be forgiven for zealously defending their most sacred place?

Chapter 53- Picked Off

Windigo reveled in the strength his new body afforded. And it was well and truly *his*. The Bear had been vanquished, trapped in the recesses of his own mind.

Windigo had worn countless forms over a near-infinite lifetime, but none had been as powerful as Yosemite. The Great Bear brimmed with power, one of Isis's most potent creations. Yet, for all his power, the Bear's mind had been shockingly easy to overcome. The Bear had been naive to the extreme, and it had been a simple matter to manipulate him.

Now, the Bear's consciousness had retreated to the dim recesses of his mind. He'd given up, recoiling from the carnage he knew Windigo had planned, the carnage he was even now about to execute.

Windigo gave a ghastly, skeletal grin and walked silently toward the row of cars the locals had fashioned into a crude wall. He could smell the dogs prowling in the darkness on either side, could hear their hearts beating.

They smelled something on the wind, something they couldn't recognize. A few began to bark, while others sprinted across the darkened field. They'd alert their alpha, one of the Ka-Dun who protected this place. That Ka-Dun would come to investigate, and when he did, Windigo could finally sate his endless hunger. Every meal increased his strength, his knowledge.

It had been so for countless years, long ages before humans had first arrived on this continent—before their ancestors found the courage to leave the trees. Windigo was older than they could comprehend, and in all that time he'd longed for the ability to control an Ark.

At long last, that possibility danced within his grasp.

Tonight, he'd send the first message that would draw inexorably toward the Ark Lord's death. Windigo walked in shadow, approaching the wall silently. Several dogs lounged atop it, staring out at the darkness. They were alert, ears cocked and noses twitching. He gave them nothing, walking boldly to the wall of rusting automobiles. They didn't react.

Windigo extended both arms, then he slashed. Once, twice, a third time.

There was a single yelp, then the rest died silently. Windigo bent and began to feed. He ate swiftly, knowing that the alpha would soon be upon him. Ka-Dun were easily manipulated. Kill one of their pack, and it sent them into a rage. That rage blinded them, making it a simple matter to overcome their mental defenses.

Windigo finished his meal, wiping at his fanged mouth with a gore-soaked claw. Any time now.

A few heartbeats later there was a rush of wind as a Ka-Dun blurred into a crouch perhaps forty paces distant. He knew he'd been seen, but the fire in his eyes made it clear that he didn't care. Excellent.

Strangely, the Ka-Dun was an old man. He had a long grey braid and hard eyes. He burned with fire, and was likely a talented shaper. As recently as two moons past Windigo would have leapt to possess this Ka-Dun.

The Ka-Dun tensed, and Windigo realized he was about to flee. His survival instinct was overpowering the rage. Windigo could not allow that.

He cackled, hefting the remains of one of the dogs into the air and flinging it at the Ka-Dun. Even as the ghastly remains left his claws, he shaped, sending a probing tendril of energy at the Ka-Dun. The Ka-Dun was distracted by the flung remains, his rage at the desecration overpowering all other emotion for a split second.

It was long enough. Windigo slipped his tendril into the Ka-Dun's mind, fueling the rage.

"Know that I am John Rivers," the Ka-Dun roared, "and I protect these lands. I'll rip out your spine, you monster." He charged forward, shifting to warform as he blurred toward Windigo.

The force of his charge knocked Windigo into the row of cars, crumpling one. The Ka-Dun savaged Windigo's throat with an impressive set of jaws, but his host's body was simply too tough. The thick hide he'd inherited from the Great Bear turned away the Ka-Dun's attacks.

Windigo lunged, wrapping his long arms around the Ka-Dun. He crushed the wolf to his chest, funneling more rage into the Ka-Dun's mind.

"Kill—you," the Ka-Dun choked out, all rational thought driven away by the madness. Then Windigo lunged again, wrapping enormous jaws around the Ka-Dun's head and shoulders. He ripped loose half the man's body, and began to feed. He'd save enough to taunt the Ark Lord, but he would savor the rest.

The flurry of barking dogs became a mournful howling, one that echoed over the fields into the hills. The pack rushed to save their master, but by the time they arrived Windigo would be long gone.

Chapter 54- Under Seige

Blair trotted down the ramp to the stage. The seats were filling up quickly, and the nervous rustle was growing. They needed to get in front of this, but he didn't see how it was possible. He hopped up on stage and joined Liz and Alicia at the podium. The teen looked lost, with dark red circles under her eyes. No one could blame her for that. Blair knew that in many ways John Rivers had been her father.

Liz wrapped an arm around Alicia's shoulders, looking pointedly at Blair. He nodded. Liz led Alicia to the back of the stage, and Blair stepped in front of the podium. Hundreds of eyes were on him, and every face wore a mixture of grief and fear. These people had been shaken to their core, and somehow Blair had to find the words to make that better.

"I know that many of you don't know me very well," Blair began. "I've only just come to Santa Rosa, and I'm still a stranger to a lot of you. I've got some dark news to report, news that most of you already know." He licked his lips, watching the expectant faces. "John Rivers was attacked and killed tonight. He was working the Petaluma border, and his surviving pack tells us that he battled an antlered monster. We all know exactly who that is. Windigo has finally returned, and he started with a victim we all knew well."

He watched them, waiting for a reaction. No one spoke.

"John was a leader here," Blair continued, "and Windigo chose him for a reason. He wants to shake us to our very core, to spread fear and anger. If we allow him to do that, he'll pick us off one by one."

"So what are we supposed to do?" called a blond Ka-Ken whom Blair didn't recognize. "We can't hunt him down. We can't hide. I don't care how strong the Ark makes you, you can't kill Windigo if you can't find him. You can't protect us all the time, and Windigo will just wait until we're alone."

"You tell him, Eleanor," called an older man. "Alicia, this place ain't safe any more. Do you really want this to end like Angel Island? We need to get out now, cut our losses. Some of us aren't gonna make it, but the survivors can rebuild somewhere safe."

"Somewhere safe?" Blair interrupted. He thumped the podium with a fist, glaring hard at the old man. "Where might that be exactly? Where is it you think you can go that Windigo can't follow? If you leave, he'll finish those who stay here. Then he'll hunt you down, and feed on you wherever you end up."

"So what the hell can we do about it?" called Zee. He folded his arms, eyeing Blair balefully. "You've done a lot of talking about protecting us. If you've got some plan, tell us."

Liz walked proudly to the podium, standing next to Blair. "Hey, I get it," she said. "People are lashing out. You're angry, we all are. Right now we're *all* wrestling with grief. We're scared. That's normal, and no one can blame us for that. But making decisions when scared and angry is never a good idea. That plays right into Windigo's hands. We need to consider our next moves carefully. We can fight Windigo, but we need to be smart about it."

"She's right," Alicia said. She stalked to the edge of the stage, stabbing a finger at the old man. "Pat, you have no right to bring up Angel Island. This is different. We've built a home here, and I'm not going to just abandon it. We'll fight Windigo, and the Ark Lord will find a way to stop him once and for all. We'll ensure that he never does to anyone else what he's done here. We're going to avenge John Rivers, aren't we?"

Alicia turned to Blair, and all eyes moved to him. He had absolutely no idea how he was going to stop Windigo, but right now that didn't matter. "Damned straight, Alicia. For starters, no one goes anywhere alone. You always travel with a pack. Those with territories out in West County will stay here for the time being. Windigo will strike again, we know that. We can't make it easy for him. We need to be ready to fight back, and that means staying together. Meanwhile, I'm going to get some answers. The Ark has a massive database. I'll see what I can learn about Windigo's origins. Maybe he has a weakness."

No one looked happy, but people were nodding. Most looked mollified. Liz leaned in to the mic. "Alicia and I will start pairing people. Line up along the left wall, and we'll get started." She covered the mic with her hand, whispering to Blair out of the corner of her mouth. "Do something flashy.

These people are scared. They need to see a god."

Blair nodded. "I'll be back as soon as I can."

Then he light-walked. He lingered in the brilliant white light, letting it flood the room. When it faded, he stood in the Ark's central repository.

Hopefully that had been impressive enough.

Chapter 55- Outmaneuvered

"Moment of truth," Jordan muttered. He stepped through the portal, into the golden city. One moment he was standing in a humid jungle, the next he was in a warm, dry city. The transition was instant, and he could feel the sweat all over his body beginning to dry.

Trevor was the next through, then Anput. Leti was the last to enter, and despite her soiled white skirt she wore a beatific smile. Jordan knew this meant everything to her, finally reaching the city she believed to be the holy land prepared by the Mother. Hell, she might even be right about that.

Jordan offered her his hand. "Congratulations, Leti."

She ignored the hand, gathering him into a hug.

Jordan laughed. "I can't speak for your people, but the city has clearly accepted you or we'd never have made it this far."

"I thought that if I ever saw this day it would be centuries away," Leti said. She stared around in wonder, giving a delighted laugh when a massive butterfly launched itself from a basketball-sized scarlet flower. The garden was a riot of colors, each flower giving off a soft, pleasing fragrance. None of the vegetation looked at all familiar—from the jungle, or anywhere else. It was all contained in small gardens and parks between the clusters of golden pyramids.

"So what now?" Trevor asked. There was an edge to his voice that brought Jordan back to the present.

Two groups were approaching from opposite directions. At first glance Jordan couldn't discern any differences in the two groups. Each wore the same white clothing he'd seen Leti and Elia wear, though nearly every one had at least one piece of golden jewelry. Many wore bracelets, though a few had necklaces or a belt—scavenged when they'd found this place, probably.

"Oh, shit," Jordan said. His heart sank. "Looks like Elia got here first. She's at the head of that second group."

"These are the interlopers I warned you of," Elia called, loudly enough for her voice to carry to the second group. "As you can see, two are the ancient enemy the texts speak of, the horrible deathless. Their hearts no longer beat, and they survive by devouring the flesh of the living. The Mother's command toward such creatures is clear."

A hard-eyed old woman with snowy hair and a dark, pockmarked face led the second group. Her eyes studied Elia sharply, and she raised a hand. Her followers halted, and the old woman approached Elia alone. "What are you going on about, Elia? Who are these people, and how did they reach the city?"

"A renegade from the Temple of the Ark has betrayed our kind," Elia said. She pointed accusingly at Leti. "One of our most trusted sisters has forsaken our ways. Leticia serves the usurper, and it is he we must be most wary of. Wherever he goes he brings corruption, and his unclean companions are the proof of it."

"You twist words like a snake, Elia," Leti snapped. Her eyes blazed. "Ark Lord Jordan is the direct progeny of the Mother." She stepped forward protectively in front of Jordan. "He has fought at her side. Learned shaping from her. She entrusted him with control of her Ark."

"Did she?" Elia countered. She gave a cruel smile. "If I recall, he took the key from a defeated foe, not from her hand. She did not bequeath it to him. He took it. Isn't that the truth, Ark Lord?"

"Yeah, it's the truth," Jordan admitted. He removed his sunglasses and his hat, so they could see his face. "I claimed the key from a guy named Steve, a guy that Isis asked my pack to eliminate. She didn't specifically say she wanted me to have the key, but I was the only option at the time. Like Leti said, I am the Mother's direct progeny. I've fought at her side. She's also kicked my ass several times, and I don't mind admitting that she scares the piss out of me."

"I notice you're no longer so quick to spout your blasphemies," Elia said. The cruel smile intensified. "Why don't you tell them about the Mother's death. She is dead, isn't she, Ark Lord? That's what you told us."

Horrified gasps went up from both groups. The wizened woman's face hardened. Elia had just scored a significant blow, one that Jordan didn't have an easy way to counter. Jordan had no idea who the white-haired woman was, but the strength in her was impressive.

"I don't see how she could be alive," Jordan admitted, reluctantly. "She was in the First Ark when it blew. Her, Osiris, and Ra battled together for the first time in millennia. They united to stop Set, who I think is talked about in your scriptures. They succeeded, but the cost was high."

"Why have you come to this city?" the snowy hair woman asked. "That is the real question, the only one that matters at this instant." She'd remained calm during the conversation, but studied everything like a bird of prey.

"It's complicated, but I'll do my best to uncomplicate it," Jordan said. He gave a heavy sigh. "Set worked for a group called the Builders. They're the ones that originally created the Arks, and this city. Those Builders left this world long before humanity had even come down from the trees. Those Builders are about to come back, and they consider us squatters. They plan to wipe us out, though we don't know how exactly. Just that they do. Isis fought against the Builders, and I'm carrying on the fight. This city is critical to that war, and the grey men know it. They're after something here called the Proto Ark."

"Grey men?" the snowy-haired woman asked.

"Like I said, it's complicated." Jordan scanned the crowd. There was still a good deal of hostility on most faces. "The grey men were created by the Builders. Think of them as shock troops. Listen, I know that this is a lot to accept. I know you're not really sure what to make of me. Trust me when I say we're allies."

"How do you explain these two?" the woman asked, her tone accusing. He gestured at Trevor and Anput. "They are clearly the ancient enemy, the ones we are sworn to protect against. Their kind ravaged this land for thousands of years—and for just as long, the champions have pushed them back. Our goal was to keep them from this city, yet you've willingly brought them here. Why? And how can you expect us to trust you after doing such a thing?"

"You have to understand that things aren't black and white," Jordan countered. His best chance was in being honest. "I've fought against

Trevor more than once, but if Isis could put aside her differences to work with Ra and Osiris, then I can learn to work with deathless. They share the same goal we do: stopping the Builders. We need each other, or we're all going to be wiped out."

"Again he blasphemes," Elia said. "The idea that the Mother would work with the ancient enemy is madness." She glided forward, stopping near Jordan. "We can debate this in council, but I am not comfortable having these people loose in our city. I think they should be imprisoned with the other interloper until we decide what to do with them."

"I am not comfortable imprisoning the progeny of the Mother," the snowy-haired woman said. "He might be misguided, but we must accord him the proper honor. Leticia certainly believes in him, and she has always been highly regarded here." That last seemed to surprise Leti, who blinked rapidly. "Yet you are right about the ancient enemy. I suggest we imprison the deathless with the other interloper, and we bring the Ark Lord to the council chambers. We can deliberate this matter with the full council. Do you agree, Elia?"

"Of course, Matron Davina," Elia said. She beamed a triumphant smile, and Jordan realized he was really starting to hate this woman. They didn't have time for this political nonsense.

Chapter 56- Jordan

Jordan was led to a golden pyramid on the west side of the city, about four hundred meters from the portal. He was still using that to orient himself, and made damned certain he stayed oriented. He wanted to be able to flee if needed.

"The white-haired woman was Matron Davina," Leti was saying. "She's the strongest councilor, the champion who first discovered this place. Elia was the second, and holds nearly as much sway. They are the two who really determine what will happen."

"I thought they mentioned a council," Jordan replied. He studied the building they were entering, a tiny golden version of the Ark. It was clear both had been built by the same people. The similarities in the symbols lining the walls were impossible to ignore, even for a soldier.

"They did, but the other three members hold very little sway," Leti explained. "Most of us have gravitated toward one of the two camps. Elia's is centered around the world outside, which is why she leads from the Ark. Davina spends her time here, which is why her faction is slightly stronger. She's also the only one considered a matron, and, as we have no clearly defined rules on who may become one, she is essentially first among equals."

Leti bowed before the pair of severe-looking guards, so Jordan mimicked her.

Once they were inside the structure, Leti spoke again. "This is Awa's temple. He speaks primarily for the young and the radical, those who are looked down upon by Davina and Elia both. Our order is very much a matriarchy, and the fact that he is a Ka-Dun hurts his standing with many."

"So we're allying with the misfits and renegades? Sounds about par for what I'm used to." He'd had less to work with. At least they had some allies.

Leti led him down several maze-like corridors, until they finally emerged in a wide room. The walls were covered with gems in strange configurations, and Jordan could feel the faint power pulsing within. He had no idea what the place had originally been used for, and he doubted the current occupants did either.

They'd converted the room into rough barracks, and had set up two rows of cots against the far wall. One corner of the room held boxes of provisions and other supplies, and bordering it was a crude boxing ring where two Ka-Ken were sparring in warform. There were probably a dozen people all told, most between the ages of sixteen and twenty-five.

Most watched him and Leti with curiosity, but no one approached until they were spotted by a short, dark-skinned man. He looked much like the natives in the village they'd passed through, though he wore the same white garb as the other priests.

"Leti, it gladdens me to see you again." He gave the same bow she had, and his face lit up at her approach. This guy had it bad. "I see you've brought the Ark Lord with you. I don't know what to think of the situation. Have you come to discuss it?"

"I have. Councilor Awa, this is Ark Lord Jordan. Jordan, this is Councilor Awa." Leti gave Awa a friendly smile, one that drew a smirk from Jordan. He'd seen girls play the boys they knew were into them, and Leti was playing Awa like a violin. "As I said in the square earlier, he is the Mother's direct progeny. None stand closer than he, and only a few stand equal."

Awa looked impressed. He glanced quickly at Leti as if struggling to figure out how best to impress her. "You are both welcome to stay here, and I will offer whatever aid I can. I am not, ah, as respected as some councilors. But my voice still carries a little weight. I will speak for the Ark Lord when we are called to session."

Jordan could feel the potential within Awa, which might be why they all followed him. Next to Jordan, the little native was strongest shaper in the room. The body language of the other priests was almost subservient, despite the fact that most were larger and stronger than Awa.

Leti bent forward and kissed Awa on the cheek. "Thank you, Awa. We will gratefully accept your hospitality. When do you think that the council will be called to session?"

"It will probably take an hour or so for them to organize it," Awa said.

"Possibly a little longer, though I am certain there will be some urgency in the matter. Nothing like this has happened since the interloper was caught."

Leti smiled, and the kid perked up like a plant reaching for the sun.

"You've mentioned this interloper twice," Jordan interjected. "Who is he?"

"He is an explorer named Percy," Awa explained. "Apparently, he'd been trapped in the city for many years before the sun changed. He was skulking about when we discovered the city, and he was able to hide from us for some time. Eventually he was caught, and the council decided he'd done nothing worthy of punishment—but we couldn't release him, or he might bring others to the city." Awa looked troubled. "We imprisoned him in a large pyramid on the eastern side of the city. It's large and possesses the means to feed and house him, but we do not allow Percy to venture beyond its walls."

"Awa, what do you think the council will do about the Ark Lord?" Leti asked.

Again, Awa looked troubled. He reached out and took Leti's hand. "I do not know for certain. Elia's hatred is clear, so she will do whatever she can to thwart the Ark Lord. Matron Davina is more impartial, but still has little reason to trust you. Elise will vote as Davina votes, and Garret will follow Elia. I do not think they will try to harm anyone, but then we've never had the ancient enemy within our walls before. It is possible they could order the execution of your friends, and I am not sure they'd be wrong to do so."

"They are not the enemy, Awa," Leti said, even if she said it grudgingly. "I've travelled with them. They are different, and their ways are barbaric, but they do not seek a war with us. They are here to help us vanquish a terrible enemy, and the Mother fought alongside them. If she can set aside her hatred for the deathless, can we not do the same?"

"I make no promises," Awa said. He let Leti's hand drop and turned back to Jordan. "I will head to the council chamber to speak with the others. We will send for you when we are ready."

Trevor didn't resist as he was shoved roughly through the doorway, into the pyramid. The white-furred Ka-Ken who'd pushed him touched the panel on the wall outside, and a golden door slid down. Trevor and Anput were left sealed inside a wide hallway. It led to a large, very empty room about sixty feet across, with walls set with clusters of gems every few feet. There were four pedestals in the room, all humming faintly with power. A faint light came from the ceiling—not enough to read by, but enough to see.

"What do you think this place is?" Trevor asked. He walked to the middle of the room, examining one of the pedestals. He could feel the signals emanating from it, but had no idea what they were.

"Don't you think we should be more concerned about how we're going to get out of here?" Anput asked. "Or about what those genocidal savages are going to do to us? You don't remember the war between our species. I do. They're going to have their little vote, and then they're going to kill us." She stalked to the other side of the door, bending to inspect the panel next to it. "I'm going to see if I can get this thing to open."

"Odds are good we're stuck for the time being, and the best way for us to find a way out is understanding where we are," Trevor said. He knelt beside the pedestal to examine the base. "The gems on this thing look like an interface of some kind. I've seen similar ones in the Ark. I don't know what this place is, but we might be able to control functions with these. Functions like opening the door."

Anput finally looked up. "Now you have my attention."

"There's some risk, obviously. This thing could fire disintegration beams for all I know," Trevor said. He rose, inspecting the gems near the top of the console. "Guess there's only one way to find out."

Trevor put his hands on a pair of gems, an emerald and a ruby. A jolt of power shot through him. It wasn't painful, but he still jerked back in surprise, releasing the console.

"Are you okay?" Anput asked. She blurred over to his side. "Hmm, you seem fine. What did the gems do?"

The air next to them shimmered, and a holographic figure flickered into existence. A familiar figure. It stood about five feet tall, with translucent green skin. A pair of wide, black eyes contrasted with its tiny mouth. The hologram's limbs were too thin, its head too large for its tiny body.

"Ka, is that you?" Trevor asked. He knew almost instantly that it wasn't, though. This hologram looked a great deal like Ka, but the face was slightly different. It looked like a brother, or close relative of some kind.

"You have met one of my fellow keepers?" the hologram asked. Its voice was about half an octave higher than Ka's. "That is most intriguing. My name is Ark Keeper Ba, and I have been assigned to watch over this facility." It gave a deep bow.

"How about we ask the questions for now?" Trevor suggested. "Why did you suddenly appear?"

"You've accessed the system, and I have responded." The hologram gave a low power flicker, dimming considerably. "Oh dear, we've lost another conduit."

"Many people must have touched those pedestals." Trevor folded his arms, unsure whether he should trust this thing.

"Indeed. At least one individual has attempted to access the system in the last twenty-four hours, without success. The safety protocols keep them locked out."

"But not us?" Anput asked.

"Well, not *him*," Ba corrected. "An Ark Lord may come and go as they choose. The system was designed to serve them."

"Are you serious?" Trevor asked, blinking. "You're just sitting here waiting for an Ark Lord to tell you what to do?"

Ba nodded its bulbous head. "Precisely."

Anput laughed. "I can't believe it. Those fools locked us in the control room, and left us unsupervised."

"Let's start with our current location," Trevor said. "What was this room originally used for?"

"This portion of the facility is a laboratory belonging to Kek-Telek," Ba said. "The pedestals tap into the helix repository, allowing you to manipulate genetic matter. Many experiments have been conducted here, though not in several hundred thousand years." He cocked his head again, giving a very human sigh. "Unfortunately, damage to this facility has eroded my control. Despite the Builders' use of time dilation, this city has still existed past its projected life span. Many systems are badly in need of repair. My cognition is currently tied to this building, because my awakening damaged the energy converter. I can project elsewhere in the city, but not access any systems."

"So you're stuck here, alongside us," Trevor said. He turned to Anput. "At the very least we might be able to make use of this place. Maybe we can experiment using some of your theories."

"Possibly, but before we do that there's something that concerns me." Anput walked to the far side of the room, and Trevor followed. A stairwell led down into darkness. "They mentioned that there was an interloper. If he's in here, I'm not sure I want to let our guard down. Let's find him, and then we can see about some experimentation."

"Ba, can you access the internal sensors?" Trevor asked.

"I'm afraid not." Ba's hologram flickered, then appeared next to them again. "My functionality is quite limited, though I can answer any question you might pose. I am well versed in this place's history. It was created by Builder Kek-Telek himself."

"We can check that out later. For now, we need to find out if there is anyone else in this facility. Are there any weapons here we can use?"

"I'm afraid not," Ba said, its tiny mouth in a pout. "You will have to rely on your own shaping. This facility has four levels, each used for different types of experiments. If there is another individual in this facility, they have to be on one of those four floors."

"Break the floors down by type," Trevor ordered. If they were going to proceed, he wanted as much intel as possible.

"The top floor is modulation, the next floor is used for time-accelerated growth. Level three is reserved for direct mutation, and the last floor contains several banks of reclamation chambers, and access to the full data archive." Ba flickered again.

Trevor turned to Anput. "I don't think they would have put us in here with something lethal, but let's proceed with caution. If it were me, I'd spend my time at the data archive, so I expect that's where we'll find him."

"Or her," Anput said. "Your logic is sound enough. Let's explore this place and see what we can find." She slid into the shadows, her words retreating into the distance as she started down the stairs.

Trevor followed, wrapping the shadows protectively about him. He walked quickly down the stairs, allowing his superior vision to adjust to the limited illumination provided by the gems set into the wall. He followed the stairway down another hundred paces, where it opened into a wide chamber. Similar to the one above, the room held half a dozen terminals, each next to a clear crystal tube.

"Those things are large enough to hold an elephant," Anput whispered. Her voice came from several feet ahead. "Think of the creatures that could be created here. Entire species, wholly from the imagination of the creator."

"Yeah, it's a hell of a lot of power, that's for damned sure. I wonder why the Ark doesn't have chambers like these. This place is supposed to have preceded them, right? That's why it's the Proto Ark?"

"Precisely. This place is undoubtedly older. One has to wonder why the Arks were, apparently, given more limited functionality." Anput's voice didn't move as she spoke, so Trevor paused as well.

"Let's take a look at the next floor. The stairwell is right next to the one we came down," Trevor suggested. He crept forward, moving slowly down the next stairwell. The chamber on the floor below them was several times larger than the previous floor, which made sense given the pyramid structure.

Chambers similar to the tubes above lined the walls on two sides of the room, but their walls were comprised of much thicker crystal. At the base of each cell sat a faintly glowing ruby the size of a VW Bug. Trevor could feel the faint pulses of energy, unlike anything he'd encountered thus far. They were primal somehow. Chaotic.

"There's the stairway down to the next floor," Anput's voice came from about a dozen paces away. They were doing a pretty good job of staying close given that they couldn't see each other.

"I wonder what these vats are," Trevor asked. He passed within an arm's length of a cylindrical golden vat. There were nearly a dozen scattered across the level, each with gems set in the side.

"No idea," Anput replied. "Ba can probably shed some light on them, after we find this interloper."

"And found me you have," an old man huffed. He paused at the top of the steps, leaning heavily on a cane. He reached into a tweed jacket to withdraw a handkerchief, then mopped his forehead. "Those stairs make coming down here a major excursion. Now, my eyesight's not too good, so you'll have to come closer if I'm going to get a look at you."

Trevor studied the man. His clothing was completely out of date. Trevor wasn't a historian, but he'd been a fan of H.P. Lovecraft growing up. This guy was wearing clothes from the 1920s. His long jacket was made from a coarse fabric, with rows of matching buttons, and he had a newsboy style hat. His tan pants were tucked into knee-high leather boots. A grey-black handlebar mustache overpowered his lip, and a short goatee covered his chin.

"Who are you?" Trevor asked. He stepped from the shadows, moving closer to the old man. He could hear the old man's heart thundering in his chest, as one would expect from a normal human. If he had the ability to shape, Trevor certainly couldn't sense it.

"My name is Lt. Colonel Percival Harrison Fawcett, formerly of Her Majesty's Royal Artillery." The old man spoke with dignity, offering Trevor a trembling hand. "How do you do?"

Chapter 58- Percy

Trevor took a step further into the light, wincing at the horrified expression on Percy's face. The old man recoiled, shrinking against the wall as his mouth worked. Sometimes Trevor forgot just how monstrous he appeared.

"First there were werewolves," he whispered, "and I thought…I must be mad. Then I got used to the idea. I thought I was sane." Percy clutched his cane like a talisman, scrunching his eyes shut as if that would banish the situation. "But now? I just don't know. Am I even seeing you? Or are you some sort of demon conjured by this hellish place to torment me?"

"My name is Trevor. The woman in the shadows is Anput." Trevor spoke slowly, and made no move to approach the man. "You're not mad, and we are not a vision. We were created by the same people who made the werewolves. They locked us in here with you."

"You, ah, I realize this is horribly rude, but you aren't going to eat me, are you?" Percy opened one eye, peering at Trevor.

"Quite the opposite," Anput breathed. She sauntered toward Percy in that succubus-like way of hers. "Clearly, you're an explorer of some kind. You must have been, to have reached this city. And you've been here longer than we have. Would you be willing to give us a tour?"

"Of course, of course. How very rude of me." Percy perked up instantly. "How do you do, Ms…?"

"Anput," she supplied. She shifted her weight, the motion somehow managing to emphasize her chest.

"Anput you say? As in the Egyptian goddess? Wife of Anubis?" Percy adjusted his spectacles, studying Anput's face. "You have the right complexion for it. I'd definitely say you are Egyptian. Dark skin, dark hair."

"You're a scholar?" Anput's surprised was total. She dropped the seduction. "How long have you been here? What can you tell us about this place?"

"Why don't we begin with that tour, and I'll tell you the tale as we walk? I'm afraid I'm quite frail these days. Would you be so kind as to assist me?"

Percy offered his arm to Anput, and she took it, leaning against the old man as they started down the stairs to the fourth level. "I'm assuming you've seen the two upper floors already, as you had to pass them to get here. The top floor is some sort of control room, and I believe this is a laboratory of some kind. The apparatus on the second and third floor suggests they were experimenting with living creatures. The last floor is the most troubling, but as that will take an old man some time to reach, why don't I tell you how I came to be in this place?"

Percy stopped speaking, breathing harder as he made his way to the next landing. He paused there, mopping sweat from his forehead.

"I was fortunate enough to have a distinguished career with Her Majesty's Royal Artillery. During my travels, I spent a great deal of time learning about the local cultures. From Egypt to the New World, I was privileged enough to see the world's wonders. After my retirement, I decided I wanted to find the lost city I believed lay behind the tales of El Dorado. I called that city Z. Most didn't believe it existed, but I was *certain* this place was out there."

Trevor glanced down the stairs to the room below. It was cavernous, many times larger than the floor above. Banks of strange pods lined the room, but he couldn't see much detail from this distance.

"My son Jack, the Rimmell boy, and I set out along the Xingu River in 1925. I'd been there often, you see, and knew the ways of the local tribes." Percy's eyes took on a faraway cast. "The trip was long, and difficult. At one point we lost most of the gifts we'd intended for local tribes, and both Jack and the Rimmell boy contracted malaria. I tended to them best I could, but our pace was hobbled. They worsened, until they lacked the strength to walk. I stayed with them until the end. It's a hard thing, watching your child die and knowing there's nothing you can do about it."

Anput made a sympathetic noise. It was difficult seeing the old man's pain, and Trevor didn't know what to say, so he patted Percy on the shoulder.

"Eventually, I continued on. I don't know why I didn't contract malaria. I don't know how the Xavantes tribe never found me, the murderous savages. I kept pushing further into the jungle, never really expecting to find the city. I don't know how long I walked. Weeks? Months? Time loses meaning in the jungle, as you're no doubt aware." Percy was interrupted by a fit of violent coughing. He dabbed his mouth with a handkerchief, and Trevor could smell the spots of blood staining the white cloth. The scent was sickly somehow. "I couldn't even send word to Nina, and it ate at me that she'd never know what happened to her boys. But I wouldn't let it all be for nothing. If I was going to die, at least I'd see Z before I did.

"One day, I discovered a shimmering doorway in the middle of the jungle. It was wide enough to drive an automobile through, and on the other side I could see gold. I climbed down the valley, and found this place." The old man grunted as he started down the stairs again. They'd nearly reached the fourth floor. "I spent a good month exploring the city. It was maddening. All around me was proof of a culture more advanced than anything Mother England had produced. It made the ancient Egyptians look like children, yet I was powerless to make sense of any of it. I couldn't read even a single passage, and had no idea how to translate it. I spent months exploring every inch of Z, prying what secrets I could from her. Many buildings have exquisite artwork that told me a great deal about the beings who built this place. This may come as a bit of a shock, but they were not human."

"It's not as shocking as you might expect," Anput said. She helped Percy down the last few steps, leading him slowly onto the fourth floor. Dozens of banks of pods lined the room.

Trevor followed, walking over to one of the pods. It was cylindrical, with a thick golden conduit connecting it to a bank of similar pods. "These things are about the right size to hold a person, and they have little windows at about face height."

"What do you think they are?" Anput asked. She disengaged from Percy, moving to inspect the pod.

"Ba called them reclamation pods," Trevor said. "They look like something we saw routinely in science fiction. Cryogenic suspension pods. I have no idea what their actual purpose is, but there are hundreds of them." He turned in a slow circle, scanning the room. Row after row of pods, and that was it.

"This building isn't the only one with those pods. Nearly every pyramid has a similar number of them, and the largest pyramid in the city leads to a cavern with countless pods. Literally countless. I spent days trying to count them, and eventually gave up when I reached a hundred thousand." Percy hobbled over to the pod, leaning heavily on his cane. "I've no earthly idea what they might be used for. I'd considered livestock, but never that they might put people in these things. What is this 'cryogenic' thing you mentioned?"

"It's a way of keeping a living being in stasis indefinitely," Trevor explained. "They're theoretical, but if they worked as expected someone could go to sleep in a cryo pod, and wake up after thousands of years without having aged."

"Similar to the rejuvenation chamber in the Arks." Anput walked in a slow circle around the pod. "This looks different. Not just in appearance, but the signal it gives off. Perhaps Ba might be able to tell us more."

"The what chamber in the what? I'm not following." Percy removed his spectacles, squinting at Anput as he cleaned them on his jacket.

"It's a lot to explain," Trevor supplied. "So you reached this city and explored it. What happened then?"

"Ah, yes. As I said, it was maddening. I tried to document everything, but eventually I ran out of paper. I decided to go back through the portal to get tree bark, as I figured it would make a suitable substitute. But the portal was gone. The city is as you see it now, surrounded by a dome of gold. I've walked the entire edge of that dome, and the only way in or out is the portal." Percy withdrew a canteen from his belt, lifting it to his mouth with a trembling hand. He took several mouthfuls, then replaced the canteen. "Over time, I realized that the portal wasn't static. It would open and close, seemingly without cause. I was terrified. I didn't know if I should flee back into the jungle. I hadn't found any source of food, and my supplies were dwindling. That's when I realized something profound. I wasn't hungry. I'd been having meals because it was habit, but I was never truly hungry. I stopped eating, and as the days passed it became clear that city was somehow sustaining me."

"That explains much," Anput said, her tone sympathetic. "This city is using energy to sustain you, but that energy is degrading your helixes. Eventually, what is keeping you alive will kill you."

"I suspected that part," Percy said. He gave a half-smile. "I always knew this place would be the end of me, but it was worth it. This place was a fitting greatest adventure for a man of my disposition. I suspect that you two can provide many of the answers I seek."

"We're happy to do that," Trevor said. "It's also possible that Anput might be able to help you recover."

"Help how?" Anput asked, raising a delicate eyebrow.

"We have access to the deathless virus, the werewolf virus, and the vampire virus," Trevor said. "We're in a Builder laboratory. What he's experiencing is basically radiation poisoning right? We should be able to create a strain of the virus that will give him the same protection we have."

"It's worth a try, I suppose," Anput allowed. She studied Percy critically. "Why don't we get you back to the first floor? Let's get you comfortable. You can tell us the rest of your story while I prepare a mutagen."

Chapter 59- Time Dilation

Anput helped Percy onto his cot. It was a clever little contraption made from thin wooden dowels and a length of thick cloth. It kept the old man nearly a foot off the ground, which was no doubt helpful in an insect-infested jungle.

"The fact that you survived this jungle with such primitive equipment is really quite impressive," Anput said. She offered Percy a blanket, and the old man accepted it gratefully.

"I've noticed that both your attire and your apparatus are unfamiliar to me. They seem advanced, yet more akin to modern technology than to that of these mysterious ancients. Where did you come by it?" Percy was breathing easier now, and color had returned to his face.

"Perhaps Trevor should explain, as all these things are from his own time. My world is far removed, from both yours and his," Anput explained. She couldn't help adding a dash of mystery. It was nice flirting with someone who didn't just stare back impassively, like Trevor.

"You said that your expedition left in 1925, right?" Trevor asked. He looked up from the pedestal he'd been inspecting. "What year do you think it is?"

"Well that's a very good question," Percy said. He stroked his mustache, considering for long moments. "I believe I was in the jungle for several months, certainly no longer than a year. I've been here for a number of months, perhaps twice as long as my stay in the jungle. Let's call that two years. That would make it somewhere between 1927 and 1929, by my estimate. How'd I do?"

"You're off by almost a century," Trevor said.

Anput was more than a little surprised at his bluntness, though by now she shouldn't have been. It was a refreshing departure from the endless political games in Ra's court.

"It's been almost ninety years since you found this place."

"That's impossible. I've kept a rough count of time, and even if my methods were wildly inaccurate it couldn't be more than a few extra years.

If ninety years had passed, I'd be a skeleton long since." Percy sat up on his cot, smoothing his mustache. "How do you account for that?"

"He's right," Anput realized aloud. "The energy sickness would long since have killed him. There's no way it could keep him alive for that length of time. He might survive another year, two at the outside. Definitely not another five."

"Ba, are you monitoring our conversation?" Trevor asked.

"Indeed," Ba's disembodied voice said. "How can I assist you, Ark Lord?"

"How long has Percy been in this city?" Trevor asked.

Anput could have kicked herself for not thinking to check with the construct.

"Seven months, nine days, eleven hours," Ba's voice said.

"Can you explain the time discrepancy then?" Anput asked.

Ba was silent until Trevor repeated the question. It irked her, but she'd long grown used to living in the shadow of an Ark Lord. At least Trevor was less insufferable than Ra had been.

"This city was the crowning achievement of the species you refer to as the Builders," Ba began. "They constructed it in a subterranean location, one carefully protected from all outside influence. Then, the Builders created an energy field that warped the space around the city. This was done to extend the longevity of the city, though this measure has not been entirely successful. The time dilation factor is currently set to ten, so for every hundred days that passes outside a single day will elapse here. The portal allows the city to connect briefly to the current flow of time."

Anput merely blinked. The implications were staggering.

"I need you to cancel that time dilation immediately," Trevor said. "Can you do that?"

"I can do so, but this will accelerate the destabilization of this city," Ba cautioned. "Once the field is deactivated, I will not be able to reactivate it without first enacting extensive repairs. Do you wish me to disable the field?"

"Do it," Trevor ordered. "We can't afford to have that much time pass." A moment later a tremor passed through the room, and the lights dimmed even further.

"It is done, Ark Lord," Ba said.

"Trevor, do you realize what this means?" Anput asked, laughter bubbling up. "For time dilation to function, time would have to be non-linear."

"Einstein was right," Trevor said. He gave one of his boyish smiles. "It might even be possible to travel backwards in time."

"Such travel is inadvisable," Ba interjected, "and outlawed in the Builder Codex."

"But it's possible," Anput shot back, throwing her arms around Trevor.

"Pardon the intrusion," Percy said, "but I have so many questions." He tried to rise from the cot, but Anput disengaged from Trevor and moved to intercept him.

"And we'll answer them, but you need to rest," she ordered. "We still don't know the rest of your story. At some point, you were imprisoned here. What happened?"

"Of course, of course. I owe you the conclusion of the tale." Percy settled against the cot, dabbing his mouth with his handkerchief. "One day, the portal opened differently. It was far, far larger than it had been. I don't know why it changed, but this time it stayed open. It would move sometimes, each time showing a different part of the jungle. Yet it never again closed. I watched it every day, and eventually a group of natives entered the city. At first I thought they were local explorers, but then they turned into hairy, brutish monsters. They were more akin to the kind of werewolf described in English folklore than anything I'd have associated with the Amazon."

"We can explain how and why they exist when you're done with your story," Trevor offered.

Percy nodded, then continued. "I tried to hide from the monsters, and was successful at first. By then I understood the city's layout better than they did. I watched as they explored Z. They seemed very excited by the writings, and by the jewelry they found." Percy reached into his pouch and withdrew a thick golden bracelet. "These are highly prized. At first I thought they're merely decorative, but then I saw some of the werewolves use them. I could never figure out the trick of how they did it." He offered the bracelet to Anput.

"Are you giving this to me?" she asked, blinking.

He nodded.

She accepted the bracelet, snapping it around her wrist. She could feel the power within it, linking instantly to her. It was unlike the few sunsteel weapons she'd touched, as if this somehow possessed its own primitive intelligence. "Do you have any idea how priceless this artifact is?"

"Lady Anput, I realize you are a married woman, and I am a married man. Still, I cannot see either of our spouses objecting to me making a gift to a beautiful woman." Percy gave her a wink, paired with a grandfatherly smile. "I can't use that thing. Maybe you can. You wished to hear the rest of my tale? When the werewolves finally caught me they put me inside this pyramid, and sealed it behind me. I was caught without most of my research materials, and had little more than a chronometer and a few flares. They didn't give me a chance to explain, nor did they ask my opinion. That, in my mind, makes these creatures the enemy. You, then, might be my allies."

"They don't want us here any more than they want you, I can promise you that," Trevor said. He looked to Anput. "What do you need from me to conduct your experiments?"

"Ba, are you capable of reading a data crystal?" she asked. No answer, of course.

"Ba, I order you to answer Anput's questions as if she were an Ark lord," Trevor commanded.

"Very well, Ark Lord. I am capable of reading data crystals, as they were the primary means of data storage used by the Builders. My databanks can handle conversion of most numeric systems, and can decrypt most symbol sets." Ba finally shimmered back into view, drawing a gasp from Percy.

"Here," Anput said, tossing a fist-sized ruby to Trevor. "That's what I was working on with Project Solaris. The experiments were mostly conducted on David, to find out what the grey men had done to him. I have enough of an understanding to map the desired traits into the virus—at least I think I do. It shouldn't take that much modulation to scale the virus back. If we do that, we give Percy a higher chance of surviving, though he's unlikely to manifest much in the way of shaping."

"I only understood about one word in three," Percy said, his confusion evident, "but it sounds like you may have the means to my survival. You want to expose me to some sort of sickness?"

"Something like that," Anput explained. She put a hand on his. "For the time being, please just relax. Trevor and I might be able to cure you, but it's going to take time, study, and experimentation."

"Well, we've got plenty of time and nothing else to do," Trevor said. He moved to the console, inserting Anput's data crystal.

Chapter 60- Stand Off

Jordan wasn't having the best day. Three of the five councilors had denied his request for an audience, and he hadn't even bothered to ask Elia. He suspected the only one who'd agreed had simply done it out of politeness.

He hoped it was politeness, anyway.

"Welcome, Ark Lord," Matron Davina said, gesturing at a foam chair across from him. It was similar to those in the Ark, and Jordan sank comfortably into it. Davina waved a hand and a white-robed acolyte brought forth a tray with two wooden goblets on it. She filled them with a clear liquid, then offered a mug to Davina. The matron took it, and waved at Jordan to do the same.

Jordan shook his head. "I'm too dehydrated to drink alcohol. I was in the jungle this morning. Thanks for the offer though."

"As you wish." Davina studied him for long moments, so Jordan took the opportunity to do the same. Davina's grandmotherly exterior was backed by the toughest steel. "You've placed us all in a very difficult predicament, Jordan. Did you realize that?" Davina asked mildly.

He noticed that she'd dropped the *Ark Lord*.

"I apologize for that. I know our arrival was unexpected, but we really didn't have a choice. If the grey men and Hades want this city, then we need to deny it to them. That means getting the city fortified for battle." Jordan knew it sounded desperately inadequate.

"This place *is* fortified for battle. We have over two score of the toughest champions on this continent. What is it, exactly, that you think will enable an enemy to breach this city?" Davina asked. Hard eyes locked onto Jordan. Her jovial expression melted. "That's assuming they were even able to find the city, which I assure you they cannot. Unless your friends are here to reveal the location."

"I found it," Jordan pointed out. "You're also assuming that there's nothing out there that can deal with forty plus champions. I assure you, there are things that could sweep aside this defensive force in a matter of hours."

"You're no doubt referring to Nox, and his puppet Camiero," Davina said. The matron seemed unconcerned. "If you think we fear him, then you are a fool. Nox has his armies clearing jungle in a futile effort to find this place. Every day we pick off troops."

"Yeah, and I'll bet you're losing troops too," Jordan countered. He shook his head, sadly. "You think you've got a handle on this situation, but I promise that you don't. If Hades is coming for this place, he'll hit it with overwhelming force. Not just deathless, but demons. Stuff you haven't had to deal with. If Nox really took apart Mohn Corp, he can back all that up with the most sophisticated technology in the world. He's funded by a god that Isis herself was wary of. Do you really think that's worth treating lightly?"

"You mistake my intent, Jordan." Davina sipped her drink calmly. "I am not treating it lightly, I'm simply saying that we're beyond his reach. No matter how powerful he is, he cannot harm what he cannot find. You've shown me nothing to prove that he has the means to locate this place. Or is there something you wish to tell me?"

"No, there isn't. And it's your call whether you mount a defense, I just want you apprised of the facts. So let's ignore the imminent threat for now." Jordan knew he wasn't changing the matron's mind; might as well see what else he could accomplish. "How about my friends? You've got them locked up. How and when do we sort out what's going to happen with them?"

"The council meeting will be starting in less than an hour," Davina said. The corners of her mouth were turned down in the kind of frown Elia would have envied.

"I thought you already had your meeting. Awa said that he was leaving for the council meeting," Jordan protested. He folded his arms, forcing even breaths. He couldn't afford to lose his temper, not now.

I disagree Ka-Dun. These are champions. They respect strength. Take her position for your own.

Jordan knew it wasn't that simple, or he'd have already done exactly that. A hostile takeover wasn't going to work, and would only weaken them when they most needed strength.

"We met to plan the trial itself," Davina said. "That trial will be held in full view of every sister and brother, so they may witness justice taking its course." She took another sip, eyeing Jordan distastefully. "That trial will be held this evening, just after moonrise."

"Then I guess we're done here," Jordan said. He rose to his feet. "I don't know why you dislike me so much, and I have to be honest. I don't much care. You and I want the same thing, Davina. We want to see this city—and your people—survive. You might think I'm being overly paranoid. You might think I'm power-hungry, or whatever the hell else you believe about my motives. I don't much care. We need each other, and the sooner you realize that the more of our people will survive what's coming."

"Goodbye, Ark Lord. I believe this will be the last time we meet, and that after the council meeting you may find your short stay in the Holy City at an end," Davina said. She also rose to her feet, seemingly unperturbed by the relative difference in heights. Jordan towered over her, in human form at least. "When that time comes, I urge you toward restraint. If you try to resist, you will find that your abilities avail you little here. We are also powerful, and we've learned more than you can imagine about shaping."

"Davina, you're one of the least intimidating adversaries I've had to deal with. I'll extend the same courtesy you've offered me, a warning." Jordan leaned forward, lowering his voice to a near-whisper. "If you threaten the safety of this city, none of your fancy toys, none of the shaping tricks you've learned, none of your allies will save you. I'll put you down, Davina. I'll put down anyone and everyone I have to, so if you pronounce that judgment be ready for a fight."

Trevor raised a hand, deftly spinning the hologram. It moved to a different fragment of DNA, what Anput kept referring to as helixes. Ba hovered nearby, eyes scrunched as it observed Trevor's work.

"I believe Anput's assertion is accurate," Ba said. "Changing this segment would likely affect the subject's ability to shape. This gene is present in all strains of the virus you've provided. However, its interactions with nineteen other genes are slightly different in every case. Slight modifications to this gene will almost certainly trigger unpredictable results."

"Not necessarily unpredictable," Anput countered. She tapped lightly on her glasses, lips pursed as her eyes shifted between the various strains. "We know the capabilities of each strain, and we know the desired end result." Anput pointed at the last of the DNA sequences, the one that differed the most from all the others. "David's DNA was modified by the grey men to allow him to interface with Builder technology. That's, unsurprisingly, the same reason I believe Hades would seek this city. If they can find a way to control Builder technology, they can seize full control of the Nexus, and find the Black Knight satellite."

"And you want to get that ability first," Trevor said. He didn't understand enough about genetics to see the patterns that Anput casually understood, but the concepts weren't that hard to understand.

"Doesn't that make sense? We lost one of the keys when the First Ark detonated. You're young, and can't really understand what an incredible blow that is—far greater than losing Isis herself." Anput turned to face Trevor, her oval face bathed in the blue glow of the hologram. "If we could manufacture deathless with the ability to become Primary Access Keys, we could guarantee victory in this war against the Builders. They know that, too, which is why I think they're seeking the same thing. Hades isn't stupid."

"I get it. I'm not stupid either. I did see Blair wield that thing. It's a potent weapon." Trevor tried to stifle his irritation, but it was difficult. Being cooped up in here was wearing on him, and throwing himself into work he barely understood wasn't much help.

"You *don't* get it." Anput removed her glasses and began to pace. "Blair used the staff in the most blunt force way. It is capable of incredibly intricate shaping, especially when linked to a nearby Ark. You can destroy an Army with a thought. Reshape an entire species, every member within a hundred miles."

Trevor was a bit taken aback. "Okay, I can see the importance. We have to get there first." He turned to Ba. "Can you replicate David's segments in all nineteen affected genes?"

"Of course," Ba said. His large eyes closed, then opened a moment later. "Done. I've modified the current template to include the requested change. However, I would caution against using the mutagen in its current form. It is likely to have very detrimental effects. It might be wise to conduct tests on other lifeforms before risking your own helixes."

"Perhaps we can test it on me," Percy's shaky voice came from the shadows against one wall. He rose haltingly to his feet, leaning heavily on his cane as he limped into the light. "I don't appear to have much time in any case."

Anput frowned at Percy. "It's highly unlikely you'll survive. Most people exposed to any strain of the virus simply die, or don't come back with the capacity for real intelligence. An unstable version? It would disintegrate your helixes."

"What would you suggest then, Lady Anput? Should I resign myself to an ignoble end? Testing this virus would contribute to science in a small but measurable way. I am first and foremost a scientist, just as you are. Let me contribute." Percy rested against one of the pedestals, regaining a bit of color.

"We don't have anything to test just yet," Anput said. "We've got a lot more simulations to run before I'm comfortable testing anything on anyone. When we reach that phase, we can decide if we want to allow Percy to test it."

Trevor focused on the hologram again. "Ba, given the differences between all viruses, can you extrapolate any possible side effects?"

"The mutagen will likely exhibit entirely different side effects for each being exposed," Ba said. "If given to a normal human, that human is unlikely to survive. If they do, they'd likely be very similar to the original subject. The altered helixes would allow the subject to shape in a variety of ways, and to further modify their helixes as desired. However, this ability could be extremely dangerous. Some modifications could terminate the subject. Even if they do not, such radical alterations will often send a body into shock. This shock can trigger systemic failure."

"He's right," Anput said. She played with a lock of hair, her gaze fixed on David's DNA. "The amount of energy needed to shape is immense. If the subject has the same kind of adaptation David does, that could explain why it took the grey men so much testing to create a viable subject. It could also explain why they haven't been able to duplicate their work with him, so far as we know."

"Just so I'm clear," Trevor said, "a normal human that survived the process could modify how they shape. This could make their shaping stronger, but their bodies aren't equipped to process that much energy. That about sum it up?"

If you consumed the right kind of human mind you wouldn't need to feel this ignorant, his risen taunted. *Your squeamishness limits you in countless ways, and you know that Anput would agree.*

"It mirrors my understanding, Sir Gregg." Percy dabbed at his mouth with his handkerchief. The gesture had become reflexive. "I still do not fully understand this shaping you go on about, or who these 'grey men' fellows are. What I do understand is that I'm not of any use to anybody if I am dead. Please create whatever this pill is so I can take whatever—what did you say it was called?"

"Mutagen," Ba provided.

"Yes, this mutagen. I'd say create it, and I will take it," Percy continued. He seemed to gain strength as he spoke, driven by pure hope. "If it doesn't work, why simply put my body in one of those—" Percy turned to Ba. "What did you call the strange man-sized tubes in the basement?"

"Reclamation chambers." Ba said. The hologram seemed pleased to answer. "I begin to see what potential subject Percy has planned. If the mutagen is unsuccessful, he could be placed into a state of suspended animation until a shaper of sufficient skill was able to modify the mutagen in the appropriate way."

"Precisely, my short green friend, precisely." Percy attempted to clap the hologram on the back, and seemed puzzled when his hand passed through.

"I'm on board with letting him take it," Trevor said. He turned to Anput. "What do you think?"

"It's his life." Anput shrugged. "It will probably take at least several hours to come up with a set of modifications that take every possibility into account. I can do a lot of that on my own, but I need space to think. Interruptions are catastrophic to creativity. That's one of your era's more insightful quotes."

She bent to one of the pedestals, and Trevor took the hint. He helped Percy to his feet.

"Let's go examine those tubes," he suggested. "I want to make sure we understand the sequence needed to freeze you, if necessary."

Chapter 62- Calculated Risk

Jordan removed his sunglasses as he stepped inside the temple's shaded corridor. He'd needed them for the glare, which he suspected was artificial. The domed sky was too white, the sunlight not quite right.

It made him uneasy, and he was happy to leave it for the cooler confines of the temple.

"You realize that the council will react very poorly when they hear that we've entered this place," Leti said. Her tone was disapproving, but she'd stepped inside just the same. "It will destroy what little chance we have of swaying them to help us."

"I know," Jordan replied. He kept walking, and waited until Leti followed before he spoke again. "Respectfully, your council is impotent. They're too busy bickering over power to see a real threat. They think they have Nox right where they want him, but I know him. The Director always has a plan. We might not see it coming, but the blow *is* coming. We need to be ready."

"And how does coming to this place make us ready?" Leti asked. She grabbed him by the arm, stopping him. "Listen to me, Jordan. I have sacrificed everything to support you, because I believe that is what the Mother wants. I deserve to know what you are thinking."

"You're right." Jordan paused, shoving down the surge of guilt. They'd nearly reached the makeshift prison's control room, but were still far enough off that he doubted their conversation would be overheard. He turned to Leti. "I'm sorry. In the military we learned to give and accept orders without question. Command rarely explains themselves to subordinates."

"I am not your subordinate." Leti's eyes narrowed dangerously. "I support you, but I do not serve you."

"I know," Jordan said, maybe a tad quicker than he might have with a less angry Ka-Ken. "I'm not suggesting you're a subordinate. I'm just used to dealing with them in combat situations, and I have a feeling this is about to become one."

"Do you really believe this Nox is that dangerous? It took us weeks to find this city, and we had advantages no demon will possess."

Leti's anger seemed to have ebbed, and Jordan relaxed a hair.

"Far, far more dangerous than you can imagine," Jordan explained. "The Director, Mark, was the finest strategist I've ever seen. He was always a dozen moves ahead of his enemies, and even when he made a mistake he usually turned it into an advantage. Now? He's got powers we can't even guess at. He'll find this place. I'm actually a little surprised he hasn't already."

Leti released his arm. "You were going to tell me why coming here would help us prepare," she prodded.

"The Director is incredible, and there's only one other person I've met that might approach his level. Every damned time I've gone up against Trevor, he's pulled ahead somehow. I don't know what he can do to help, but I'm damned well going to bring him into the loop. That will piss off the council, but they don't really have the power to stop me." Jordan gestured at the control room. "Shall we?"

"Very well. I'm unsure if your friend is worth risking the council's ire for, but we've already acted. We may as well see what he can tell us."

Jordan was mildly surprised by her use of the word friend, but he said nothing. Instead, he walked boldly into the room, raising his voice. "Trevor, you around?"

A soft blue glow came from a cluster of holograms around one of the room's four pedestals. Trevor and Anput were both peering at a segment of DNA, speaking in low tones.

A few feet away a familiar hologram hovered.

"Ka, is that you?" Jordan asked.

"Ah, I see that you too have met my fellow Ark Keeper." The hologram disappeared, then appeared in front of Jordan. It flickered, the same way Ka had when the Nexus had been nearly out of power. "I am Ark Keeper Ba, custodian of this facility. Welcome, Ark Lord. It has been many millennia since we've had one Ark Lord, let alone two. I almost believe the old days have come again."

"Trevor, this thing trustworthy?" Jordan asked. It looked remarkably similar to Ka, but now that he was studying it he could spot differences. The head was a slightly different shape, and the unreadable black eyes were a little further apart.

"Jury's out, but it's been helpful so far. No idea if it will betray us to the Builders if given a chance." Trevor rose from the pedestal, then approached. "Let me guess, you're here to deliver more bad news? Hey, Leti."

Leti gave a cool nod, then folded her arms. Anput stayed at the pedestal, darting occasional glances their way as she continued her work. She seemed irritated at the interruption.

"I'll keep it brief," Jordan said. "Looks like you guys are in the middle of something." He approached the holograms, but couldn't make heads or tails of what he was seeing. He turned back to Trevor. "The council is going to meet shortly. I suspect it will be a lot of posturing with a healthy dose of denial. They think they're secure here—in fact, they're certain of it. Because of that, they spend their time bickering and jockeying for power."

"Yikes," Trevor replied. "They have no idea what the Director is capable of. If anyone can find this city, it's him."

"Yup," Jordan agreed. "So you see the problem. Maybe it won't be today, and maybe not tomorrow, but sometime very soon Nox is going to find this place. The werewolves will get overwhelmed, and he'll take over the city."

"Then you're really not going to like what we've learned," Trevor said. He let out a long breath. "This place warps time. The interloper they were talking about? He arrived in 1925. To him, only seven months have passed."

"Oh, shit," Jordan said. The news sent him reeling. "How much time has passed in the outside world since we arrived?"

"Weeks maybe? We shut off the time dilation, but we'd already been here for a while."

"We're so fucked," Jordan whispered.

"I couldn't agree more," Anput said. "The question is, what can we do about it? I feel so powerless." Her tone was bitter, and her beautiful face twisted with distaste. "These fools have no idea what they're dealing with, no idea of the stakes. They will keep us penned in until it is too late, and there seems to be little we can do about it."

"That's why I'm here. There's an element among the werewolves, a disenfranchised bunch. We can at least sway them to our cause," Jordan explained. He darted an uncomfortable look at Leti, who was eyeing him disapprovingly. "We may need to orchestrate a coup. After we're in charge of the city we can bring in forces from Peru, and if Blair is willing maybe even from San Francisco. This place needs to be protected, and it's going to take a real army to do it."

"You seek to incite rebellion among my people?" Leti was aghast. Her eyebrows knit together, like thunderclouds. "You go too far, Jordan."

"Do I?" he shot back. "This city needs to be protected. If Isis were here she'd agree with me, and I think you know that. We can't let petty politics endanger this place. Am I wrong?"

Leti's fire sputtered out. She was a long time in answering. "No, you aren't. The council won't act. I do not know if you are correct about this approaching threat, but if Nox really is able to find this city, I do not think my people can stop him. Not distracted as we are. Even I must admit that. It is, after all, why I supported you in the first place."

"Anput and I have been working on something that might help," Trevor said.

The way he said it made Jordan pause.

"What's the catch?" He knew there had to be one.

"The virus is unstable," Anput admitted. She sighed. "We need more time, weeks at the very least. Without that time, the best we can do is make educated guesses at what this virus might do. It could kill you, quite spectacularly."

"What if the virus works? What sort of tactical advantage would it give us?" Jordan asked. He'd take anything at this point.

"If it works, it will give the host most of the functionality contained in the Primary Access Keys," Trevor explained. "It allows the host to adapt their shaping to suit just about any situation. Basically what David can do, but a stronger version when combined with Isis's original virus."

"That might be a game changer." Jordan suppressed the slight tremor of hope. "If it works, that is. I have no idea how long you have to work on it, but assume it needs to be ready to go at a moment's notice. I'm going to go deal with the council. If things go south, get ready to act in a hurry."

Chapter 63- Found You

Nox winged silently over the jungle, hugging the treetops as he passed into another valley. Behind him flitted a dozen shadows, invisible to all but him. He could feel them, through the demonic link he'd forged. Only Kali was exempt to that, lurking somewhere in the darkness. He hated not knowing where she was.

He'd have preferred to come alone, but the chance of encountering champions was too great. The search had taken over two weeks, a slow spiral ever deeper into the jungle. His pattern was meticulous, and at long last it had borne fruit.

A deep thrumming came from the valley below, and he could smell the power down there. Nox smiled, dropping silently into the canopy. He glided toward the jungle floor, his many shadows following.

Nox gestured, and three winged demons emerged from the shadows, visible to anyone or anything that might lurk below.

As expected, a Ka-Ken lunged from the shadows. She landed on the demon's back, riding him to the jungle floor. Bone cracked with the impact, and the female began tearing at the demon's gut. She tore through his thick hide, ripping out a handful of entrails.

The demon screamed, struggling futilely to escape.

Nox drifted silently down, extending his right hand. He willed his weapon to emerge. A pool of dark metal flowed into his palm, elongating into a wickedly curved blade. The demonsteel vibrated faintly, anxious to taste another essence. It wasn't alive, exactly, but it hungered all the same.

So Nox fed it. He rammed his blade into the unsuspecting female's spine, pinning her to the ground. His lieutenant wriggled away from her, a trail of blood in his wake. He'd live. The Ka-Ken wouldn't.

Nox willed the demonsteel to drink, mouth opening in pleasure as power flowed into him. A heady mixture of memory, ability, and raw energy. Nox continued to drink until the lifeless husk tumbled to the wet earth, then he willed his blade back into his body, bringing himself back to his surroundings. Shadows had landed all around them, but no other threat had presented itself. Could they really have only one sentry?

"Fan out through the jungle," Nox ordered, just loudly enough for the others to hear. "Find the portal, and encircle it."

His words were swallowed by the hum of the jungle, a million insects singing that they existed. The place teemed with life, more so than any other place Nox had visited. He loathed it—loathed the chaos and disorder.

His shadows flowed through the jungle, moving toward the potent energy source near the heart of the valley. Nox flitted after them, careful to allow them to get there first. If there were other sentries, they might include a male. That male could, conceivably, detect them even though they were cloaked in shadow. If that happened, Nox wanted it happening to an underling.

They made amazing time, cloaked by the jungle as they approached the shimmering portal. It was far larger than Nox had expected, which would make his task even easier. If he'd had to assault the city sending in two people at a time that would have been problematic, but as it stood he could send an entire battalion all at once.

He studied the city on the other side of the portal. Golden pyramids stretched into the distance. The place was massive, though not so massive as a Great Ark. Not unless those pyramids extended a lot further underground than he expected.

A few figures walked leisurely down the wide marble thoroughfares, mostly between a trio of pyramids near the city center. Nox glided closer, stopping less than a dozen feet from the portal. He could feel his warriors around him, ready to spring into action should a threat present itself. None did. It appeared that the sole guardian of the portal had been the jungle sentry. If that kind of mistake was indicative of the defender's caliber, he strongly suspected this would be over very quickly.

Nox mentally ordered ten of the shadows through the portal, holding his breath as they passed through. If there were an alarm or countermeasure, this would be what triggered it. Nothing happened. None of the champions seemed to react. They continued into the largest pyramid, moving with the same unhurried pace. Nox was cautiously optimistic. He stepped through the portal, moving swiftly toward the edge.

A massive golden obelisk stood at the very edge of the portal. Immense power flowed through it, into the portal. Nox crouched next to it, obscured from the rest of the city by the obelisk. "This appears to be the emitter. Kali, head to the opposite side and set up the modulator."

Kali knew what to do, so Nox focused on his own task. He removed a wide demonsteel box from his pack, ordering his shadows to do the same. They materialized around him, winged demons who matched his own form —his children, in a way—and began silently erecting the modulator, affixing it to the side of the obelisk.

Nox stepped back into the shadows. He watched the city, but there was still no visible response. Their work would take another few minutes, and when it was complete the invasion could begin. The werewolves had concentrated their forces at the jungle's edge. There was no army in this city, just a small enclave.

In a matter of hours, the city would be his.

Jordan squared his shoulders, walking proudly into the coliseum. Every member of the council, and every other werewolf in the city, seemed to be in attendance. They lined the lowest rows of the golden seats, all watching him with a mixture of curiosity and animosity. The curious faces were mostly young, and he recognized quite a few from his meeting with Awa.

The council was arrayed across a wide dais, each councilor seated on a golden throne. Jesus, the Builders had loved gold. The council watched him with varying degrees of hostility, clearly waiting for him to find a seat. The only friendly face was Awa, and he was watching Leti, of course.

"Where you choose to sit will occasion a great deal of comment," Leti whispered without facing him. She walked a half-step behind, allowing him to pick their destination.

Jordan scanned the crowd one more time. Most of the seats in the first row were taken, though he might be able to squeeze in. He could sit in the second row, but suspected that doing so would lose him some face.

What would his rebellious young supporters most appreciate?

"Follow me," Jordan muttered. He walked toward the dais, pausing at the edge. He drew a sliver of power from his link to the Ark. Molding the air around himself and Leti was simple. In a moment, he had created two chairs that shimmered like a desert mirage.

Jordan sat, and gestured for Leti to do the same. She did, though Jordan noticed that she avoided looking at the council.

Jordan had purposely placed the chairs opposite the council, highlighting the adversarial role he knew they were about to play. It had the desired effect. Elia's eyes blazed, but it was Davina who spoke. She made a great production of it, gesturing expansively to everyone around them. "You mock our ways in front of all. This, on the heels of defying our decree that the deathless were to be kept in isolation. The meeting has not even begun, and already you are disrupting it. Do you delight in chaos, Ark Lord? Or are you merely that contemptuous of our ways?"

Jordan risked a glance at the crowd. More faces were growing hostile.

Davina had chosen an excellent opening gambit. No one liked seeing their faith mocked, not even the young, rebellious types. This wasn't starting out well. He needed to recover some ground.

"Who appointed you as matron and councilor, Davina?" Jordan asked. It was a risk, as he didn't know the answer. He strongly suspected it, however.

Davina's eyes narrowed, and she stared hard at Jordan. "I am not on trial here, nor are our ways. If necessary, I can have you removed from these proceedings."

"You've taken the time to have all your people come to witness this. Let them see how their leadership works. Are you transparent? Or are you a tyrant? Pick. You can't be both." Jordan leaned back in his chair, waiting.

"Very well, we'll play your little game, outsider. No one elected me to the council. I was the first found worthy by the city, and I founded the council with those who followed." Davina's confidence was undiminished.

"So, you found the city," Jordan said mildly. "The next four people who found it were also considered important. Everyone who found it after that is less important, right? They're not worthy of a voice on your council?"

Whispers rippled through the audience.

"Silence," Elia roared. She rose to her feet, and the crowd subsided. Elia glared around her, sitting only when there was complete silence. She waved at Davina to continue.

"Thank you, Elia." Davina nodded graciously. She rose magnanimously from her throne, turning in a slow circle as she addressed the audience. "The council is guided by our strongest members. It has always been so, and is as the Mother willed. Did she not say that only the strongest rule?"

Leti's clear voice rang out through the room. "Did she not also say that compassion is what separates us from the ancient enemy?" She rose from the invisible chair, also addressing the crowd. "Did she not stress the importance of wisdom, the danger of hubris? Of her own mistakes? Each time Isis faltered, it was because she believed herself above others. She admits this, though we don't often like to talk about it. If this council is fixed, if we do not listen to the voices of the people, then we make the same mistake she did."

"Speaker, may I address the floor?" Elia asked. She nodded deferentially toward Davina.

"Of course, Councilor," Davina said. She returned to her chair and sat. Leti strode back to hers as well.

Elia rose, walking to the middle of the floor before she spoke. "Ark Lord Jordan brings change. At first, I was frightened by this change. After all, he possesses power that we do not. He stands higher in the Mother's grace than we. The Ark Lord is powerful. Yet, as Leti reminds us, even the most powerful are fallible. Power does not make us immune to mistakes. I am certain that the Ark Lord means well, but he has no idea the threat he has leveled at our culture, at everything we have built here."

Elia raised her arms, turning slowly. Every eye was fixed on her, many in rapture.

Jordan could feel the subtle signal emitting from the bracelet, though no one in the audience seemed to react to it.

"Let us tend to the matter that brought us here today, the fate of the deathless. Once that has been dealt with, we can adjourn to discuss the weighty matters that sister Leticia has put before us. If there are truly those who feel disenfranchised, we will see your concerns addressed. Just not right now. Not as a distraction used by the Ark Lord to protect the ancient enemy. Let us show the deliberate patience the Mother advises."

Jordan knew he'd lost them. This side of Elia was new, and he suddenly understood how she'd amassed so much power. Somehow, she'd casually derailed Leticia's argument, quashing the crowd's anger. Part of that was no doubt related to the bracelet, but only part. She'd spoken masterfully, and probably would have succeeded even without the aid of shaping.

"I'm amicable to that," Jordan said. "Let's discuss the fate of my friends —but if we're going to do that, I'd like to remind you that they're directly tied to the fate of this city."

All eyes were on him again, but this time nearly every gaze was filled with animosity. He was breaking protocols he knew nothing about, and Elia was using that to her advantage.

"I assure you that I don't like chaos," he said, "nor am I contemptuous of your ways. I'm doing what the Mother would want me to do: protecting this city. Many people in this room are males; there are enough of us to mindshare. I am happy to show you my encounters with her, the encounters that Elia and Leticia have already seen. You want to see what's lurking out there, the danger that might be approaching even now? Let me show you."

"If that danger is real, then of course we will address it," Davina said. She looked contemptuously at Jordan. "You say you respect our ways. If you do, you'll remove yourself from this stage. You will allow us to conduct our business, and wait until you are recognized before speaking."

"Nah," Jordan said. He closed his eyes, feeling the cluster of minds surrounding him.

Jordan reached into his memory, beginning with the day he'd first put on the demon armor. He broadcast that memory to the audience, conscious of the gasps and cries as his shaping pushed outwards.

He showed them Mohn Corp gathering to fight, the battle outside the First Ark. He showed them Set's power, and everything he'd seen of the last confrontation.

"That's what we're facing, people. An army of demons capable of overwhelming this place."

"What you have shown us is most troubling," Elia said. Again she rose to her feet. She spoke directly the crowd, who stared at her in near rapture. "These demons are a real threat, but let me remind you all that we have safely contained that threat. Nox's forces push all along the border, and all along the border our bravest champions push them back. The spirits of the jungle assist us, and we keep that enemy at bay. These demons must be stopped, clearly, but they are hardly the imminent threat the so called Ark Lord would have you believe. Now, will you leave the stage, or must we attempt to remove you by force?"

"I'll leave," Jordan began, "but before I go let me say this." He rose, taking in the audience the same way both Leticia and Elia had done. "You have no idea who we are dealing with. I knew Nox as a mortal, before all this happened. I've never met a more canny, more devious person. If you think you're winning against Nox, you can be certain you aren't. We might not see the blow coming, but it is. We are all in danger."

Jordan leapt into the stands, landing in an unoccupied section in the third row. Leticia joined him a moment later. She avoided looking at him, eyes downcast. He couldn't blame her.

"Now then, on to the more pressing business," Davina said. She clasped her hands behind her back, giving the crowd a grandmotherly smile. "We must discuss the issue of the deathless brought to our city. Ark Lord Jordan claims they are allies. The scriptures, however, are clear. The ancient enemy can never be trusted, even when it appears we have common goals. I will serve as arbiter in this matter. Who wishes to present arguments?"

Jordan stood, waiting for Davina to acknowledge him. Instead, the elder turned smugly to Elia. "You wish to present an argument, Councilor?"

"I do," she said, nodding graciously. "Having just been impressed with the gravity of the situation with the demons, I understand why the Ark Lord might consider working with the ancient enemy. Wait, wait…hear me out." She raised a hand to forestall the crowd, who'd begun to mutter. "We need allies, and our world has been overrun with deathless. Is it not natural then, to seek them out? Can we then not see how someone could do something so misguided, but do it from a rational, understandable place?"

The crowd was eating out of her hand. Many were nodding, and more than a few darted sympathetic look Jordan's way.

"And what if the possibility exists that he is right? What if they could be useful? For that reason, I suggest a course of moderation. Just as we did with the interloper, we imprison the deathless. They are not allowed to leave, which risks carrying knowledge of the sacred city. Yet neither should we kill them, not if the possibility exists that they might become allies."

The applause was thunderous.

Chapter 65- It Begins

Nox placed one hand on the modulator, and pointed toward Kali's end of the portal with the other. Both modulators had been set up, and both seemed to be working. Now it was time to redirect the portal.

A beam of dark energy shot from Nox's hand, arcing toward Kali several hundred yards distant. A similar bolt shot from her hand, and the two met in the middle. There was an explosion just beyond hearing, then a wave of crackling black energy rippled out from both obelisks.

The portal flickered, and when it stabilized it showed an entirely different vista.

Instead of the lush jungle that Nox had labored to pass through it now showed his forward command base in Brasilia. Rank upon rank of demonic troops stood waiting for orders.

Ahead of them was a line of something special Vulcan had cooked up: the Rottweiler. It was a four legged robot with an energy cannon mounted on the back. If gunning down an opponent failed, the claws were lethal enough to take down champion or deathless alike.

Clustered around the Rottweilers were scores of hellhounds, hairless beasts with dark hides. They had once been dogs, but Hades had reshaped them into tireless killers who hunted in packs. Their skin was thick enough to stop a rifle round, and they were fast enough that they might just dodge that bullet to begin with. By themselves, they weren't much of a threat, but given time, an entire pack could overwhelm a Ka-Ken.

Those were all shock troops, of course. The real combatants were the demons themselves. Over the past five years, Nox had done a great deal of experimentation. He'd corrupted werewolves, deathless, and vampire alike. Each retained their parent abilities, but gained the benefits of being a demon as well. That meant they were stronger and tougher, more resistant to shaping.

All demons, regardless of parentage, had some traits in common. Each had a pair of horns curling from their forehead, and ragged bat wings. A thick tail curled behind them, itself a weapon most foes underestimated. They ranged in height from about eight feet to a full twelve, and every last demon was thickly muscled.

Towering over the winged demons were a trio of demonic Anakim, what Vulcan had termed Demokim. Each stood forty-five feet tall, and had thick, black demonic hide. Enormous demonsteel plates had been woven into their skin over vital areas, and their right arms had been replaced with massive beam cannons, another of Vulcan's inventions. They'd not yet been battle-tested, but Nox was confident they could dominate the battlefield if the werewolves put up significant resistance.

His demons were divided into squads of five. Every five squads was a division. There were four divisions in the platoon, which Nox wagered would be enough to overwhelm whoever was defending this city, even without the Demokim. Even if they failed, they'd provide enough of a distraction for him to fulfill his true mission.

"We should already be attacking," Kali said, stepping from the shadows.

She was careful to keep in front of him, and for good reason. He'd told her that he'd kill her if she ever came out of the shadows behind him. She knew he meant it.

Kali frowned. "We're losing the element of surprise."

"Have a little patience. They may not even know we're here, and if they do they haven't done anything about it. In a matter of minutes my troops will sweep over the city." Nox hated explaining himself, but he'd learned the hard way that Kali could be vindictive if she thought he was patronizing her. He didn't have time for her antics right now.

"What are we waiting for?" she asked sourly.

"I need to report to Hades," Nox admitted. That, too, galled him. He didn't mind answering to a superior, but for so long that had been a superior whose motives Nox had known fairly well. With Hades, Nox knew he was out of his depth. Worse, he had no idea what Hades' true motivations were. Did his master want to rule the world? Help the Builders succeed? Stop them after allowing everyone else to die?

Nox simply didn't know.

"I see," Kali said. Her tone was as contemptuous as it was unsurprising. Kali answered directly to the grey men, and served Nox at their pleasure. She had a low opinion of Hades, and didn't mind showing it.

"Organize the corrupted into scouting groups," Nox ordered. "Have them prowling the city. Locate only, do not engage. We want to know what we're dealing with before we invade."

Kali hesitated for a long moment, then finally nodded. She turned on her heel, then leapt into the air. Her powerful wings carried her upward, and she glided toward the center of the portal.

She was in plain sight of course, almost daring the defenders to rally. Hopefully, her brazenness wouldn't endanger the mission. Nox wished, for the billionth time, that he could arrange an "accident." But Hades had been very clear. Kali was not to be harmed, under any circumstances.

Nox withdrew a tiny marble from his pocket, then channeled a bit of energy into it. The marble swelled, rising from his hand as it grew. It hovered several feet in the air, bobbing slowly up and down. When it had finished growing, it was roughly the size of a person's head. The surface was iridescent at first, but then resolved into Hades' very annoyed face.

"Days without a word." Hades spoke quietly, but the rage was simmering just under the surface. "*Days*. I will remind of you this only once, Nox: *you* serve *me*. We are not equals. You do not get to improvise. You do what I tell you, exactly how I tell you. You were to contact me daily. Why have you not done so?"

"I haven't wanted to risk breaking radio silence," Nox explained. "These things use energy. Any male champion within a few miles would have felt me using it."

"Yet you feel it is safe to use now?" Hades demanded.

"Now it's worth the risk. Look behind me." Nox gestured at the city. "We've arrived, and I've successfully connected the portal. The invasion will begin in moments."

"Very well. Contact me when you have conquered the city. Do not fail me, Nox. If ever there were a time your considerable talents were valuable, this is it. Everything hinges upon you, remember that."

The globe went dark.

Nox took a deep breath, stifling the rage. Hades was devious, but sometimes he behaved like the worst third-world despot.

Yet there was little Nox could do. Hades could jerk him about like a puppet, and thus far Nox had found no way to escape the demonic hold. Fortunately, he had a suitable target to take his rage out on.

He leapt into the air, gliding through the portal. Nox lowered an arm, and the army began marching into the city.

Chapter 66- Perfect Target

Windigo's plans were nearing their apex. He could smell the fear, taste the horror radiating from the city of Santa Rosa. People cowered in their homes, terrified that he might find them. They knew that their champions could not protect them, that one of their greatest had been felled in their very midst.

But that wasn't enough. It was time to shake them to their core.

Windigo gave a hideous smile, picking a piece of dog from his teeth with a slender claw. He began loping through the darkness, moving up cracked asphalt streets. He picked his way past terrified families, savoring their fear as he approached his quarry. He picked his way up the steep hillside, winding past an abandoned factory.

As he neared the top of the hill, he passed the first cluster of houses. These ones were larger, and more of them were occupied than down below. The heartbeats in these houses beat calmly, their owners full of misplaced confidence that they could deal with a threat like Windigo.

No one could. Not even the treacherous creatures that had birthed it had escaped Windigo's wrath in the end.

Windigo approached the summit, loping silently toward a three-story house overlooking the entire city. He slowed his pace, creeping toward the house as his senses strained to detect anything. A single steady heartbeat came from within—just the one. There were no guards, unless they were lurking in the shadows. That meant Alicia was alone. No doubt her guardian was out leading his pack, looking for him. They protected their perimeter, ignoring their most important assets.

He placed a hand on the side of the house, feeling the worn wood. The paint flaked, exposing the beginnings of rot underneath. The heartbeat came from the other side of the wall, less than two feet away.

Windigo lunged, punching through the wall with his long arms. He seized the sleeping figure, digging his claws into her throat. She began to thrash, but Windigo jerked her back against his chest. He crushed her against him, choking off her scream.

"That won't do. We need them to hear you," Windigo taunted. He repositioned his grip, grabbing the scruff of her neck with one hand. He grabbed her thigh, yanking with the massive strength afforded by this new body. The limb tore free with a horrific pop, and a spray of hot blood. Windigo smiled.

Alicia screamed.

"Yes, that's more like it. Louder." Windigo sank the claws of his free hand into her side. "Sing for them."

He let her agonized screams continue for a few moments longer, then slammed her head against the ground. She groaned, still conscious. He did it again. This time she went limp in his grasp.

Windigo slung her body over his shoulder, then began loping down the hillside. He made his way west, toward the ocean. The closest forest lay not too many miles away. It was the perfect place to set his ambush, now that Windigo had acquired suitable bait.

"Ka, are you around?" Blair called into the vast chasm bordering the Ark's heart. The titanic blue stone rotated slowly in the center of the stadium-sized room. It gave off a soft blue glow that refracted endlessly from the crystals lining the chamber's walls, ceiling, and floor.

"Of course, Ka-Dun," Ka said. The hologram shimmered into view not far from Blair. It gave a quick bow. "How may I be of assistance?"

"We're dealing with an entity that calls itself Windigo. I can show you everything I know about it. Will you search the Ark's datastore to see if you can figure out what this thing is?"

"At once, Ka-Dun. You may begin the sharing when ready."

Blair tapped into the well of energy offered by the Ark, using a tiny drop to transmit key memories to Ka. It was far more efficient than speaking, conveying information Blair would never have thought to relay.

"Ah, I see," Ka said—cheerfully, like it did everything. "We do indeed have a record of this creature. It was originally created by the Builder Ra-Ket, an experiment gone awry. Ark Lord Ra-Ket oversaw this continent for the Collective. Observe."

Something like a DNA helix appeared, plus a wall of scrolling symbols Blair couldn't read. Images of something that strongly resembled a house cat, but it sat hunched like a hominid. Its hand had three distinct fingers and a thumb. A tiny pair of antlers jutted from its head.

"Ra-Ket found this species exhibited high degrees of problem-solving intelligence. More so than any other species found on this continent. He believed that, with the proper manipulation, this species could become sentient. Ra-Ket conducted four thousand twenty-two experiments utilizing this creature as a base. Nearly all of those resulted in failure, but an anomaly was recorded. Many of the subjects were highly aggressive, but subject 3199 was exceptionally so. It killed the other subjects in its litter, devouring their corpses. Each time a new subject was introduced, subject 3199 immediately killed and devoured them. Subject 3199 showed increased cognitive ability each time it consumed another subject. This intrigued Ra-Ket, and he decided to see what the creature could achieve if allowed to pursue its full potential. He released subject 3199 into the wild."

This answered so many questions. "How long ago did all this happen?" Blair asked.

"Subject 3199 was released into the wild two point four million years ago," Ka answered happily.

"It's millions of years old?" Blair asked. "And presumably it's been out there all this time? How did it survive for so long? Does this thing sleep between sun cycles? It would need shaping." He was mostly thinking aloud.

"You are correct, Ka-Dun. Subject 3199 does possess the ability to shape. Ra-Ket's logs show how it survived between sun cycles."

The hologram shifted to show a redwood forest. The realism was impressive, like Blair had always imagined virtual reality. He could almost step out into those trees.

One of the cat-like creatures prowled through the trees, seemingly unaware that it was being recorded. It froze, ears cocked toward something imperceptible. The cat crept backward into a fern, a pair of eyes just visible in the shadows.

A few moments later, a bipedal figure came up the path. It had pasty skin and large black eyes. The bulbous head was familiar, though not identical to the grey men he'd seen in the Nexus. It carried a crude spear in one hand, but wore no clothing. It had no discernible genitalia.

The cat creature waited for the grey man to pass, then leapt onto its back. It sank its claws into his throat, and it snapped at the grey man's face. An invisible force flung the cat backwards into a tree with bone-cracking force. The grey man raised his arm, and hurled the spear. It zipped unerringly toward its target, pinning the cat thing to the tree. It mewed pitifully in pain, writhing futilely as its life bled away.

The grey man approached the creature cautiously, pausing near the tree. It rested a hand on the spear, not approaching further until the cat's thrashing had ceased.

A bolt of red lightning crackled from the cat's lifeless eyes, arcing into the grey man's face.

The energy transfer was brief, and when it ended the grey man slowly rose to its feet. It knelt next to the cat, and began devouring it.

"What am I seeing, exactly?" Blair asked. He had theories, but he wanted more data before leaping to conclusions.

"This was the first time Subject 3199 was exposed to the Progeny of the Builders, what you call the grey men," Ka explained. "They were created to serve as mindless drones, and often sacrificed in experiments your species would consider brutal. In this case, Ra-Ket was attempting to feed a grey man to Subject 3199. Instead, 3199 responded in an entirely unpredictable way. Observe."

The hologram began playing again, but at an accelerated rate. It showed the grey man returning to a village with six identical peers. At first, the grey man was greeted and accepted. He did things that seemed entirely normal for a simple hunter-gather society.

Then, after the rest of the grey men had gone to sleep, he slit each of their throats. The surviving grey man fed, devouring his companions—all of them. He fed until there was nothing left to eat.

"This next image is from two weeks later," Ka said, gesturing at the hologram.

It shifted to show the grey man, but his body had begun to change. His skin stretched across his ribs; all his fat was gone. A pair of small antlers sprang from his forehead, and his features had become more feline. His arms were much longer, razored claws dragging in the dirt as it walked.

"Over the next several cycles, subject 3199 killed dozens of grey men. Each time, it grew smarter. Ra-Ket continued to conduct tests for many millennia, and according to his logs was proud of the fact that he'd created a new consciousness. He was the first of his contemporaries to do so."

"None of that explains how Windigo, Subject 3199, survived between sun cycles. Where does its consciousness go? How does it transfer to a new host?"

"Subject 3199 survived many sun cycles during the tests Ra-Ket performed. The creature's energy essence contains a specific set of helixes, and it uses that energy to imprint on the host. Once that is done, the host will begin to exhibit traits similar to Subject 3199. However, the host retains many of its own abilities."

Nearly a dozen different holographic creatures appeared. Each spun slowly in place, allowing Blair to examine them.

"All of these creatures existed during Subject 3199's early life. Each had a remarkable method to store the sun's energy. All were capable of primitive shaping. Subject 3199 simply transferred itself to hosts that were capable of surviving between sun cycles. It would feed as much as it could, always looking for a stronger host. Then it would hibernate, sleeping in the body of the host. When the sun changed again, it could abandon that host and find another."

"That's why Windigo left," Blair said. It was all clear now. "He headed to the mountains, and took Yosemite as a host. He's using the Bear's body to pick us off. That's why the pack said they smelled the Great Bear. Ka, how much information do you have on the specifics of how Subject 3199 transfers bodies?"

"The data is limited. Ra-Ket's experiments were designed to find the answer, but in that regard they failed. He was never able to duplicate Subject 3199." Ka cocked his bulbous head. "However, he did record one other relevant ability. Over the many millennia of feeding on grey men hosts Subject 3199 picked up some of their rudimentary shaping, which is very similar to your own. Subject 3199 was particularly adept at manipulating emotions, specifically rage and hatred. Subject 3199 would often use this ability to cause subjects to lower their guard, then strike when their mental defenses were down. Be wary when dealing with this creature."

Chapter 68- Taken

Liz knew something was wrong the moment she walked up the driveway. Her house was fine, but Alicia's had clearly been the site of a battle. One of the front walls had been smashed in, and Liz could smell blood. She shifted almost without thinking.

"Oh, no," she breathed. She sprinted across the street, leaping through the gaping hole in the wall.

She landed lightly, instantly cloaking herself in shadow. There was no sign of any survivors, but the moonlight showed the puddle of blood on the floor. There was a shape in the darkness, a person maybe. She crept closer, raising her muzzle. No heartbeat, or sweat. She could smell Alicia, and smell something awful, but she didn't think anyone was still here.

So what was that on the floor?

Moonlight illuminated the shape of fingers, she was sure of it. She knelt next to the hand, recoiling when she realized what she was seeing. Those weren't fingers. They were toes.

It was a severed leg. Alicia's severed leg.

"Oh my god."

"Liz?" called a voice from the shadows. "I-is that you?"

"Yes, Kathy. It's me." Liz stepped from the shadows, standing clearly in the moonlight. "What happened here?"

"I don't know." Kathy sobbed. She stepped from the shadows as well, and even in the thin moonlight Liz could see her tear-streaked cheeks. "I heard screams, and came as quickly as I could. Alicia was already gone when I got here, dragged west by this…monstrosity. I knew I should go after her, but…Alicia's stronger than I am, and that thing overpowered her. What could I do? So I waited until someone stronger came back. Where is Blair?"

"He's at the Ark, studying. He should be back in the morning. Yukon is on patrol, and won't be back until then either." Liz took a deep breath. She didn't like the idea of charging after Windigo by herself, but she had a feeling that Alicia didn't have very long. "We're going to have to do this ourselves. I need your help, Kathy. Are you with me on this?"

"We might be able to get others to—"

Liz silenced Kathy with a look. "We don't have time. You know what Windigo will do to her. This was a warning. He's baiting us, and Windigo doesn't strike me as the patient type. If we don't find her now, we're going to find nothing but pieces of her come morning. Are you ready to face that? Because I'm not." Liz couldn't afford to babysit this woman, not right now.

"I'll do my best," Kathy managed. "Lead the way." She stepped back into the shadows.

Liz leapt back out the hole she'd used to enter, testing the air with her muzzle. She could smell the blood, and the trail leading into the darkness couldn't have been clearer. It traced a path toward Highway 12.

Ka-Ken, be wary, Wepwawet rumbled in her mind. *The anger you feel is justified, but it feels…enhanced in some way. I believe that someone or something is shaping us. If we truly cannot wait for dawn, then be mindful of your emotions. They may not be your own. I have encountered this before, and it is a subtle kind of shaping. My wife is adept at such things.*

She concentrated for a moment, using an ability Blair had shown her back in London. Bones popped as her body began to rearrange itself. The process was unfamiliar, and thus slower than her normal shifting. She felt every tendon popping, every bone shifting. It was a horrifying experience, and it still shocked her that she'd grown used to it.

When the process was complete Liz stood on four legs, a massive wolf.

She sprinted into the darkness, finally replying to Wepwawet. *Windigo is cunning. He's using our own fear and anger against us. That makes us sloppy, and easy to manipulate. But we have an advantage too. I know Windigo wants me to catch him, and that gives us the chance at a straight-up fight. I still have the sword Blair gave me. What do you call them?*

A Na-Kopesh, Wepwawet growled. *It is a weapon from my time, one of our most common blades.*

And you know how to use one, right?

Indeed. I am a master. I begin to see where this line of questioning will lead us. If you wish, I will share my knowledge with you. You will fight as you've never fought before.

Windigo is powerful, but so are we. Let's find this bastard, and get my friend back.

Liz loped through the darkness, eating up the miles with surprising swiftness. She made her way through Santa Rosa, and into a town called Sebastopol. She crossed rolling fields covered with grapes, and here and there large stands of oak trees. The further she went, the more rural things became.

Eventually, she began to reach redwood trees, the remains of the gravel road leading up and down steep switchbacks. Liz followed them, crossing into the redwoods. They led her to a river, and she crossed a rusting metal bridge. Midway across, Liz could smell flesh. She trotted over, bending to sniff at a puddle.

It was blood, and in the center lay a human ear.

Liz bared her fangs, turning toward the dense forest blanketing the hillside ahead of her. He was in there somewhere, waiting.

A single female scream split the night, echoing down the hillsides. Liz saw red, rage fueling her as she sprinted toward the sound.

She was going to catch this bastard, and he was going to pay for harming Alicia.

Chapter 69- After Her

Blair popped into existence in the backyard, the cool wind ruffling his fur. He cocked an ear, listening for breathing. There was none—of the human variety anyway. A few foxes, a pack of coyotes, and countless field mice. That was it.

Liz wasn't home, and neither was Alicia. It was nearly dawn, so that didn't make any sense at all.

He leapt to the top of his house, tasting the wind. Recent blood, from Alicia's house.

Blair closed his eyes, his mind questing for the packmind. He found them everywhere, all competing to mindshare. Over and over he saw variations, each a piece of a large puzzle. Screams from the house. Big scary creature carrying fierce little sister. Heading to the mountains, west. Angry red Ka-Ken following.

He focused on the link he'd forged with Liz, paying close attention to the emotions bleeding through. Liz was furious. He could feel her somewhere to the west.

Blair expanded his reach, seeking Yukon. He found him to the north, prowling the forests in lower Mendocino County. *Yukon, we need you back home. Alicia has been taken. Liz went after Windigo alone.*

I will come swiftly, whelp, Yukon thought back. Blair could feel his sudden fear, that either Alicia or Liz might be in danger.

Blair shared the fear, but fought not to let it overwhelm him. Windigo preyed on desperation. Defeating him was going to take cold pragmatism.

He used telekinesis to rip the hood from an old abandoned Ford. He flipped it onto the road, stepping onto the curved steel, then concentrated, willing his makeshift raft into the sky. He stopped a hundred meters up, the height most hot-air balloons hovered at.

Sonoma County sprawled before him: houses, trees, fields. It stretched westward, toward Guerneville.

The wind was bitterly cold, but Blair ignored his chattering teeth. Liz was somewhere west, possibly as far out as Guerneville. He could reach that spot in moments, but going alone was foolish. That was exactly what Windigo was counting on: emotional mistakes.

So Blair was as calm as he could be, given his fear for Alicia and his even greater fear for Liz. They'd finally admitted their feelings, and begun a rather awkward courtship.

He loved her, and he'd be damned if he'd let anyone take her away.

Hear me. Blair pushed his thought to every member of the Great Pack, every dog, fox, coyote, and Ka-Dun within fifty miles. He touched them all, the packmind swelling to thousands. *I know now what Windigo is, and how it came to be. I know how to fight it, and that requires all of you. Only the pack can stop this menace, and we have to stop him now. This morning, Windigo kidnapped Alicia. Liz left in pursuit, even though she knows it is a trap. I'm sure of that. She did it because she loves Alicia, and we all know what Windigo will do to her.*

I'm going to show you an ability, one that I invented. I call it a ping, and Ka-Dun can use it to locate anyone walking the shadows.

Blair blazed through the packmind, seeking every Ka-Dun. He found them by the dozens, and once he had gathered them all he shared the memory of the first time he'd used the ping—against Bridget, inside the Ark's sparring ring.

It's a simple shaping, and all of you have the strength to do it. When we reach the forest where Windigo has taken Alicia, you'll use this ability to find him. Don't engage. Just find him. I'll deal with the bastard.

Blair hovered there, watching as the sun threatened to appear over the eastern horizon. The first rays of dawn illuminated golden fields and patches of forest. So many familiar landmarks stretched beneath him.

This is our home, and we will defend it. Find her.

He stretched out a hand toward the south, where the Great Ark lay like a pulsing beacon. Blair pulled deeply at the reserves, feeding the power into the packmind.

The Ka-Dun drank the power directly, but the rest of the pack manifested that power physically. They grew stronger, tougher, and much faster. Hundreds of canines blurred into the trees, flowing westward. Their barking startled birds into flight, the flock heralding the pack as it ran through West County.

Blair followed, staying airborne as they crossed the rolling golden fields.

The link to Yukon grew stronger as the dog made his way south, but he was still far off. He'd be here in a few hours, but by then this would all be decided one way or the other.

It was up to Blair, and those he'd gathered to help.

Chapter 70- Hunter or Hunted

Liz crept silently into the parking lot, not spotting any immediate movement. On the right was a steep ridge, with a hiking trail picking up switchbacks. The hillside was covered in thick redwoods, with clusters of ferns carpeting their feet. Across the parking lot lay a large visitor's center, and beyond that lay the valley floor.

It was the most beautiful forest Liz had ever seen—not that she was in a position to appreciate it.

The mighty trees were far enough apart that they didn't limit visibility, but they did provide ample hiding spaces, even for something as large as Windigo. He was out there somewhere, watching. She could feel his gaze, even if she couldn't see him.

"Face me, Windigo," Liz yelled. "That's why you drew me in, isn't it? You wanted me out here alone. I'm here. Let's get this over with."

Her voice echoed through the trees, and in the distance a few ravens answered. There was nothing else.

She walked boldly across the parking lot, in plain view, and approached the visitor's center, leaping onto the roof to get a better view of the forest.

"Are you really going to draw this out?"

A sharp scream echoed through the trees, far enough away that Liz couldn't tell where it originated. She was pretty sure it was from the southwest, so she sprinted that direction. She resisted the urge to cloak in the shadows around her, reminding herself she wasn't the hunter here. She was the hunted. She needed to stay in the open, or Windigo would never show himself.

It means conceding the opening attack to a powerful opponent, Wepwawet cautioned. *It is not too late to gain your Ka-Dun's help, or— failing that—to at least approach with cunning. We are rushing headlong into whatever trap this creature has laid. You must realize that, Ka-Ken. I know you care for this child, but your value is incalculable. Risking yourself is foolish.*

"I wish we had time for that, but you live in my head. You know exactly what's at stake. I left Alicia once. I can't do it again." Liz knew it might not be the most logical choice, but she was damned tired of always doing the "right" thing.

Fuck the greater good. Sometimes you needed to do the right thing in your own life, or you couldn't live with yourself afterwards.

Another scream, this one closer. It was definitely coming from ahead. Liz redoubled her speed, kicking up a spray of leaves as she cut between the trees. She came up short next to a sign proclaiming the name of the tree as *The Colonel*. She'd never have noticed it if not for spray of blood across the sign. It was fresh, droplets still tracing lines down the sign's glossy surface.

The sun had risen over the valley, but the high ridges on either side of the valley preserved the dimness. It was just enough to thicken the shadows in a very hackle-raising way. Liz cocked her ears, straining to pick up anything. The valley was still; only the squirrels were brave enough to chatter. They sensed a predator in their midst—they just didn't care, because they assumed they were safe in the trees.

Another scream, this one back the way she'd come. Liz darted back into the trees, sprinting toward the cry. She caught sight of a stone stage, ringed on one side with benches. It was an outdoor amphitheater, the kind of place that locals used to host concerts or plays.

A prone figure was curled into a fetal position on the middle of the stage.

Liz rushed to Alicia's side, crouching next to the teen. Her eyes were closed, and blood pooled on the uneven granite beneath her. Liz felt for a pulse, breathing in relief when she found one.

Roll, Wepwawet roared.

She reacted, dropping her shoulder and rolling to the right. Long claws skittered across the stone where she'd been, sending up lines of sparks. They were attached to the kind of monster that would haunt her dreams forever.

Wide antlers jutted from a skeletal face, and bits of flesh hung from the bony protrusions. Its arms were thin, but Liz had a feeling the thing was stronger than it looked—especially if it had beaten Alicia. She might be a teen, but she'd become an impressive warrior.

"Hello, Ka-Ken," the creature taunted. It walked slowly, circling her.

Liz interposed herself protectively in front of Alicia.

"Ahh, I see I chose the right bait. I violated her, Ka-Ken, in so many ways. And I will do it again, in so many more."

Rage pressed down on Liz's vision, condensing it to a tunnel. Windigo's mocking laughter broke something inside of her, shattering the floodgates. She came for him then, in a tide of fury.

She leapt forward, slashing at his face. Windigo fell back, and Liz danced backwards into the shadows. She darted right, then slashed at his belly. Claws found flesh, but Windigo's hide was thick. The wound was superficial, and healed before she even had time to dart away.

Windigo brought down both arms, smashing Liz in the back as she leapt away. The blow knocked her into a bench, stone splintering as she tumbled into the next one. She scrambled forward, but Windigo gave her no quarter. It slashed at her with those awful claws, drawing hot lines across her back, then her muzzle.

Give over to me, Ka-Ken. Let me fight this monster.

Part of Liz wanted to bite and snap at Wepwawet, but a distant part of her mind remembered that she was being shaped. Emotions couldn't be trusted. She relaxed a hair, enough for Wepwawet to seize control.

The change in her combat abilities was both instant and educational. Her body flipped backwards, a golden sword flowing into her hand. She brought the sword down in a tight arc, lopping off Windigo's clawed hand even as it plunged toward her heart.

The creature recoiled with a deafening shriek, but now it was Liz's turn to press. She landed in a crouch, wrapping the shadows around her. Then she sprinted left, circling wide while Windigo scanned the forest in a vain attempt to locate her. It clutched at its bloody stump, hissing pained little breaths as it hunted.

"I can kill her right now, Ka-Ken. You aren't fast enough—"

Liz took three quick steps, then vaulted into the air. She came down on Windigo, bringing the blade down so swiftly it hummed. The creature was quick enough to escape death, but not injury. Her blade severed one of his antlers, sending the rotting bone to the forest floor.

Windigo scrambled backward with a screech, then vanished into the shadows.

Liz did the same, moving to stand near Alicia's unconscious form. Now, all she could do was wait.

"Very impressive, Ka-Ken. You're stronger than you should be—a good deal stronger. And your mastery of the blade is too great. What secrets are you hiding, I wonder? How did you come by these abilities?"

The voice trailed off. It had been moving the entire time, and she couldn't use it to locate the bastard. Silence stretched, until Windigo taunted her again.

"I'm going to keep her alive while I feast on her. I promise you that her pain will be the stuff of legend, but that is only the beginning. After her, I'll kill your little golden puppy, and then I'll kill that absent-minded Ka-Dun. I'll take his key from him, and then the fun will really begin."

Liz began to approach the voice, but it stopped just as she was sure she knew where it originated. Blast it. This kind of cat and mouse drove her nuts. Should she appear again? Did she even have a choice?

You always have a choice, Ka-Ken. Just be sure you understand the risks you take. If you appear, he will be on you instantly. He is wounded, but likely already healing. The wisest course is to wait him out. When he tries to kill Alicia, you attack.

The advice made sense, but Liz resisted. If she waited for Windigo to attack, Alicia might not survive.

True enough, Ka-Ken. But if you reveal yourself now, you *may not* survive.

There was no real choice. Liz stepped from the shadows, feet sliding into a practiced combat stance. There was no warning, not even a breath of wind. Claws punched into her back; Windigo's arm emerged from her gut in a shower of blood.

Liz coughed, specks of blood coating her lips. The wound was grievous, but she wasn't going to let this be the end of her.

Her blade swept down in a fluid motion, and the sunsteel blade cut off the horribly thin arm at the elbow. She jerked forward, rolling away from Windigo.

The creature launched a swipe with its newly regrown hand, but Liz was faster. She sliced through this arm, too, leaving Windigo with two severed stumps. She charged, kicking Windigo in the chest with both feet.

The blow caught him off guard, flinging him backward. Liz leaned into the kick, lunging with her blade. The weapon took Windigo through the shoulder, pinning him to the granite near the edge of the stage.

Windigo lunged at her with a muzzle full of wicked fangs, but Liz seized the side of his head and slammed his skull into the granite. Then she did it again. And again.

"End it, then," Windigo slurred. He panted, twitching feebly under Liz's weight. The sunsteel blade was already pulling strength from him, washing away her fatigue. If she pulled harder, it would grant Windigo's wish. "I've never seen a Ka-Ken with your raw ferocity, not even Isis. I must know: how did you become so skilled with a blade?"

Inexplicable fury welled up in her. What right did this…this *creature* have to continue drawing breath? Alicia was unconscious, maybe dying. The day before, it had killed John Rivers. Who knew what atrocities it had committed before that. How many lives had it destroyed? And all she needed to do was draw a little harder, and the creature would be gone forever. It would never hurt anyone again.

She waited to see if Wepwawet would offer his advice, as he always did. As her beast had done before. Yet he was strangely silent.

There was no one here to make the decision but her, so she chose death for Windigo. She'd drink his essence, and he'd never bother anyone again.

"Ark Lord, a situation has arisen that requires your input." Ba's digitized voice came from behind Trevor.

He looked up from the console, facing the hologram. "What is it?" he snapped. "We're almost done with this strain."

He hated letting irritation get the better of him, but his nerves were jagged glass. Ba didn't seem the frivolous type, so it must be important. Still, the interruption was jarring. They were so close.

"Unknown entities have entered the city, and tapped into the portal control obelisks." A flickering holographic screen appeared behind Ba, showing a cluster of black, winged brutes fanning out around the obelisk at one end of the portal. "Nearly every other life form in the city is currently inside the central pyramid. As of yet, they seem unaware of the incursion."

"Fuck," was all Trevor could manage.

"What are they doing to the obelisk?" Anput asked. She approached the hologram, squinting at the demon crouched next to the obelisk.

"Ah, their motivation has become clear," Ba said. He raised a too-thin arm, pointing through the portal. "They've shifted the modulation. The portal control has altered the portal's point of egress."

"Well, where is the portal pointing now?" Trevor asked, though he was positive he didn't want to know.

The hologram adjusted, bringing the point of view closer to the portal itself. The expected wall of jungle on the other side had been replaced by a busy tarmac—and what looked to be a full platoon of demonic troops.

"It looks like they've got some high tech armaments," Trevor said. "Those angry kitchen-appliance-looking things have got a shoulder-mounted energy weapon. I don't know what the hairless dog things are, but they don't look too friendly. What are the giants? They look like Anakim, with some technology thrown in."

"I recognize neither the giants nor the dogs," Anput admitted. "I've seen most of Hades' forces, and I can tell you about the winged demons, at least. Nox is the same breed. They're corrupted Ka-Dun, Ka-Ken, and deathless. They'll use everything we do—plus be stronger, tougher, and more resistant to shaping."

"So individually, they're tougher than us. And they outnumber us, by what looks like a lot." Trevor watched in horror as the demon army began to advance. They moved with military precision, more like Mohn Corp than any supernatural army. It was a terrifying fusion of everything Trevor had battled since Liz and Blair had come to him for help back in San Diego. "There's what, twenty-five werewolves here? They'll be overrun in minutes."

"And we're locked in here, unable to even warn them," Anput said. She scraped the wall with her claws. "Damn it. I tire of being powerless."

"We're not, not entirely," Trevor pointed out. "We've got a workable virus." He started walking toward the stairs.

"Wait, you want to take it, don't you?" Anput asked, blinking. "Trevor, it isn't ready. We have no idea what it will do."

"We're out of time, Anput. Either we take it now, or we get wiped out by that demon army when they seize the city." Trevor walked back to the pedestal. "Ba, how long will it take you to synthesize the mutagen I've been tinkering with on this terminal?"

"It is best administered on level three. I can have the chamber prepared by the time you arrive," Ba said.

"Do it." Trevor sprinted for the stairs, accelerating into a blur.

"Are you mad?" Anput called, darting after him. She matched his blur. "This could destroy you. The potential benefits might take you weeks to master."

Trevor dropped his blur when he reached the third level. One of the chambers glowed green, setting it apart from the rest. He turned to face Anput as she arrived next to him. "If we're lucky one of us will survive the transformation. If we do, we can try to help stop that army. It's the only play, Anput. I don't like it either. We're dead either way. This is at least a chance to make a difference."

"I'm sorry, but I'm not taking that virus. I'm confident I can escape this place undetected, and if I've learned one thing in my centuries its that only death is final. You can escape with me, Trevor. We can fall back. But staying and fighting is suicide. Taking an untested virus is even more so." Anput's eyes were filled with emotion she normally kept cloaked. "I like you, Trevor. You remind me a great deal of Anubis when he was young. You'll be just as powerful one day—maybe stronger. But only if you live. Don't do this."

"I have to," Trevor said. He stepped into the chamber. The glass flowed into the opening, sealing him in. "I understand the risk, and I'm willing to take it. This war is too important, and we know what happens if Nox gets this place. Hades being able to make access keys seems like his endgame. Once that happens, we'll never recover. The Builders will come, and we'll be wiped out. We stop them here, or it may as well be over."

Chernobyl-green light shone from the ceiling, bathing Trevor in intense heat. The light vibrated through his body, and his vision blurred. His entire body lost all motor control and he tumbled to the floor of the chamber, twitching and spasming as the light began pulsing in an odd staccato. He jerked and thrashed, struggling in vain to exert any control. Anything at all.

In the back of his mind, in the place where the risen lurked, he heard a scream. It was distant, and getting fainter. Trevor felt the risen struggling for its existence, and felt it keenly when the risen failed. It was eradicated—every trace scrubbed from his mind.

"The purging is complete. Next, we will administer helix replication. Results may be...unpredictable," Ba cautioned.

The green light shifted to violet, and the pulses began again. This time, they were at a much deeper frequency. Trevor's teeth rattled, and his vision went blurry. It wasn't painful, exactly, just extremely uncomfortable. His entire body was being rewoven, but unlike the virus Isis had created this was happening in a measured, controlled way.

Trevor thought he was getting used to the process when his spine snapped into a rigid bow. His arms and legs were extended, every muscle as taut as it could go. His eyes began to bulge, and a ringing noise overpowered everything. He could feel blood leaking from his mouth, but couldn't make sense of why. He struggled to rise, but slipped, tumbling back to the glass at the bottom of the tube.

Jordan rested his forearms on his knees, letting his head dip. There wasn't even much point in listening any more. Elia had launched another self-congratulatory speech about how wise and cautious they were being, and Davina and the rest of the council were nodding along. The audience reaction ranged from agreement to apathy.

There wasn't any anger, which told Jordan everything he needed to know. The disenfranchised weren't so disenfranchised that they'd oppose the establishment.

"I am sorry, Jordan," Leti said, resting her hand on his arm. She leaned closer. "At the very least, I doubt they will attempt to imprison or bar you in any way. While you are free, there is still hope."

The air flickered and hummed next to Jordan, and he blurred into a combat stance. Ba's wavering hologram resolved into view, bobbing its head apologetically. "Greetings, Ark Lord Jordan. Ark Lord Trevor has asked that I apprise you of a developing situation. May I continue?" Ba blinked those huge black eyes, making Jordan's skin crawl. The motion reminded him of Set.

"Jordan," Leti cautioned from behind him.

Jordan looked around. Elia had stopped her speech. She was staring at Ba, slack-jawed. So was the rest of the council. One by one the audience realized something had happened, and they, too, were turning in Ba's direction.

"What is the meaning of this, Jordan? Have you brought yet another enemy into the very heart of our stronghold?" Davina demanded.

"I didn't bring him to the city. Ba has been here the entire time, before us, and before even Isis found this place. He's what the Builders looked like. Ark Keeper Ba, why don't you tell everyone how long you've been custodian of this city?" Jordan didn't try very hard to hide the smugness.

"I've been custodian of this city for approximately 2.4 million years. I can provide a more precise figure, if desired," Ba offered. He shifted from foot to foot in a very human way. "Ark Lord, apologies for my impertinence, but the news I carry is rather time-sensitive."

"What did you come to tell me?" Jordan asked. He turned to the audience. "Say it loudly, so everyone can hear."

"It appears the city is under attack," Ba explained. "An army of entities that Ark Lord Trevor has referred to as demons has massed outside the portal. Even now, they are marching."

"Nox." Jordan's blood went cold. He glared at Elia. "I told you he'd find us. Now he has. The time for your political games is over. Now it's time to think about survival."

Elia was undaunted. She took a threatening step forward, that special blend of petulant anger rolling off her in waves. "You expect us to believe that this thing has been here the entire time? What proof do you—"

Jordan straight-up Vadered her. He lifted a hand, squeezing two fingers as he pinched off her larynx. She began to choke, her hands shooting to her throat.

"I exist to solve problems, Elia. That's what Isis used me for, and she wasn't too particular about my methods, as long as I got the job done. Right now, you're part of the problem. Think very carefully about your next words. If you continue to be a part of the problem, then you're about to get solved." Jordan released her with a wave, turning back to Ba. "Show me this army."

Ba summoned a large holographic screen in the air near Jordan. It was a topdown view of the portal, and it showed a mass of figures sprinting through. Clusters of brutish demons commanded large packs of sleek black dogs, and their squads were stiffened by mechanized units Jordan was unfamiliar with.

Towering behind all of them were a trio of forty-five-foot-tall monstrosities. Their thick black hide was lined with hardened steel plates. Where their right arms should have been, they had sleek black cannons. The barrels glowed with green circuitry.

That kind of sophistication could only be managed by one corporation, even before the world had ended. It confirmed that Nox had control of their facilities, in Syracuse at least. It also confirmed that Vulcan was still working for them.

"Ba, pan this image back," Jordan ordered. "I want to see the whole city." The hologram adjusted, rising to show the marble thoroughfares linking the various pyramids. Nox had sent patrols to watch his flanks, but the bulk of his army had a clear destination. Jordan turned back to the council. "Nox is coming straight for us. He knows we're in here, and it isn't accidental he chose this exact moment to attack."

Chaos erupted. Three councilors began speaking at once, and half the crowd rose to their feet. Jordan suppressed his frustration. This was what happened in an organization with no discipline.

"Everyone shut the fuck up and sit the fuck down," Jordan boomed.

He harnessed his parade voice, backing it up with a touch of shaping. The result was thunderous, and it had the desired effect. People slid timidly back into their seats.

"I wasn't done speaking. The time for strife is over. I'm going to do everything I can to keep us all alive. To do that, I need you to follow orders. If you can manage that, we have a chance to live, and a chance to save this city. If not, we're going to die and the place you consider most holy will fall into the hands of the Mother's sworn enemies."

Davina stepped forward. "Just because—"

"Are you part of the problem, Davina? Because I'm out of patience and out of time."

Davina's eyes narrowed. "I will do as you ask until the end of this current crisis. I'd advocate everyone else do the same. All in favor?"

Jordan could have stopped her, but chose to let the woman keep her dignity. Embarrassing her here would only make her more of an enemy. They could have their little vote.

Each councilor nodded in turn, with Elia giving the last one. Grudgingly.

Davina licked her lips. "What now, Ark Lord?"

"Okay, let's see how Nox is playing this," Jordan said. He studied the hologram. The demons were moving swiftly, already reaching the building's perimeter. "Ba, are there any other ways in or out of this building besides the entry tunnel?"

"Negative. That is the only means of ingress or egress."

"Perfect," Jordan said. He smiled grimly as the beginnings of a plan formed. "Elia, Davina, organize the council into squads. Each councilor will work with their supporters. Your job is to support and protect each other during combat, understand?" Many nods. "Excellent. Here's what we're going to do. Nox can't take the city until we're eliminated. He knows that we can't get out, which means he can take his time coming in. He's going to make sure there's no back entrance, then his forces will charge the entryway.

"Elia, Davina, your groups will be flanking that doorway. Your job is to tear apart everyone who comes through. Councilman Awa, you'll be waiting at the stairwell leading to the next level. Leti, you'll be leading everyone else. Your job will be to ferry any wounded down the stairs. We'll hold the entryway as long as we can, then fall back to the second level. We'll repeat, falling back until we reach the bottom level," Jordan continued. Everyone was still standing there. "Are you people high? Fucking *move*."

That did it. People sprang into action, fanning out to obey the orders they'd been given. It was a start at least.

He trotted to the entryway, pausing behind Elia. "I'm going to go get us a few more allies. I'll be back in a minute. Elia, you're in charge until I get back. Hold this door for as long as you can."

Trevor awoke with a gasp. He was lying on Percy's cot, on the first floor. He struggled to rise, but the room spun drunkenly. Whispers came from every direction, but none of it made sense. It wasn't even real words, just fragments of sound he could nearly hear.

"Don't try to move," Anput murmured. Her hand pressed him gently back into the cot. He tried to look at her, but his eyes refused to focus. A million tiny motes swam through his field of view. "The mutagen has nearly finished its work. I think the worst of it is over, though obviously I can't be sure. Can you speak?"

"Percy?" Trevor managed.

"Yes, in a manner of speaking. After your little stunt he insisted on taking the mutagen as well. I administered it, then moved him to a reclamation pod. His vitals began to fail, so I placed him in stasis. If the controls are accurate, his life signs are still active. He should be safe until we can find a way to stabilize his helixes," Anput explained. She placed a hand on Trevor's forehead. "How do you feel?"

"Like I was hit by a truck, then that truck backed over me a couple more times," Trevor wheezed. Then it hit him. He'd wheezed. He was breathing. His hand shot to his neck, and he took his pulse with two fingers. "I've got a heartbeat. How the hell is that possible?"

"We knew the virus would be unpredictable. It has pieces of both the werewolf and super viruses. Both are designed to work in living creatures. One of the changes must have had this as a rather unfortunate side effect," Anput theorized. She gave him a sympathetic look.

"Unfortunate? Are you serious?" Trevor said. He gave a whoop, offering Anput a fist bump. She left him hanging. "I'm alive. I'm breathing. I have a heartbeat. Anput, I know you've been dead a long, long time, but I was alive six months ago. I remember eating, and sunburns, and needing to sleep. I remember having sex, and taking a crap. You might not miss all of that, but they're a core part of my identify—a part I just got back."

"Congratulations on your newly reacquired ability to defecate," Anput said. Her mouth was twisted in distaste. "I'd be considerably less, ah, exuberant were my circumstances to have changed in the same way."

"What did I miss?" Trevor asked. He tried again to struggle into a sitting position, this time with more success. The strange sensations suddenly made more sense. His entire body was being re-written at a molecular level. Hopefully it would pass soon. The double vision was improving slightly.

"Nothing that I can see," Anput said. She gave a frustrated sigh. "Ba left to go warn Jordan, and hasn't returned. Anything could be happening out there. Presumably, that army is roaming the streets. Anyone can enter this temple from the outside, so if they start going door to door we're not going to have anywhere to run."

"I'm still an Ark Lord," Trevor rasped. His throat was on fire now, the change altering new parts of his body every few moments. "Ba, can you show us what's happening outside?"

"Of course, Ark Lord," Ba answered pleasantly. He appeared at the foot of the cot. "Though, you may find Ark Lord Jordan's more colloquial explanation of more use. He will be joining us presently."

The air next to Ba warped, and the outline of a man appeared. The outline resolved into a very troubled looking Jordan. "Shit's hit the fan. How up to speed are you two?"

"Not very," Trevor admitted. He stifled a groan, clutching his side with both hands.

"What's the matter with him?" Jordan asked Anput.

"He took the mutagen. So far as we can tell, whatever changes it's making are nearly complete."

"I hope so," Trevor got out between gritted teeth. "Sounds like now is not a good time to be flat on my back."

"Not at all. Ba, get up the same footage you were showing me in the temple," Jordan ordered.

Ba obligingly created a holoscreen within Trevor's field of view. It showed a mass of black specks clustered all along the perimeter of the central pyramid in the middle of the city. "Let me guess—that's where the council was holding their little party?"

"Yup, here's the quick version. Nox somehow hijacked the portal and pointed it to his own army. They flooded the city, and now everyone is trapped inside the council's cheerleading center. Ba can light-walk them out, though, if it comes to that. For now, I've left them there in as fortified position as they can make. They've got some pretty fancy toys, and some of the shapers are strong. They can hold whatever initial probes Nox sends," Jordan said.

He didn't sound all that confident, but Trevor didn't press the issue.

"What do we do in the meantime? That's just a holding action."

"We don't have many options, so I'm playing for time. We need help, and a lot of it. Pretty much right now. At the very least, we need to cut their supply lines, stopping their flow of reinforcements. That means shutting down that portal. You two have had a little time to get your bearings. Do you think that's something you can do?"

"He can barely walk," Anput protested. She poked Jordan in the shoulder. "Why don't you send a couple werewolves? You've got dozens."

"Because I want to make sure this actually gets done. You two are the only ones I trust. If Blair or Liz were here I'd ask them. Since they aren't, I have no other choice. I know Trevor can get this done."

"And I will," Trevor said. He rose shakily from the cot. "I'm not a hundred percent yet, but I'm getting there. Anput and I will find a way to stop that portal. After that, I'll link back up with you in the temple. Light-walking should let us stay one step ahead of them for a few days. Maybe longer."

"It could, but I don't think we have that kind of time," Jordan said. He shook his head, frustration all over his chiseled face. "The Director is after something specific. Whatever that thing is, he'll make a play for it as soon as he's certain we're not a direct threat. If we go to ground, he'll just keep us there until he gets whatever it is he's after. And even if that's only taking over the city, we'll still lose eventually."

"So what do you propose?" Trevor asked.

"Hell if I know. I'm just buying us time and praying for a miracle."

Chapter 74- Desperate Defense

Jordan's light-walk dropped him into chaos. He appeared at the edge of the council chamber, where a pitched battle was being fought. Demons had flooded the room, and pockets of werewolves were battling them. No one had attempted to fall back to the stairs. Instead, they were just brawling. Half a dozen werewolves were down and dying, though Leti and her team were trying to pull them to the relatively safety of the stairwell.

The room was lit by a ragged staccato of green blasts from the werewolves and their bracelets, and the sharp muzzle flares of answering automatic weapons fire. The room stank of blood and gunpowder, plus something so rancid it made Jordan tear up.

He sucked in a deep breath, then activated his blur. He pulled deeply from his link to the Ark, though the flow of power was sharply diminished this far away.

It was enough.

He reached for half a dozen of the closest demons, the winged ones carrying black swords. They seemed to be doing the most damage, so they had to go. Jordan pulled them upward with immense force, slamming them into the ceiling forty feet above. Bones cracked from the first impact, but he was pretty sure they were tough enough to take it—so he slammed them into the floor, then into the ceiling again.

After a little more encouragement, all six went limp, and Jordan hurled their corpses at a pack of demon dogs that had surrounded Elia. The dogs jumped nimbly away, but the distraction gave Elia time to counterattack. She pounced on one of the dogs, digging her fangs into its neck. She yanked upwards, ripping out its spine in a spray of gore.

The sudden absence of the six demons strengthened the werewolf position on that side of the room. Leti and her companions darted into the gap, pulling the wounded to the mouth of the stairs.

"Push them back to the doorway," Jordan boomed. He leapt into the fray, landing on the back of a winged demon. The creature began to spin, its tail wrapping around Jordan's leg. It yanked Jordan to the ground, its sword arcing toward his face.

Jordan blurred out of the path, ramming two fingers into the demon's eye. He jerked it forward, slamming the skull into the golden floor. It splattered with a sickening crunch.

"You heard him," Elia shrieked. She killed another dog, then bounded after a third. All around them, werewolves were ganging up on the surviving demons. The last few seemed to realize their predicament, but not a single one attempted to run. They stood and fought, each inflicting as much damage as they could before dying.

When it was over Jordan stood panting, still in human form. He wiped the blood from his fingers onto his cargo pants, then trotted over to the mouth of the hallway. It was empty, but somehow Jordan was positive that Nox was watching. He studied the corridor a moment longer, then headed back into the room. All around him survivors were climbing to their feet.

"Start piling those bodies around the doorway. We can use them as a barricade," Jordan ordered. He grabbed a dazed looking kid in his twenties. "Hey, it's going to be okay. Just focus on one task at a time. Start moving bodies."

The kid nodded dumbly, then started hauling a winged corpse over to the doorway.

"Jordan," Leti called from the stairway. She was covered in blood, though he couldn't tell if any belonged to her. "I do not know how you did it, but you've driven them back."

"For now," Jordan allowed. He heaved a stinking demonic corpse onto the growing pile.

"Can't you use your telekinesis to move those?" Leti asked.

"I could, but I already feel the cost of that combat. I can't fight forever, and Nox knows it. He'll keep sending waves to deplete our strength, and we need to conserve everything we can." Jordan heaved a final body, then turned to survey the room. "I only see about fifteen people on their feet. How are the wounded?"

"Recovering, for the most part. We've had two fatalities." Leti's face hardened, her smile evaporating. "We're weaker now, and it seems Nox has a near limitless army."

"I'm working on that," Jordan said. He trotted over to the stairwell.

Leti followed. "How?" she asked, pitching her voice low. It was nearly drowned out by the moans of the injured, and the bravado from Elia and Davina as they talked about a counter attack.

"I've sent Trevor and Anput to shut down the portal. If they're successful, we limit Nox's reinforcements. We're still vastly outnumbered, but that will force him to be more cautious. That buys us time." Jordan moved down the stairs into a makeshift infirmary.

"To do what?" Leti asked.

"Get these people down to the lowest level. Odds are good the next wave will push us back, and we might lose this floor," Jordan said. He didn't have an answer, so he focused on what they could accomplish. "I need to go stop Elia from doing something stupid."

Trevor crept toward the obelisk, convinced that his ragged breathing was going to give him away. He sucked in deep lungfuls, lightheaded from the exertion. It had only been a light blur, which scared the hell out of him. Trevor shook his head, focusing, and studied the cluster of demons standing around the obelisk. All five were the same winged variety, and now that he had a closer look he was pretty sure that these were the toughest of the lot. All stood at least nine feet, and all were female.

They are corrupted Ka-Ken, I believe, spoke a familiar female voice. It was cultured, and pleasant to the point of flirtatious. *If that's the case they are nearly impervious to shaping. You'll need to find another way to best them.*

"Anput?" Trevor whispered.

Not exactly, the voice replied, giving a musical laugh. *She served as my template, of course. I mean, she did design the new virus after all. You can't really begrudge her that.*

Well, at least you're more pleasant than my risen was. Trevor glanced toward the far obelisk at the opposite end of the portal. The real Anput was creeping up on it, just as he was creeping up on this one. She faced a similar group of demons.

You said they're impervious to shaping. Illusions bend light. Will that still work on them? Trevor thought.

It should, the voice suggested. *What would you like to call me, by the way?*

Uhhh, let's call you Ann.

Trevor circled around the demons, maintaining a hundred-foot gap. The other side of the portal showed an airport surrounded by jungle. Ranks of demons were assembled, close enough to rush through the gate at a moment's notice. It was the closest look he'd gotten, and it filled him with dread. There were so many demons, each a powerful champion or deathless. Nox had well and truly created an army of gods, and nothing in this city was going to stop them.

Hey, none of that, Ann said sternly. *Focus on the immediate problem. How do we get rid of ten feisty demons who will tear us apart in a straight up fight? Impress me, hot stuff.*

Trevor knew she was right. Fix the first problem, then worry about the next one. All ten demons looked bored. Instead of watching the portal, they were jealously watching the rest of their forces surround the pyramid.

That would change the instant either he or Anput came out of the shadows to disable the portal. They could blur, but who knew what the demons could do? If they could blur, too, Trevor would be overwhelmed before he could complete his work.

He needed them to leave the obelisk entirely, long enough for him to do what needed to be done. But how did you get guards to leave a post?

Hmm. Trevor smiled.

He studied the base on the other side of the portal, mapping the size and layout in his mind. Then he thought back to the single craziest battle he'd ever seen. Set's army had attacked their camp, giant winged dragons raining gunfire from the emplacements bolted into their demonic hide.

Trevor envisioned the battle with as much detail as he could, then began to shape. It was more difficult than it had been, requiring both more concentration and more energy.

He conjured the illusion of dragons strafing the cluster of buildings at the far side of the base. He added a layer of sound, simulating gunfire and explosions. The realism of the illusion shocked him. Prior to this new virus, his illusions had lacked sound and were really just tricks of light. Now he could see—and apparently manipulate—more types of signals. Just as they'd hoped.

The reaction among the demon guards was swift and professional. One demon from each group sprinted toward the pyramid, kicking off buildings then using their wings to get altitude. Both could blur. The rest of the guards sprinted through the portal, onto the base. They rushed toward the combat, fanning out as they approached. These demons didn't blur. Hopefully that meant it would take them time to get there, realize they'd been had, and then get back.

Suddenly, Osiris strode onto the battlefield. He was rushed by a cluster of demons, and cut them down ruthlessly.

It took Trevor several moments longer than it should have, but he eventually realized it had to be Anput's handiwork. Nice, a great way to signal to him that she was there and paying attention.

Oh that's devious. Well done, both you and my flesh-and-blood counterpart. See? Things aren't so hopeless after all.

We still need to disable the modulator, Trevor thought back. He blurred to his assigned obelisk, bending to examine the equipment the demons had attached. A rectangular box had been affixed to the side of the obelisk.

Trevor didn't recognize the metal, though he suspected it was a more advanced version used in Hades' power armor suits. The box sucked in power, and Trevor could feel the signal it broadcast into the modulator. He materialized, reaching for the box.

A thick ropey tail wrapped around his leg, and he was jerked from his feet. Trevor slammed face first into the marble, and his nose shattered.

The pain exploded through him in a way it hadn't done since he'd become deathless. He was unprepared for the shock of it.

Oh, that's an unfortunate side effect of reactivating your full nervous system. I probably should have mentioned that. Ann's tone was contrite. *I can make it up to you, though. Let's harness those shiny new abilities. First, activate a blur.*

Trevor did so, his flight slowing as the demon who'd grabbed his leg raised him into the air again. He wasn't eager to repeat the whole face-smashing thing. He tried to turn to mist, his normal defense when attacked by something larger and stronger.

Nothing happened. The place where that ability had been was simply... gone.

Hmm, that's unexpected. Dematerialization was a desired trait. Sucks that we lost that. Okay, next option. Unfortunately, the demon is stronger than us. I'm not sure you can get loose by sheer physical strength.

I'm open to suggestions, Trevor thought back frantically. He'd reached the apex of the demon's swing, and was already starting back toward the marble. He tried to accelerate his blur, but it felt weaker than it had. *This new virus sucks. Give me some options.*

Umm, well at the very least we can stop the marble from crushing our skull. Take a careful look at the demon, study the skin with your new senses. See how the molecular bonds are formed. You can replicate that. Make your skin into demon hide.

Trevor tried to do as she asked. He looked closely at the demon, sucking in a quick breath when his vision zoomed in to show a microscopic view. He saw mites on the demon's skin, tiny bacteria invisible to the naked eye. Trevor zoomed again, now seeing the molecules making up the epidermis. He saw how they fit together, a series of interlocking tetrahedrons. It was amazing in its simplicity.

Good, good. Now, use that on your own body. Will it to happen, just like you'd shape anything else.

So Trevor did. It proved far easier, and felt more natural, than blurring now did. Trevor reshaped the molecules of his skin, willing them to become a thick carapace. The process took time, completing as his cheek slammed into the marble again. This time, there was almost no pain.

Now we need a better way to fight back. Unfortunately, I don't have any suggestions.

Trevor didn't need one. In exploring the demon's defenses, he'd also spotted a flaw: the molecular bond joining the tetrahedrons was the weakest part. A sustained burst of powerful radiation might get those bonds to break—the kind of burst that came from the grey man's boomerang.

He'd seen exactly how the boomerang amplified the signal, creating the green beam. Could he mimic that?

I don't see why not. All the device does is amplify the signal through modulation. You should be able to do the same thing.

He looked at his hand, balling the fingers into a fist. That fist became translucent, then hardened into a dark green gemstone. Trevor aimed it at the demon, willing a flood of power into his fist. An emerald beam washed over the demon's face, illuminating every feature as the skin began to flake away. Trevor roared, forcing more energy into his fist. The beam intensified, and the demon's entire head disintegrated. The now headless corpse tumbled limply to the ground, the tail finally releasing Trevor's leg.

He stood, panting, the smell of cooked demon filling the area around the obelisk.

Well done. We make a great team. You keep doing the work, and I'll be over here cheerleading.

Chapter 76- Parlay

Jordan folded his arms, staring hard at Elia. She still had a wild look in her eyes, but at least she had stopped ranting at her followers.

"Fine," Elia snapped. She, too, folded her arms. "If you think trapping ourselves here is smarter than breaking loose, I'll defer to your 'wisdom.'"

"You're damned right you will. There's no way I'm letting you abandon a fortified position. We have a choke point. The second we step outside, we get attacked by the entirety of Nox's army, instead of just the few that he can force down this tunnel. Do you want to find out what those giants can do? Because you'll find out the second you go out there."

Jordan unfolded his arms, walking over to Davina's group. He'd left to allow Elia to save some face. Embarrassing her right now was counterproductive, so as long as she obeyed orders he was happy to concede the field of battle.

"Jorrrdaaan," a deep voice boomed from somewhere in the city outside the temple. It had to be enhanced with shaping, and it sounded tinny, like a bullhorn. "Come out and meet with me. I'll give you safe passage for the duration of the conversation, and you know me well enough to know that I'll honor it."

Just like the Director. Succinct, and reasonable. Jordan turned back to Elia. "I'm going out there to talk to Nox. I'm leaving you in charge, but I want your word that you will not follow me out there. You remain here, ready to defend this place. Agreed?"

"Agreed," Elia said warily. "Why are you doing this? What do you hope to gain?"

"Nox knows me, and he knows I'll make taking this place both difficult and time consuming. He wants me out of the way," Jordan explained. "By meeting with him I gain the same thing he's playing for…time. I'm trusting you and your desire to keep this place safe. Don't disappoint me."

Elia gave a grudging nod.

Jordan started walking up the tunnel, moving deliberately toward the artificial sunlight in the distance. He walked slowly, using the time to think.

How much had the Director changed? If he was the same man, he was indescribably dangerous. More so than anyone they'd dealt with—certainly more so than Set.

Set had been unbalanced and easily manipulated. Nox was neither.

Jordan paused at the mouth of the tunnel, donning his sunglasses. The Director stood about fifty feet outside the tunnel. He wore a tailored suit, tasteful sunglasses, and a silver watch. So far as Jordan could tell there was nothing to imply that the man was also a demon, which meant that he could somehow shapeshift like a werewolf.

"Hello Jordan," the Director called. He walked slowly toward Jordan. "It's been quite some time since we last saw each other. I was quite convinced that you'd died. I'm pleased to be wrong."

"I thought you were dead too. What happened when the base was overrun? How did you survive Set's attack?" Jordan offered a hand as the Director approached.

"Set blunted the explosion somehow." The Director accepted his hand, giving a firm handshake. "The next thing I remember, I was crawling out of a chrysalis. Hades uses them to create demons, like the army you see behind me."

"Hades? Not you?" Jordan asked. He eyed the demons ringing the temple. There were at least fifty, and he'd estimate another fifty hidden from sight. Maybe as many as double, so chalk it up to two hundred adversaries, assuming Trevor found a way to disable the portal.

There were also the giants, and more demon dogs than Jordan could count.

"Fair enough. I've created my fair share, though I give them more choice than Hades does. I've never forced anyone," the Director said. He sounded more defensive than Jordan expected, betraying a great deal. Unless that was done intentionally. With the Director, you never knew. Ruses within ruses. "The point is, I survived. Apparently, so did you. How?"

Jordan was a long time in answering. Anything he told Nox would be used against him, but he also needed time. Jordan decided to take a chance.

"Something called TSDS. Apparently, the Ark exploding messed with our light-walk." That was all he was willing to give—for now, at least.

"Interesting. Who else survived that blast?" Nox asked. He gave an easy smile, but it never reached his eyes.

"You know I'm smarter than that, Nox," Jordan said. He folded his arms. "However you slice it, you work for Hades. If you were in my position, that would make you an enemy."

"True, if your politics were from five years ago. A lot has changed since then," the Director countered. "Trust is a valuable commodity, especially when you're dealing with a literal demon. I do work for Hades, and I won't claim he's a saint. He's better than the grey men, though. Have you been brought up to speed on them?"

"I've heard the name, but I'd hesitate to say I've been brought up to speed?" Jordan made it a question, though the Director's expression made it clear he knew Jordan was trying to change the subject.

"Here's the short version. The species that preceded us has sent a task force to ready Earth for their return. When these Builders get back, it means the end of the human race. We'll be exterminated." Nox gestured at his troops. "I know what this looks like. I'm using the same troops that Set did—demons. Let me be clear, demonology is a science just like every other type of shaping. It's got a bad rap for a good reason, but it's still ultimately a tool. Just because I have the same tools Set did, doesn't make me evil."

"So, let's see if I'm getting all this, sir," Jordan growled. He leaned in close, looming over Nox. "You serve Hades, who worked alongside Set with these grey men. The Ark in Africa has three of their ships floating over it, right next to Olympus. Are you seriously going to stand there and tell me you're not in league with the grey men?"

"On the surface, yes," Nox replied calmly. He stared placidly at Jordan. "Hades works for the grey men, helping them. In secret, we've been building an army to resist them. When the time is right—"

"You'll stop collaborating and save the human race?" Jordan interrupted. "Yeah, there's no way that can backfire."

"I had a feeling you'd feel that way." Nox shook his head sadly. "I'd ask you to surrender, but we both know you won't. So I'm going to explain how this will go. I'm going to overwhelm your troops, and kill those who resist. Those who survive will become demons, and that will include you. After that process, we'll speak again. I look forward to having you on my side."

"You seem awfully confident you're going to win. You can feel the power in me. I'm an Ark Lord, Mark. I will not go down easily."

"Maybe. Maybe not. Your Ark is hundreds of miles away, weakening the energy you can pull from it." Nox shrugged, as if none of this mattered. "I'll give you two minutes to prepare for my assault. Make the best of it."

Chapter 77- Modulators

Anput had little choice but to wait for Trevor to make the first move. She'd never been a powerful god, not in the combat sense. She could fight, of course; no one reached her age without being able to defend themselves. But her weapons had always been cunning and seduction.

She surveyed the modulator affixed to the obelisk, but didn't leave the shadows. Instead, she focused most of her attention on the opposite end of the portal. Eventually Trevor appeared next to the modulator, and just as unsurprisingly a demon leapt on him. Any good commander would mirror that defense at her modulator, meaning that if there was a demon watching hers it was likely by itself.

One demon she could take. Anput summoned a simple illusion of herself stepping from the shadows to kneel next to the modulator. Claws raked from the shadows, passing through the illusion. Anput raised her boomerang, channeling as much power into it as she could. The blast took the demon in the back, knocking its smoking form to the ground.

The corrupted Ka-Ken's tail snaked around her leg, yanking her from her feet. She fell with a cry, trying to escape the much stronger demon. Her adversary rolled onto her, pinning her. Fangs descended toward her face, but Anput blurred. She readied a teleport, but before she could execute it a wave of brilliant light burst from the bracelet Percy had given her.

The Ka-Ken scrambled away with a shriek, pawing at her eyes. "What did you do? I can't see."

Anput swiftly raised her boomerang and disintegrated the demon's face. Plums of disgusting smoke clogged the area around the obelisk, and she had to wave it away with her arms to make out the dark metal box.

"Now how do I get inside of that thing?" she muttered. Anput placed a hand on the metal, probing it with a signal. The housing blocked it, meaning that it probably served as a shield for the delicate inner workings. She might be able to tear off the panel, but it was unclear what kind of effect that might have.

"Well, one way to find out, I suppose."

Anput seized the housing with both arms and tugged. She groaned, pulling with all of her strength. There was a tremendous popping sound, and she tumbled onto her backside, box in her lap. The portal flickered wildly between the jungle and the tarmac. Anput leapt triumphantly to her feet, allowing the box to tumble to the ground. She considered studying it, but they had more urgent matters to deal with.

Still, she couldn't just leave it, or Nox might be able to establish the portal.

After a moment's consideration, Anput used her boomerang to vaporize it. Only a slick sheen of oily ash remained on the marble. That dealt with, she stepped into the shadows and blurred toward the opposite side of the portal. Trevor was still there, crouching next to his box. His eyes were closed, and she could feel him broadcasting a complex series of signals into the box. She zoomed closer, stopping in the shadows near Trevor.

"My modulator is gone," Anput breathed near Trevor's ear, "and I think that was enough to render the portal unusable. We need to get out of here before Nox sends a team to investigate. It won't take the scouts long to report to him." She took several hasty steps backward, conscious that even now demons could lurk in the shadows around them.

"I just need another minute," Trevor muttered. He placed a hand against the side of the box, and the metal heated at his touch. The angry red glow continued to grow, until hot drips of metal washed down the side of the device. A hole appeared, and Trevor gave one of those infuriatingly boyish smiles. Then he adopted a look of concentration, broadcasting a dizzying array of signals through the hole he'd created.

Anput studied the signals, trying to ascertain what he was doing. Their goal had been to close Nox's portal, which removing the second modulator would clearly do. So what the hell was Trevor trying to accomplish? She peered over his shoulder at the device's internals. If she understood what she was seeing, the modulator tapped into the portal's coordinate system somehow.

Then she realized what he was doing. "Where are you shifting the portal?"

"Well," Trevor said, peering into the box, "I'm betting that this thing has a massive range. Possibly global. You and Jordan both agree that we can't beat the demons on our own. We need an army, and I think I might know where we can find one."

Chapter 78- Yosemite

The pack filled Blair with awe. It swept across the hills, following Windigo's trail unerringly forward. They picked up a hundred different signs, from the blood to cracked branches. The chase led them on, and within minutes they'd reached the Russian River. Blair was shocked. It was a half-hour drive to cover the same distance, and the blur had brought hundreds of enhanced dogs in a fraction of the time.

A lanky greyhound began baying, and others took up the call, barking and howling, sprinting down Armstrong Woods Road toward the state park. It was a place Blair knew better than his own apartment. He'd spent countless hours exploring miles of trails, listening to audiobooks and pretending that he'd do great things some day.

Blair accelerated, zipping through the giant redwoods. He followed the pack, who were bolting through the underbrush toward the amphitheater. Blair caught a flash of auburn, and blurred even faster. Time slowed as he zoomed toward the stage. Liz was crouched over Windigo, her curved golden blade pinning him to the stone. Pulses of sickly scarlet energy, made lazy by his blur, flowed up the sword into Liz.

It wasn't too late.

"Liz, stop!" Blair yelled. "Don't kill him." He landed a few feet away, trying to get her attention.

She blinked, then slowly looked up at him. Her eyes flared red, a supernaturally imposed rage overpowering her. Then she took a deep breath, and grimaced like she'd eaten something sour. She blinked several times, and her eyes returned to normal. "I was going to drink his essence, just like I did Cyntia, and Wepwawet."

"That's exactly what he wants, Liz." Blair extended a hand toward Windigo, feeling his aura. Subject 3199 was still broadcasting some sort of signal, aimed directly at Liz. She seemed to be resisting it, but the signal hadn't slackened since he'd arrived. "He's shaping you, right now. If you kill him, he'll invade your mind and take over. That's how he jumps bodies."

"Oh. Well, that seems like a terrible idea." Liz rammed her sword deeper into Windigo's shoulder, pinning him more firmly to the stone. "I'm going to take just a little more energy, to make sure he doesn't give us any fun surprises while we figure out how to deal with him."

"How are you resisting me?" Windigo hissed through clenched fangs. "Why won't you break?"

"Are you even serious?" Liz asked. Her fist rabbited forward, knocking Windigo's skull against the stone with a sharp crack. "I dealt with the Master's committee at Florida State. If their bullshit couldn't get me to lose my temper, your amateur-hour crap isn't going to cut it."

Blair laughed. "See? This is why I love you."

"Plus you think I'm hot," Liz pointed out. She seized Windigo's head, then snapped off his remaining antler. "So how are we going to deal with this asshole? I think I may like him even less than I liked Steve."

"I think I have an idea about that." Blair squatted next to Windigo. "The key gives me a lot of leverage. I'm going to reach into Windigo's mind, and see if the Bear is alive in there somewhere."

"Be careful." Liz moved to put her head against his chest. She gave him a quick squeeze. "He's tricky, remember that."

"I will be," Blair said, and meant it.

He visualized the mental dagger, thrusting at Windigo's skull. The creature's defenses were considerable, but the force provided by the key was more than sufficient. He slipped past Windigo's defenses, into the strangest mind he'd ever encountered.

The landscape was a simple, rich forest. Granite jutted between stands of pine and redwood, backed by a clear blue sky. Overhead an eagle wheeled, crying its defiance. The wind carried the scent of rotting flesh, sharp enough to sting Blair's eyes. He shifted to wolf form, loping through the trees toward the stench. It grew worse, and was overpowering by the time he arrived at the meadow.

The corpse of a large black kodiak lay in the sun, an army of flies roosting in sunken eye sockets. As Blair approached, the kodiak twitched, then jerked violently erect. Something began to bore its way through the Bear's skull; spits of bone emerged from either temple. They grew swiftly, branching into a pair of misshapen antlers.

"The Bear is dead," the corpse rumbled. "I have swallowed his mind. He was a simple creature, simpler than your species, which is saying a great deal."

"You've been alive a very long time, Subject 3199." Blair approached the Bear slowly, keeping his defenses up. He didn't know what Windigo was capable of, beyond the little he'd learned from Ka.

"Where did you hear that name?" The Bear lumbered forward, rising onto its hind legs and flexing its claws. Its arms elongated, and its furry body grew ever more emaciated.

"I know all about you," Blair said. "About your creation and your abilities." He shifted into warform, eye to eye with Windigo. "You know I'm an Ark Lord, that I have control of the same forces used to birth you in the first place."

"If you had the power to destroy me, you already would have." Windigo relaxed onto his haunches. The stench was intense, even from ten feet away. "I think you lack the strength, little pup."

"You're still hoping to bait me into devouring you, aren't you?" Blair gave a hearty laugh. "Six months ago, maybe you could have. But I'm not that guy anymore, Windigo. You're just a footnote—a villain no one will remember. I know you've survived for millions of years, but that ends today."

"You genuinely believe that. I sometimes forget how arrogant your species can be." The Bear's rotting face somehow managed smug.

Blair felt a moment's hesitation. Was there anything, absolutely anything, he was missing about this situation? A way that Windigo could turn the tables? Blair didn't think so.

He extended a hand, and chains erupted from the ground. They swarmed over Windigo like snakes, yanking it to the granite. Every limb was pinned; struggle as it might, the twisted thing was unable to free itself.

"Maybe we are arrogant. Maybe I need the help of a different species." Blair turned from the dead bear, shifting back to wolf form as he loped up the hillside. He needed a better vantage point.

"Wait," Windigo called, naked desperation in its voice. "There is much I can tell you, much you don't know about the species that created the Ark. I know why they left. I know when they will return. There's much I can tell you if—"

Blair kept moving, ignoring Windigo as its voice faded into the distance. It was possible he could learn from Windigo, but some creatures were too dangerous to deal with. Irakesh and Steve had taught him that lesson. Blair wasn't risking it. He needed to remove Windigo from the world, and he needed to do it before Windigo figured a way out of the situation.

It didn't take long to reach the summit, a thick spire of granite that jutted over the valley below. It looked familiar, but Blair couldn't place it. He turned slowly in a circle, pausing when he spotted a familiar landmark. Was that the back of Half Dome? That made this Cloud's Rest. Below him lay a shimmering blue lake, the kind too virgin to have ever known the touch of man. Tenaya Lake?

A massive California grizzly prowled along the shore, wading into the water in search of fish. A silver-haired woman approached, tiny beside the massive Bear. A golden staff with a familiar scarab tip was clutched in her right hand. She gestured at the Bear, and the creature looked up curiously from the water. Blair thought the expression comical, especially on a creature that large. He could feel the energy washing over it as Isis shaped the Bear. He studied the signal, but it was impossibly complex. Isis wielded the key with casual skill, and Blair had no idea what she was doing.

The shaping went on for long minutes, altering the Bear at a genetic level. When Isis was finished, the Bear stood erect. It looked down at hands now graced with opposable thumbs.

She'd shaped it into something resembling a werewolf, but ursine in nature. A werebear, Blair decided to call it.

Time accelerated below, and Blair watched as seasons unfolded. Isis stayed with this Bear, teaching him. She showed him the ways of man, in time introducing him to a local tribe. The Bear was accepted into that tribe. He was given a name. The Great Bear. Yosemite, in their language. Blair leaned against the granite as the implications spilled over him, the sudden understanding of where Miwok myth must have begun.

Yosemite's children spread across the mountains, settling much of the sierras. They lived in small, isolated villages. They weren't warlike, or interested in conquest. Years continued to roll by, and Yosemite grew larger and larger. He spent less and less time among men, keeping to the wilds. Finally, centuries after his birth, Isis left the Great Bear. Blair could feel the hole in the Bear's heart, the loss of his mother. He could feel the jealous rage as her attention turned to her newest creation.

Isis had forsaken the Bear, in favor of the wolf. Blair experienced the loss as if it was his own, and he empathized with the Bear. He understood why Yosemite was so full of rage, why he'd attacked Yukon when the pack had entered his territory. Yosemite had been abandoned, left to wonder endlessly what he'd done to drive his mother away. Why she'd chosen another.

Blair had seen enough. He concentrated, warping the fabric of the Great Bear's mind. It was different than a person's, more malleable in many ways. He could see why Windigo had overcome Yosemite so quickly. Blair entered the Bear's vision, joining him near a rushing stream. Yosemite was lazily killing trout, giving Blair a disinterested look.

"I cannot believe I'm walking *toward* a grizzly," Blair muttered. He hopped onto a boulder in the middle of the stream, picking a path to the area where Yosemite was fishing. The Bear's ear's perked up, and he rose onto his haunches. Blair raised both hands, stopping on a stone a good dozen feet away from the grizzly. The water burbled and flowed around them, just a few feet deep. No barrier at all to a bear that size.

"I know the pain of loss. I know what it's like to feel abandoned. But Windigo is using you. He's taking advantage of your pain. He's using your love for the Mother. That's not what she would have wanted, Yosemite. Come back to us, Great Bear."

The Bear roared, lumbering closer to Blair.

He froze as it approached, wincing as a giant snout sniffed at his face.

The Bear spoke in a rumbling voice, "You are also of the Mother. You have a part of her scent. Why have you come to my valley?"

"You are trapped in memory, mighty Yosemite." Blair remained still, and kept his tone as soothing as he could manage. This Yoda crap was a lot harder than blurring around killing things. "A horrible being called Windigo invaded your mind. He's hidden the memory of his arrival. Look."

Blair raised a hand, and the sky shimmered. It showed the confrontation between Yosemite and an old woman. Yosemite killed the woman, feasting on her. Bright red light flared from the corpse, flowing into Yosemite's eyes. Those eyes flared red, then the Bear continued feeding.

"This…cannot be. It must not be," Yosemite rumbled. His body began to tremble. "Where is this creature? I will tear it apart."

"That's the spirit." Blair raised a hand to Yosemite's chest. He concentrated, pouring energy into the Bear. Yosemite grew larger, and more swift. Blair continued the flow of energy until the Bear was roughly double the size he had been. "You'll find Windigo chained to that hill over there. He's all yours."

Chapter 79- We Need An Army

Blair laughed as the colossal Bear bounded down the mountainside, growing even larger as he approached the meadow where Blair had imprisoned Windigo. Blair closed his eyes, leaving Yosemite's mind and willing himself to return to his own body. He opened his eyes, blinking as he took in the area around him.

Liz was still crouched over Windigo, her hands wrapped around the hilt of her sword. It looked far more natural in her grip than it ever had, and her expression was one of relaxed and confident determination.

"How did it go?" she asked.

"Yosemite's got the upper hand now," Blair said. "It may take some time, but I think he can expel Windigo. After that happens, I can help him become as he was." He summoned the access key, the staff's enormous power providing comfort as it flowed into his hand. "I don't think I can hurry the process any more, though. It's just going to take time."

"Well, we've got that. Still, I think I'm going to stay right here until we have confirmation that this thing is no longer a threat." Liz shot him a wink and a half-smile. "Can you look after Alicia?"

Blair moved to the teen's side, pressing two fingers against her throat. "She's breathing evenly, and her pulse is steady. I'm no doctor, but I imagine she'll wake up shortly."

"Can't you use the Ark to, I don't know, juice her healing or something?" Liz suggested. She nodded toward the man-sized dogs clogging the trees around them. "I see you've already done it for the pack."

"I don't think so," Blair said, studying Alicia's prone form. "A female's defenses are incredibly strong, and designed to stop exactly this kind of shaping. I might be able to do it with you, though, using the bond."

"Something to think about if Windigo wakes up instead of Yosemite," Liz said. She shifted her attention back to the prone monstrosity.

Blair felt something immense to the south, powerful beyond imagining. It was an unfamiliar shaping, emanating a powerful rhythmic pulsing. The strength of it was incredible, the kind of thing he'd only ever seen Isis do.

"Someone is right outside the Ark, using abilities I don't fully understand."

"Never a dull moment. Do you want to go investigate while I babysit? I think you've already done your part," Liz suggested.

Blair was torn. The situation here was contained, but that could change quickly if Windigo woke up. "I don't like the idea of leaving. If Yosemite kicks Windigo out, he's going to look for a new host. I don't know if I can stop him from doing that, but I have to be here if I want to try."

"True, but if something powerful just showed up at the Ark we *need* to know what it is. Maybe scout it out and come back?"

Blair nodded. It was a good plan. He pulled at his reserves, light-walking to his familiar perch atop the Golden Gate Bridge. It was one of those rare clear days where fog didn't blanket the bay, and Blair could see the source of the shaping.

A tear in reality stretched across a hundred meters of shoreline, facing the Ark. A single figure stood on the shore, and even from this distance Blair could make out the shock of red hair. He light-walked again, appearing on the beach.

Trevor's hand shot to his sidearm, but he stopped himself from drawing. "Shit, man, I hate it when you do that."

"Holy crap," was all Blair could manage. He blinked, reaching out to touch Trevor's hand. "You're alive. You have a pulse. What the hell happened in that city?"

Trevor gave a reluctant sigh. "It's a great story, but we're kind of in a hurry. If we survive, I'll tell you the whole thing."

"So, uh, why is there a rift on my beach?" Blair asked. He peered through the portal at a golden city. "Am I looking at what I think I'm looking at?"

"Yeah, but take a closer look. Center of the city, at the base of the large pyramid." Trevor pointed to indicate a pyramid that had clearly been central when planning the city. It was easily four times as large as any other. That pyramid was besieged by winged black figures, made small by the distance. A trio of titanic figures moved across the battlefield, easily thirty or forty feet tall.

"Oh, crap," Blair whispered. "I haven't seen an army like that since Set. Are those demons?"

"Yup. They don't go down easy, and Nox brought an ass-ton of them." Trevor gave sheepish grin. "I know it's asking a lot, but we're kind of in need of an army. Do you think you can help us out?"

Blair grinned back. "Just give me a few minutes to get some friends together. I think Liz is going to want to be in on this one."

Chapter 80- Marshalling

Liz cupped her furry hands around the blue camp cup, enjoying the warmth seeping through the plastic. The coffee was black, but she sipped at it anyway. "Yuck."

Yukon had arrived shortly after Blair left, and was boiling more water over a camp stove. Alicia sat on the ground nearby, her back against a redwood. Her face was too pale, her pupils dilated. She was in shock, and Liz knew from experience there was nothing anyone could do to alleviate it. Alicia had to come out of it on her own.

"Liz," Yukon snapped, knocking over the camp stove as he shot to his feet. Liz spun toward Windigo's prone form, ready to defend Alicia. Her blade still pinned Windigo's shoulder to the stone stage, but his massive body had begun to thrash wildly.

Windigo's stubby antlers fell away. His skin darkened, and fur began to sprout all over his body. Liz darted forward, yanking her blade from his shoulder. She assumed a defensive position, watching as the transformation accelerated.

"The Bear, he is returning," Yukon said. He also moved to stand protectively before Alicia, shifting back to his oversized dog form. The dog bared his teeth at the Bear, giving a low growl.

Windigo's skeletal face began to crack and pop, a thick muzzle pushing its way outward. Fur sprouted over a thick, jutting forehead. Beneath that forehead, the eyes changed. Gone were the hollow furnaces; in their place was a pair of large brown bear eyes.

Those eyes closed, and a sixteen-foot-tall bear lay curled in a fetal position, shivering.

Liz prodded him with a foot. "Hey, do you speak English? Hellloooo."

The Bear moved faster than she'd thought it could, scrambling away from her. It stared at Liz with those big eyes, sniffing at the air with a fist sized nose. "You…are not her. I thought, for a moment… It is not important. Yes, I speak your tongue. You are the Ka-Ken who watches over the Ka-Dun, the one who came into my mind. He freed me from Windigo."

The Bear sat up on its haunches, and Liz glided back a step. She adjusted the grip on her blade.

"I really don't want to have another fight," she said. "You're going to be a good bear, right?"

Behind her, Yukon growled.

"I do not wish to fight. I am tired, and weak. Even so, I have bested every Ka-Ken I have ever battled. Even Jes'Ka." That last was said with pride, and the way he watched her suggested he was waiting for some sort of acknowledgement.

"I seriously doubt that," Liz countered. "Blair said that Isis made you. If I can take you, and trust me when I say that I can, she'd have kicked your ass nine ways from Sunday." She willed her blade back into her body, shifting to human form. "It sounds like you don't want to fight, though, so I'm going to give you the benefit of the doubt. Where is Windigo now? Is he still hiding in your head somewhere?"

"I— I do not believe so," the Bear said. He raised a paw to his forehead. "I cannot feel him any longer. The pressure is gone. But I am afraid. I hurled him from my mind, yet I do not know if he is still there, toying with me."

"Yeah, that's a possibility," Liz replied. She looked around the stage, eyeing Yukon, then Alicia. The teen seemed the most vulnerable, and if Windigo were hunting for a new host he'd probably begin there. She walked over to Alicia, placing a comforting hand on her shoulder. "Hey, kiddo, how are you holding up?"

"Liz?" Alicia looked up at Liz, blinking. "I'm sorry. I just feel...I don't know. Last night was a lot. The things Windigo did..."

"You don't have to process it all at once, or even talk about it. As long as you know that you're safe." Liz scanned ceaselessly, watching for any sign that Alicia wasn't herself. She saw nothing obvious.

Brilliant light filled the forest, radiating from a second sun that appeared a few dozen feet away. The light faded, revealing Blair in human form. He looked majestic, his staff glowing with a nimbus of power. Behind him stood a familiar figure.

Liz leapt to her feet. "Trevor!"

She rushed forward and threw her arms around her brother. He hugged her back, just as fiercely.

Then Liz stepped back. She sniffed twice, cocking an eye. "Trevor, you're….alive."

"Yeah." Trevor gave one of her favorite grins, then he punched her lightly in the arm. "Hey, I realize this will shock you, but there's yet another world-ending crisis we need to deal with. We're kind of on the clock. Blair?"

"Liz, I'm gathering the entire pack. Nox is overrunning the Proto Ark."

"How are we getting there?" Liz asked. "And have you told Melissa yet?"

"I'll grab her next. I just wanted you brought up to speed so you could lead the pack into battle. We're assembling on the shore near the Ark."

"Great, then enough wasting time. Let's be on our way." Liz shot a final glance at Alicia, but the teen still showed no sign of Windigo.

If he hadn't found her yet, the safest thing Liz could do was get her as far from here as possible. She picked up Alicia, carrying her over to Blair.

Chapter 81- Change of Plan

Nox glided across the sky, circling the army below. There was no substitute for aerial recon, and that was one of the reasons he was grateful to have wings. Below, his army was beginning the final mobilization. They'd send in the hellhounds to soften resistance, then rush in with his most talented demons. The demokim were waiting outside, ready to gun down anything that emerged from the temple.

The key was taking Jordan down fast, giving the Ark Lord no time to react. Jordan was fast on his feet, and had immense power at his command. Fortunately, Nox had an answer to that power.

Nox hefted his staff, admiring it as he glided to a perch atop an obelisk. The amplifier was an ingenious invention, possibly the most devastating weapon Vulcan had ever created.

It would break the back of Jordan's defense, effectively ending the resistance here. That would free Nox to accomplish his assigned tasks, and might possibly allow him to station a permanent garrison here.

Even if it didn't, the real gain here would be the champions he was able to convert to his cause. Corrupting powerful Ka-Ken and Ka-Duns was why his forces were now so terrifyingly effective. He'd taken the best every continent had to offer, giving powerful people access to even more power.

A winged shape shimmered into view a few dozen yards away, atop another obelisk. Nox glided closer to the corrupted Ka-Ken, hovering next to her with powerful beats of his wings. "What is it, Dakota?"

"My lord, the base at Brasilia is under attack. We sent scouts to investigate, but the forces appear demonic in nature." She came up sharply, pointing at the portal. "They appear to belong to Set, my lord."

"Set's dead. Did you leave the portal unguarded?" Nox asked, turning to glide in that direction.

"Of course not. I left our two best Ka-Ken there," Dakota said. She glared at him. "I'm not an idiot, my lord."

"There's only one Ka-Ken at each obelisk? Yes, you are an idiot."

Nox took a deep breath, knowing the next minute was vital. Jordan was somehow launching a counter attack at the portals, and Nox needed to deal with it swiftly.

He kicked off an obelisk, blurring toward the edge of the portal. He saw no movement as he swooped closer. Marble cracked as he landed. There was blood, but no sign of the guard. The modulator had been removed from the obelisk.

Nox looked at the portal, his heart sinking. Instead of his forward operating base, the portal overlooked a glorious San Francisco morning with several feet of fog blanketing the bay. The Ark there appeared to be floating on a sea of clouds.

He didn't know what was happening within the Bay Area, as his three top spies had all died during Smith's purge. He did know one thing, however: Smith had a Primary Access Key. If he entered the fray, he might be able to overcome Nox's forces.

"My lord?" Dakota asked.

"Follow me," Nox snarled. He leapt into the air, blurring toward the pyramid. He glided over his forces, winging toward a cluster of his most powerful servants. Kali was at their center, a queen holding court.

Nox glided smoothly into a walk, stalking up to Kali. "The game has changed. We're about to be under assault."

"Does that mean you're finally going to let me burn some wolves?" Kali straightened, a malicious grin making her young face ugly.

"It does. We're going to hit them with everything we have. Ready your best and get them assembled into a vanguard." He checked his watch. Jordan still had fifteen seconds. "Oh, and Kali? I'm changing the plan. You're going to like this twist, I think."

Chapter 82- Firefight

"Here they come," Jordan roared. "Remember, hold the goddamned line as long as you can."

A flood of huge black dogs began sprinting into the room, scrambling across the marble as they fought to find purchase. They had huge, slobbering mouths—and where that slobber landed, it hissed and sizzled. These things were going to be a real treat to fight.

"Don't let them get close," Jordan ordered. He used his telekinesis to sweep most of the dogs from their feet. Ka-Ken darted in, slashing at bellies and snapping necks.

Another wave of demon dogs burst through, this one larger than the first. Jordan knocked down as many as he could, but the tide was endless. His people were being forced back, and they hadn't even fought the real threat yet.

"Fall back to the stairwell!" Jordan set up a wall of telekinetic force that neatly bisected the room. He opened gaps for his people, swiftly closing them once each was safe. "Those of you with boomerangs or those fancy bracelets, get ready to open up when I yell fire."

Jordan waited for his people to form a ragged line, straining as dog after dog hurled themselves against the shield he'd erected. Thousands of pounds of demonically enhanced flesh snapped and snarled just a few feet away.

"Three, two, one, FIRE," Jordan bellowed. Then he dropped the shield.

A flurry of green and blue bolts shot from his people, burning into the enemy ranks. Dog after dog fell, but some still reached his ranks. Most were cut down by waiting champions, but two Ka-Ken and a Ka-Dun were swiftly torn apart. Their skin sizzled and hissed, and the stench of it filled Jordan's nostrils.

Just like that, the last dog was down. Jordan crept warily forward, one hand raised toward the mouth of the tunnel. He called out to Elia, who was also creeping up. "Get ready. Nox won't give us time to catch our breath."

A winged demon burst from the shadows, her tail encircling a Ka-Dun.

She yanked him up into the air, using both hands to tear his head from his shoulders, then discarded the body and darted back into the shadows.

More demons leapt from the shadows—dozens of them. Jordan erected another barrier, this time blocking the entrance to the stairwell they'd retreated to. The last few survivors turned to flee.

A young woman almost made it before a demon crushed her to the marble. The demon wrapped a clawed foot around her skull, popping it with a disgusting spray of gore. Jordan met that demon's gaze. It was Nox, in his demonic form. He had a black staff in his right hand. Two rubies glittered near the tip, hellish eyes sizing up prey.

Jordan didn't know what the staff could do, but he had the uncomfortable suspicion he was about to find out.

He expected something from Nox, some comment or plea. Nox said nothing, instead grinning cruelly as he aimed the staff at Jordan. That kind of cruelty seemed out of place, even knowing the Director was now a demon. The staff began to glow, and Jordan blurred down the stairs. He didn't want to be anywhere near what was about to happen.

There was no explosion, nothing flashy at all. At first, Jordan thought it was some sort of trick. Then, a few moments later, people began to scream —not in pain, but in fear. They stampeded from their posts, abandoning the stairwell.

"Stand and fight," Jordan roared. He knew if they broke they were done for.

Something crept up his spine, a tingling terror that reduced him to a frightened six year old. The desire to flee was impossible to resist.

You are stronger than this shaping, Ka-Dun. Do not let it overpower you. Strengthen your mental defenses and weather the storm.

Jordan gritted his teeth, staring at the darkness at the top of the stairs. A flood of demons flowed down, leaping on the slowest of the fleeing Ka-Ken. That included Davina. Nox tackled the old woman to the floor, ramming the staff's spiked end through Davina's spine. It pinned the matron to the marble, and pulses of golden energy began to flow up the staff.

Jordan had seen enough people drained to know what was happening, but it took everything he had not to flee. He wanted to help, but he... couldn't. The terror was immense, so much so that he couldn't even find the words to yell commands.

Not that anyone was listening. The defenders were going down fast, the only survivors those who could hide in the shadows.

"Do you see now, fool?" Nox taunted, evidently having finished draining Davina's now desiccated corpse. There was nothing of the Director in that voice. "Your powers are feeble, your Ark far away. After I've killed the rest of this offal, I'm going to take that key from you. Then we're marching on Peru. Everything you've tried to build will be swept away."

Jordan cowered, paralyzed, as Nox approached.

Chapter 83- Payback

Blair surveyed the army around him with immense pride. When Isis had first mentioned the Great Pack he hadn't understood the size, or the grandeur. The power, or the sense of belonging.

Before him stretched a seemingly endless cluster of dogs, coyotes, and foxes. Sprinkled between them were champions. Ka-Ken, each with a Ka-Dun and his pack.

Liz stood at the head of the pack, her auburn fur rippling in the cold wind rolling off the bay. Yukon nuzzled her side, the too-large dog standing to Liz's waist. Given that she was nearly twelve feet tall that was no mean feat. On her other side, a few steps away, stood Yosemite.

It was the first time Blair had really seen the Great Bear, and he was impressed. Despite the thick folds of skin showing how much weight the Bear had lost, he was still one of the largest creatures Blair had ever encountered. He was half again as tall as Liz, and his claws were easily a foot long. His thick black fur added to his size, as did a muzzle large enough to bite off a man's head whole.

Alicia stood with the Bear, one hand against the creature's flank. The two seemed to share a bond now, shared suffering from Windigo's depredations. The fact that they had no idea where Windigo was terrified both of them, and their wide-eyed gazes never stopped moving. Blair was no psychologist, but he hoped it wasn't permanent for either of them.

The last group was the strangest, and it kept away from everyone else. Fifty deathless of all shapes and sizes, all armed with assault rifles. He could feel their strength. Some rivaled Melissa herself.

Melissa nodded at Blair, indicating that her forces were ready.

"It looks like we're good to go." Liz beckoned him forward, so Blair moved to join her. "They're going to need a rousing speech," she whispered. "I hope you've got something good."

Blair smiled at her, giving her hand a squeeze. Then he turned to face the crowd. He enhanced his voice, drawing power from the Ark behind him. "We're out of time so I'm going to make this quick. We've been asked to help protect one of the most important places in the world, a city that may determine the fate of us all. If we fail here, the enemy we face will spread across the world like a cancer."

He pointed at Melissa and her deathless.

"I know that fighting alongside deathless feels strange. Some of you have fought them, and even those that haven't…well, we've all lost someone to the virus. I'm asking you to put that aside. We need the deathless. They've come because I've asked for their help against a common foe."

Blair swiveled his arm, now pointing at the portal. "You can all see through the portal, to the city where we're going. We are the only thing standing between that army of demons and the potential end of our world. So, who's willing to fight?"

A chorus of shouts and barks rippled through the crowd, growing into a throng of cheers and howls. Those cheers combined into a single word, chanted by deathless and werewolf alike.

Fight. Fight. Fight.

It filled the packmind, the word charged with rage and hope and pride.

"No demon leaves this battlefield alive," Blair roared. He raised the key, aiming it at the pack. Wave after wave of immense power flowed from the Ark, a river of white light that he passed on to the Great Pack. They became larger, stronger—and much, much faster. A tiny shih tzu grew to the size of a wolf. A german shepherd was now cow-sized. "I can do more. I know I can."

Blair concentrated on the Ka-Dun, on their ability to shape. He divided the flow of energy from the Ark, feeding it equally to every shaper. Faces lit with wonder as the Ka-Dun felt the strength he'd given them. He wished he could do the same for the Ka-Ken, but saw no way to help any of them.

Except Liz.

Blair turned to her, feeling her emotions through the bond. He was humbled by the affection and awe he felt there. He took her hand again, feeding her a river of light, then gave that river shape, channeling it into a single manifestation: speed. He wove into her helixes the ability to blur, mimicking his own ability perfectly.

"You can blur now, as fast as I can. At least until the energy I've given you runs out. I genuinely feel bad for these demons." Blair shifted to warform, staring up at her much taller form. "Now get out there and defend my honor while I hang back and look pretty."

Liz laughed. "Liz kill demons. Testosterone. Grrr."

She blurred toward the portal. The pack followed her lead, flowing into the portal by the dozens. They sprinted forward, moving to engage packs of demon dogs. They snapped and snarled at each other, squaring off into dozens of skirmishes. The Great Pack were faster, but the hellhounds were tougher and stronger, even after Blair had modified his pack.

The battle devolved into chaos, yips and growls competing with the shouts of the Ka-Dun. Blair felt every dog's death, but he compartmentalized them. He needed to be focused right now, for all their sakes.

The Ka-Ken and their Ka-Dun were engaging the larger demons, the winged ones. They were having mixed success. On one flank, a Ka-Ken was picked up and carried high into the air by her demonic opponent—then the demon dropped her. She tumbled toward the earth, slamming into the marble with incredible force. She didn't rise. Her Ka-Dun went into a frenzy, he and his pack leaping on the demon who'd killed his mate. They tore it apart, then looked for another target.

Anger smoldered, but Blair refused to give it reign. He strode through the portal at the rear of the pack, instantly diminished in strength. On the other side of the portal he was a god. Here, the Ark was a distant candle flame. He could barely feel the flicker of power it offered. Still, his own strength was considerable. If he could leverage the key, he could still be a potent force on the battlefield.

He watched the battle unfold, trying to pick the best way to utilize his abilities. Melissa and her deathless fanned out ahead of him protectively. She darted back toward him. "Where do you want me?"

"Back up the Ka-Dun, Blair ordered. "Pick off those dogs as quickly as possible."

Melissa nodded, blurring toward the combat. Her deathless followed.

Blair turned to Alicia. "I want you to—"

"I'm going with Liz," Alicia interrupted. She glared at Blair, daring him to protest.

He considered contesting the point, but didn't have time to convince the teen. "Okay, find Liz. Tell her to drive a wedge through their ranks, and cut us a path to the pyramid. See if you can get the other Ka-Ken to help her."

"I will." She nodded and sprinted after Liz.

Blair glanced in Liz's direction, awed by what he saw. She was squaring off against a pair of corrupted Ka-Dun, each armed with a black sword. They flanked her, blurring toward her at exactly the same time.

Liz was faster. She blurred between them with her sword. Limbs flew, and when the blur stopped both demons toppled lifelessly to the ground.

A thunderous roar shook the entire battlefield. Blair spun, unsure how to deal with what he was seeing. Three demonic giants were laying into his forces with their laser cannon arms. Beams of sharp green energy lanced into his forces, cooking dogs and Ka-Dun alike.

Yosemite charged forward, leaping for a giant's throat. He tore into its flesh, worrying at the throat with his enormous fangs. Yosemite looked comically small next to the giant, but the move knocked the giant onto its back. A tremendous crash shook the entire battlefield.

Yukon took advantage of the giant's weakness, darting in to sever a hamstring. He darted away again, narrowly dodging a kick. Then the Anakim breathed, and a dense black cloud enveloped Yukon. It took Blair a moment to realize that the cloud was made up of a small flying insects. Wasps, maybe?

Yukon began yelping, desperately blurring away from the insects. They pursued, and the dog yipped frantically, running in Blair's direction.

Blair raised the staff, firing a blast of white light that disintegrated the wasps. He turned to the trio of Anakim, wracking his brain for options. He could already tell that thing was tough enough to survive a blast from the staff. So what could he do?

He glanced at Yosemite as the Bear was knocked away from the giant's throat. The Bear crashed into the side of a small pyramid, shaking his head as he rose. Then Yosemite gave a roar of his own, and rushed toward the much larger giant again.

"Hmm. Yeah, the Godzilla defense." Blair aimed the staff at Yosemite, channeling almost all his remaining strength into the Bear. He sent out a complex signal, reshaping the Bear's DNA just like he'd done to the pack. Yosemite grew larger, stronger, and tougher. Twenty feet tall. Twenty-five. Thirty. Forty feet tall. Finally, Yosemite stood eye to eye with the giants. "That's more like it."

Yosemite lumbered up to the giant he'd been battling. The two titans seized each other wrestling back and forth until Yosemite got the upper hand. He picked up the giant, hurling him into the middle of the battlefield.

The Great Pack were smaller, and much more nimble. They blurred out of the way of the impact. The demon dogs were too slow, and many were crushed under the giant.

Melissa and her deathless took advantage of the distraction caused by the impact, adding automatic weapons fire to the screams and blasts.

The tide was turning in their favor, the pack slowly overwhelming their demonic counterparts—mostly due to Liz. She and her Ka-Ken were tearing through winged demons, slowly forcing a path toward the pyramid. Resistance was stiff, but every demon who faced Liz died. Her mastery of the sword was beyond incredible. It was at a level he'd previously only seen exhibited by Osiris.

"That's my girlfriend." Blair laughed and turned back to the portal. He was out of juice, but there was no reason he couldn't go get more.

Chapter 84- Flanked

Jordan's breaths came in short, ragged gasps. He scrabbled across the floor until his back met the warm stone wall. His forces had been routed and Nox was advancing on him, a palpable aura of fear flowing from a menacing black staff that seemed to drink in the light. Jordan knew he should fight, but inexplicable terror blanketed everything.

Behind Nox, his army of demons were mercilessly cutting down the defending champions. Councilor Awa was tackled to the ground not far away, and all Jordan could do was wince when the demon began noisily feeding. Awa fought weakly, but was unable to push the demon away.

This fear is unnatural, Ka-Dun. Use the past. Remember Set, who also used this ability. In the end, you defeated him. You can defeat this threat as well. The terror isn't real. Do not let it control you.

Jordan focused on that memory. He relived the humiliation of losing control of his own bladder, of being forced to work for Set against his own friends. He was tired of being trampled over by bullies, and he'd be damned if he let it happen again.

The anger ran deep, and Jordan jumped into the river, letting it carry him. He moved by instinct, baring his fangs as he raised a hand.

"What are you going to do, little puppy?" Nox asked, laughing viciously. "You can't even stand up."

The words bit into him, and the anger surged. Jordan focused on the staff, forcing himself to look at the source of his terror. He used every bit of will, every ounce of discipline, all focused into one action…and jerked the staff from Nox's grasp with his telekinesis.

It flew into Jordan's hand, freeing him instantly from the fear.

"Don't call me puppy." Jordan drew on the distant flow of power from the Ark to fuel his blur. It proved a wise decision, as Nox blurred, too. The Director was nearly as fast as him, shifting into a defensive stance as Jordan approached.

Jordan wasn't sure how the staff worked, but he didn't really care. The top looked pretty damned pointy. He slipped it past Nox's defenses, ramming it through the Director's chest in a spray of stinking black gore. Jordan slammed into Nox, pinning the demon against a thick stone column. He slammed his forehead into Nox's, and the demon's skull bounced off the hard stone.

Nox's tail coiled around Jordan's leg, yanking him off his feet. The demon slammed Jordan into the floor repeatedly, and Jordan just barely kept his face from smashing into the stone. Bones snapped, but Jordan battled past the pain. He seized Nox's tail in both hands, then bit down hard.

Nox screamed as Jordan worried at the tail, finally tearing it loose. The blood tasted awful, but Nox's screams made it worthwhile.

Jordan rose shakily, raising a hand. The staff ripped free of Nox's chest, shooting back to his hand. All around him, beleaguered werewolves were being overwhelmed. Awa's struggles were feeble now. The demon continued to feed.

He had to stop it. Jordan concentrated on the staff, feeding it an experimental flow of energy. A black signal pulsed from the staff, and Nox's features changed from smug anger to utter horror.

Nox vanished, leaving his forces leaderless.

Jordan fed more energy to the staff, focusing on the demons still scattered throughout the room. The black signal washed over them, and they broke and ran just as Jordan's own forces had done when faced with the staff. "Cut them down. Don't let them leave the temple."

The surviving werewolves followed Jordan into battle, cutting down their tormentors. Demon after demon fell as they fought their way to the front of the temple.

He'd nearly reached the tunnel on the first floor when a familiar shock of red hair stepped from the shadows next to him.

"What the hell is that thing?" Trevor asked, nodding at the staff.

Anput stepped from the shadows a few feet from him.

"Something Vulcan created, I'm betting. It inflicts the same kind of fear Set used." Jordan's chest was heaving, and he was happy for the break. All of them needed it. He did a quick count, frowning when he realized only seven werewolves were still standing. "Please tell me you have some good news to report. I'll take anything at this point."

"We've got a chance." Trevor looked inordinately proud of himself. "I was able to redirect the portal. We cut off Nox's reinforcements, and we brought some of our own. Blair and Liz are here. They've brought the Great Pack, which just engaged Nox's forces."

"We have to move quickly then," Jordan said. He started trotting up the tunnel, which was now empty save for a dozen or more demonic corpses.

"Why? What do you have in mind?" Trevor asked, trotting alongside.

"We need to stop Nox, right now. As soon as he realizes he's losing, or there's a chance he'll lose, he'll vanish. We'll never have a better shot than right now." Jordan didn't wait for a reply, blurring out of the tunnel and into the artificial sunlight.

More chaos greeted him. A quick scan suggested Nox still had maybe sixty winged demons, and about ten times as many dogs. Most of the mechanized dog bot things were already down, but the few surviving ones were laying into their enemies with enviable fury. Two out of the three titanic Anakim were laying waste to their foes, seemingly unstoppable. The last was being torn apart.

"That is the biggest goddamned bear I have ever seen," Jordan said. "It has to be fifty feet tall."

Trevor just laughed.

Opposing the demons was the answer to Jordan's unuttered prayer: the Great Pack. It couldn't be anything else. Hundreds of cow-sized dogs were blurring through the enemy ranks. Between them were dozens of Ka-Dun, backed by Ka-Ken leaping from shadows whenever a threat presented itself. Deathless with automatic weapons were chewing up the demons' right flank, forcing them to engage the pack.

Overshadowing both groups was the struggle between the giants. The Bear had finished his first target, and roared at the next Anakim. The pair approached each other like wrestlers, grappling each other as they struggled for dominance.

"Now there's something you don't see every day," Jordan said.

"Tell me about it," Trevor agreed. "Any sign of Nox?"

"He'll be in the most protected position, assuming he hasn't fled the battlefield." Jordan scanned the field again, trying to determine where the Director would go. He'd want a high vantage point, ideally with concealment.

Jordan looked up, studying the pyramids and obelisks, looking for any sign of Nox. If Nox stayed out of the battle, there'd be no way to find him. But if he were still fighting, he'd have to come out of the shadows to shape. There was no sign of him, at least not that Jordan could find.

"Is that him?" Anput asked, pointing at the thickest part of the battle.

Jordan was shocked to see Nox mixing it up on the front lines. A burst of superheated flame came from his hand, incinerating a Ka-Ken. It was totally unlike the Director, going against everything he'd taught Jordan. Perhaps being a demon had robbed him of that level of control. Maybe whatever lurked in his head forced him to act differently. Or maybe that wasn't the Director at all.

"Looks like it. Let's take him out," Jordan said. He wished Leti were here too, but last he'd seen her she was tending to the wounded. Instead, Jordan turned to Elia, who led the ragtag cluster of combat-ready champions. "I want you to hold the mouth of this tunnel. Keep the survivors inside safe, and don't risk anyone else."

Elia's face softened. She took a step closer to Jordan, staring searchingly into his eyes. "You really are trying to protect this city, aren't you? You're doing your best to make sure that the enemy is defeated, even if that means risking your own life. What's more, you aren't asking the same sacrifice of my people. We treated you like offal, but you're still protecting us. Why?"

"Because my job as Ark Lord is to help build a future for everyone," Jordan answered without hesitation. "If I fall here, someone else will take up the mantle, but only if champions survive long enough to do that. Stay safe, Elia. I have work to do."

"Of course." She nodded, stepping back into the mouth of her tunnel. For the first time, she eyed Jordan with respect.

Chapter 85- Saw That Coming

Liz flipped over the demon, her blade darting down three times in rapid succession. Each cut hit the same spot at a different angle, where the right wing connected to the demon's back. The third strike finally sliced through the thick bone, and the wing fluttered away in a spurt of black blood. The now flightless demon cartwheeled awkwardly toward the ground, but Liz decided to help it along with a roundhouse to the face. She landed in a crouch, the demon's broken body slamming into the marble behind her.

Move. Wepwawet roared.

Black claws materialized in the shadows next to her, streaking toward her face. Liz blurred backwards, slicing upwards with her sword. The sunsteel severed the hand, and the demon retreated back into the shadows with a shriek. Liz did the same, cloaking herself as she continued to cut a path through the fighting.

Nox was battling a grey-furred Ka-Ken, and it looked like her sister was getting the worst of it. The grey began retreating into the shadows, but Nox raised both hands. A river of blindingly hot flame engulfed the grey, and her sister's scream was choked off as she was reduced to oily ash. Liz had never seen a power quite like it, though the end result wasn't too much different than melting someone with one of the boomerangs Blair had talked about.

"Hey," Liz roared, leaping from the shadows. "Remember me, Director?" It was risky, but she didn't want any more of their people to die. Nox was the toughest thing out here, more powerful even than the titans battling the Great Bear behind her.

"Ah, you must be Ark Lord Blair's pet Ka-Ken," Nox taunted. There was madness in those black eyes, and his voice wasn't quite right. "Come then, try that blade against me."

The demon extended her left hand, and a pool of black metal formed. It extended into a wide, curved blade, nearly identical to Liz's own. Nox smiled wickedly at her, then blurred toward Liz.

Liz brought up her blade smoothly to block, drawing as much on the skill

Wepwawet imparted as she did on the speed Blair had lent her. She blocked several more strikes, matching Nox blow for blow. He was incredibly fast, using his tail and wings to increase his considerable speed. That tail darted forward, and Liz leapt over it. At the same time Nox launched a wide slash, and Liz barely blocked it. The momentum knocked her back several feet, and she rolled with the blow.

She came to her feet swiftly, dodging to the right as a blast of intense white flame shot through the space she'd occupied. It passed several feet from her, but the heat was so intense it still singed skin. The scent of her own cooked flesh made her eyes water.

We are outmatched, Ka-Ken. Wepwawet rumbled. *Fall back to your lines, this fight is beyond us without more aid. I have never seen a creature like this, and we do not know what else he is capable of.*

"Easier said than done," Liz muttered, ducking into a slide as she avoided another blow from Nox. She got mostly out of the way, but the black sword drew a hot line across her forearm. Liz flipped to her feet, slashing at Nox's leg. He dodged nimbly backwards, and she used the opportunity to wrap the shadows around herself.

"Coward," Nox raged. His eyes bulged, and his fangs grew. That kind of rage seemed alien on the Director, the calmest man she'd ever met. Nox extended his arms, firing off fans of fire in a vain attempt to hit Liz. She blurred further away, circling.

The energy lent to us by the Ka-Dun is not infinite. Spend it wisely, Ka-Ken.

I get it, watch for an opportunity, and don't strike until I have it. Liz thought back. She didn't like it, but that might mean allowing Nox to attack more of her people.

"Turn around and face me, Nox," a familiar voice boomed across the battlefield. Jordan strode into battle, a black staff clutched loosely in one hand. "You've talked a good game, but you know I can best you in a fair fight. Are you going to run like a coward, or stand and fight me?"

Liz circled slowly around Nox, moving into his blind spot. She crept closer, but waited to strike. She wanted Jordan to be closer first, so they could flank this bastard. It was the only way they were going to be able to overcome him.

Nox turned to face Jordan, flicking Liz's blood from his blade. "You're even more arrogant than he said. If it's death you're craving, I'm happy to give it to you."

Jordan stalked closer, holding the staff defensively before him. "Yeah, that definitely cinches it. The Director would never engage in a battle he had a chance of losing. He's not stupid enough to fall for the 'one v one me bro' crap. If you were really Nox, you'd have ordered all your demons to attack me while you fled for the back line. So who the hell are you?"

"Well you're not stupid, I'll give you that. My name is Kali," a feminine voice came from the Director's throat. Nox's body rippled, shifting into a woman Liz had never seen before. She was short, with dark hair and a perfectly oval face. Liz guessed her to be about twenty, maybe a year or two older. She looked like any other college kid. "Nox also said you were dangerous, but I'm not sure I believe that. You have some good moves, but you're nothing compared to me. The grey men have given me powers you can't even begin to understand. And that was before I pried even more power from all the champions I've killed and eaten."

"I understand that you're dumb enough to stand in one spot," Jordan taunted. Liz assumed he was talking about her, and prepared to strike. Before she could, two more combatants entered the fray.

The first was Anput, who emerged from the shadows above Kali long enough to fire a thick beam of intense green light. Trevor appeared to Kali's right, a similar beam of green energy shooting from his fist. Both Trevor and Anput were blurring, but not fast enough that Kali couldn't dodge. The demon started a graceful leap, but the motion was suddenly arrested. Jordan's arms trembled, but his telekinetic grip held. Both beams found their target, the first burning away one of Kali's wings, while the other put a gaping wound in her side.

Liz didn't need Wepwawet's combat experience to recognize an opportunity. Kali was vulnerable. Liz leapt into the air, bracing her sword against her leg just as she'd done when she killed Cyntia. The blade pierced's Kali's thick hide, sinking deep into her spine.

"Jordan, hold her still," Liz yelled. She drove the weapon in deeper, dodging a clumsy swipe from Kali's tail. Trevor and and Anput fired smaller blasts, concentrating their fire where the tail met the back. The third shot sent the tail flopping to the ground, where it continued to thrash. Liz dug the claws of her right hand into Kali's shoulder, the other still wrapped tightly around the hilt of her sword. Kali bucked wildly, and Liz struggled to keep her seat.

Kali's arms shot out, one aimed at Trevor and the other at Anput. She blurred, sending out bursts of super heated flame. Neither Anput, nor Trevor was fast enough to avoid the fire. Both were blasted backwards, landing in smoking heaps.

"That was a dumb move, bitch. You just torched two of my friends," Jordan roared from somewhere far away. A wave of black energy surged from his staff, washing over Kali.

Kali froze, quivering in abject terror. Her eyes widened, and her mouth worked silently. The demon's eyes were fixed upon the staff, and Liz took advantage of that lapse. She used the last of the energy she'd taken from Blair, slicing off Kali's head, then slicing her skull in two. Jordan lifted Kali's body high up into the air, then slammed it into the marble with a satisfying crack.

Liz waited just long enough to be sure the body didn't rise, then rushed to Trevor's side. She knelt next to him, feeling for a pulse. It was there, but ragged. The entire left side of his body had been cooked, and if he was healing she certainly couldn't see it. One eye was covered in charred flesh, and the remaining eye was unfocused.

"Trevor? Trevor, can you hear me?" she shrieked, looking around for help. Jordan had moved to Anput's side, and was helping her into a sitting position. The vampire's hair had been burned away, as had most of her clothing. But her flesh was already healing, and Liz knew in a matter of minutes she'd be good as new.

Trevor wasn't so lucky.

Chapter 86- Plans Within Plans

Nox blurred through the bowels of the Proto-Ark, far underneath the city. It amazed him that the locals seemed not to have made it this far down. The place that had forged the destiny not just of mankind, but of the species who'd created the Great Arks, was ignored completely. It was mind boggling.

He passed through golden corridors, finally stopping in a stadium-sized cavern at the heart of the Proto-Ark. It was similar to the Great Arks themselves, but smaller and clearly a precursor. The gems were more simplistic in their arrangement, and the flow of power less focused than the Arks managed.

Yet only here were certain feats possible. Feats like the one he was about to attempt.

This is madness. If we create this tool for Hades, we give him the tool of our destruction, Set-Dun.

"Madness would be not following Hades' orders," Mark shot back. "If we take the weapon and run, he'll find us. When he does, you know we can't resist him." He reached into the pack he'd brought, withdrawing the components Hades had given him.

Then do not make the weapon at all. Lie. Tell him the plan failed.

Mark knelt next to to a wide tray directly under a massive blue gem. He arranged the gemstones around the long rectangular block of sunsteel, creating a mockup of the staff he wanted to create. Moving back to the control console at the far side of the room, he placed a hand against it. The console hummed to life.

"Hello, unfamiliar life form," came a pleasant voice from behind him.

Mark whirled to see a holographic grey man. The physiology was unmistakable.

"Ka?"

"A common mistake," the construct corrected. "I am Ark Keeper Ba. I was tasked with watching over this city, and assisting the Builders upon their return. As you are unauthorized to be here, it is my duty to report your presence."

"Wait. I'm also assisting the Builders," Mark said, reaching back into the pack. He withdrew a glowing blue sigil about the size of a fist. "Do you recognize this?"

"Of course, Emissary," Ba said, bowing. "The sigil is the mark of Kek-Telek himself. You have full access to our local systems. How may I assist you, Emissary?"

"I'd like to create a Primary Access Key. Can you guide me through the attunement process?" That would save Mark long minutes, and given how many demonic servants had been snuffed out while he was down here, he might not have much longer than that.

"Of course. It is why I was designed: to assist in creation." Ba glided over to the console. "I have examined the materials to be used, and find them of sufficient quality. All you need to do is initiate the process."

Mark placed his hand against the console again, willing the process to begin. The gigantic sapphire glowed with an inner light. That light began pulsing, slowly at first, then with increasing frequency. The light poured into the sunsteel and the gems, so blinding that Mark took several steps back and looked at the opposite wall.

As the light pulses continued, he used the time to stare around him in wonder. The idea that there was virtually no security here seemed out of keeping with the very reason he'd come. Why make the Arks require keys, but allow the Proto Ark to be accessed by anyone who had a sigil they recognized? They'd even provided a helpful AI to walk visitors of an entirely separate species through creating what was arguably the most powerful artifact in the world.

The Builders are a species apart from ours, and from our petty problems, his risen said. *They did not war on each other as we did. They lived in perfect harmony. There was no need for security.*

Mark seriously doubted that. The pulsing light finally stopped behind him, so Mark turned to the tray under the giant gem. The materials had been fused into a familiar golden staff, complete with the scarab head. He picked up the staff reverently. Mark could feel the power within it, feel the staff's ability to both amplify and modify nearly any type of shaping. Even now the staff offered him control over the city. He could tap into the Proto Ark just as an Ark Lord tapped into an Ark.

"Is there anything else I may assist you with, Emissary?"

"There is," Mark said. He leaned the staff against the edge of the tray, then summoned his demonsteel blade, setting it on the tray. He reached into his pack, withdrawing several handfuls of gemstones. These were arranged around the hilt, and several were placed along the blade. "I'd like to make another primary key."

"The materials provided are insufficient," Ba cautioned. "The resulting object will lack critical functionality."

"But it will function like an access key in most ways?" Mark asked.

"Indeed." Ba nodded eagerly, pointing at the console. "I've set up an attunement that should include the most important functions. What will this key be used for? That knowledge will help me further modify the attunement."

"Above all, the key needs to control Arks, and other forms of Builder technology," Mark instructed.

"As you wish. You may begin the creation when you are ready."

"There's one more thing," Mark said. He prayed this next part would work. It was an insurance policy of sorts. "I want you to remove all memory I have of the second key we create. Can you do that?"

"Of course, Emissary. I can show you how to eradicate specific memories using the terminal," Ba confirmed happily.

Chapter 87- Saving Trevor

Blair sprinted back through the portal, assessing the combat. The most obvious fight was the one between Yosemite and the two remaining giants. One had his arms pinned behind his back, while the other was attempting to force the barrel of its gun into the Bear's mouth. Blair vibrated with energy, holding as much as he could have taken from the Ark. That energy begged for release, and Blair was happy to oblige. But how did one deal with a nearly impregnable giant?

If this giant is based on the Anakim, then that creature has a rudimentary mind. His beast rumbled.

"Good point," Blair said. He pointed the staff at the giant's head, unleashing a torrent of energy. He burst past the giant's rudimentary mental defenses, and was instantly overtaken by vertigo. His perspective shifted, and he was now observing the world from the vantage of a fifty foot giant.

Blair stopped trying to shove the barrel into Yosemite's mouth, instead aiming it at the other giant's face. Blair fired, and the giant's face melted. It released Yosemite, grabbing at its face with its hand as it roared in pain. Blair fired again, catching both its face and the hand covering. The hand melted down to bone, and another layer of the face peeled away.

Yosemite, now free, rounded on the wounded giant. He seized the head in both hands, pushing the mouth toward the barrel, just like they'd been trying to do to him. Blair fired into the other giant's mouth, and the head exploded. Black ichor, plates of metal, and large bone fragments shot in every direction. Both the giant Blair had seized, and the Bear were covered, and Blair had to wipe at the giant's eyes before he could see again.

The now headless giant collapsed with a crash, crushing a small temple. Yosemite was already turning toward the body he inhabited, and he looked pissed. There was one more thing Blair wanted to do before vacating the giant, though. He aimed the laser cannon down, and made the giant blow off his own knee. The crippled giant began to topple, but Blair had released its mind and returned to his own by the time it crashed atop the body of its companion.

Blair blinked as his perspective adjusted. He was standing near the portal, and watched as Yosemite began dismembering the wounded giant. That freed Blair to turn back to the battle at large. The demons were clearly getting the worst of it. Their demon dogs were few in number, and their surviving demons had been forced into several tight clusters. Those clusters were surrounded by packs of dogs, led by fierce Ka-Duns. Ka-Ken darted from the shadows, dragging demons out into the waiting pack. Those demons never regained their feet.

He scanned for Liz, sucking in a panicked breath when he found her. She was kneeling next to a charred form, sobbing. Not far from her Jordan was helping Anput to her feet. The charred body had to be Trevor. Blair blurred closer, leaping over corpses as he crossed the battlefield. He stopped next to Trevor's prone form. Liz was already crouched there, crying.

"He's still breathing," she said, staring in agony at her brother's hideously burned form. "I don't know for much longer. I was so happy he was alive again, but now? I wish he'd stayed deathless. He'd have had a better chance of surviving this."

Blair moved to Liz, squeezing her shoulder. "He's not dead yet, and we're not giving up on him."

"Thank you," Liz whispered. She buried her furry face in Blair's equally furry chest, sobbing hot tears against him. He wrapped an arm around her, but turned his attention to Trevor. There had to be something they could do.

"Blair," Anput croaked weakly. "Come. Closer."

Blair released Liz, rushing over to Anput. She was badly burned as well, her face and throat especially. "What is it?"

"Staff. Use, the staff," Anput managed. She lifted a trembling hand, pointing at Trevor.

Blair rose to his feet, moving back to Trevor. He aimed the staff at his fallen friend, fueling the artifact with what power remained. The universe seemed to open, showing Blair Trevor's wounds. He could see every molecule at once, understanding in some primal way how to regenerate the destroyed cells.

Power flowed from the staff into Trevor, the potent signals encouraging his organs to regrow. Trevor jerked up with a gasp, then fell back to the ground, seizing like an epileptic. Blair poured more power from the staff, sagging weakly to one knee as he continued to shape. The signal rippled outward, affecting Trevor's skin now. The burnt sections flaked away, exposing new pink skin underneath.

Trevor was staring down at himself in wonder, and Blair couldn't help but do the same. He offered Trevor a hand, "Good to see you breathing, man."

"I can't believe you can heal people. We totally needed a cleric in our party," Trevor said, laughing. He rolled his arm in the socket. "You did a hell of a job. I thought I was done."

Liz threw her hairy arms around Trevor, "I'm so glad you're all right."

"Guys," Jordan called, striding over. He held a black staff, one that made Blair uneasy. The signals coming off it very wrong. Inhuman somehow. "I promise we'll do a reunion soon, but we've still got a mess to clean up."

"I think the fight's over," Trevor said, gesturing at the city around them.

He was right. Combat had stopped, the demons eradicated to a man. The pack was lounging now, licking wounds and panting furiously. They'd won.

"It's not the fight I'm worried about," Jordan said, frowning. "There's no sign of the Director. It's possible Nox fled, but I seriously doubt it. He came to this city for a reason. If it was conquest, he'd have brought a much larger army. This was surgical. He was after something."

"He wanted to make an access key," Anput rasped, rising shakily to her feet. She waved off Trevor's offer to help. "This place is capable of it. The grey men need one to win the war. It's the only thing that makes sense."

"Unfortunately, I agree," Jordan said, grimly of course. The man looked even more dour than usual.

A small group of werewolves walked up, led by a large blond female.

She nodded deferentially to Liz, then dropped to one knee before Blair. He was taken aback. "Welcome to our city, Father."

"Uh, what are you doing?" Blair reached down, helping the woman to her feet.

"Blair, meet Elia," Jordan said. "Elia is the leader of a sect of champions, the ones who protect both the jungle and this city. Until recently, she was custodian of my Ark."

"Why did you call me Father?" Blair asked the Ka-Ken

"I am honored to meet you, Ark Lord Blair. You are the father of our species in this epoch. Most of us are descended from you," Elia said, tone reverent. She bowed low, then straightened. "You have saved us all. We are eternally grateful that you chose to intercede on our behalf."

"Yeah, it's a good thing those evil ancient enemies decided to go find him, huh?" Trevor said, shooting Elia an accusatory glance.

"I take it you two don't get along?" Blair asked.

"Elia locked Anput and I up, and tied Jordan up with political games." Trevor glared hard at Elia. "She's making all nicey-nice, but only because she thinks you match some of the dogma they've cooked up around Isis."

"Do not mock our faith, cur," Elia snarled. Blair was amazed at the transformation, the depth of hatred in the woman.

"I know you're not growling at my brother," Liz said, taking a protective step in front of him. She raised her blade into a guard position. "I will cut you in half, bitch."

Elia looked horrified, bowing repeatedly as she backed away. "This— this thing is your brother, eldest sister?"

"You're damned right he is, and from the sound of it he just saved your collective asses." Liz poked Elia in the chest with the tip of her sword. "If I hear another word out of your mouth about Trevor, I'll remove your ability to make words." Liz's eyes blazed, and Blair felt a little sorry for Elia.

Jordan cleared his throat. "I'd suggest we gather in the main hall. We can tend to the wounded, and talk about where to go from here," Jordan said. He scooped up Anput, carrying the wounded vampire toward the temple. The others followed.

Blair took one final glance at the battlefield. They'd won a sizable victory, even if it wasn't perfect.

Chapter 88- Ark War

Hades paced before his throne in a most undignified manner. He'd received a brief communication from Nox that he'd succeeded, but there were no details. Just how well had he succeeded? Was that blasted city theirs at last? Had he actually created a real Primary Access Key, and if so, was he wise enough to turn it over, or would he try to use it to free himself from demonic control? So many questions.

The air near the entryway of the throne room popped and sparked, then the outline of a figure appeared. Over several seconds the figure gained shape and definition, finally resolving into Nox's demonic form. He dropped to one knee, bowing his head.

"Not for the first time I regret the amount of autonomy I've granted you," Hades spat the words at Nox. "It's not too late to destroy your will. Always remember that."

"Of course, master. I never forget that fact," Nox said, with just the right shade of deference.

He extended a hand, gold pooling within it. That gold flowed into a staff that filled Hades with a very physical hunger.

Nox rose, offering the staff with both hands. "You know I disagree with your plan, but I am not a fool. I've created what you asked for."

Hades leapt down the landing, seizing the staff from Nox. He clutched it to him, taking a cautious step backward. He took a long moment to compose himself. "I'm glad you see reason, and that you did not think to challenge me. Now, what of the city? Tell me everything."

"You're not going to like this," Nox admitted. He gave a heavy sigh. "Somehow the enemy sabotaged the portal, and pointed it at San Francisco. Ark Lord Blair brought the Great Pack to the defense of the city, and our forces were annihilated to a man."

"No," Hades moaned. He refused to accept this. It couldn't be. He buried his face in his hands, but was unable to hide from the implications. He looked up. "Do you see what you've done? Not only have you not secured the city, but you have cost us nearly a fifth of our army. We are greatly diminished thanks to your inept bungling of the situation."

"I thought you might feel that way. You're going to be even less happy." Nox folded scaly arms over his chest. "Kali was among the dead. She was killed by Jordan and his friends."

"Are you trying to doom us all?" Hades shouted.

He leapt from his throne, pointing at Nox. An arc of black lightning shot from his hand, crackling over Nox's entire body. The demon flopped about like a fish, smoke rising from his body. Hades did not abate. He continued the torture for several minutes, using Nox's pain to calm himself.

When he finally felt composed he stopped the lightning. "You may rise, Nox. Your short life may well be at an end. I won't hesitate to offer you to the grey men. The only reason you live is that you have delivered the staff, even if you did it in the most disgraceful of circumstances."

Nox didn't rise immediately. It took him long moments to crawl to his feet, streamers of smoke still rising from his body.

Hades had brought him close to death, and had very nearly finished the job. Yet he needed Nox still. For now. "Now, compose yourself. We must contact the grey men."

Hades hurried back up the stairs, reveling in the power offered by the staff. With both the staff and the crown, he was the equal of any Ark Lord now—at least for as long as the grey men allowed him to keep the staff. Would they really deliver on their promise?

Nox bowed wordlessly, moving to stand on the step below the throne. He clasped his hands behind his back, the dutiful bodyguard. It bothered Hades just how adept Nox was at donning and shedding such masks. He had to continually remind himself of just how devious his creation was. He must watch Nox even more closely going forward.

Hades whispered to the crown, willing it to initiate the connection to the device that the grey men had provided. The golden cylinder cast forth a shimmering wave of light that perfectly mimicked life. A hologram, Nox had called it. The hologram showed a forest of tiny black obelisks. Three equally tiny grey men stood among the obelisks, using golden devices that, to Hades mind, were truly magical.

He didn't buy into this technological religion that Vulcan had picked up from the moderns. Hades knew divinity when he saw it.

"Greetings, honored emissaries of the great Builders," Hades intoned. He gave a seated bow.

"Entity Hades, that you have contacted us must mean you have successfully acquired the Access Key. Is this statement accurate?" one of grey men asked. Its tiny mouth didn't move, but the voice came from somewhere.

"Yes, honored Emissary. I have acquired the key, as you have asked." Hades licked his lips, darting a nervous glance around the room.

"Entity Hades, what of the Proto Ark? Have you secured it for our use?" the grey man asked, cocking its head.

"Regrettably, your enemies arrived first," Hades admitted. He clutched the staff to his chest. "We were unable to wrest the city from their grasp, and were forced to retreat. My incompetent servant Nox led the assault."

"Unfortunate," the grey man said. It turned to its companions, and they seemed to confer silently. When they were finished the lead grey man turned back to Hades. "Entity Kali is no longer functional. Explain."

"She was killed in the battle, great Emissary. This wasn't an attempt to remove your servant, I assure you." Hades hated how subservient he sounded. "If you'd like to assign another, I promise that I will keep them from harm."

"Her death is insignificant," the grey man said. "Another servant will be provided."

"What of my reward? May I use the staff to take the Ark of the Cradle?"

"We will come for the key. Until then, you may use it as you wish," the grey man said. He conferred with his companions, then turned back to Hades. "We will arrive in a quarter rotation. Prepare yourself."

The hologram winked out of existence. Hades leapt to his feet with a whoop. He laughed at Nox. "I told you they could be trusted. The Ark of the Cradle is *mine*. At long last, I have exceeded my brother. The first sorcerer god to become an Ark Lord."

Nox turned to face him, all respect gone from his face.

Hades blinked, unable to grasp the change in the man's demeanor.

Nox's voice was contemptuous. "They gave you the Ark of the Cradle, because by creating that key you made some powerful enemies. Jordan and Blair are working together. Blair has resurrected the Great Pack, and Jordan is an unparalleled military leader. They're coming for you, Hades. The grey men are all too happy to allow us to fight it out, weakening us both. They know that sooner or later you're going to betray them. They're just using you until their masters arrive. Then we're expendable."

"You will *never* speak to me in that tone again," Hades snarled. Only his brother Zeus had ever dared say such things, and Hades had vowed he'd never allow another to do the same. "You are fortunate that I need you, Nox. But you are not so clever as you think. Open your mind to me, and pray that I find no subterfuge."

Hades pulsed power through the mindshackle he'd attached to Nox at the moment of the demon's creation. Hades rifled through Nox's memories, seeking any deception that might give him cause to destroy Nox. He needed the treacherous fool, but if Nox had already turned on him, Hades would mete out justice here and now.

There was nothing, not beyond the kind of treacherous thoughts he himself had been guilty of when serving Set. Hmm. Removing the will of such a valuable servant seemed...hasty. "Perhaps I will allow you to retain some will, since it appears your insolence is the worst of your crimes. But remember this, Nox: my patience is not infinite. If you cannot keep your tongue, I will replace you with someone who can."

Hades waved a hand at Nox, and the frightened demon scurried from his presence.

Now that the unpleasant tasks were dealt with, Hades turned his attention to the staff. With it, he would finally claim that which he had sought his entire life.

"These young gods wish to come for *me*?" Hades shouted. His powerful voice echoed from the walls, bringing a dark smile. "Let them come, and I will teach them the true power of an Ark Lord. Let the Ark War finally begin."

Epilogue

"Hold still," Liz said, straightening the sleeves on Blair's ivory robe. Blair stood as patiently as he could, trying to distract himself by reading the glyphs on the temple wall. It didn't help.

"I look like the villain in a bad Kung Fu movie," Blair muttered. "Why don't you have to wear one of these?"

"Because I didn't populate an entire continent with crazy werewolves," Liz countered. She finally stopped, taking a step back to inspect him. "Also, I didn't save the city with a big pack of super dogs. Besides, you look great."

"I'm still not sure that I even understand what's happening here," Blair said. And he wasn't. It was some sort of coronation, but he wasn't sure what Elia and her friends expected him to do. "I hope they don't think we're sticking around. We have a home, and this isn't it."

"I think Jordan beat that into them," Liz said. "Plus, I suspect that this Elia doesn't want you sticking around making her look bad." She took a step back, beaming a smile and nodding approvingly. "You really look the part. Let's go."

Liz shifted into warform, summoning her blade. Blair trailed after her as she stalked up the narrow corridor. It dumped them into a small coliseum, made large only by the sparsely populated stands. There simply weren't enough of them to fill the place, even with a few Ka-Dun from the Great Pack having stayed. Some of them were electing to stay permanently, and to Blair's mind that was a good thing. The things they learned here could be brought back to the Bay Area.

"I wish John were here to see all this," Blair said. He missed the old man, despite not having spent much time with him.

"Me too. He won't be the last casualty in all this," Liz rumbled, her furry ears twitching as she watched the new council.

Blair marched toward the raised dais at the center of the ring. Elia stood before a golden throne wide enough for a monarch with a very large ass. She held a neck torque, simple gold with an oval sapphire set in the center.

It would have been at home in Old Kingdom Egypt.

He paused next to Elia, turning slowly to face the crowd. Jordan's friend Leti had coached him, and she'd drilled into him the importance of the ritual.

"Yesterday our ranks numbered forty-three," Elia's clear voice rang through the chamber. "Forty-three champions, who swore to live as the Mother." She paused masterfully, waiting until the crowd held a single collective breath. "Twenty-eight of those champions fell today. They gave their lives in defense of this place. Nor were they the only blood price paid today. Our Father brought his pack to save us, and many of our brothers and sisters will never be going home. We owe the Father a great debt for his service, but now we must ask an even greater service. In the Mother's absence we need a real leader. Our Father, Ark Lord Blair, is that leader. He shall steward our faith, his faithful Ka-Ken watching over him."

Elia placed the torque around Blair's neck. A thrum passed through it as the clasp snapped shut, and for a terrible moment Blair was reminded of the collar of Shi-Dun. He probed the collar, and could feel a reservoir of energy within. It was small compared to the staff, but potent in its own way.

"Please," Elia called, smiling magnanimously, "welcome Ark Lord Blair, Steward of Isis."

The crowd burst into applause, which somehow managed to fill the room despite the small audience. Blair suspect shaping, and scanned the audience looking for the culprit. Trevor shot him a guilty smile.

Testing out the new shaping? Blair thought at him.

You know it. Trevor thought back. The words were tinged with joy, the kind Blair hadn't seen since Trevor had died.

Much to Blair's surprise he realized that Jordan was sitting next to Trevor. He'd taken the time to shave his blond curls, going back to the severe buzz cut he'd had when Blair had first met him. Somewhere he'd found a black t-shirt, and camo fatigues.

Next to Jordan sat Leti, and Blair smiled when her hand found Jordan's.

Blair raised both arms, and the crowd fell silent. He slowly lowered them, taking a deep breath. "Today was both horrible and miraculous. We lost many, as sister Elia said. But those who survived are stronger. We've learned to put aside differences—for deathless, champions, and unblooded to work together. We stopped Hades and his demons, showing them that we will not be taken easily. They are powerful, but together so are we." He left out the part where Nox had gotten away.

And the part where Nox had probably created a Primary Access Key.

"Many threats still remain. Hades is in Cairo, squatting over the Ark of the Cradle. Sobek and his nameless master are in Australia, and they could decide to attack us at any time." Blair stopped, considering his next words carefully. "I thought long and hard about telling you this next part, but you not only deserve to know, you need to. Hades works for the beings who built this city. They also built the Arks, and created the technology Isis used to create all of us. Those creators, we call them the Builders, will be returning soon. Their shock troops are already here."

He raised his voice to a roar.

"Until now, we've been on the defensive—scattered groups just trying to hold onto what we have. *That ends today*. We are going to take the fight to our enemies. We didn't ask for this war, but we are damned well going to win it."

The crowd went berserk, and this time it didn't take shaping from Trevor to make the applause echo.

Blair reveled in the collective joy, the relief they all felt at still being alive. He reveled in the power of this place, and the possibilities it offered.

Trevor had been quite clear. The city had somehow manipulated the flow of time, and they'd seen something similar when they'd light-walked from the exploding First Ark. Trevor believed that time was a signal, just like any other.

If that was true, then Blair had no doubt that Trevor would learn to master time travel. When he did, Blair already knew how he planned to use it.

If they were going to win this war, they needed to save the Mother.

63892449R00206

Made in the USA
Lexington, KY
21 May 2017